Secrets of Whiskey River

A.J. Turner

Turner House Press

Content Warning

This book contains depictions of human trafficking, sexual assault, physical assault (including graphic violence), abduction, and murder. These elements are integral to the story and may be distressing or triggering for some readers. Please take care while reading.

PROLOGUE

"You're really pissing me off," Enzo said, his footsteps clicking down the concrete aisle of the stable. "You know what happens to people who piss me off?"

He stopped in front of Zorro's stall, where Alex stood unbraiding the gelding's mane, fighting back tears of anger.

"They end up in dumpsters."

Alex flinched. Until now, she had tuned out his tirade, biting back the urge to say I told you so. But when her eyes met his, cold and black and utterly soulless, she knew he meant it.

She had convinced herself she was safe because he needed her. A man of his age, with his back problems, couldn't handle the lesson schedule or the number of horses in training. He needed her.

Until he didn't.

A month ago, he had hired an assistant without asking her. Today, the truth snapped into place. She had been training her replacement. Fear twisted low in her gut, frustration tightening her throat, but anger was the one that broke through. It surged through her, drowning out everything else.

"Are you kidding me?" she shouted, hurling her brush against the stall wall. Zorro jerked on the crossties, startled, but settled the moment her hand touched his neck. This morning, Enzo had shown up unannounced with a potential buyer for Zorro. The showing had gone exactly as she predicted—poorly.

"You're trying to blame me for what just happened, even though I told you he wasn't ready. I begged you to postpone. I just started him over jumps last week. We can't sell him as a kid's jumping pony yet. The horse wasn't even trained to be ridden until last month."

Tears spilled down her cheeks. She angrily wiped them away with the back of her hand and bent to retrieve the brush.

Enzo shifted in the doorway, uncomfortable. "Oh, don't cry," he said, scrunching his face in distaste. Alex could have sworn he winced.

"Go fuck yourself," she said. He didn't get to be uncomfortable, not when he was the one causing the situation.

Enzo fell silent. Alex resumed grooming, though her hands trembled with adrenaline.

"Go fuck myself," he repeated with a low chuckle.

His lips curled into a sadistic grin. The shift in him was immediate and predatory. Sweat prickled along her hairline. His threat wasn't hollow. People had ended up in dumpsters, if not by his hand, then by his orders.

Alex stiffened and forced her expression into something neutral.

Enzo was a small man—five-six on a good day, maybe a hundred and fifty pounds soaking wet, and pushing sixty. They stood eye-to-eye, but he still had about fifteen pounds on her. Alex, at twenty-two and in peak physical condition, knew that if it ever came down to a fight, she could take him.

But that wasn't how he operated. He waited, watched, and struck when his target was vulnerable.

"Maybe I will go fuck myself," he said, "since you won't."

She'd had enough. His daily jabs about her unwillingness to sleep with him grated on her last nerve.

"No, Enzo. I'm here to train horses, not to be your mistress. I don't recall 'fucking an old decrepit sleazeball' in the job description."

The words shocked even her. She rarely lost her temper, but when she did, she never held back.

Enzo's face twisted with malice. "You can't even do what I hired you for. If Brittany had done the showing, we would have sold the horse today."

Alex barked out a laugh. His frown told her he hadn't expected that.

"Oh, please. We both know the only thing Brittany is good at riding is you. That's why you hired her. The girl has never trained a horse in her life. But sure, keep deluding yourself. If you'll excuse me, I have work to do."

She unclipped Zorro from the crossties and led him toward the pasture, praying Enzo would be gone when she returned. Her back burned under the weight of his stare as she exited the stable.

Outside, the February air was mild. Snowmelt dripped from the eaves. In New Hampshire, this was fool's spring, and a second winter lurked around the corner. If she wanted to escape, she had to move fast.

A truck engine roared to life behind her. She exhaled shakily and turned Zorro loose in the pasture. Determined, she latched the gate and hurried back to the barn. The familiar scent of sawdust and manure enveloped her as she hurried to the office. The sound of her footsteps echoed through the empty stable.

She slipped into the office, rounded the desk, and turned on the ancient computer. Her fingers flew across the keyboard as she emailed the parents of her lesson kids, informing them she was leaving Great Valley Farm and that Enzo would refund any prepaid lessons.

That would piss him off. Probably not smart. But she needed every dollar, and he could afford it. Next, she grabbed the cordless phone. Her hand trembled as she dialed the woman who had surrendered Zorro to her. The entire escape plan hinged on this woman's cooperation. The woman answered on the second ring.

Alex's voice shook as she spilled everything—her fear, her plan, her desperation. The woman listened quietly, then agreed without hesitation.

Relief washed over her.

She could take Zorro to her family's stable if she had to, but that would be the first place Enzo looked. And despite her strained relationship with her uncle, she wouldn't put him in danger. Working with horses was all she had ever wanted. She had spent the last year at her family's barn, suffocating under her uncle's refusal to acknowledge her skill. She'd been so desperate to prove herself after leaving her family's farm that she'd ignored the whisper in her gut telling her something was off here. The way her shoulders tightened whenever Enzo walked into the barn. The lesson books that never quite added up. The uneasy silence that followed his temper. She'd been so focused on escaping her uncle's shadow—on finally being seen, finally being valued—that she'd run straight into the hands of someone far worse.

Tears burned her cheeks as she looked around the office, at everything she'd built here. Walking away would be the hardest thing she'd ever done, but there was no version of this where she left unscathed. Alexandria True knew too much. She'd seen too much. Staying meant waiting to be silenced; leaving meant becoming a target the moment she stepped off the property.

Unlike Enzo, she always kept her cards close. There was one person she could call, someone capable of ending this nightmare with a single phone call, but his help always came with a trail of bodies. She wasn't sure she could stomach being responsible for that kind of carnage. Enzo was terrifying, but his boss was worse, and the fallout would never land on just them. Innocent people would be caught in the crossfire.

The only smart move was to disappear.

And she knew exactly how to do it.

Henry was still waiting for an answer to his proposal. Sweet, steady Henry, who had no idea of the danger closing in around her. Marrying him would solve everything in one clean, decisive move. A new town. A new name. A new identity. She could become someone Enzo had never even heard of. It was fast, legal, and—most importantly—completely off Enzo's radar.

All she had to do was say yes.

The countdown began.

In one week, Alex True would vanish. All she had to do was stay alive until then. It was a chessboard in motion, pieces sliding into place around her. She wasn't playing to win, she was playing to survive. Pawns didn't get second chances. Pawns got sacrificed. She might not be in control of the board, but if she played smart and stayed moving, she could outmaneuver the pieces hunting her.

Chapter One
ALEX

Alex sat at the kitchen island, sipping her coffee and savoring the quiet before the day exploded into chaos. Six months into her job at Southeast Regional Hospital, she still had mornings where she couldn't quite believe she'd made it this far. Five years ago, she'd been a twenty-five-year-old divorced single mother, thirteen hundred miles from home, working as an EMT, and barely scraping by. Now she was a registered nurse with a stable job, a plan, and a future she'd carved out herself.

Behind her, Alyssa shuffled to the coffeepot, poured herself a cup, and leaned against the counter, looking half-awake.

"Morning," Alex said.

"Morning," Alyssa mumbled.

Moving in together had been a practical decision. Both were single mothers with little support, both had survived messy divorces, and both were starting from scratch. They'd met on their first day at Southeast Regional—two strangers trapped in the same windowless conference room, enduring the hospital's infamous death-by-PowerPoint orientation. Three hours in, they were trading looks of mutual suffering. By lunchtime, they were swapping stories. A week later, they were friends.

Alex had stayed in Arkansas after her marriage fell apart. Her service in the Air National Guard and Collin's father made for simple explanations, but the truth ran deeper. Returning to New Hampshire wasn't safe, and staying here kept her off the radar.

She was proud of what she'd built since then. Eight years earlier, she'd uprooted her life in New Hampshire to marry her high school sweetheart, Henry, an Air Force officer stationed at Little Rock Air Force Base. Their relationship had always been rocky, and the whirlwind of military life only widened the cracks. Four years ago, when Collin was still a baby, the whole thing finally collapsed.

A chime sounded from Alyssa's phone. She smiled down at the screen. It was the same secretive smile she'd been wearing all week.

"Lover boy?" Alex teased.

Alyssa smirked and headed upstairs. "I'm gonna get the boys up."

The familiar stampede erupted overhead. Alex finished her coffee and started packing lunches. She'd gotten good at juggling mornings like this—school drop-offs, shift work, Guard weekends, and the never-ending grind of her Doctor of Nursing program. She'd used her GI Bill to get through school, and she was determined to finish her doctorate no matter how long it took. Last month had been her last weekend in the Air National Guard, and she still wasn't sure how she felt about not reenlisting. Part of her missed the structure, but another part knew she was being pulled in a different direction.

Twenty minutes later, the boys barreled down the stairs. Collin ran straight into her, wrapping his arms around her waist.

"Love you, Momma!" he said before grabbing his lunchbox.

"Bye, Miss Alex," Luke added.

Alyssa came bouncing down the stairs in leggings, a loose T-shirt slipping off one shoulder, and sneakers. She had even done her makeup—something she never bothered with for school drop-off.

"Where are you off to?" Alex asked.

"I'm going hiking!" Alyssa smirked, not meeting Alex's eyes.

"Alone?"

Alyssa flashed that same secretive grin and slipped out the door.

Alex shook her head and headed upstairs to get ready for work.

She paused in front of the bathroom mirror. Her medium-length mahogany hair was a mess, a mix of loose waves and a few stubborn curls. Her hazel eyes looked tired from two back-to-back night shifts. She stripped down to her underwear and studied her reflection. Athletic. Average height. Mostly toned. A few stretch marks from pregnancy. A few insecurities still whispered in her ear, echoes of the comments her ex-husband used to make.

She pushed the thoughts away and pulled on her riding pants. Before nursing school, before the divorce, before Arkansas, horses had always been her escape. They still were.

The barn was jumping with activity. The warm-up ring had too many horses going in all different directions, with riders who didn't know what they were doing. Alex wasn't feeling the crowd. She stood at the entryway to the ring, holding Zorro by the reins, and contemplated whether it was worth the bother.

Jeremy, one of the other boarders, was down at one end of the ring, exercising a horse Alex didn't recognize. The mare was skin and bones. Her eyes were dull and glazed over. She half-heartedly trotted at Jeremy's request.

Honestly, he shouldn't be exercising her at all. It was clear she had no reserves and needed to gain some weight. She was a beautiful chestnut with a big white blaze, approximately sixteen hands tall. Jeremy was getting frustrated and cracked the whip on her butt to get her moving better. A flash of white-hot anger shot through Alex.

Jeremy reeled her in; disgust etched on his face. He turned to the trainer and shook his head.

"I'm sending this thing back to the auction to become dog food. I can't believe I let you talk me into buying her," Jeremy barked.

As he led her back into the stable, Alex saw the fear in the animal's eyes and knew she had to do something.

"I'll buy her from you," Alex said as Jeremy walked past her.

He stopped and turned, thinking for a moment. "Fifteen hundred, and you've got a deal." Jeremy's eyes narrowed, sizing her up.

Alex knew the mare wasn't worth that much in her current condition but saw the potential of what she could be. Before she could talk herself out of it, she gave a curt nod.

What had she just done? It was too late now. She was the proud owner of another horse that she knew nothing about. The thought of that poor soul heading to an auction house almost broke her heart, though. Alex turned to follow Jeremy back to the stables. She tied Zorro's reins in a knot and shut him in his stall while she went to fetch her checkbook.

Jeremy handed over the papers, his expression unreadable. Alex glanced down at the registration papers. *Star Maker's Set Me Free*. An American Saddlebred. A soft laugh escaped her. She had wanted to get back into the Saddlebred world. What were the odds?

"I'd try to keep that sense of humor if I were you," Jeremy said tartly. "That horse isn't worth a nickel, let alone fifteen hundred."

Before he turned to leave, his gaze swept over her with a slow, measuring intensity that made her breath catch. Something in his eyes sharpened, a flicker of recognition or interest she didn't understand. The moment lingered, unsettling in a way she couldn't shake.

Then he blinked, the look gone as quickly as it appeared. "Good riddance," he muttered, heading toward the parking lot.

A faint chill crawled up Alex's spine at the odd interaction.

After settling Freedom in her stall, she decided a trail ride would probably be her best bet today. Zorro was feeling feisty after a week off. After she had warmed him up in the arena, she steered him toward the trail that wrapped around the base of Pinnacle Mountain. She didn't have time for the full loop, but an hour in the saddle was enough to clear her head.

About five minutes in, she had the distinct sense that someone was watching her. She glanced around casually but saw no one. The woods were quiet. She shook her head. She was being paranoid. Stress did that.

An hour later, she and Zorro returned to the upscale stable where she boarded him. The board was expensive, but she made it work with extra shifts. She'd saved enough for a down payment on a house, and her dream was to find a property with a barn—a place where she, Collin, and Zorro could finally settle. Nursing was her practical career, but horses were her long-term plan. Five years, she told herself. In five years, she'd open a small stable again.

After brushing Zorro and settling him in his stall, Alex grabbed her bag and headed to the locker room. She changed into her work clothes, left her riding boots in her locker, and checked the time. She still had more than an hour before her shift. Her stomach growled. Lunch first, then chaos.

Today was shaping up to be a good day.

The shift had become a full-blown dumpster fire.

She pulled into three ambulances in the bay and an overflowing waiting room. She had been running nonstop since she had clocked in. Now it was six-thirty p.m., shift-change chaos. Every nurse in the department huddled together at the small nurses' station, giving reports to the oncoming shift. Alex worked the one-to-one swing shift and sat charting, waiting for the crowd to thin. She hated feeling boxed in.

"Hey, Alex."

She turned to see Joe, the night-shift charge nurse, standing beside a tall man in navy scrubs and cowboy boots. Only in Arkansas.

"This is Troy," Joe said. "New travel nurse. Tonight's his first night. He'll train with you."

Alex blinked. Six months on the job and somehow she was the one training a travel nurse. Perfect. What could possibly go wrong?

"Hey, Troy. I'm Alex," she said. "You can take the station next to me. I'll show you the charting system, then give you a tour of the department."

Troy turned out to be knowledgeable and quick to learn. It was a relief to have someone competent helping with the patient load.

The night was flying by until Alex glanced at the board and saw her newest patient: a twenty-three-year-old female, sexual assault.

"I'd better take this one alone," she said.

"Absolutely," Troy replied.

She had only done one rape kit before, with a senior nurse guiding her through every step. She tried to recall the process as she walked down the hall toward room five.

"Have a good night, Miss Alex."

She turned to see Martha, one of their regulars, heading out.

"You too, Martha."

Her coworkers groaned when Martha came in, but Alex had a soft spot for her. Martha was homeless and often came in for a warm bed and a turkey sandwich. Alex never minded taking care of her.

She refocused and knocked twice before entering room five.

Nothing prepared her for what she saw.

The girl lifted her head, and the full extent of the damage slammed into Alex. Bruises swallowed her eyes until they were barely slits. Blood streaked her torn clothes. Her lower lip hung open in a raw split. She sat rigidly on the bed, shivering, staring at nothing.

The brutality of it hit Alex hard, sharp enough to steal her breath.

Alex steadied herself and stepped closer. "Hey, hun. My name is Alex. I'm going to be your nurse tonight. Can you tell me what happened?"

If the girl pressed charges and the case went to court, her medical records would become a legal document. She needed the full story for her charting.

The girl suddenly broke into sobs and threw her arms around Alex. Alex froze for a heartbeat, then wrapped her arms around her and held her. She murmured soothing sounds—at least she hoped they sounded soothing—until the girl's breathing slowed. Alex blinked hard, fighting back her own tears. Falling apart wouldn't help either of them, but the wave of empathy was almost overwhelming.

"What's your name, hun?" Alex asked gently.

"Liz."

Alex waited a moment, then kept her voice soft. "Tell me what happened to you."

Liz didn't let go. She clung to Alex as if she were the only solid thing in the room. After a long, tense silence, she finally spoke.

"I was walking home from work. The weather has been so nice; walking felt like a good idea." Her voice trembled. "When I turned down Elm Street, something moved in the bushes. I looked over, and then it felt like I got hit by a truck. Someone tackled me to the ground. I couldn't breathe. I couldn't scream. Then someone hit me in the face, and that's the last thing I remember."

She took a shuddering breath, her fingers twisting together in her lap. For a moment she couldn't speak; her throat worked around the words, her eyes fixed on a spot on the floor as if steadying herself.

"When I woke up…" She paused again, swallowing hard. "My pants were around my ankles. I'd been dragged off the street into the bushes." Her voice thinned, trembling at the edges. "I looked around to make sure no one was there. Then I pulled my pants up and walked here." She shook her head, a helpless, broken motion. "I didn't know what else to do."

Her breath hitched, and the tears she'd been fighting spilled over, tracking down her cheeks as she tried to hold herself together.

Alex hugged her tighter, then eased back and met her eyes.

"Okay," she said softly. "We have a couple of options. I'm a mandated reporter, so I do have to let the police know what happened. But whether you want to talk to them or pursue charges is completely your decision."

She paused, giving Liz a moment to breathe.

"If you want, we can collect evidence with a rape kit. That includes things like your clothing and swabs that help preserve DNA. It doesn't mean you're committing to anything. It just keeps your options open later. If you're not ready for that, we can still take care of you medically—get you changed, check for injuries, and give you medication to prevent infection or pregnancy."

She kept her voice steady, gentle. "You're in control of what happens next."

As she finished explaining, Alex realized Liz's torn clothing pressed against her during the hug. Evidence could have been transferred. She closed her eyes for a moment. These were her favorite scrubs. Now they were evidence.

Liz stared at the floor, thinking. "What do you think I should do?" she whispered.

"I can't make that decision for you, hun," Alex said. "But if you come forward, it might keep someone else from going through what you did tonight."

Liz lifted her head and took a long, steady breath. "Let's do the rape kit. I want whoever did this to pay."

Alex gave her a small, encouraging smile and stepped out of the room. She walked back to the nurses' station and told the doctor the patient wanted to proceed.

"Was it bad?" Troy asked quietly.

Alex nodded as she picked up the phone. She dialed the police. The line rang twice before a bored voice answered.

"Little Rock Police Department."

"Yes, hi. My name is Alex, and I'm a nurse in the emergency department at Southeast Regional. I have a patient here who was sexually assaulted, and she would like to file a report."

The woman's tone shifted immediately. "Okay. I need to get some information from you, then I'll send a detective over."

Five minutes later, Alex hung up and turned to Troy. "They're sending a detective to talk to her."

Chapter Two
DECLAN

Declan Wallace sat in the cramped interrogation room across from a tall, weaselly looking man, who couldn't stop fidgeting. He hit play on the security footage showing the man ripping a purse from a little old lady down at the River Market. When the suspect turned toward the camera, Declan paused the video on the full-frontal shot.

The man giggled nervously. "That could be anyone, man. That footage is static."

Declan gave him a flat look. "Unless you have a twin or a doppelgänger, that's you."

Mrs. Wentworth hadn't gone down without a fight. It had been cold and raining, the kind of day that made sane people stay home. She'd been walking down President Clinton Avenue, toward the parking deck, when this idiot came up behind her and tried to snatch her purse. She'd just spent a small fortune on her granddaughter's birthday gift and wasn't about to let it go.

Declan almost smiled remembering the footage. A full-on tug-of-war, and Mitch's face when the woman jabbed him with her umbrella was priceless. She'd fought like hell. Mitch shoved her to the ground and bolted.

"My officer just called from the emergency department," Declan said, rising from his chair. "Mrs. Wentworth broke her wrist when you pushed her. So, we'll add battery to your already impressive list of charges."

"But I didn't mean to hurt her!" Mitch protested.

"So, it was you?" Declan asked, lifting an eyebrow.

Mitch's shoulders sagged. "I want a lawyer," he whispered.

"That's the first intelligent thing you've said today. Sit tight."

Declan walked out, shutting the door behind him. His expression didn't change, but the shift from interrogation mode to everything-else mode was immediate. His shoulders relaxed as he prepared to head home for the night.

He headed down the hall to his office. It was a little after seven, which meant he was already late picking up the boys from his ex. He let out a long breath and grabbed his keys, ready to call it a night.

His office phone rang.

"Wallace," he answered, clipped and automatic.

"Uh, yes, sir," the dispatcher said. "A nurse from Southeast Regional just called. They have a rape victim in the emergency department. Sounds pretty bad. She wants to file a report."

Declan closed his eyes for a moment and rubbed his brow. "I'm already two hours over my shift. Detective Haggerty is on tonight; call him."

Declan was just about to place the phone down on the receiver when the woman spoke again. "He was just called to a murder scene."

Of course. The universe had a sick sense of timing. He was on call until midnight tonight, so there was no getting out of this.

"Tell them I'm on my way."

He hung up harder than necessary, then sat for a moment, forcing himself to breathe. Work-Declan didn't get rattled. Work-Declan handled the job, kept his voice steady, kept his head clear. But the man underneath was tired. Bone-deep tired. And every time a call like this stole another evening from his kids, it scraped at him. He hated letting them down, hated losing precious time with them for the never-ending depravity of the world they lived in.

He pulled out his phone and dialed Susan. She answered on the second ring.

"Hey," he said. "Sorry I'm late. A rape case just came in, and I have to head to the hospital. I'll wrap things up as fast as I can and then come get the boys."

"There's always a case," Susan said, exasperated. "The boys will be in bed at nine. If you're not here by then, just come after Andrew's soccer game in the morning."

Declan stared at the wall for a beat, jaw tight. He wanted to argue. He wanted to tell her that he was doing his best. But he'd learned a long time ago that arguing with Susan was like arguing with a brick wall—except the wall had better listening skills.

"Okay," he said quietly. "I'll do what I can."

He hung up and grabbed his jacket. Another night, another mess to clean up. Another weekend with his kids cut short.

He locked his office behind him and headed for the exit, slipping back into the version of himself the job required, the one who didn't flinch, didn't hesitate, didn't feel.

Alex

Both physicians working that night were men, so they asked Alex and another nurse, one of the few certified Sexual Assault Nurse Examiners on staff, to collect the rape kit. While the two of them handled the evidence collection, the doctor completed his initial assessment. He ordered a head CT to rule out fractures, and Alex drew basic labs as she worked through the kit.

She had just sat down to finish the paperwork when a voice behind her made her jump.

"Excuse me. I'm looking for the nurse of Elizabeth McCoy."

Alex turned. A man stood on the other side of the nurses' station counter, dressed in black slacks and a blue button-up. He was tall—easily six-foot-three—with short dirty-blonde hair and stormy blue-colored eyes that seemed to take in everything at once. Broad shoulders, a serious expression, and a presence that filled the space without effort.

She stared a moment too long before she spoke.

"Y-yes. That's me. I mean—yes, she's my patient. Hi, I'm Alex." She stood and shook his hand.

"Detective Declan Wallace," he said, eyes dipping to the box sitting beside her. "I see you've already completed the rape kit. Does she want to press charges?"

"Yes, she does."

"How bad is it?"

Alex looked away. "Bad."

"Shit," he muttered under his breath.

He straightened. "Alright. I'm only gathering basic information tonight. I'll follow up next week and set up interviews with both of you."

The thought of seeing him again made her pulse skip in a way she absolutely did not want to unpack right now.

"Okay," she said.

"If you have a minute, would you mind coming with me while I talk to her?" Declan asked, patting his pockets for his notebook. "She might be more comfortable if we go in together, since she already knows you."

"Of course. I'll show you to her room."

They walked down the hall in silence. Liz sat cross-legged on the bed, HGTV flickering softly in front of her, the bright colors on the screen at odds with the bruised stillness of her expression. Alex had cleaned most of the blood from her skin while the physician stitched her lip, but the effort could only do so much. She looked a little less battered, but the brutality of what she'd survived was still visible in every swollen contour of her face.

"Liz, this is Detective Wallace with the Little Rock PD," Alex said gently. "He's just going to get a statement from you tonight. We're waiting for the rest of your labs, and then we'll get you home."

Alex glanced at Declan. The muscle in his jaw worked; his expression settling into something grim. She recognized the look; she'd worn it herself the first time she saw Liz.

Declan cleared his throat. "Hi, Liz. Can you tell me what happened tonight?"

Liz shifted, hesitated, then repeated the story exactly as she had told Alex earlier. Declan listened without interrupting, then handed her a notebook.

"Write everything down for me. I'll step out for a minute."

He and Alex stepped into the hall to complete the chain-of-custody paperwork. Once the signatures were done, he returned to Liz's room.

Alex caught her reflection in the security mirror near the main doors and winced. Her hair was a disaster, and the puke-green scrubs she'd changed into were doing her no favors. She straightened herself quickly before Declan came back out.

"Okay, Liz," he said from the doorway. "You did the hard part tonight. I have your written statement and contact information. Tomorrow you'll get a call to schedule a full interview, and we may also set up a session with a sketch artist."

"That sounds good," Liz said.

Declan handed her a card. "If you remember anything, call me." Declan turned to leave, then paused. "Do you need a ride home?"

Liz shook her head. "My mom's coming. But thank you."

Declan stepped into the hall and glanced at Alex's badge.

"Alexandria... what's your last name, and what's a good number for you?"

"Kelley," she said, giving him her number while he scribbled it down.

"Great. I'd like to get you both in as soon as possible. When can you come by the office?"

She flipped through her schedule in her head. It was the weekend; she worked, and he probably wouldn't be in the office, anyway.

"I can come Monday morning, if that works," Alex said, cutting off the mental rambling.

"Perfect." He wrote it down. "Nine o'clock?"

Alex noticed the absence of a ring on his finger.

"Sounds good," she said, smiling before she could stop herself.

He returned a brief, warm smile. "Have a good night."

He turned and walked toward the exit. Alex watched him go, admiring the way his slacks fit across his backside.

She immediately regretted the zero effort she'd put into her appearance today. Normally, she did it on purpose to keep the creeps away. Today, she wished she'd tried. Monday would be different.

She checked the clock. It was just after nine p.m. The waiting room was still packed, and three new patients were waiting for her. In trauma room one, her coworkers were doing compressions on a patient. She scanned the department and realized she was the only nurse left on the floor.

She dropped into her chair with a tired sigh.

It was going to be a long night.

Four hours later, she clocked out, still buzzing from the hectic shift. Instead of heading straight home, she swung into the Friendly Quarter Bar on impulse. The bar scene wasn't really her thing anymore, but after the day she'd had, she needed something strong enough to take the edge off. The room was dim and warm; the lighting softened the rough edges of the world. A live band played in the corner, low and bluesy, and the air carried the familiar mix of whiskey, fried food, and old wood.

She slipped onto an empty barstool and ordered a whiskey sour.

While she waited, she let her gaze drift toward the stage. The moment she turned, she froze. Detective Wallace sat on the stool beside her, shoulders tense, staring into his glass as if it held the answer to all the world's problems. The low light carved shadows across his face, making him look even more worn than he had earlier.

She opened her mouth to say hello, but the hard line of his jaw told her he wasn't in the mood for conversation.

The bartender set her drink down. She paid in cash, thanked him, and turned back toward the band.

Declan was watching her.

She offered a shy smile. "Hello."

"I thought I recognized that voice."

His smile was warm and unexpected, and it hit her harder than she wanted to admit. She had to look away for a moment to collect herself.

"You needed a drink after that too, huh?" she asked.

His expression shifted, the warmth fading. "Unfortunately, that's nothing new for me. Tonight, I needed one after talking to my ex."

"Oh?"

"I was supposed to pick up my boys. I was walking out of the station when the call came in about the assault. By the time I finished at the hospital, they were already asleep." His tone carried a bitter edge. "So, I'll get them after my son's soccer game in the morning."

"That's tough. Couldn't they send someone else?" she asked, though a small part of her was relieved they hadn't.

"There are other detectives, but they all caught cases. I was on call until midnight. Now"—he lifted his glass—"I'm officially off duty."

His southern drawl was more noticeable now, warm and slow around the edges. "You don't sound like you're from around here."

"I'm originally from New Hampshire."

"I had you pegged for a WASP."

Alex frowned. "What's a WASP?"

"White Anglo-Saxon Protestant," he said, as if it were obvious.

She almost laughed. With her face, her hair, her whole, painfully predictable aesthetic, she knew she practically screamed PTA-meeting energy. But she wasn't letting him off that easily.

"Did you use your detective skills to deduce that?" she asked, rolling her eyes.

Declan shrugged, amused. "I bet you grew up riding horses and sailing." A grin tugged at his mouth. "Probably even have an aunt named Miriam."

Alex opened her mouth, searching for a comeback, but he wasn't wrong. Not even a little. Instead, she finished her drink in one gulp.

"You got all that from me saying I'm from New Hampshire, huh?" she said. "Maybe I'm Catholic."

He raised an eyebrow. "Are you?"

"No," she admitted, smiling.

He nodded toward her empty glass. "Are you having another one of those?"

"No. I should get home."

"I should do the same." He finished his whiskey and stood. "I'll walk you to your car."

Outside, the night air was cool and quiet. When they reached her SUV, Alex fumbled with her keys, suddenly aware of how close he was. When she looked up, he was watching her with an intensity that tightened something deep in her stomach, a look that felt far too direct for how little they knew each other.

For an instant, she thought he might close the distance between them. The air shifted, charged with the possibility of a kiss that would pull her in before she had time to think, the kind you lost yourself in without meaning to.

He pulled his gaze from hers and stepped back; the tension dissolving as quickly as it had formed.

"I'll see you on Monday," he said, hands sliding into his pockets.

"See you Monday."

He didn't leave until she started her car; then he turned and walked away. Alex stayed in the driver's seat, forcing herself to breathe. Heat flushed her cheeks, and her pulse hammered. Declan Wallace was impossible to read, playful one moment and quiet and serious the next. Their banter had been easy enough for two strangers, but she hadn't assumed it meant anything more. Not until she caught the way his gaze lingered on her, a sudden intensity that startled her and stirred something inside her she had forgotten existed.

By the time she pulled into the driveway, it was nearly three in the morning. The living room light was still on. Alex parked her black SUV beside Alyssa's bright-blue Subaru, killed the engine, and sat there in the quiet.

Exhaustion settled over her like a weight. Today had wrung her out completely. All she wanted was to climb the stairs and collapse into bed.

Locking the door to the garage behind her, Alex rounded the corner and found Alyssa curled up on the couch, fully absorbed in *Grace and Frankie*. Two glasses of wine sat on the coffee table. Alex dropped onto the couch beside her without a word. Alyssa leaned forward and nudged one glass toward her, eyes still on the screen.

"Figured you might need this since you're getting home two hours late," Alyssa said.

"I had a rape victim tonight. It was the worst I've seen. Someone beat her to hell," Alex said, shaking her head. They both loved working in the ER, but some shifts carved pieces out of you. Alyssa seemed to sense she didn't want to talk about it, so they sat in comfortable silence until the episode ended.

"I also wanted to see you when you got home to tell you about this amazing guy I've been talking to," Alyssa said, brightening.

Alex perked up. "Finally. I've been waiting for over a week. Spill it."

"Well... we started talking on Tinder."

Alex gave her a dramatic eye-roll.

"I know, I know," Alyssa said quickly. "He's different, I swear."

Alex raised a skeptical brow. "Okay. Continue."

"His name is Dean. He's a firefighter in Little Rock, and he has three kids. The divorce has been dragging on for a while, but he's really sweet. We went hiking today. It was a little awkward, but... I've never felt this way about someone before. It's scary."

Alex saw the vulnerability on her friend's face and softened. Tinder was a minefield of people looking for hookups. She hoped, for Dean's sake, that he was different. If he hurt Alyssa, Alex would have to kill him.

A reluctant smile spread across her face. She had never seen Alyssa this giddy.

"Do you have a picture?" Alex asked.

Alyssa pulled out her phone. The man in the photo had dark hair streaked with gray, a square jaw, and warm eyes. He was clearly older than Alyssa, maybe five-nine, and muscular beneath a fitted black long-sleeved shirt. There was a hint of George Clooney about him, though his features were sharper.

Alex realized Alyssa was watching her reaction.

"He's cute. I'm happy for you. Just be careful and take things slow."

"Thanks, girl."

"How old is he?" Alex asked, noting the speckles of grey throughout his dark hair.

"Thirty-eight," Alyssa admitted sheepishly.

"Robbing the grave, I see," Alex teased. He was ten years older than Alyssa.

"Yeah, well, we're going to be the real-life Grace and Frankie because we'll outlive our spouses. Whenever you find someone who finally catches your attention, that is."

Alex blushed, and Alyssa pounced.

"What are you not telling me?"

"It's nothing," Alex said quickly.

"Oh no, ma'am. Spill it."

Alex sighed. "The detective who came to take my patient's statement tonight was literally the most beautiful man I've ever seen in my life." She looked up at Alyssa with a grin.

Alyssa's jaw dropped.

"Oh, yeah?" Alyssa prompted.

"Yeah. I stopped at the bar after work because I wasn't ready to come home yet. I looked over, and he was sitting beside me. We talked while we finished our drinks, and he walked me to my car."

"And...?"

"And nothing. He said he'd see me on Monday and left. He couldn't have been less interested."

Alyssa waved that off. "I'm sure that's not true."

"I'm sure it is. I have an appointment with him on Monday to give a statement. He wanted to interview me in case I forgot anything tonight."

"Alex, how many times have you had a rape or assault victim and had to talk to the police?"

Alex frowned. "More than I can count."

"And out of those times, did any officer ask you to come to the station for an interview?" Alyssa asked, raising a single brow.

There was a long pause. "Never."

"Exactly. They get everything they need from you then. If it goes to court, then you get called in."

A slow smile spread across Alex's face. "You're right. I told him everything tonight. There's no reason for him to have me come in... unless he wants to see me again."

"Now the wheels are turning," Alyssa said playfully. "Looks like we'll have to give him something else to focus on besides the interview."

Alex laughed and shook her head. She finished her wine and stood.

"I need to pass out. Goodnight."

"Goodnight," Alyssa called after her. The scheming tone in her voice made Alex regret saying anything. Alyssa would spend the entire weekend plotting how to capture the detective's attention.

Alex finally collapsed into bed, drained from the emotional weight of the day. She tried not to think about the upcoming semester, or the interview, or the man with the stormy eyes who had walked her to her car.

When sleep eventually pulled her under, she dreamed of him anyway.

Chapter Three
DECLAN

Declan pulled the blackout curtains closed, stripped down to his boxers, and collapsed onto his bed. Exhaustion settled into his bones, but his mind refused to quiet. The ceiling fan spun lazily above him while he tried to force his thoughts to stop being so loud.

Missing the evening with his kids gnawed at him. He rarely let work interfere with his time with them, but tonight had been unavoidable. Stopping at the bar afterward had been out of character, yet he didn't regret it. He'd been in a foul mood, trying to drown the frustration in a glass of whiskey, when he heard a voice he recognized from earlier that evening.

Alex.

He'd wanted to see her again, and there she was. At the hospital, he'd asked her to come in for a formal interview only because he couldn't think of another appropriate way to see her. Asking her out then would have crossed every professional line.

By the time she walked into the bar, he was on his third whiskey, and the mild buzz had lowered his guard more than he liked to admit. His reaction to her had blindsided him. When she fumbled with her keys and bit her lip, his attention snapped to her mouth. His mind drifted, imagining the feel of her lips under his, imagining her in ways he had no business thinking about.

Her soft gasp had snapped him out of it. He realized he was staring at her like a predator circling its next meal. What truly surprised him was the way she leaned in, lips parting slightly, as if she felt the same pull.

It had taken every ounce of discipline he possessed to step back and tell her goodnight. The short walk home had done little to settle the pounding in his chest. Even in her frazzled state, she'd been beautiful. He'd noticed the absence of a ring while they signed the chain-of-custody forms. That minor detail had stirred something he didn't want to examine too closely.

He was looking forward to seeing her again on Monday, but he'd already decided he would keep things strictly professional until the case was closed. That didn't stop his thoughts from drifting back to her, no matter how hard he tried to focus on the hum of the fan or the distant traffic outside.

He exhaled sharply, irritated with himself. Rolling onto his side, he grabbed his phone and set an alarm for nine. In the morning, he planned to revisit the crime scene to make sure nothing had been missed.

To distract himself, he queued up a documentary about ancient Egypt. The narrator's monotone voice usually knocked him out within minutes. Tonight, it didn't stand a chance. He drifted off thinking about hazel eyes and a smile that had no business being that captivating.

The next morning, on his way to Andrew's soccer game, Declan pulled off the road near the spot Liz had described in her statement. He stepped out of his vehicle and walked along the shoulder with his hands in his pockets. It was a habit he'd developed early in his career—arrive, observe, and let the scene speak before touching anything.

He scanned the area slowly, taking in the brush line, the sidewalk, and the drainage ditch. No disturbed foliage. No discarded clothing. No drag marks. Nothing contradicted Liz's account, but nothing new appeared either.

He turned to head back to his car when the screech of tires shattered the quiet morning. A blue Honda blew through the red light and slammed into a white Ford pickup in the intersection. Metal crunched, glass exploded, and the Honda spun to a stop.

The driver of the Honda jumped out and bolted.

"Damn it," Declan muttered. Not how he'd planned to spend his morning.

He didn't bother chasing the runner. They had the license plate, the prints, and the entire collision on the traffic cam. The guy wasn't going anywhere. Instead, Declan jogged toward the Ford to check on the driver.

As he called in the accident and waited for medics to arrive, something clicked.

The traffic camera.

It pointed directly at the intersection, right toward the area Liz had been dragged through the night before. If the timing lined up, the camera might have caught her attacker.

Once EMS took over, Declan headed back to his car and made the call to request the footage. It would be Monday before the street department pulled it, which irritated him more than he liked to admit. Still, the possibility of catching a break in Liz's case outweighed the inconvenience of the delay.

For the first time since last night, he felt a flicker of optimism. With the right angle and a little luck, he might have this wrapped up by the end of the week.

Declan's office phone rang at ten minutes to nine on Monday morning. He didn't need the receptionist to say a word.

"I'll be right down."

He hung up and caught his reflection in the office mirror. He paused long enough to straighten his tie. Red shirt, black tie, black slacks. People always told him he looked good in red. Normally, he was lucky if he ran a comb through his hair before leaving the house. He wasn't in the mood to analyze why he'd put in more effort today.

As he stepped into the hallway, Bishop passed by.

"Damn, Wallace. Got a hot date?" Bishop asked.

Declan shot him a confused look.

"You brushed your hair, and you're wearing cologne. No more 'rolled out of bed' look."

Declan shook his head, but a faint smile tugged at him. Bishop had been his rookie once, all raw talent and too much energy, and now he'd worked his way up to detective. Declan was proud of the kid, even if he'd never say it out loud.

He shrugged, pretending not to know what Bishop meant, and headed for the stairs.

He scanned the waiting area as he descended. It took two passes before he spotted her—standing near the bottom of the staircase, hands clasped in front of her, trying to look composed. The sight of her knocked the air out of him.

She looked nothing like the frazzled woman he'd met at the hospital. Her hair fell in loose curls past her shoulders, soft and deliberate. The hunter-green off-the-shoulder sweater dress skimmed her figure, paired with brown knee-high boots that made her look both put-together and... stunning. There was a quiet confidence about her, but he could see the nerves in the way she shifted her weight.

He paused for half a second to collect himself. When their eyes met, she smiled, and something flipped in his stomach.

Get it together, Wallace.

She straightened as he reached the bottom of the stairs.

"Miss Kelley," he said, clearing his throat. "How are you today?"

"Good. How are you?"

"Great." His tone came out curt. He winced internally. "Follow me."

Small talk had never been his strength. He wanted her to feel comfortable; he just had no idea how to make that happen.

At the top of the stairs, Bishop walked by again. He glanced at her, then at Declan, and muttered a knowing "mm-hmm" before continuing down the hall.

Declan caught Alex's curious look. "Ignore him. He played football in college and took one too many hits to the head. We let him file paperwork now."

Bishop turned as if to respond, but Declan was already ushering her into his office and closing the door. He shot Bishop a smirk before shutting it completely.

Alex took the seat opposite his desk. Declan sat as well, fingers brushing the edge of the blotter before he forced them still. He wasn't entirely sure how to start. The room felt too quiet, too small, and he was suddenly aware of the faint trace of her perfume drifting across the desk.

"Alright, Miss Kelley. Let's start with what Liz told you, as close to verbatim as you can remember."

Straight to business. It was safer that way.

Alex took a steadying breath and repeated everything Liz had told her. Declan listened without interrupting, committing each detail to memory. Some of it he wished he could forget. The more she spoke, the more the shape of the case solidified in his mind, and none of it pointed anywhere good.

He nodded in the right places, kept his expression neutral, but his focus kept slipping. Every few seconds, his eyes flicked—against his better judgment—to the low neckline of her dress. It wasn't intentional. It was instinctive, distracting, and completely unprofessional.

He realized she'd stopped talking a beat too late. Clearing his throat, he pretended to flip through the stack of papers in front of him, buying himself a second to pull himself together.

"Did anything during the exam stand out to you?" he asked.

Alex thought for a moment. "She had a pretty serious bite mark on her left inner thigh."

"A bite mark?" His attention sharpened instantly.

"Yes. We photographed it with a tape measure and included it in the kit. It was deep. The marks will be there for a while."

"That's good," he said, already thinking ahead. "We can get a warrant for a dental mold and compare it to the bite. The kit's at the crime lab now."

"Do you have a suspect?" she asked.

"Not yet. But the street department is sending over traffic cam footage this morning. I'm hoping we'll find something."

Alex smiled faintly and looked down. Silence settled between them, thick and awkward. Declan felt it too—an awareness that had nothing to do with the case.

He finally stood. "That's all I need for now. I'll call if anything else comes up. Thanks for coming in so quickly."

"No problem." She rose with him.

He should've let her go. Should've kept the moment clean and professional. But when she looked up at him, something unguarded in her expression cracked his restraint.

"Are you seeing anyone?"

Her gaze snapped up to his as if she wasn't sure she'd heard him right. He cursed himself silently.

Alex blinked. "No."

Relief unfurled through him. He masked it with a controlled smile. "Alright, then." His voice stayed even, almost too even. "Let me walk you out."

They stepped into the hallway, the shift from the privacy of his office to the bustle of the station making the air between them feel strangely fragile. Their footsteps echoed down the stairwell, neither of them speaking, both too aware of the other. Declan kept his hands in his pockets, trying to look composed, trying not to think about how close she was or how easily he could reach out and touch her arm.

At the bottom of the stairs, she slowed. "Can you keep me updated on the case?" she asked over her shoulder, stopping in front of the double glass doors. "I know you can't go into detail, but it'll make me feel better, knowing whoever was capable of doing that isn't wandering the streets near the hospital."

"I can do that," Declan said. He pulled the front door open for her, the cool air rushing in around them.

She stepped through, offering him a small, grateful smile before turning toward the parking lot. He watched her walk away, the green dress tracing every curve, her hips moving in a slow, effortless sway. Something tightened low in his stomach. His jaw worked as he dragged his gaze off her and forced himself to look anywhere else.

He let the door close and turned back toward the stairs, the echo of her footsteps fading behind him.

One thing was certain: he needed to solve this case, and he needed to solve it soon.

By midday, the street department finally sent over the footage from the intersection near the crime scene. Declan fast-forwarded to the night of the attack, then backed up several hours. He knew the approximate time Liz had given, but he wanted the full picture. Sometimes offenders circled the area beforehand, testing the environment, waiting for the right victim. Sometimes they came back afterwards.

He settled in and watched.

Liz appeared on the screen, walking up the sidewalk and away from the intersection. A figure in dark clothing burst from the bushes and tackled her. Declan winced as her head struck the pavement. Three heavy blows followed, each one snapping her head back. His stomach tightened; he'd seen hundreds of assaults, but this one hit differently.

He rewound the tape and watched again, looking for anything identifiable: height, gait, a limp, a tattoo, a logo. The traffic camera was too far away and the lighting too poor. The attacker wore a black hoodie, and the camera quality was barely a step above that of a VHS tape.

Of course, he couldn't see his face. These ancient cameras ought to be endorsed by Mr. Magoo for all the good they do.

He let the footage loop while he finished paperwork and made calls.

After lunch, Martin wandered in and pulled up a chair beside him. Declan didn't ask for help, but he didn't turn it down either. They watched the footage in silence until Martin suddenly grabbed his shoulder.

"There," Martin said, pointing.

It was dawn the next morning, just before Declan had arrived at the scene. A man in a black hoodie lingered near the bushes, scanning the ground as if searching for something he'd dropped. He turned slightly, and Declan froze the frame.

Billy Caruso.

A frequent flyer. Petty theft, vandalism, drug possession. Nothing like this. But people escalated. Meth made them unpredictable, and Billy had just graduated from petty crimes to a Class Y felony.

Declan felt the shift in his gut. This was their guy.

He'd stay late. If everything lined up, he could close the case before the end of his shift. First step: find Billy. Get him talking. Pray he was still wearing the clothes from the attack. He needed a warrant for Billy's arrest and a dental mold to compare to the bite mark on Liz's thigh. A confession would seal it.

He worked diligently the rest of the day, obtaining warrants, coordinating with patrol, and fielding calls from Liz's family demanding updates. Billy managed to stay off the patrol's radar.

Declan had packed it in for the night around six and headed home. He'd barely sat down to dinner when the call finally came in. Patrol officers had picked Billy up at one of his usual hangouts, surrounded by his deadbeat friends and a pile of used needles. Declan threw on jeans and a T-shirt, grabbed his gun and badge, and headed back to the station.

Billy started talking before Declan had even entered the room. He barely had time to read him his rights before the kid launched into a frantic, drug-fueled ramble. Declan let him go, interrupting only long enough to get the Miranda rights on record. Thankfully, the patrol officer had already gotten him medically cleared before bringing him in, which might be the only thing keeping the confession from getting tossed.

Billy was a mess. Six-foot-three and rail-thin, jittery from meth, his whole body seemed to vibrate with restless energy. He kept picking at the scabs on his arms, rubbing at his nose, his jaw working in that constant, involuntary chew. His ginger hair hung in greasy, matted clumps, and he was still wearing the same clothes from the night of the attack, the fabric stiff and unwashed.

Declan made a mental note to collect them once Billy changed into a jumpsuit.

"Why did you do it, Billy?" Declan asked, keeping his voice even.

Billy's eyes darted. "I asked her out a few nights ago, and she laughed at me." Bitterness twisted his voice. "Like she was too good for me. I showed her what she was missing out on."

He tried to look tough, but the bravado cracked when Declan slid a photo of Liz's bruised face across the table. Billy's expression collapsed.

"I was high," he sobbed. "Only bits come back to me. I didn't mean to hurt her that badly."

Declan shook his head in disgust. "Sit tight. Someone will take you to county for the night. You'll see the judge in the morning."

The interview wrapped up in under thirty minutes. A patrol officer would escort him for a dental mold before booking him . The lab might take months to process it, but that was irrelevant. Between the confession and the footage, Billy was going away for a long time.

Declan stepped out of the interrogation room and called Liz. Relief flooded her voice when he told her they'd caught the man who attacked her.

It was nine p.m., and he wasn't even close to tired. Adrenaline still thrummed through him. One more predator off the streets. One more case tightened toward a close. It had come together with an ease that felt almost unreal; most cases dragged on for weeks or months, but every so often the universe lined things up and handed you a break wrapped in a neat little bow.

He thought of Alex—and the promise he'd made to keep her updated. Flipping through his notebook, he found her address and plugged it into his GPS. He typed her number into his phone and sent her a quick text to let her know he was on his way over with news about the case.

He shut off the lights in his office and stepped into the brisk night air, suddenly more awake than he'd felt all day. The case was nearly closed, but something about the night felt unfinished.

Chapter Four
ALEX

Alex curled up on the couch with *Grace and Frankie* playing in the background, waiting for Alyssa to get home from work. She'd just made herself a bowl of ramen when the garage door rumbled open. Finally, she was ready to decompress and catch up.

She had come straight from the stable and was bone-tired. Zorro had made her work for every stride today. It was her own fault; between work and school, she hadn't been able to ride as often as she wanted. He was turning eighteen this year, still in great shape, but she knew the time was coming to let the old man enjoy retirement. She pictured him giving pony rides to Collin and beginner lesson kids once she opened her own barn. The thought made her smile. Eight years ago, she would've laughed at the idea of Zorro ever being a kid's horse.

She was excited to see what Freedom could do once she put a little weight on. She would love to offer saddle seat lessons. No one else in the state offered them, and she would have the market. The idea of working for herself again lit something inside her. And as a nurse practitioner, she wouldn't have to rely on the barn's income to survive. That freedom made the dream feel possible.

Her thoughts drifted back to that morning's interview. Declan might have been abrupt, but she was almost certain he was interested. He'd stayed professional, yet she'd still caught his gaze dipping to the V-neck of her dress more than once. Maybe Alyssa had been right about the outfit after all.

She sat on the couch in an oversized gray sleep shirt and pink shorts, stray pieces of her messy bun threatening to dive straight into her ramen. She looked like a feral goblin who'd just discovered carbs and was shoveling them in with the frantic determination of someone defending her meal from five ravenous siblings.

A sound from the kitchen made her pause long enough to remember to breathe. Alyssa walked in from the garage. She looked exhausted, even though she was home earlier than usual.

"How was it?" Alex asked.

"Not terrible." Alyssa dropped her things on the counter and flopped onto the couch beside her. "Tell me everything."

Alex grinned. "Well… I think he might be more interested than I thought. The dress was a good call."

"I know," Alyssa said smugly, and they both laughed.

"I caught him looking a few times. He tried to hide it, but there was definitely something there. I hope I'm not imagining it."

"I doubt you are," Alyssa said. "Women know."

"He asked if I was seeing anyone," Alex added, smirking.

Alyssa's jaw dropped. "Okay, that's not subtle."

"He went right back to being professional afterward, though. I can't tell what he's thinking. He's giving off mixed signals."

"Alex, you've been out of the game for a while. Men don't profess their undying love on day two," Alyssa said, rolling her eyes as she stood to pour herself a glass of wine.

She was heading back toward the couch when a knock sounded at the front door. They both froze.

They exchanged a look. Neither was expecting anyone.

Alyssa set her wine down and whispered, "I'll grab the bat. You get the door."

Alex nodded. She tiptoed to the entryway and tried to peek through the window, but the angle was terrible. Alyssa crept up behind her, bat in hand, breath held like they were about to breach a cartel hideout.

Heart pounding, Alex opened the door.

"Hello?" she said cautiously.

The man turned toward her.

Their eyes met.

"Oh, shit!" Alex yelped—and slammed the door in his face.

Alyssa's eyes went wide. "Is that him?"

"Yes!" Alex hissed.

"Let him in!"

"No, I look terrible!"

Alyssa ignored her entirely. She reached around Alex and swung the door open again.

Declan stood on the stoop with a smirk tugging at the corner of his mouth. He had definitely heard their exchange.

"Hi! You must be Detective Wallace. Alex has told me all about you. Please come in."

Alex shot Alyssa a murderous glare, but Alyssa breezed past her, grabbed her wine from the counter, and continued her performance.

"I was just heading upstairs to bed. It was nice meeting you!"

She smiled sweetly, pretending not to notice Alex's frantic headshaking or the sheer look of panic on her face. Then she disappeared up the stairs. Alex leaned against the door, watching her go. She made a mental note to smother Alyssa in her sleep tonight. Declan turned toward her, the shift subtle but unmistakable, and she felt the weight of his attention settle on her before she even met his eyes. He was watching her with that unreadable expression of his, taking in the chaos he had just walked into. She straightened a little and tried to look casual.

"Come in," she said, pushing off the door and walking into the living room. She gestured toward the couch. "Have a seat."

Declan sat on the middle cushion, shoulders slightly tense, looking unexpectedly vulnerable. Alex's gaze drifted to her wineglass. She wished she could down the whole thing in one gulp.

"Would you like a glass of wine?" she asked. Maybe he needed the courage as much as she did.

"I'd love one. Thanks."

She hurried into the kitchen, checking over her shoulder to make sure he couldn't see her. She used the reflection in the window to fix her hair and pinch some color into her cheeks. It was the best she could do.

She returned with the wine and handed it to him before curling up beside him, legs tucked under her. They both took a sip.

Declan broke the silence. "I texted you earlier to let you know I was heading over. We caught the guy."

Alex's eyebrows shot up. She swallowed quickly. "Oh—I left my phone upstairs." Of course, her phone was upstairs. She treated it like a nomadic pet she kept forgetting to feed. One day she'd learn to keep track of the thing. "You caught him already?"

Declan gave a modest shrug. "What can I say? I'm good at my job."

She smiled. "So what happens now?"

"He'll either take a plea deal or it'll go to trial. He confessed, so there isn't much wiggle room."

"That's great. Does Liz know?"

"Yes. I called her after the confession."

Alex nodded, but she knew he hadn't driven over at nine-thirty on a Monday night just to give her a procedural update. She opened her mouth to shift the conversation, but Declan beat her to it.

"Sorry for dropping by so late," he said. "Closing the case had me wired. Thought you might still be up since you work late, and I promised updates. Really hope this didn't come off as creepy."

"No, not at all," she blurted. "Really."

Declan's attention drifted to the photos on the mantel. He stood and walked toward the fireplace, studying them quietly. His gaze lingered on a picture of a younger Alex laughing on a beach with two other girls. Then his eyes moved to the next frame—Alex standing beside a black-and-white horse in front of a weathered gray barn.

"Those are my two best friends from back home," Alex said, joining him. "I haven't seen them much since moving here. I miss them."

Declan nodded, then pointed at the horse photo with a faint grin. "Is that your horse?"

Alex paused, then sighed. "Okay, fine. You were right about the horses." She rolled her eyes, bristling a little. "My family owns a stable. But it's not like we were rich. We did the work. We trained the horses for the rich people."

She took another sip of wine. "And I definitely do not have an Aunt Miriam." She shot him a pointed look.

Declan's grin widened, slow and warm, and something in Alex's chest tightened in response.

He laughed, the sound rich and annoyingly pleased with himself. "And the boat?" He leaned back slightly, all confidence and smug amusement.

Alex sighed, already regretting admitting anything. "Speedboat. Although I've always wanted to learn to sail."

His smile reached his eyes. "So I was right."

"You correctly guessed a few things about my past. That doesn't mean you've figured me out."

His expression shifted, the humor fading. "No," he said quietly. "I'm sure it doesn't."

Alex blinked, thrown by the sudden change. One moment he was all smirks and swagger; the next, he was watching her with something sharper—something she couldn't name. Interest? Heat? Curiosity? Whatever it was, it pressed against her skin, unsettling her in a way the teasing hadn't. She shifted, trying to shake off the weight of his gaze.

"So," he said, breaking eye contact and looking back at the photo of her and Zorro, "have you been riding long?"

"Since before I could walk. That's my horse, Zorro. I keep him at a stable in Little Rock until I can get my own place." She tilted her head. "What about you? Any hobbies?"

"Not really. More of a computer nerd. I finished a computer science degree last year, started designing games, and now the plan is to leave policing and build my own business."

Alex perked up. "Really? Tell me about your game."

"It's still a work in progress. Have you seen *Lost in Space* on Netflix?"

"I've seen a few episodes."

"It's going to be similar. Different ships, different characters. It's a MMORPG... you probably don't know what that means..." His voice trailed off.

"I used to play *World of Warcraft*," she said. "So, yes, I know what it means. I'm kind of a dork too."

Declan stared at her as if she'd just sprouted a second head.

Alex shifted under the weight of it. "What?" she asked, suddenly aware of how exposed she felt.

A slow smile tugged at his mouth, softer than his usual smirk. "There's more to you than meets the eye."

Heat crept up her neck. Great. Now he was looking at her as if she were some kind of puzzle he wanted to take apart piece by piece. Before she could respond, *Grace and Frankie* timed out, and the TV returned to the Netflix homepage. *Lost in Space* was front and center.

"You want to watch an episode?" she asked, not ready for the night to end.

"Yeah," he said, smiling. "Let's do it."

They spent the next few hours watching, talking, laughing, and learning each other's rhythms. She wasn't sure how many episodes they'd gone through, but when she finally glanced at the clock, it was half past midnight. She had to be up early to get the kids to school.

As if sensing her thoughts, Declan stood. "I should get going. I have an early interview."

Alex rose with him. "I'll walk you out."

They drifted toward the door, the quiet between them thick with tension. Her pulse thudded in her ears, embarrassingly loud. She wanted him to kiss her, wanted it so badly it ached, but she knew she'd never be the one to make the first move.

He opened the door and stepped outside, the cool air brushing past her as if urging her forward.

He turned back, looking down at her with a soft smile. "Have a good night."

He lingered for a moment, then turned and headed down the steps.

Disappointment washed over her. "Goodnight," she said, closing the door.

"Hey, Alex," Declan called from the bottom of the stairs.

She yanked the door open again. "Yes?"

He looked up at her, breath visible in the cool night air. "Will you go to dinner with me tomorrow night?"

Her heart flipped. "I would love to… but I work tomorrow night."

"Friday?" he asked, smiling now.

"Friday works."

A warm, nervous thrill curled through her chest, equal parts excitement and panic. She tried to keep her expression neutral, but she could feel the smile tugging at her mouth anyway.

"Alright, Friday it is. Goodnight," he said, turning towards his car.

It wasn't a kiss, but it was something. And it was enough to make her lean against the door with a grin she couldn't fight.

Chapter Five
ALEX

Alex was the last one up the next morning. Thankfully, Alyssa had already made breakfast for the boys. Luke and Collin were on the couch, glued to a commercial featuring a very pregnant woman.

Collin turned to her, eyes wide. "Mom, when I get big, I wanna have a baby in my belly."

Alex raised her eyebrows and shot Alyssa a look. Alyssa smirked and shrugged. Alex hadn't had caffeine yet. She was not equipped for this conversation.

"That's... not how it works," Alex said. "Only girls can have babies in their bellies."

Collin looked devastated.

"Boys put the babies in the bellies, though," Luke interjected.

Alex dropped her head into her hands, mentally preparing for the onslaught of questions heading her way.

"How do boys get the babies in there?" Alyssa asked sweetly, sipping her juice with a wicked grin. The question was clearly meant just for Alex—but the boys had the hearing of bats and the impulse control of squirrels.

Alex shot her a murderous look.

Collin perked up instantly. "I think I know!" he announced, practically vibrating with confidence. "The boy goes to the store, picks out a teeny tiny baby, and brings it to the girl. Then the girl eats it, and it grows in her belly until it's so big it has to come back out!"

Alex paused. "That's exactly right, honey. You're so smart."

Collin beamed. Alex prayed the conversation was over.

"The baby comes out of the pachina," Luke announced.

Alex closed her eyes. So close. She had been so close to escaping without an anatomy lesson.

"What's a pachina?" Collin asked, face scrunched.

"It's down there," Luke whispered, pointing vaguely at his lower half.

"Yeah, Alyssa," Alex said dryly. "What's a pachina?"

Alyssa only smirked and took another sip.

"So the baby comes out of the girl's pee-pee?" Collin asked.

"Girls don't have a pee-pee, silly," Luke said confidently. "They just have a hole down there where pee, poop, and babies come out."

"Okay!" Alyssa cut in brightly. "Time to get dressed for school."

The boys looked ready to argue.

Alex closed her eyes for a beat, pinched the bridge of her nose, and let out a slow breath. "Go. Now."

They bolted up the stairs.

Alyssa slid a hot cup of coffee toward Alex. "You did not just tell him girls eat babies."

"I panicked," Alex said, laughing. "I didn't exactly see you correcting Luke's misperception of a 'pachina' either."

"We probably should sit them down and have a very generalized talk about the birds and the bees soon," Alyssa said in a resigned tone.

Alex gulped her coffee and noticed Alyssa staring at her with a grin on her face.

"So! Tell me everything!" Alyssa said excitedly.

Seeing an opportunity to give Alyssa a taste of her own medicine, Alex grinned.

"I would, but I need to get ready to take the boys to school."

"I hate you," Alyssa called after her.

"I love you too," Alex said, heading upstairs.

When Alex clocked in to work, the ER was eerily calm. Only six patients, no one in the waiting room. Her coworkers were sitting at their desks, scrolling on their phones. She wasn't about to jinx it by commenting.

She grabbed an assignment sheet and took over her one patient. Everything was done except waiting for labs.

With nothing else to do, she pulled up Amazon and started browsing for new shoes. Her ten-dollar Walmart specials weren't cutting it for twelve-hour shifts. Sunday was her birthday, and she decided she deserved something nice.

Thirty.

The number made her cringe. Where had the time gone? At least she still looked young enough to pretend she wasn't approaching a new decade.

Several hours into her shift, the ambulance radio toned out a multi-car collision with multiple injuries. The entire unit groaned as they got up to prepare the trauma rooms. Alex had just returned from stocking trauma room two when Lindsay, the charge nurse, called out that the injuries were minor. The patients would be assigned to regular rooms, leaving the trauma bays open.

All the incoming patients were assigned to other nurses.

Today might actually be her lucky day.

Alex settled back at the desk, pulled up Amazon again, and opened a bag of Sweet-Tart ropes. She had just taken a bite when a delivery tech approached the nurses' station holding a small bouquet of roses.

"Delivery for Alex Kelley," he said.

Alex blinked. "Uh... okay."

She signed for it, confused. Declan wouldn't send flowers. Not after one almost-date and a case update. Would he?

A cream-colored envelope was tucked between the roses.

She opened it.

"I hope the detective's visit last night was... professional.
You looked beautiful.
You always do."

No name.

No signature.

Her stomach tightened. A cold prickle crawled up her spine. She set the flowers aside, but the unease clung to her like static. Someone had been close enough to see Declan at her door. Close enough to see what she was wearing. Close enough to know she'd looked... beautiful.

Someone had been watching her last night. Were they watching her now?

She had just turned back to her computer when something caught her eye.

A patient was lying in her trauma room.

A patient who looked dead—or very close to it.

"What the fuck!" Alex shot to her feet and sprinted into the room.

Shelly rushed in behind her. "Sorry, Alex! This is my guy from room thirteen. He came in from the accident. He looked stable at first. Vitals were fine until he came back from CT and started throwing up blood. His pressure dropped to seventy-five over forty."

"Great," Alex muttered.

"I'll grab supplies for another IV. Put a pressure bag on those fluids," she called as she ran out.

Passing the physician's station, she glanced at the man's X-ray. His femur snapped clean in half and drove upward into his pelvis, the jagged end hovering centimeters from puncturing his bladder.

Of course, this day was too good to last.

She grabbed what she needed and hurried back. She had just inserted the second IV when the patient suddenly vomited blood. The tech caught most of it in a bag, but the man gasped, choked, and coughed, spraying warm droplets across Alex's face.

She froze.

"Oh, my God!" Memory, the tech, exclaimed. She grabbed a towel and wiped Alex's face. Alex sucked in a breath, realizing she'd been holding it since the blood hit her skin.

"Thank you," she managed, securing the IV before moving to place the Foley catheter.

The doctor entered as she worked. "He has a small subarachnoid hemorrhage. We need to transfer him to St. Mary's. No neurology coverage tonight. We also need Hare traction on that leg before transport. He has multiple vertebral fractures in his C-spine and T-spine. Get a C-collar and backboard."

Alex looked at Shelly.

Shelly shook her head. "I've never put anyone in traction."

"Me neither." Alex headed for Lindsay, who also shook her head.

"Call the medics and have them come show you," Lindsay said.

"Okay. I'll be tied up here for a while. Can you call St. Mary's and give report so we can get him out as soon as possible?"

Lindsay nodded.

Five minutes later, the medics walked in. Jason shook his head at Alex and Shelly.

"What?" they both said defensively.

"We've never had to put someone in traction before," Shelly explained. "And apparently no one else knows how either."

Jason laughed. "Alright. I'll show you."

Ten minutes later, they rolled the patient out for emergency transfer. Alex stepped out of the room and exhaled hard. She'd kept him alive. Now he was someone else's problem. She hoped he made it. He seemed like a sweet man.

Shift change hit. They were a nurse short, which meant Alex would take two extra rooms. She settled in as the day-shift nurse began report. She saw she had a patient in room fourteen she hadn't met yet, but labs had already been drawn while she was busy in trauma two.

She breathed a sigh of relief.

Memory squeezed through the cluster of nurses. "Alex, I need you in room eight. Like right now."

Alex had just picked up room eight, and the report she'd gotten suggested nothing critical. Just a sweet elderly woman with dementia and a touch of pneumonia.

"Is she okay?" Alex asked, alarmed by Memory's tone.

"Uh, yeah, she's fine. Just... come here. You'll see."

Alex followed Memory down the hall. Memory was in the waddling stage of pregnancy, and the sight made Alex think of Collin's baby-in-the-belly conversation that morning. She snorted quietly to herself.

They reached the door of room eight.

"Deep breath," Memory warned, then pushed the door open.

Alex was not prepared.

Her sweet little old lady was covered head to toe in feces. The walls, the sheets, her gown, her hair—everything.

Alex froze in the doorway, mouth open, until the smell hit her. She snapped her jaw shut and took a step back.

"Okay, hon," Alex said, voice tight. "We're going to go get some wipes, and we'll be right back."

She closed the door behind them.

"What the actual fuck?" She whispered to Memory.

"I put her on the bedpan and came back two minutes later to that. She said she had to 'get the impaction out.'" Memory said, making air quotes.

Alex didn't know whether to laugh or cry. "Maybe we can put her in the decon shower?"

"The decon shower doesn't have warm water. We'd freeze her to death. We can do an impromptu bed bath with wipes and towels," Memory suggested.

"Oh my God, I cannot handle this day," Alex groaned, heading for the supply room.

They gathered supplies and returned to the room. Fifteen minutes later, they were elbow-deep in cleanup. Memory was trying to scrub feces from under the woman's fingernails.

"I wish we could just cut her nails off," Memory muttered. "It'd be easier."

"Or the entire hand," Alex mumbled.

They both burst out laughing. A pang of remorse hit Alex the moment the words left her mouth. The woman wasn't in her right mind, and if she had been, she would've been mortified. Alex said a silent prayer that she never ended up with dementia.

When they finally emerged, Alex walked past the secretary's desk. The secretary flagged her down.

"Lab called. Blood's ready for room fourteen."

"Blood?" Alex asked. "Why?"

The secretary shrugged. "I'm just the messenger."

Alex sat at her computer and pulled up the lab report on the computer and skimmed it. The woman's hemoglobin was three.

How is she even alive?

She checked the computer for an upstairs room assignment. She silently said a prayer while she waited for the screen to load. Nothing yet. A groan slipped out. The transfusion would have to happen down here. ER nurses rarely had time for blood transfusions, but there was no choice.

She grabbed her phone and headed for the elevator. Blood products had to be hand-carried from the lab. The elevator doors closed. She checked her phone for the first time in hours.

One new message from Declan.

Hey, it's Declan. Hope you're having a good day.

Alex smiled despite herself.

Today has been crazy! I haven't even sat down to eat yet. AND! I've already gotten blood spit in my face.

Okay, whose ass am I kicking?

Alex laughed out loud.

He didn't do it on purpose. It was a little old man trying not to die.

Oh, okay, then. I guess he can live. I've got a new case, and I'll be working late. How about Denny's after you get off? Can't have you getting hangry.

Her heart sped up. Tonight? She wanted to see him—but not looking like she'd been dragged through a biohazard.

I'll have to go home and change first.

Okay, I'll pick you up at your place.

Sounds good! See you then!

The elevator dinged open. Alex walked to the blood bank. The technician was new; Alex had never seen her before. She read off the verification details.

"Patient is Sharon Roberts, DOB 02/05/1947, MRN 3009873, blood type B-, unit number W009754872, blood band EU4658, expiration 02/24/2020."

"It's a match," Alex said, signing for the unit.

Back in the ER, she grabbed tubing and saline. In her haste, she connected the tubing to the blood before the saline and forgot to clamp the other side. When she squeezed the reservoir, blood splattered onto the floor.

"Damn it!" she hissed, clamping it quickly.

She glanced at her patient, who was grinning.

"Sorry," Alex said.

"No worries, honey. I've seen you running around like your tail's on fire. Take your time."

Alex threw a towel over the spill and started the transfusion. She didn't know why she'd deviated from her routine. Her conversation with Declan had left her distracted.

She glanced at the clock.

Three more hours.

By the time she clocked out, she was utterly exhausted. Part of her wanted to cancel dinner, go straight home, shower, and collapse into bed. But the thought of seeing Declan—of sitting across from him, hearing that low voice again—was too tempting to pass up.

She clocked out ten minutes late and practically jogged to her car. Thankfully, she and Alyssa lived right down the street from the hospital. She pulled into the driveway, hurried inside, and came to an abrupt stop. A man she'd never seen before was sitting comfortably on her couch.

"Uh... hi, I'm Dean," he said, standing and offering his hand.

"Alex," she replied, shaking it. "Where's Alyssa?"

"She just ran upstairs to grab something."

"Okay. Nice to meet you." She nodded politely and headed for the stairs. She met Alyssa coming down the hallway.

Alyssa grinned. "I see you've met Dean."

"I did," Alex said, giving an approving nod. "Can't chat—going to Denny's with Declan."

She didn't wait for Alyssa's inevitable squeal or interrogation. She darted past her, straight into the bathroom, and turned on the shower.

She had exactly one goal: wash off twelve hours of chaos and look like a woman who hadn't been sprayed with blood, covered in feces, or traumatized by a stalker's anonymous flowers.

Tonight, she was seeing Declan.

And she would not show up looking like she'd survived a natural disaster.

Chapter Six
DECLAN

Declan was at a standstill with his latest murder case. He glanced at the clock and sighed. An hour and a half left before her shift ended. He tapped his pencil against the desk, trying to push through the fog settling behind his eyes. He was more tired than he wanted to admit after the late night he'd had. The fatigue made it hard to focus, and his thoughts kept drifting to Alex.

Finally deciding he needed a break, he stood and grabbed his coat. A quick shower before picking her up would help. The thought of seeing her again gave him a small surge of energy, enough to cut through the exhaustion that had been dragging him down all afternoon.

He wasn't sure why he'd asked her out so late. Maybe it was the way she had looked at him when he left her house. Or maybe it was the nagging thought that she'd had a rough day and he wanted to be the one to make it better. He knew little about nursing, but he knew the ER must be brutal.

He parked in his designated spot outside his industrial-style apartment building and headed for the lobby. Living on the third floor, just blocks from the station, had its perks. It was convenient, although it also meant work was always close.

He bypassed the elevator and took the stairs two at a time. At his apartment, he let the shower run while he stripped. The water always took forever to warm up. He caught his reflection in the mirror, noticing the dark stubble shadowing his jaw and the faint lines of fatigue around his eyes. The beard suited him. He hated shaving every day for a job he didn't particularly like, but regulations were regulations.

Knowing he wouldn't want to deal with it later, he grabbed his razor and stepped into the now-steaming shower.

He glimpsed himself in the mirror and made a mental note to start hitting the gym again. Between earning his degree, working full-time, and building his game, workouts had slipped lower on the priority list. Riding a desk would make him soft if he wasn't careful.

He hadn't always been a detective. He'd started as a beat cop, then joined SWAT a couple of years in. Not long after that, he'd been promoted to detective. Little Rock kept him busy. There was always something happening, always another case waiting.

After drying off, he pulled on jeans and his Deadpool hoodie. As he stepped outside, he spotted Mary sitting on the stoop. She was homeless, eccentric, and somewhere between her mid-fifties and early sixties. Declan talked to her whenever he saw her and gave her food when he remembered. He handed her the five-dollar bill he had in his pocket.

"Get something warm," he said.

Mary smiled and thanked him. He headed for his red Chevrolet Impala. The idea of replacing it had crossed his mind more than once, but no car payment beat shiny upgrades. He'd drive the Impala until the wheels fell off.

The closer he got to Alex's house, the more his nerves tightened. He hated that—hated how she could get under his skin without even trying. He wondered whether she would still want anything to do with him once she really knew him. Very few people ever had. Keeping everyone at arm's length had started as survival and calcified into habit.

His fingers flexed on the steering wheel.

He wasn't the casual type. Never had been. Two serious relationships, two endings that carved scars deep enough he still felt them.

Brianna came first—Darla's mother. He could still see the dim, filthy rooms he'd dragged her out of, the meth houses where she'd disappear for days. He'd been barely more than a kid himself, working odd jobs and grinding through night school to get his GED, doing everything he could because Darla needed him. Most boys his age would've folded. He didn't. He couldn't.

His stomach tightened as he turned onto Alex's road.

The night he came home to find nine-month-old Darla alone in her crib, Brianna nowhere in the house—that had been the breaking point. He filed for sole custody the next morning. She never showed up to the hearing. A few weeks later, he packed up, moved back to Arkansas with his daughter, and never looked back.

He exhaled slowly, trying to steady himself.

His mother, Katherine, had carried him through those early years. She'd scoop Darla up without complaint, settling her on her hip while he worked whatever jobs he could find—roofing, hauling, anything that kept them afloat. Dating wasn't even a thought. His life was simple: work, then home to his daughter.

Then came Susan.

Their relationship had moved fast—too fast, maybe. Late-night talks turned into early-morning coffee runs, and they were married before their first anniversary. She worked shifts at a steakhouse, always smelling faintly of grilled onions and fryer oil. He took a job as a roughneck in the Texas oil fields. Hard, dirty work, but it paid well.

He had loved her. Or at least he had tried to.

Declan swallowed, jaw tightening as Alex's house came into view through the trees.

He hadn't planned on becoming a cop. That started with a chance conversation in a parking lot with the Malvern chief of police. The chief had pushed him to take the civil service exam. Declan had laughed it off—until the oil rig started wearing him down. When his exam score came back higher than anything the department had seen in twenty years, they hired him on the spot.

He'd built a career from there. Detective Sergeant. Criminal Investigation Division. A reputation for being relentless, sharp, and unshakably calm under pressure.

But none of that had saved his marriage.

He came over the hill just before her driveway, headlights sweeping across the trees.

He still remembered the day everything with Susan snapped. He'd come home for lunch after an overnight shift, skipping his usual McDonald's stop because he didn't have the energy to flirt back at the drive-thru girl. The house had been dark, quiet. The kids asleep at the far end of the hall.

Then he'd heard Susan's moans.

Low. Breathless. Coming from their bedroom.

His hand had gone to his holster before he even realized it. For one terrifying second, the weight of the firearm felt like gravity itself, pulling him toward a decision he could never take back. But down the hall, his children slept. That was the only thing that kept him rooted. That, and the knowledge that once you cross a line like that, there's no coming home.

He blinked hard, dragging himself out of the memory.

He'd nearly missed Alex's driveway.

Declan eased the car to a stop behind her car and sat there for a moment in the dark, steadying his breath. Pushing the memories back where they belonged. Because whatever waited for him inside her house—whatever this thing between them was becoming—he needed to meet it with a clear head.

And God help him, he wasn't sure he had one left.

He had no idea what he was doing. After the divorce, he'd sworn off anything resembling a relationship. The bachelor life had been simple, predictable, and safe. Yet here he was in the middle of the night, parked in Alex's driveway with his pulse thudding like a rookie on his first call. Something about her pulled at him in a way he didn't understand, a quiet gravity he kept trying—and failing—to ignore. He wasn't the kind of man who got nervous about dates. At least, that's what he'd been telling himself for years. But his pulse had other opinions—loud ones.

Taking a reluctant breath, he stepped into the garage and knocked

Alyssa's smiling face greeted him at the door. "Hello again! Come in. Alex is still upstairs getting ready."

Declan stepped inside. A man stood near the sofa with his back turned, slipping on his coat. Alyssa leaned up and kissed him.

"Declan, this is Dean. Dean, this is Declan."

Recognition hit both men at the same time.

"Hey, man," Dean said with a grin.

"Hey," Declan replied, shaking his hand.

"You two know each other?" Alyssa asked.

They both nodded.

"We ran into each other pretty regularly on calls when I was working patrol," Declan said. "He's not bad for a hoser." The playful glint in his eye made Dean snort.

Dean clapped him on the shoulder and shook his head. "Good seeing you, man. I should get going."

Alyssa walked him to the door, then returned to Declan. "I'll run upstairs and let Alex know you're here."

A minute later she reappeared at the top of the stairs. "She'll be right down."

"Thanks," Declan said.

A couple of minutes passed before Alex appeared on the landing. Their eyes met.

"Hi," she said, smiling.

She stepped out in fitted jeans that hugged the curve of her hips, brown knee-high boots, and a white three-quarter sleeve boho top. She'd straightened her hair, and her bracelets jingled softly as she moved.

She looked beautiful. Fresh. Nothing like someone who had just survived a twelve-hour ER shift.

"Ready?" she asked, reaching the bottom of the stairs.

"After you." He opened the door for her and followed her to the car.

Once they were on the road, Alex broke the silence. "So, what's the new case you were working late on?"

"Murder. Looks drug-related. Fentanyl is everywhere right now. Stupid and extremely deadly."

"Yeah, we've been seeing a lot of overdoses in the ER. It's scary."

Declan nodded, eyes on the dark stretch of highway ahead. The wipers clicked softly across the windshield, pushing aside a mist that wasn't quite rain. Streetlights flashed over the hood in slow, rhythmic pulses. The heater hummed low, filling the cab with a dry warmth that contrasted sharply with the chilly night outside. Alex sat angled toward the window, her reflection faint in the glass, her expression thoughtful.

The parking lot at Denny's was packed. Cars squeezed into every space, headlights sweeping across the asphalt as people came and went. Declan eased into a spot near the back, the engine ticking as it cooled.

Inside, the noise hit them immediately—clattering dishes, overlapping conversations, the hiss of the grill. Declan glanced at Alex and caught the subtle way her shoulders tightened, like the sudden chaos pressed in on her more than she expected.

"Are you okay?" he asked.

"I hate crowds," she yelled over the noise.

Thank God. So did he. He didn't want to ruin the date he'd suggested.

"Wanna get something to go?"

She nodded quickly.

They grabbed menus, ordered, and were back in the car a few minutes later.

"Do you want to go back to my place and watch another episode of Lost in Space while we eat?" she asked.

"Yeah, that sounds good. I've been wanting to rewatch it since we started it the other day."

As Alex unpacked the food, Declan queued up the show.

"Thank you," he said when she handed him his plate.

She smiled, already halfway through her meal. She hadn't eaten in over twenty-four hours, and hunger had taken over.

Declan took a bite of his sandwich and groaned. "This is amazing. Want a bite?"

It looked incredible, and her stomach had been complaining for the last ten minutes.

"Sure."

He held out half of the sandwich, waiting patiently. She leaned in and took a small bite from the corner, trying not to take more than her share. The flavor hit instantly, rich and perfect, and she couldn't stop the quiet hum of appreciation.

"Momma?"

They both jumped at the small, sleepy voice behind them.

"Is he feeding you a baby?" Collin asked, rubbing his eyes.

Declan's eyes went wide. Alex groaned.

"Am I feeding you what?" Declan choked, as his eyes danced between Alex and Collin.

"No, Collin. Nobody is feeding anyone a baby." Alex forced a smile, doing her best to ignore Declan's raised brows and the heat creeping up her cheeks. "Why are you out of bed?"

"I heard a noise."

"Come, give me a hug," Alex said. He shuffled around the couch and wrapped his arms around her.

"Collin, this is my friend Declan. Declan, this is my son."

"Pleasure to meet you, Collin," Declan said.

"Nice to meet you too," Collin yawned.

"All right, mister. Back to bed. You have school in the morning."

They said their goodnights, and Collin trudged upstairs.

As soon as he was out of earshot, Declan turned to Alex. "I feel like there is a story behind that question." A sly grin curled the edges of his lips.

Alex blushed from head to toe. "The other day he came up with this story about boys buying babies at the store and feeding them to girls so they grow in our bellies. I... didn't correct him. I may have even agreed. He's five. I wasn't prepared for that conversation."

Declan's laugh boomed through the house, warm and unrestrained. It was contagious. Alex laughed with him, the tension melting from her shoulders.

"So, is Collin your only child?" he asked.

"Yes. His dad and I split up when he was a baby. It's been just us for five years. Moving in with Alyssa has been amazing. It's nice having help and someone else to rely on."

A thought came out of left field, sharp and uninvited. He wanted to be someone she could rely on.

"Do you have any kids?" Alex asked.

"Yeah. I have three."

Her eyebrows shot up. "Three?"

He nodded, bracing for the usual reaction. "Yeah. Darla is eighteen. I had her when I was seventeen. Her mother made some poor choices and disappeared soon after she was born. I moved back to Arkansas with Darla when she was nine months old and raised her myself until I met my ex-wife, Susan. Then we had John and Andrew. John is eleven; Andrew is seven. Susan and I split up three years ago. I get the boys every other weekend and during the summer. Darla's in college now."

He tried to keep his tone light. "Did I scare you off with my brood of children?"

"Not at all." She hesitated, studying him with that quiet, careful curiosity of hers. "Do you... want more kids someday?"

A sharp, instinctive no punched through his chest before he could soften it. His jaw tightened, and he forced a slow breath before answering.

"No." The word came out too fast, too firm. He cleared his throat. "I mean, no. I'm good with the three I have."

He didn't add the rest: that he'd spent too many years letting someone else dictate his life, his choices, his worth. He'd promised himself he'd never hand that kind of power to anyone again. Loving his kids was easy—trusting another adult with his future—his kids' future—was not.

Alex didn't press. She only nodded, letting the subject settle between them.

"Where did you live before moving back to Arkansas?" she asked.

Declan shifted, the old memories stirring like dust in a room he rarely entered. He didn't want to scare her off with his past, but he'd opened the door. "My childhood was complicated. My brother, Josh, and I ran away when I was fifteen. We lived in Austin for a while, then Ohio. Josh stayed there. I came home."

She had questions—he could see them flicker across her face—but she tucked them away with a gentleness that eased something tight in his chest. Declan let out a slow breath, the earlier tension loosening. Her weight against him felt... safe. Uncomplicated. Something he didn't have to guard against.

He wrapped an arm around her, letting her settle against him, and resolved to stay awake until the end of the episode. Now that he'd eaten, exhaustion crept in slowly, tugging at the edges of his awareness. Twenty more minutes, he told himself. Then he'd head home, crawl into his bed, and let the quiet swallow him whole.

Chapter Seven
ALEX

Morning light pooled across her face, coaxing Alex back to consciousness. She shifted, feeling the unfamiliar give of the couch cushions before her mind caught up. She must've fallen asleep on the couch.

Her pillow moved.

"What the—?" Alex shot upright.

Declan was half-sitting, half-slumped against the couch cushions, blinking blearily like he wasn't entirely convinced morning was real. Her head had been in his lap. At some point, they'd both just... given in to sleep.

He scrubbed a hand over his face. "Is it morning?" His voice was rough, sleep-thick.

"Yeah," she murmured, glancing toward the soft wash of light spilling through the window. "Sun's just coming up."

"Oh, crap." He let out a low groan. "All I remember is trying to stay awake until the episode ended."

"Same," Alex said, though her cheeks warmed at the realization of how they'd ended up tangled together.

Declan stretched, joints popping, and let out a jaw-cracking yawn. "I should get out of here before Collin wakes up."

"Yeah... probably not a bad idea," she agreed, even if a small part of her wished he'd stay just a little longer.

They rose slowly, still shaking off sleep, and padded toward the kitchen. The house was quiet except for the faint sizzle of something on the stove.

When they rounded the corner, Alyssa sat perched at the island, chin propped in her hand, smirking like she'd been waiting for them to appear.

"Well, good morning," she chirped, far too bright for the hour

The smell of bacon wrapped around them.

"Breakfast before you leave, Declan?" she asked, returning to the skillet.

Declan glanced at Alex.

"Asking was just a formality," she said. "You'll have to eat something if you want to escape."

"Breakfast sounds good."

"Great. Sit. It's almost ready."

They had barely taken their seats when a stampede thundered down the stairs.

"Momma, why is he here again?" Collin demanded.

"He wanted to eat breakfast with us," Alex said, hoping that would be enough.

It wasn't.

"Why are you both wearing the same clothes from last night?"

Luke's eyes widened. "He was here last night?"

"Yeah," Collin said proudly. "I heard a noise and came downstairs. He was putting a baby in Mommy's belly."

The sip of juice Alyssa had just taken rocketed out of her nose in a violent spray, splattering the counter like a crime scene. She lurched to the sink, wheezing with laughter.

Alex groaned. Declan tried to smother a laugh with a forced cough.

"Collin! For the love of God, Declan was not trying to put a baby in my belly. I took a bite of his sandwich. That's it. Why are we still talking about babies? Where is this coming from?"

"I want a baby sister," Collin said matter-of-factly.

"Well, that's not happening anytime soon. When you go to your dad's this weekend, ask him where babies come from. He can tell you."

"I already asked him. He told me to ask you."

"Of course he did," Alex muttered, scrubbing a hand over her brow.

"Alright, boys," she said, pointing toward the table. "Go sit down. Breakfast is almost ready."

Alyssa had regained control of herself, though tears still streamed down her face as she plated food. Alex wanted to curl up into a ball and die. They ate in relative silence. When the boys finished, they ran upstairs to get dressed for school.

Declan stood. "I should get going. I need to get home and change before work."

"Okay. I'll walk you out."

They stepped into the garage.

"Sorry I fell asleep last night," Declan said, brushing a hand through his hair. "I was more tired than I thought."

"I was too. I don't even remember falling asleep," Alex said with a laugh.

"I hope I didn't make things awkward between you and Collin."

Alex let out a full-belly laugh. "You? Make things awkward? We haven't even been on a proper date, and my son has already accused you of trying to impregnate me. Twice. You're definitely not the awkward one here."

Declan grinned. She was blushing again, and the sight hit him hard. He reached out and brushed her cheek. She leaned into his touch. He slid his hand behind her neck and pulled her up for a kiss.

He meant it to be gentle. Her eager response ruined that plan. He backed her against the garage wall and deepened the kiss. Her hands slipped under his shirt, exploring the warm lines of his chest.

Neither of them heard the door open.

"Ew!" Luke and Collin shouted in unison.

Alex and Declan broke apart instantly, trying to look like they hadn't just been making out like teenagers. The boys hurried past them and climbed into Alyssa's car.

"Have a good day at school, boys," Alex called.

"Try not to get pregnant while I'm gone," Alyssa teased, sliding into the driver's seat.

Alex waved as they backed out of the garage.

"We really need to hang out somewhere other than my house," she said.

Declan glanced over, that small, crooked smile tugging at his mouth. It did ridiculous things to her pulse. "I was thinking the same thing."

"Are you free tonight?" he asked.

She nodded before her brain caught up. "Yes."

"How about an actual date?"

Heat rushed up her neck. "That sounds... good."

"Great. I'll pick you up at six." He leaned in and kissed her cheek.

"I really have to get going," he said.

"Alright. Have a good day at work."

Alex watched him drive away, her pulse still fluttering. When she stepped back inside, the stiffness hit her all at once. Her neck ached from the couch; her back protested every movement, and the late night clung to her like a heavy coat. She was exhausted, but her mind refused to settle.

She stripped off her jeans and collapsed into bed, fingertips brushing her lips as if to confirm the kiss had actually happened. It had. And it had been perfect.

She reached for her fan, turned it on, and plugged in her phone. Cool air drifted over her skin, easing some of the tension.

Her phone buzzed in her hand before she could set it down.

Unknown number.

She frowned. Too early for spam. Too late for anyone she knew.

She answered anyway. "Hello?"

Silence.

Then, the faint sound of breathing. Slow, heavy, and loud enough not to be accidental.

A cold ripple moved through her.

"You have the wrong number," she said, keeping her voice steady. She hung up and stared at the screen for a moment before placing the phone on the nightstand.

Her gaze drifted toward the hallway. She mentally retraced her steps, trying to remember if she had locked the front door. After a moment, she exhaled. She had. She remembered turning the deadbolt before heading up the stairs.

Still, unease lingered.

Maybe it was nothing. Maybe someone misdialed. Or maybe one of her coworkers was messing with her again. They loved their pranks, and she had been an easy target more than once. Her mind flickered to him for a split second before she shut it down. She would not spiral over one odd phone call.

She lay back against the pillows and focused on her breathing until the tension slowly loosened. The fan crooned, the cool air brushing her skin. Little by little, her heartbeat steadied. The phone lay silent on the nightstand, and she drifted into sleep with a lingering sense that something about the call was not as harmless as she wanted to believe.

Declan

Declan was still in a good mood when he pulled into the parking lot of his loft, but it thinned the moment he killed the engine. The drive home had given him plenty of time to refocus on his case, yet the details refused to settle into anything that made sense.

Everyone wanted to write it off as a drug deal gone wrong. Martha had been a familiar face in the city's underbelly, drifting from alley to alley, known to every patrol officer by name. Petty theft. Solicitation. Public intoxication. Nothing violent. Nothing to suggest she had any enemies.

But someone had put two bullets in her back and taken her left pinky finger.

Declan leaned back in his seat, replaying the scene in his mind. Martha had weighed maybe a hundred pounds soaking wet. She couldn't have fought off a determined attacker. If someone had killed her in anger, they would have faced her. They would have wanted her to see it coming. Shooting her in the back felt wrong. Cowardly. Unplanned.

And the finger. That was the part that wouldn't let him go.

The medical examiner had been clear. The finger was severed perimortem. Not a trophy taken after the fact. Not a cleanup mistake. Whoever did it had either been trying to get something out of her or had enjoyed hurting her. Neither option fit the woman he knew.

They searched the alley three times. Officers had dug through the dumpster until their gloves tore. No finger. No weapon. No sign of a struggle. The only thing found on her body was a crumpled scrap of paper clenched in her fist.

Help me.

The handwriting had been messy, frantic, almost childlike. Declan couldn't shake the feeling that the note wasn't meant for the police at all.

As Declan climbed the stairs to his loft, his thoughts drifted to Alex. A grin tugged at his mouth. He hadn't laughed that hard in years. Collin was a character. And Alex's mortified reaction to her son's accusations had been adorable. For a moment, he had thought she might be more innocent than he had originally assumed.

Then they kissed.

That fleeting thought had vanished as quickly as his erection when Luke and Collin caught them in the garage.

He shook his head, still smiling, and changed into clean clothes. After a quick check in the mirror, he headed back downstairs. He had been inside for less than five minutes. He was already running late and wanted to make progress on the case today.

As he approached his car, he noticed a folded note tucked under the wiper blade.

He scanned the parking lot but didn't see anyone.

He lifted the wiper and unfolded the paper.

STAY AWAY FROM HER!

An engine roared to life across the street. Declan looked up just in time to see a brown van peel away from the curb. He took two steps toward the road, trying to catch the license plate.

He never made it.

Something slammed into him from behind. His body flew forward and hit the concrete hard. Pain exploded through him. Car alarms blared somewhere nearby. A high-pitched ringing filled his ears until he thought his skull might crack open. He tasted the metallic tang of blood.

The edges of his vision darkened as he fought to stay conscious. He tried to push himself upright, but the moment he moved his right arm, a sharp, blinding pain shot through him. His strength gave out.

His head hit the concrete again as darkness swallowed him.

Chapter Eight
ALEX

Alex finished getting ready just before six. Alyssa had eagerly agreed to watch the boys so Alex could go on her date, and now Alex sat on the couch, nerves fluttering in her stomach. She wondered where Declan planned to take her. He hadn't texted all day, which she chalked up to his new case, but the silence still gnawed at her.

Collin and Luke were deep in a heated debate about the best way to catch Bigfoot. Luke insisted that a simple net trap would do the trick. Collin argued passionately for digging a pit, covering it with a trapdoor, and camouflaging it with leaves. Their animated discussion made both women smile.

At a quarter past six, Declan was officially late.

Alex noticed Alyssa's concerned glances from the couch where she sat knitting. Each one made Alex feel more exposed. She opened her messages with Declan and hesitated before typing.

Are we still on for tonight?

Thirty minutes later, the message remained unread. She tried calling. It went straight to voicemail.

A sinking feeling settled in her chest. Either something had happened, or she had misread him entirely.

She stood abruptly, drawing Alyssa's attention.

"Everything okay?" Alyssa asked.

"I don't know. His phone keeps going to voicemail. Maybe he got wrapped up in the case and forgot about tonight." Alex tried to sound casual, but her voice wavered.

"With the way he was looking at you this morning, it would have to be a pretty serious case to make him forget," Alyssa said.

"I think I'm going to call it a night," Alex murmured, heading for the stairs.

"Love you!" Alyssa called.

"Love you, too."

Upstairs, Alex peeled herself out of her low-cut sweater and dark denim boot-cut jeans, then stepped into a hot shower. Uncertainty washed over her. She had never been stood up before, and the sting of it sat heavy in her chest. She allowed herself the length of the shower to wallow, then forced her insecurities back down where they belonged.

She crossed the hall to her room and froze when she saw an unread text. Her stomach sank when she saw it was from her boss.

> Can you come in for a few hours? We are short-staffed tonight.

Disappointment slapped her. She sighed and pulled on her scrubs. Sleep was out of the question anyway. Work would keep her from spiraling. And if Declan showed up, she wouldn't be sitting here waiting like an idiot.

Alyssa looked up from her knitting when Alex came downstairs.

"Ah, they got you, huh? I'm ignoring her text."

"Yeah. I need to keep busy. And the extra money won't hurt."

"Be safe," Alyssa said as Alex headed for the door.

"I will."

She stepped into the garage, the cool night air settling around her. The overhead light flickered on, casting long shadows across the concrete floor. She walked to her car, then reached back and pulled the garage door closed behind her.

Her phone chimed in her hand.

A sinking feeling rolled through her. It would be just her luck for Declan to text the moment she agreed to go into work.

She glanced at the screen.

Not Declan.

Unknown number.

Her breath tightened.

A new message appeared beneath the missed call from earlier.

I would never stand you up.

The words glowed in the dim garage, sharp enough to raise the hairs on her arms. Her pulse kicked hard. Someone had been close enough to see her. Maybe close enough to see her now. She drew a slow breath and fought the instinct to scan the shadows.

WHO IS THIS?

She stood there for a moment, waiting for a reply she knew would never come. Before opening her car door, she unlocked her phone again and typed a quick message to Alyssa.

Lock all the doors.

Alyssa replied almost instantly.

Already on it.

They both made it a habit to keep the doors locked after dark, but she felt the need to ensure Alyssa didn't forget. She would need to talk to her soon about the strange messages, just so her friend stayed alert to anything that felt off. The thought settled uneasily in her chest as she slipped her phone into her scrub pocket.

Alex unlocked her car, the sound echoing a little too loudly in the quiet garage, and climbed inside. The moment the door shut behind her, the space felt even more still, as if the night itself was holding its breath.

Work. She needed to get to work. Anything to keep her mind from spiraling.

But as she backed out of the garage, the message echoed in her thoughts, colder each time it replayed.

The house was dark when Alex returned later that night. Alyssa was already in bed. Alex set her tumbler in the sink, grabbed a glass of water, and trudged upstairs. She changed into pajamas and had just crawled into bed when her door creaked open.

"Momma, I had a bad dream," Collin whispered, rubbing his eyes.

Alex lifted the covers. "You wanna sleep with me tonight?"

He nodded and climbed in beside her.

She had just closed her eyes when he whispered again. "Momma?"

"Yes, Collin?"

"I like Declan. Is he gonna come over again soon?"

Alex's breath caught. "I don't know, baby. I hope so. I like him too."

Collin seemed satisfied. "Goodnight, Momma."

"Goodnight, Collin."

She kissed his forehead. He rolled onto his side and drifted off. Alex watched him for a moment, marveling at how fast he was growing. It felt like yesterday he was a baby. She lay back, listening to his soft breathing, and slipped into sleep.

Alex jolted awake with a gasp, heart slamming against her ribs. For a split second she was sure something was wrong, really wrong, until her eyes focused on Collin's tear-streaked face.

"Momma... I threw up!"

All traces of sleep vanished as she jumped into action. Vomit covered the bed. She forced herself to breathe as the realization that there wasn't an immediate threat to their lives settled over her.

Collin gagged again.

"Toilet!" Alex shouted, guiding him across the hall. They made it just in time.

She rubbed his back as he retched, then helped him into the shower. While he washed off, she gathered his soiled clothes and stripped the bed. Thankfully, most of it had hit the comforter. She carried everything downstairs and started a load of laundry.

In the kitchen, she rummaged through the medicine cabinet until she found an old bottle of Zofran. She checked the clock on the stove. It was four thirty in the morning. She was bone-tired.

She grabbed spare sheets and a throw blanket from the linen closet and headed upstairs. As she reached the top, Alyssa poked her head out of her room.

"Everything okay?" she asked groggily.

"Yeah. Collin got sick. I'm going to finish the bed and get him dressed. I'll keep him home today."

Alyssa nodded and started to close her door.

"Hey," Alex said.

"Yeah?"

"Can you put the laundry in the dryer when you get up?"

"Of course."

Alex got Collin dried off and dressed, then gave him the Zofran and some Tylenol. He felt warm, though she wasn't sure if it was fever or the shower. He climbed back into bed with her, and within minutes, they were both asleep again.

Alex woke again just before noon. Sunlight sliced through the blinds in warm golden slats, dust motes drifting lazily in the beams. She reached for the spot where Collin had been sleeping and found only cool sheets.

She swung her legs out of bed, the floor cool beneath her feet, and hurried down the hall. Collin's room was empty. A faint cartoon theme song drifted up from downstairs.

"Collin?" she called.

"Down here, Mom!" he answered.

He was curled on the couch under a blanket, pale and glassy-eyed, watching *Scooby-Doo*. Alex brushed her fingers across his forehead. His skin was warm and slightly clammy.

"How are you feeling, honey?"

"Not good," he mumbled.

"He ate a dried piece of toast," Alyssa said from the kitchen, the smell of coffee and butter lingering in the air. "That's all he could keep down."

"Thanks for watching him. I was exhausted."

"No problem. Hey, Thursday is your birthday, right?" Alyssa asked, pretending she didn't already know and hadn't already made plans.

Alex nodded.

"I was thinking. Since we are both off work, we should go out. Both boys will be at their dads', and we can invite some girls from work."

Alex was a homebody most of the time, but she had to admit, getting out for a night sounded fun. "You know what? That sounds like a great idea."

Alyssa's face lit up. "Great, I'll text the girls now!" Alyssa wandered out of the kitchen with her face buried in her phone. Alex walked over to the coffeepot and flipped it on. She reached into the cabinet, pulled out a coffee mug, and set it down beside the coffee, waiting for it to percolate.

She sat down at the kitchen island and switched her phone on. Nothing. She hated that she cared so much. She had just poured herself a cup when Collin shuffled in.

"Mom, can I play games on your phone?" Collin asked.

She hesitated, then handed it over. "If I get a call or text, bring it to me."

Collin was notorious for ignoring incoming calls and messages while he played on the phone.

He nodded and shuffled back to the couch. Alex finished her coffee in a few large gulps and decided to go for a run. She needed to burn off the restless energy coiling in her stomach.

Outside, the air was crisp and smelled faintly of pine and distant wood smoke. She plugged in her headphones, turned on her tracker app, and started down the driveway. Her shoes crunched over gravel before hitting the smooth asphalt of the road.

At the two-mile mark, her lungs burned pleasantly, and sweat dampened her temples. She turned back toward the house, rolling her shoulders to loosen the tightness.

As she glanced over her shoulder before crossing the street, she noticed a man running behind her, about a hundred feet back. Her music had drowned out his approach.

The road was quiet. No cars. No neighbors outside. Just the rhythmic thud of her own footsteps and the faint rustle of wind through the trees.

Seeing someone else out here felt... off.

She tried to shake the feeling as she jogged past him. He was crouched over, tying his shoe, so she didn't catch his face, but something about him made the hair on her neck lift. Alex quickened her pace, her pulse ticking a little faster.

A minute later, she slowed and checked behind her.

The man had turned around too.

A cold prickle crawled up her spine. She increased her speed gradually, trying not to make it obvious she'd noticed. Her breath grew louder in her ears, mixing with the steady beat of her music. She told herself she was just jumpy after the creepy texts from last night, that he was probably just a normal guy out for a run. Her body didn't buy it.

She risked another glance.

He had sped up. His strides were longer now. Purposeful.

Her stomach dropped.

Alex launched into a full sprint. Her feet slapped the pavement; her breath tore in and out of her chest. The air tasted metallic. Her legs burned. Only a quarter mile to the house.

She checked again.

He was gaining. Why hadn't she thought to bring her pepper spray or pocket knife?

Branches whipped in the wind overhead. Her ponytail slapped against her back. Her heartbeat thundered in her ears.

She rounded the corner and saw her driveway. Alyssa was outside, bent over the back of her car. Alex could hear the man's footsteps behind her—closer now, too close.

"Alyssa!" she screamed, voice cracking.

Alyssa jerked upright, eyes wide, as Alex stumbled up the driveway, gasping for air. Alex pointed toward the street, chest heaving.

"Alex, what the hell is going on?" Alyssa asked.

"He—he was chasing me," Alex panted, tasting copper on her tongue.

The man jogged past their house and lifted a hand in an easy wave, as if nothing were wrong. His footsteps faded down the road.

Alex stared after him, her skin crawling. "What the hell?" she whispered. Had she imagined it?

Alyssa frowned. "Should we call the police?"

Alex hesitated. Her hands shaking from the adrenaline. "I don't know. Maybe I overreacted. But he kept gaining on me. I panicked."

Alyssa studied her. "Is this about the flowers?"

Alex swallowed hard. "Maybe. That note was creepy. And Declan never texted back. And now, some guy is following me down a deserted road? It freaked me out."

"Okay," Alyssa said. "Let's get inside."

They locked every door. The house felt too quiet, too still. As the adrenaline faded, embarrassment crept in.

"I probably overreacted," Alex said. "But I still want the doors locked."

"Agreed. Maybe we should get a treadmill."

Honestly, that sounded perfect. They had space. And one thing was certain—Alex would not be running outside again anytime soon

"There's something I've been meaning to tell you," Alex said as she sat beside Alyssa on the couch.

"What is it?" Alyssa asked, concerned.

"I think I have a stalker," Alex said quietly. "I've been getting strange calls and texts. Plus the flowers at work the other day."

"Alex, what the hell?" Alyssa leaned in, eyes sharp. "What calls? What texts? What did they say?"

Alex's stomach tightened. "I know. I tried to brush it off at first, but it keeps happening. It started with phone calls—no one saying anything, just heavy breathing. Then last night someone texted me from the same number saying they'd never stand me up."

Alyssa's brows pulled together. "What? Who even knew you had a date?"

"Just me, you, and Declan." Alex swallowed. "Did you say anything to anyone? Maybe it's some kind of prank."

"No," Alyssa said immediately. "I didn't tell anyone. Not even Dean."

"Well, it is freaking me out, and that's why I reacted the way I did a few minutes ago."

"Have you told anyone else?" Alyssa asked. "Or gone to the police?"

Alex shook her head. "No. They haven't actually threatened me. The police won't do anything."

She didn't add the part she was avoiding—the part where she might already know who was behind the messages, and how going to the police could tear her life apart in ways she didn't have the strength to face.

"Let me see the messages," Alyssa said, holding out her hand.

Alex eased the phone from Collins sleeping hands, and passed it to her. She watched Alyssa's eyes widen as she scrolled, realization settling in. Someone had been close enough to watch Alex inside her own home.

"Alex, you at least need to file a report in case something happens."

Alex let out a reluctant sigh. "I'll go in the morning."

Alyssa exhaled, her expression shifting into something steady and protective. "Then we stay alert. We keep the doors locked at all times. And you tell me the second anything else happens."

A small wave of relief loosened the tightness in Alex's chest. She was still scared, but she wasn't carrying it alone anymore.

Chapter Nine
HIM

The bitch was faster than he'd expected.

By the time he reached his '88 Dodge Ram B250, his lungs burned and his breath came in sharp, irritated bursts. Sweat clung to the back of his neck, making his greasy hair stick to his skin. He had been right there, close enough to feel the air shift as she sprinted past him, when her roommate stepped outside.

That ruined everything.

He yanked open the van door and slammed it shut hard enough to rattle the frame. The steering wheel absorbed the full force of his fist.

"Five more seconds," he hissed. "Five. More. Fucking. Seconds and I would have had her."

He could still see the look on her face when he'd waved. That flicker of confusion. The hesitation. The way doubt had crept into her eyes. It had been almost funny, watching her question her own instincts.

Almost.

He scrubbed a hand through his hair, the strands stiff with old sweat and cheap motel shampoo, then jammed the key into the ignition. The engine coughed before roaring to life. Gravel spat under the tires as he peeled out of the wooded pull-off.

If they called the police, he would be long gone before anyone showed up.

She would not be happy about this. Not at all.

He still remembered the moment Alex's name resurfaced last week. Mr. Beaumont had said it offhandedly, flipping through paperwork as if it meant nothing. But the instant the name left his mouth, something inside him had gone rigid. Eight years. Eight years without a single thought of her, and then suddenly she was back in his world, dropped into his lap like some twisted joke, unraveling everything he'd built.

She had always been good at that. Ruining things. Taking what wasn't hers. Even back then.

And now she was taking things that belonged to him. Things he had worked for. Things he deserved. Not her.

For a while, he had almost let it go. He could handle the slap in the face from the old man. He could handle losing what should have been his. Forgetting it would have been easy enough. But she hadn't been willing to forget. She'd been furious, demanding they reclaim what was theirs, pushing and pushing until he finally told her to handle it herself if it mattered that much.

He might have left it at that—until he started cleaning out the old man's desk.

That was when he found the letter.

Alex's letter.

A neat little warning tucked among the files, explaining that she had copied the contents of the office computer to a hard drive and would go to the authorities if anyone came after her. No wonder the old man had never acted on anything. He barely knew how to turn a computer on. He was old-school, all paper and pen. But he had used that computer. He had kept things on it that were never meant to see daylight.

And now Alex had a copy.

A cold certainty settled in his chest. She wasn't just a nuisance from the past anymore. She was a threat. One he couldn't ignore. One he needed to eliminate from his life before she destroyed everything he'd worked for.

The likelihood of her discovering what she possessed was slim. He'd disguised it well enough. But the fact that it was out there at all—the fact it wasn't just his neck on the line—was enough to make him act. If the boss found out about his mistake, he was as good as dead.

Once he retrieved what she'd taken, everything would fall back into place. Order restored. Balance corrected. And she… she would finally be satisfied.

He had gone straight to the old files, hands shaking with something that felt too much like excitement. Her social was still there. Untouched. Waiting. It had taken less than an hour to track her to Arkansas; another ten minutes to confirm where she worked. New name, same girl.

He scoffed when he saw she'd become a nurse. Of course she had. She was always trying to save people who didn't want or deserve saving.

His grip tightened on the wheel, knuckles whitening. For more than a week, he'd studied her patterns, memorizing every routine. Trail rides. Girls' night. Those late shifts at the hospital. He had waited for the perfect moment, and today should have been it.

She had slipped through his fingers.

Only because the roommate had been outside. If another opportunity came—one that involved both of them—he decided he wouldn't hesitate. Interference had consequences.

And now he was on a timeline. Her timeline. He hadn't cared about any of it before, but she had made it clear he didn't have the luxury of letting this go. He had one week to fix his mistake, one week before everything shifted in ways he couldn't control.

The cop had complicated things, and he hadn't been part of the plan. But the man's constant visits had slowed everything down long enough. Removing him had been practical. The last thing he needed was some lovesick puppy with a badge sniffing around when the apple of his eye eventually turned up dead in a ditch somewhere.

Even now, the memory flickered through his mind like a match being struck—the orange glow in the rearview mirror, the distant wail of car alarms, the sharp jolt of knowing he'd outmaneuvered someone trained to see danger coming. It wasn't the act itself that stirred something in him, but the power of it, the certainty that he was always one step ahead. Thinking about it now sent a quiet, electric satisfaction through him, a reminder that nothing and no one could stop what he had planned next.

Yes, he had gone off-script, but his plan had worked out beautifully. But she would not see it that way. She never did. She had expectations, standards. And when he failed to meet those expectations...

He swallowed hard, throat tightening at the memory. He'd taken a calculated risk today, stepping close enough for her to really see him, certain she'd at least hesitate. But she hadn't. Not a flicker. Not even a pause. The girl who'd upended his life and walked away like he was forgettable had looked right through him, and the irritation of that scraped at him like sandpaper. When he was finished with her, she'd never forget him again.

He thought of the past week, of watching Alex from the woods. The way her posture tightened whenever that instinctive prickle ran up her spine. The quick, nervous scans of the trees. And then the moment he savored most—the slow bloom of fear across her face when she realized she wasn't alone.

He pressed harder on the gas, the van rattling as it picked up speed. The motel sign flickered weakly in the afternoon light, buzzing as if it were struggling to stay alive. He pulled into the cracked parking lot, gravel crunching under the tires, and killed the engine. For a moment he just sat there, breathing through the sting in his ribs, steadying himself before facing her.

The air inside the room hit him the second he opened the door—stale cigarette smoke, cheap floral cleaner, and the faint metallic tang of the space heater working overtime. She sat in the single armchair by the window, the blinds half-drawn, slats of pale winter light striping across her face. She didn't look up right away, but he felt her attention shift toward him like a blade turning.

"Where have you been?" she asked in a sickly sweet voice.

He shut the door behind him. "I tried to snatch the girl."

That got her attention. The full weight of her scrutiny landed on him. She didnt have an outward reaction, she never did. He had learned to read between the lines long ago. They lived in a world where outward reactions could get you killed, but the shift in her was unmistakable.

"What happened?"

"She slipped away," he said, forcing the words out steadily. "I had her. She just... got lucky."

Her gaze sharpened, cold and assessing. "Did she recognize you?"

He shook his head. "I don't think so. I got close. She looked straight at me. Nothing."

She leaned back slowly; the chair creaking under her weight. "You'd better hope that's true," she said. "If she recognized you, the entire plan is finished. Everything we've worked for—everything that belongs to us—gone."

A pulse of heat crawled up his neck. Shame. Anger. Fear. All tangled together.

He straightened, swallowing hard. "I have a new plan," he said. "Something cleaner. Something that won't fail."

She rose from the chair without a sound, the air in the room shifting as she crossed to him. Junior held still, every muscle tight, as her fingers slid into his hair, smoothing it back as if he were a child she was grooming for display. Her breath brushed his ear, cold and deliberate, sending a shiver down his spine that was equal parts fear and something darker he didn't examine too closely.

"Then tell me," she whispered, her voice soft enough to make his stomach twist. "What's the plan?"

Her touch lingered in his hair a moment too long, the way it always had, as if she could smooth him back into the shape she preferred. But the gesture didn't land the same way anymore. Not now. Not with the old man gone.

He watched her as she stepped back, and for the first time, he saw the truth she'd been trying to hide. She wasn't the unshakeable force she'd once been. The old man had been her shield—her anchor, her protection, the weight behind every command she issued. Without him, there was a tremor beneath her confidence, a thin crack running through the center of her authority.

And she was shifting that weight onto him. She thought she could wield him like a weapon, seize control for herself. Thought he was still the boy she'd raised to obey.

But that duty—the power, the legacy, the burden—had fallen to him now. Not her. She just hadn't realized it yet.

He felt it settle inside him, a solid, inevitable truth. He wasn't the child she'd molded. He wasn't the shadow she expected to stand behind her. He was the one who would carry the family forward, the one who would finish what the old man had started. The one who would decide what came next.

She believed she could sink her claws into him and steer him like she always had, but she was wrong. He wouldn't be controlled. Not anymore.

So he lowered his eyes, let his shoulders soften, let her see what she wanted to see—the obedient son, the loyal creation, the boy who bent under her hand.

But inside, the truth settled with a quiet, dangerous certainty.

He was the one in charge now.

And soon, she'd understand that.

Chapter Ten
DECLAN

Fluorescent lights stabbed at his eyes the moment he cracked them open. The brightness felt unnatural, too sharp, like needles pressing into his skull. His head throbbed in heavy, punishing waves, each heartbeat sending a whooshing pulse through his ears.

He turned his head to the right.

A surge of nausea rose so fast he didn't have time to warn anyone. He leaned over the side of the bed and vomited. The motion made the room tilt violently.

Someone shouted—a man's voice, loud and panicked—but the words blurred together, muffled under the pounding in his skull. Declan wished he would shut up. Every sound felt as if it was being driven straight into his brain.

A cluster of people in scrubs rushed toward him, their shoes squeaking against the polished floor.

Where am I?

"Mr. Wallace."

A woman in a white coat and black scrubs stepped into his line of sight. Her voice was calm, practiced. "You're in the intensive care unit at University Hospital. There was an accident."

Her words stretched and warped as his vision tunneled. The room dimmed. Then everything went black.

"You have a minor skull fracture, and you dislocated your right shoulder. We reset the shoulder."

Declan blinked awake again. The lights were softer this time, less hostile. He glanced down and saw his arm secured in a sling.

"We need to monitor you for a head bleed," the woman continued. "And we need to keep you calm. We're going to give you something through your IV to help you rest."

"No, I don't want any medi—"

The world slipped away mid-sentence as the sedative hit his bloodstream.

When he surfaced again, the pain had dulled to a heavy ache instead of a sharp blade. The ringing in his ears was gone. The room was dim, lit only by a soft glow from the hallway. An officer sat in a chair just outside the door, his silhouette still and alert.

Declan tried to sit up, but the tug of wires and IV lines stopped him.

What the hell happened?

He pressed the call button. A moment later, a middle-aged Black woman stepped inside.

"Nice of you to join us, Mr. Wallace. How are you feeling?"

The voice floated in through the fog. Declan forced his eyes open. The lights above him were dimmed, but even that soft glow felt like needles behind his eyes.

"I've been better," he croaked. His throat burned as if he'd swallowed sand.

"I bet you have. You've been out for almost three days now."

"What!" His voice cracked louder than he meant it to. A spike of pain shot through his skull. He winced. "What... happened?"

Before the nurse could answer, the officer stationed outside stepped into the room.

"It appears someone blew up your car, sir."

Declan stared at him, certain he'd misheard. "Someone what?"

"Blew. Up. Your. Car." The officer enunciated each word slowly, as if Declan were hard of hearing.

Declan resisted the urge to snap back. He wasn't an idiot; he was concussed, exhausted, and rapidly losing patience. He tried to reach back, really reach, and the last thing he remembered was driving toward his apartment that morning. Sunlight on the windshield. A podcast droning. His turn signal clicking as he pulled into the lot.

Then nothing.

Just a blank space where the rest of the day should've been.

He swallowed, the throb in his skull pulsing harder. "Do we have any leads?"

"I'm not sure, sir. Chief and Detective Martin were here earlier, but they didn't mention specifics to me. They told me to call them when you woke up."

Declan waved him off impatiently. The nurse remained at his bedside, patiently waiting for them to finish their conversation.

"Do you need anything?" she asked as the officer stepped outside.

"Water," he rasped.

She nodded and slipped out of the room. Declan let his head fall back against the pillow, trying to piece together the last thing he remembered. His thoughts felt sluggish, as if they were moving through mud.

The officer finished his call and poked his head back in. "They'll be here momentarily, sir."

Declan swallowed, throat aching. "What day is it?"

"It is Thursday evening."

Thursday.

The last thing he remembered was leaving Alex's house on Tuesday morning.

Shit.

He was supposed to take her out that night. She probably thought he'd ghosted her. He groaned out loud. She'll probably forgive him considering he couldn't exactly help getting blown up.

His gaze drifted around the room until he spotted his belongings piled on a chair. Just then, the nurse returned with a cup of water. He drank it in one long gulp. The cool liquid soothed the rawness in his throat, but the discomfort lingered.

"Why does my throat hurt so badly?" he asked.

"You were intubated for the first two days," she explained gently. "We had to keep you sedated because of your head injury. You woke up several times fighting staff, so we had to increase your sedation. Whenever that happens, we have to place a breathing tube."

The words hit him like a second impact. He hadn't realized how bad it had been.

"Can I get you anything else?" she asked, pausing at the door.

"Yes. My cell phone, please."

She retrieved it from his bag and handed it to him.

"Thank you," he murmured.

The screen stayed black when he pressed the button. Dead. Of course. He let out an aggravated sigh. He needed to call Alex.

He was drifting again, eyelids heavy, when footsteps echoed down the hallway. Sharp, purposeful. He opened his eyes.

Chief Abernathy and Detective Martin strode toward his room, their expressions carved from stone.

They stepped inside.

"Wallace," the Chief barked, "what the hell happened?"

"Funny, I was fixin' to ask y'all the same question," Declan said. His voice came out rough and thick, his southern drawl heavier than usual. It always slipped like that when he was exhausted.

"All we know is someone planted an explosive on your car and almost took you out," Martin said. He reached into his pocket, pulled out a folded piece of paper, and held it up.

"When we got to the scene, you were holding this."

Declan's stomach dropped. He scanned the note. A cold ripple crawled up his spine as everything slammed back into place—the note, the brown van, the roar of the engine, the blast.

"Alex!" The name tore out of him. He lurched forward, trying to get out of bed.

The wires and IV lines jerked him back. Panic surged. He grabbed the cluster of leads on his chest and ripped them off in one violent motion. The adhesive tore at his skin, ripping out chest hair. He didn't care. He yanked out the IV next, flinging the tubing aside. Fluid splattered across the floor.

He pushed to his feet, and the room spun violently. His vision tunneled. He caught himself on the bed with his good arm, teeth clenched.

"What are you doing, man?" Martin said, gripping his shoulder to steady him.

"I need to get to Alex. I think she's in danger."

"Alex... the nurse from that rape case?" Martin asked.

"Yes. We started seeing each other... after the case was closed," he added quickly when the Chief's eyebrow shot up.

"Sit back down, son. You're not going anywhere," the Chief said, voice firm.

"Yes, I am." Declan straightened, towering despite the sling and the hospital gown.

"You won't make it past the three of us," the Chief warned, gesturing to Martin and the officer in the doorway. The officer shifted uncomfortably, desperately looking for an escape.

Martin knew better. He'd worked with Declan for years. Even injured, Declan was a wall of muscle and stubbornness. If he wanted out, he'd get out.

Before anyone could move, a commotion erupted in the hallway. Several staff members rushed in. His nurse stormed to his side, eyes blazing.

"What are you doing out of bed?" she snapped.

"I'm leaving," Declan said flatly.

"The devil you are." She planted herself in front of him, arms crossed. "Unless you want to go through me first."

She was five-foot-four, maybe, but somehow the most intimidating person in the room.

Martin lifted both hands. "Let's all take a breath. Declan, you think Alex is the 'her' mentioned in the note?"

"Yes, she's the only one I've been spending time with."

"Do you even know where she is right now?" Martin asked.

Declan glanced at the clock on the wall. Just before midnight.

"She gets off work in the next half hour," he said. "She's at Southeast Regional. Emergency department."

Martin stepped aside and murmured something to the officer in the doorway. The officer nodded once and disappeared down the hall.

"He's going to get her and bring her here," Martin said. "Now sit down and let your nurse reconnect you."

Declan shot him a look sharp enough to cut steel, but he lowered himself onto the edge of the bed anyway. His glare swept across the room, making it clear he hated being handled.

He was just about to lie back when a familiar voice echoed down the hallway.

"Declan! Oh my God, you're awake!"

Susan barreled into the room.

Declan's head snapped toward Martin, eyes narrowed in accusation. Martin held up both hands and shook his head.

"How did you know I was here?" Declan asked.

"I'm still your emergency contact from when you had your appendix out," Susan said breathlessly. "Your nurse called and told me you woke up."

"You didn't have to come up here in the middle of the night," Declan muttered, glancing past her.

The Chief and Martin were already retreating, inching toward the door like men escaping a burning building. Declan shot Martin a silent plea to stay. Martin pretended not to notice and gave a quick wave before disappearing.

Coward.

"The boys and I have been so worried about you," Susan continued, dragging a chair to his bedside. "They were asleep, but I'll bring them up in the morning."

Declan sighed inwardly. Great. Make yourself comfortable.

He needed her gone before Alex arrived. He did not have the energy for that kind of collision tonight. The nurse reentered, brisk and efficient. She restarted his IV, reattached the monitors, and turned to leave.

A sudden rush of dizziness hit him. His chest tightened, and his limbs felt impossibly heavy.

"Whoa, what did you just give me?" he asked, gripping the bed rail.

"Some morphine for your pain," she said.

Perfect.

He needed his brain sharp when Alex walked in, not floating off into la-la land.

The pressure in his chest eased, but a thick wave of exhaustion rolled over him. His limbs felt heavy. Susan's voice blurred into background noise, a steady drone he couldn't focus on.

He closed his eyes for what he told himself would be a second. Just long enough to gather strength. Just long enough to let her finish talking so he could politely send her home.

But the morphine tugged at him, lulling him into a fitful sleep.

Darkness crept in at the edges.

And Declan slipped under.

Alex

Alex spotted the officer before he spoke—standing stiffly beside her car, hands clasped in front of him as if bracing for something.

"Alex Kelley?"

"Yes," she answered, her voice tight.

Her mind snapped straight to the worst. A break-in. Alyssa hurt. The boys terrified. Some psycho finally making good on the threats she'd been trying to outrun. Images flashed too fast to separate, each one tightening her chest until she could barely breathe.

"Detective Wallace asked me to find you, ma'am."

Her heart kicked hard against her ribs, a sharp jolt of fear giving way to a shaky rush of relief.

"He was involved in an incident on Tuesday morning and just woke up in the hospital. He's asking for you."

Alex froze. The world seemed to tilt. For a moment she couldn't breathe.

He's awake. And he wants me.

She nodded quickly, barely remembering to lock her car before climbing in and following the patrol cruiser. The short drive across town stretched endlessly. She peppered the officer with questions the moment they stepped into the hospital, but he remained maddeningly silent, offering nothing beyond clipped, polite responses.

Her stomach twisted.

He hadn't stood her up.

He hadn't ghosted her.

He'd been hurt.

Relief washed through her, followed immediately by guilt for every irritated thought she'd had over the past three days.

The elevator ride to the fourth floor felt like an eternity. When the doors finally slid open, the officer led her to a room at the end of the hall, then took a seat outside the door.

Alex stepped inside.

And stopped cold.

Declan lay in the bed, eyes closed, chest rising and falling in a slow, steady rhythm. He looked peaceful. Alive! Relief surged through her—until she saw the woman beside him.

A petite brunette sat in a chair pulled close to the bed, her fingers laced through Declan's. She leaned down and pressed a soft kiss to his lips. Alex waited for him to pull away, to turn his head, to do anything that proved she wasn't seeing what she thought she was seeing.

Instead, Declan lifted his hand, cupped the back of the woman's head, and drew her closer.

The air punched out of Alex's lungs. Her vision blurred. A sharp, physical ache bloomed in her chest, so sudden and deep it stole her breath. She didn't even realize she'd stepped back until her shoulder brushed the doorframe, a small, instinctive retreat she couldn't stop.

She backed away silently, unnoticed.

The officer outside stood when he saw her retreating. "Ma'am?"

She couldn't answer. Her throat locked around the words, a hot, burning knot she couldn't swallow past. She turned sharply and headed for the stairwell, pushing through the door before the tears could fully spill.

The metal door clanged shut behind her, the sound echoing up the concrete shaft. She descended the stairs as fast as her legs would carry her, gripping the railing when her knees threatened to buckle. Hot tears streaked down her cheeks, blurring the steps below her.

How could she have been so stupid?

Of course he didn't want her. The thought rose automatically, but another pushed in behind it, sharper and far more painful. Why had he asked her to come at all if he already had someone else there? None of it made sense. Unless he'd known exactly what he was doing.

Old insecurities stirred, the ones she thought she'd buried years ago. She pressed her palm to the wall, trying to steady herself, trying to understand why he'd called her there only to let her walk into that. It felt intentional.

Her breath hitched. She wiped her face with the back of her hand, but the tears kept coming. The stairwell hummed around her, cold and impersonal, and she stood there with her heart aching in a way she hadn't expected, wondering how she could've been so wrong.

Chapter Eleven
DECLAN

Declan had been dreaming of Alex—her soft laugh, the warmth of her mouth—when a sudden, passionate kiss dragged him out of sleep. For a split second, the boldness of it startled him, heat sparking low in his stomach. He reached up to pull her closer—and froze the moment his fingers brushed short, curly hair.

His eyes snapped open.

He was lip-locked with his ex-wife.

Revulsion shot through him. He jerked back and shoved her away. "What the hell are you doing, Susan?"

She had the nerve to look wounded. "I miss you, Declan. I didn't realize how much I still wanted you until we almost lost you."

"Let me be perfectly clear," he said, voice low and lethal. "We will never get back together. You lost me the day you slept with another man in our bed. Now get the hell out."

Susan's face crumpled, but she turned and left.

Declan caught movement in the doorway. The officer stood there, stiff and uncomfortable, eyes darting anywhere but at him.

No Alex.

"Where is she?" Declan demanded once Susan was out of earshot.

The officer swallowed. "Uh... she was here. Just a moment ago." He stared at the floor. "She came to the doorway, stopped, and left."

Declan let his head fall back onto the pillow. Pain shot through his skull, sharp enough to make his vision pulse. "For fuck's sake," he growled. "What else can go wrong this week?"

He needed to get out of there. Too much was at stake for him to rely on others to get things done. He wasn't delusional enough to think he'd get anywhere tonight, but first thing in the morning, he would find Alex himself and explain everything.

The next morning, Martin arrived early, balancing coffee and a box of donuts. Declan was already dressed, bag packed, sitting on the edge of the bed like a man ready to bolt.

"Whoa," Martin said. "They're releasing you?"

"No. I signed out against medical advice. Take me home."

Martin hesitated. Declan's irritation flared. "What is it?"

"Chief ordered a protective detail until we figure out who tried to kill you."

"No." Declan's refusal was immediate and absolute.

Martin winced. "He also said you'll be staying at the Clinton Hotel until further notice."

"Like hell I am," Declan grabbed his bag. "Take me to the station. I need to have a discussion with the Chief."

Declan was the newest—and most unwilling—resident of the Clinton Hotel. His conversation with Chief Abernathy had not tipped in his favor. He might have pushed back, but his body felt like someone had tossed him in a dryer, set it to tumble, and walked away.

The FBI had stepped in after the explosion, and whatever decisions followed were no longer coming from the Chief. The murder case Declan had been working on had suddenly become part of something larger, something with too many suits and too many opinions. Now there were federal agents in every hallway and conference room, and the moment they arrived, Declan's voice in the matter had thinned to almost nothing.

He stood at the front desk while the clerk typed in his information, and every second on his feet felt like a negotiation with gravity. A deep ache pulsed through his ribs, the kind that made breathing feel optional. The pounding in his head refused to ease, tightening his vision whenever he tried to focus. Any protest he might have made about the Chief's decision had died before it reached his mouth; pain and exhaustion had joined forces and shut him down long before he could string together a convincing argument.

The clerk slid a keycard across the counter and offered a polite smile; he didn't have the energy to return. He picked up the card and nodded, hoping it looked like gratitude and not the grimace it felt like. Even lifting his arm sent a dull ripple of pain through his side.

Right now, he was just trying to make it to the elevator without broadcasting the fact that four days hadn't been nearly enough time to stop feeling like he'd been punted across a parking lot.

Bubba—his assigned shadow—followed close behind.

Declan stopped abruptly. "Where do you think you're going?"

"Where you go," Bubba replied, tone flat and unbothered.

"Absolutely not. You can sit outside in an unmarked car, but you are not sitting outside my room." Declan glowered at the six-foot-four slab of muscle. Bubba didn't blink.

Declan crossed his arms and waited.

After a beat, Bubba sighed, pulled out his phone, and stepped away to make a call.

Behind them, a young father and his son checked in. The boy pushed the luggage cart with uncontained excitement.

"This is the best trip ever, Dad!"

"Yes, it is, buddy. I'm glad you came with me."

Declan's chest tightened unexpectedly. The only time he had ever spent alone with his father had been on those early morning fishing trips. The first half of the day was usually good. His dad would be sober, talkative, almost gentle in a way that made Declan believe things could be different. The second half never lived up to that hope. By thirteen, he already knew how to load the boat, drive them home, and pretend nothing was wrong.

Running away had taught him how to survive. He and Josh drifted through the streets for months, doing whatever they had to until Brianna found them. She was older, already settled into her own apartment, and she took them in without asking for explanations. He had done things during those years that still sat heavily in his gut. Things he rarely let himself think about, let alone speak aloud.

There were days when the badge on his chest felt like a costume he had no right to wear. Most of his youth had been spent on the wrong side of the law, and sometimes the weight of that history pressed harder than he liked to admit. Becoming a single father had been the turning point. It forced him to clean up, to grow up, to become the man his daughter deserved. He had done his best to raise her and give her the life she deserved.

If the old crew could see him now...they wouldn't recognize the man he'd become.

The idea of him becoming a detective would've been laughable back then.

But his past made him good at his job. He understood criminals: how they thought, how they moved, the angles they played. He could slip into their mindset and anticipate their next step before they made it.

"Boss is fine with my sitting outside," Bubba said, snapping Declan back to the present. He handed him a card. "If you leave, call this number to give us a five-minute heads-up."

"Absolutely," Declan said. Pretending to agree was easier than starting a fight he did not have the energy for.

Bubba leveled him with a stare. "If you try to give us the slip, we'll be so far up your ass you won't be able to fart without asking permission."

Declan smirked. "You enjoy burying yourself in people's asses at the Federal Bureau of Ineptitude, don't you?"

He didn't wait for a response. He left Bubba standing there and made for the elevators.

At least the hotel was nice. Built in 1876, the Clinton Hotel had a regal, historic charm—ornate molding, tall ceilings, warm lighting. His room was spacious, with off-white carpet, gray-and-white pinstripe wallpaper, and a separate living area with a sturdy desk.

He plugged in his phone and let it charge while he showered and brushed his teeth. When he powered it on, it chimed twice: one text, one voicemail.

He checked them quickly, then dialed Alex.

It rang twice. Voicemail.

He tried again. One ring. Voicemail.

She was ignoring him.

Martin had stopped by her house that morning before picking Declan up from the hospital. No one had been home. She was probably at the barn.

He couldn't remember the name of the stable where she kept Zorro, and a quick search showed over thirty barns in Little Rock. No way to check them all.

Resigned, he opened their messages.

Call me! It's important!

His body ached, his head throbbed, and exhaustion tugged at him. He turned his phone volume to max and set it beside the bed. The doctor had been furious when Declan signed himself out. They'd warned him it could take two weeks for the concussion symptoms to fade. They'd also told him to wear his sling for four weeks.

Yeah. That wasn't happening.

Shaking off the urge to lie down, he sat at the desk and pulled out the file Martin had given him. Per Declan's request, Martin had dug into Alex's past.

For the first time in his career, Declan felt as though he was crossing a line. Invading someone's privacy. He would've preferred to talk to her face-to-face.

But she wasn't answering his calls.

Despite what the FBI believed about the car bombing being tied to his murder case and the mob, Declan had other suspicions—ones he prayed were wrong. He'd seen it in her eyes when she thought no one was watching. That far-off stare, like her mind slipped somewhere dark and distant. Somewhere she didn't want to be. Somewhere that scared her.

Sometimes she looked as if she'd lived a hundred lives, each one heavier than the last. It was the look of someone carrying secrets—old, buried, suffocating secrets that pressed on the lungs and stole the air. The kinds of secrets that chased a person, even in their sleep. The kind that would crush them if they ever stopped running.

Alex

Alex spent her morning touring properties within thirty minutes of the hospital. Ever since the divorce, she had carried a quiet ache she could never quite shake. She wanted a place that felt like hers. She had stayed in the house she and Henry once shared because it was practical, but the moment he walked out, the house stopped feeling like home. Even now, despite Alyssa's warmth and generosity, Alex still felt like a guest in someone else's life.

She wanted a home of her own.

Seeing Declan with another woman the night before had stirred up feelings she thought she had buried years ago. Loneliness. Unworthiness. The sting of betrayal. She hated that she had let her guard down. Being alone for the last five years had been intentional. After Henry's infidelity, she had focused on Collin and her career. Now that both were thriving, she found her focus shifting elsewhere...somewhere dangerous.

Two serious relationships.

Two betrayals.

Two men who had chosen someone else.

The pattern left scars. Affection made her tense. Trust felt dangerous. She told herself she was healing, that the past was behind her, but some nights she still lay awake wondering what she had done wrong.

It was exhausting, this quiet war inside her. Wanting to believe she was enough. Trying to believe someone could stay. She needed to stay busy today, or her thoughts would swallow her whole.

The realtor led her to the fourth and final property of the day. The first three had been nice, but none had felt right. This one sat halfway down a dead-end dirt road. The road was private and poorly maintained, so she crawled along at ten miles per hour to avoid rattling her suspension apart.

When she pulled in, something inside her shifted.

The barn sat on the left, near the treeline. Each stall had its own run-in paddock. To the right, an old driveway led to a power pole with a security light still attached. A gravel pad marked where a house once stood. Further back, a small hill rose gently, and she could already imagine a home sitting on top of it.

James stepped out of his red Jeep as she parked. "This property is fairly raw. If you don't mind putting in some work, it could be a great option."

"I'm open to a fixer-upper."

"Good. The price was recently reduced. It has been sitting for six months. Most people don't want the hassle of building, but this place is in the Bryant school district while still being outside city limits. Best of both worlds.

There's also a loft apartment above the barn. I haven't seen it yet, but the listing agent says it's livable. Whether his definition matches yours, we'll find out."

Alex felt a spark of excitement. It was just her and Collin. A small apartment would be perfect while they built the house, and the money saved on rent could go straight into construction.

The barn door stood open. It took a moment for her eyes to adjust to the dim interior. Chewing damage marked the first stall on the right, deep grooves worn into the wood. Two boards were missing from the stall on the left, leaving a narrow gap near the bottom. The back stalls appeared intact. Each one measured twelve by twenty feet, suggesting the place had once been used as a foaling barn. Small tack and feed rooms sat behind them on either side of the center aisle.

Through the back door, an outdoor riding arena stretched to the right. To the left, a large pasture rolled out beneath the sky. Behind the barn was a covered area for exercising horses in bad weather.

It wasn't perfect, but it felt right.

"What do you think so far?" James asked.

Alex nodded. "So far, so good. I want to see the loft."

"After you."

She followed him to the side entrance and pushed the door open. The loft smelled faintly of dust and disuse. To the right was a coat closet. To the left, a small bathroom with a double vanity, a shower stall, and a toilet. A small bedroom sat on the left, and a larger one on the right. Straight ahead, an open living area held a compact kitchen and living room.

The kitchen sink sat beneath the picture window she had noticed earlier. It overlooked open fields. She could already imagine mornings here, coffee brewing, Collin chattering at the table, horses grazing outside.

The space was small, but it was enough.

She opened the oven and immediately slammed it shut as a foul odor hit her.

"Looks like it's never been cleaned," James said with a laugh.

Alex wrinkled her nose. Whoever had lived here before had not been tidy. Dust coated every surface. It would take days of deep cleaning to make the loft livable.

But despite the flaws, she felt a pull. She could see the potential. Collin would love it here. Woods to explore. Trees to climb. Space to run. She could already picture him playing in the fields with the animals she would inevitably adopt.

She had not expected to find the right place so quickly, but she knew this was it.

She stepped onto the back deck overlooking the arena while James locked up. The breeze carried the scent of pine and earth. She turned to him, heart pounding.

"I want to put in an offer."

James blinked, then grinned. They went over the details, exchanged information, and he promised to be in touch.

When he drove away, Alex sat in her car for a long moment, staring at the property she had just offered her life savings for. With some work, it could be beautiful again. It could be home.

She couldn't wait to show Collin.

She typed the barn's address into her GPS and pulled away slowly. A good ride would clear her mind. As she drove, she took in the area. Minutes from downtown Bryant and Benton. Five minutes from the elementary school. Another point in its favor.

She cracked her window, letting the cool air wash over her.

Tonight was girls' night with her coworkers. She just needed to keep herself busy for a few more hours.

Chapter Twelve
ALEX

Henry picked Collin up for the weekend at five-thirty. The house felt strangely quiet afterward, the kind of quiet that made Alex too aware of her own thoughts. She and Alyssa were getting ready for their girls' night out at the Clinton Bar and Grill. Alex never made a big deal out of birthdays, but this year felt different. Thirty hovered over her like a storm cloud, and the week had been a whirlwind. Declan. The hospital. The emotional whiplash of it all.

She needed air. Noise. Distraction.

Tonight she would pull on something flirty, swipe on lipstick with more confidence than she actually felt, and let her friends drown out the chaos in her head. For a few hours she would dance, laugh, and pretend her heart wasn't twisted into a knot of confusion and longing.

Tonight, she would forget about him.

She padded down the hall toward Alyssa's room, her pink knee-length robe cinched tight around her waist. She still had no idea what she planned to wear, and curiosity tugged her forward to see what Alyssa had chosen. After a quick knock, she stepped inside at Alyssa's invitation.

Alyssa stood before the mirror, adjusting the lace neckline of a white bohemian blouse. She'd paired it with fitted boot-cut jeans and green flats, her hair gathered into a loose, effortless twist that made the whole look seem casually perfect.

"I don't know what I should wear," Alex admitted, sinking onto the edge of the bed.

Alyssa studied her for a moment. "You look great in green or red. Throw on a pair of jeans and a cute top."

Alex sighed. "Alright. Are we taking a taxi, or are you driving?"

"Memory's picking us up. She's the designated driver since she can't drink."

"Okay," Alex said, pushing herself up. "I'll go dig through my closet again."

Back in her room, she sifted through her shirts until she settled on a low-cut red top with lace along the hem. She paired it with fitted jeans and grabbed a black blazer in case it got cold.

Alyssa knocked once and entered without waiting. Her eyes swept over Alex.

"You look like you're going to a business meeting, not a night out. Lose the blazer."

She crossed the room, rummaged through Alex's closet, and pulled out a black leather jacket. "This is better."

Alex slipped it on and turned toward the mirror. Red lipstick. Soft eyeliner. Long, loose waves. She looked... hot. Confident, even if she didn't think too hard about it.

Alyssa's phone chimed. "They're here."

They headed downstairs and climbed into their friend's black Buick Enclave. Ten minutes later, they found street parking and walked toward the Clinton Bar and Grill, the warm hum of music and conversation spilling out onto the sidewalk.

Alyssa had made reservations, so they were seated quickly. Alex had barely opened her menu when Emily flagged down the server and ordered a round of margaritas on the rocks for the table, plus a mocktail for Memory.

The night had officially begun.

"Y'all, I'm such a lightweight now. I'm probably going to max out at two margaritas," Alex warned. She had no intention of waking up with a hangover.

"What do you guys think of Sandy?" Emily asked. Sandy was the new emergency department manager.

Everyone made a variation of a groan or eye roll.

"I don't think she's that bad," Memory offered. She was always the optimist.

Every woman at the table turned to her and shook her head.

"She's terrible," Emily said flatly.

Alex's phone dinged. Declan again.

> I understand if you don't want to talk about the hospital, although it wasn't what it looked like. I need to speak with you about a case. Please call me when you get a chance.

Her heart skipped. Despite everything, she wanted to talk to him. What case?

Probably just a ploy to get her to pick up. But tonight was for her friends. She rarely went out. If he was awake when she got home, she'd call.

She lifted her phone. "Group photo!"

Everyone leaned in, smiling, and Alex snapped the picture.

"That's a good one! Send that to me," Alyssa said.

"I'll send it to everyone."

After forwarding the photo to the group chat, she reopened her conversation with Declan and attached it.

> Out with my friends tonight. Call you later, maybe.

The typing bubbles appeared immediately. Alex bit her lip.

> Look over at the bar.

Her head whipped toward the bar.

There he was.

White button-up, top two buttons undone. Sling on his arm. Bruising along his jaw. And those stormy blue eyes locked on her like she was the only person in the room.

"Holy shit," she whispered.

"What's going on?" Alyssa asked.

"Declan is here," Alex breathed.

She looked up just as he started toward them. No one at the table knew about the hospital or the explosion. At the sound of his name, Alyssa stiffened, ready to go to war on Alex's behalf. Alex reached under the table and squeezed her hand, silently begging her not to start anything.

"Hey, Declan," Alyssa said coolly. Her eyes widened as she took in his injuries. "Whoa. What happened to you?"

Declan's gaze snapped to Alex at the sound of her sharp inhale. She stared at him, wide-eyed. She hadn't seen his face clearly in the dim hospital lighting.

"Hazards of the job," he said, eyes never leaving her. His stare was intense, almost hungry. Alex shifted in her seat. "Hello, Alexandria."

"Hey," she murmured. No one called her Alexandria except her parents. Yet she liked how it sounded on his lips.

"This is Declan, Alex's friend," Alyssa said, drawing out the word friend.

"Hey," Memory and Emily echoed.

"I've been trying to call you," Declan said, still watching Alex.

"I know. I've been ignoring them." Her voice was overly bright, too casual. Her heart hammered so loudly she was sure the entire table could hear it. Heat crept up her neck. She hated how easily he could unravel her.

Out of the corner of Alex's eye, She saw Alyssa arch a brow.

"What are you doing here?" Alex asked, sharper than she intended.

"I'm staying here for a short time. I was grabbing dinner before heading back up to my room." He lifted his to-go bag.

"You're staying here? I thought you lived nearby."

"It's a long story. It has to do with the case I'm working on." He nodded to the group. "I'll let you ladies get back to your night. I just wanted to say hi."

He smiled at Alex, then turned and headed for the stairs.

"Oh my God, Alex. He is gorgeous," Emily said the moment he was out of earshot.

Alex blushed. "I know."

"How did you two meet?" Memory asked.

Alyssa jumped in, recounting the late-night dates, the chemistry, and the sudden cold shoulder.

"Well, from the way he was looking at you, he's definitely still interested," Memory said. The others agreed.

Alex's phone chimed.

> We need to talk. Call me when you get home or come up. I'm in room 314.

Her stomach flipped. The girls were finishing their dinners and working on their third round of margaritas. Alex had barely touched her food. Her nerves were a tangled mess. Going up to Declan's room would be the first time they were truly alone together.

What could he need to talk about so urgently?

Alyssa set her napkin on the table and nudged Alex. "Bathroom."

Alex followed her.

"What is going on?" Alyssa demanded once the door closed behind them. "You barely touched your food, and you haven't said a word since he left."

"He wants me to come up to his room after dinner," Alex admitted, cheeks flushing. She avoided eye contact. Alyssa could read her too well.

"Oh? Someone's getting lucky."

"Stop. He just needs to talk to me about... something. I don't know what, but he's very insistent."

Alyssa's raised eyebrow said exactly what she thought of that.

"Why have you been ignoring his calls?"

Alex considered telling her about the woman in the hospital but swallowed it down. "Because I thought he had stood me up."

"Well, it looks like he had a valid excuse."

"I'm nervous," Alex said, fidgeting with her shirt. "I wasn't expecting to see him tonight. Should I have worn something different?"

Alyssa grinned. "Your boobs look fantastic in that shirt. And if the way he was devouring you with his eyes earlier is any indication of what he's going to do to you, what you're wearing won't matter for long."

Alex's face flushed a deep crimson. It had been a long time since she'd been with a man, and her nerves were tying themselves into knots. She had no intention of anything happening tonight. Her plan was simple: hear whatever Declan felt was so urgent he'd blown up her phone for the past twenty-four hours, clear the air, and then call a taxi home. She would say what needed to be said, close the door on this whole mess, and move on.

Alyssa and Alex returned to the table. Memory and Emily were already standing, gathering their things.

"We paid for y'all. Happy birthday, Alex. Are you guys ready to leave?" Emily asked.

A sly grin spread across Alyssa's face.

"Alex actually has other plans... the six-foot, blonde-hair, blue-eyed kind of plans."

Emily's jaw dropped. "Shut up! Are you going upstairs?!"

Alex nodded.

"Go get you some, girl!" Memory chimed in.

Alex sank back into her chair, grabbed her untouched margarita, and downed it in one go.

"I'm going to need this, I think," she said, breathless. Her friends burst into laughter.

Alyssa sat beside her, tone softening. "You know you don't have to go upstairs, right? You can tell him it's girls' night and you'll see him later."

Alex smiled at the concern in her friend's eyes. "I know. And I'm sure. I just need a little liquid courage."

Emily and Memory were already halfway to the door.

"You ready, Alyssa?" Emily called.

"Yeah," Alyssa said, rising. She leaned close to Alex. "Call me if you need me."

"I will. Drive safely, guys!" Alex waved as they left.

The attention made her squirm. Blooming love life, she thought dryly. More like withering.

On the second floor, she ducked into the ladies' room. She rummaged through her purse, found her makeup and perfume, and spritzed herself with her salted caramel pistachio scent. A quick touch-up of blush. She refused to examine why she was doing this when she had no intention of staying longer than necessary.

It had been a couple of hours since Declan had invited her up. Hopefully, he was still awake.

She climbed the last flight of stairs to the third floor, each step making her pulse thrum harder. She paused outside his door, steadying herself. Her head was swimming from that last margarita, and she instantly regretted chugging it. She wasn't a big drinker. Her tolerance had plummeted over the years, reduced to a few glasses of wine with Alyssa during chick-flick nights.

Gathering her courage, she lifted her hand and knocked.

The door opened a moment later.

Declan stood there, still in the clothes he'd worn downstairs. His eyes softened when he saw her.

"I wasn't sure if you were coming," he said quietly.

Alex swallowed. "I wasn't sure I was coming either."

Declan smiled and pushed the door open wider. "Come on in."

The cluttered desk caught Alex's eye first. It looked as if a storm had blown straight through the room, scattering papers everywhere. Then she looked at Declan—really looked—and the exhaustion etched into his face made guilt twist in her chest. Maybe this wasn't the right time.

"You seem tired," she said softly.

"I'm exhausted," he admitted, voice low.

"I can still catch the girls before they leave and let you get some rest," she offered, though her heart wasn't in it.

"No." The word came out too fast. "I want to see you."

Alex's lips curved despite herself. She wanted to see him, too, and she'd hoped he wouldn't send her away. She set her jacket and purse on the bench at the foot of the bed and took a seat.

"So," she said, steadying herself, "what's this case you needed to talk to me about so urgently?"

Declan exhaled and sank into the chair across from her. He set down a glass of brandy she hadn't noticed him holding, then raked a hand through his hair. He slipped off his sling and stretched his arm, wincing as he worked out the tension.

"Do you have any enemies?" he asked abruptly.

Alex's pulse stuttered. "No," she lied. "Why?"

"Tuesday morning, after I left your house, I went back to my apartment to change before work. When I came downstairs, there was a note on my car that said, 'Stay away from her.'" His voice hardened. "I saw a man in a brown van pulling away. I tried to get the license plate, but I only made it a few steps before my car exploded."

Alex went pale. Her breath caught, but she said nothing.

Declan watched her closely. "I spent three days unconscious in the hospital."

Her stomach dropped. It couldn't be. Not after all these years.

Declan's eyes narrowed, studying her. She had never been good at hiding her thoughts.

"How do you know I'm the 'her' they were referring to?" she asked quietly.

"Because you're the only woman I've been spending time with."

Alex let out a sharp laugh. "It sure didn't look that way last night at the hospital."

"Alex, that wasn't what it looked like."

"Sure it wasn't. I imagined you lip-locked with another woman in your hospital bed."

"No, you didn't," he shot back. "But I guess you missed the part where I pushed her off me and kicked her out of my room?"

"Yeah," Alex said, heat rising in her cheeks. "I only saw the part where you pulled her in closer."

"Alex, that woman was my ex-wife, Susan. She's in the middle of divorce number three. She took advantage of me while I was asleep in my hospital bed. They'd just given me pain medication, and I was groggy. I was resting while I waited for you to arrive. When she kissed me, I thought it was you. As soon as I realized it wasn't, I pushed her away."

An unwelcome, dangerous hope flickered in Alex's chest. She wanted to believe him. She really did. But her instincts had failed her before. She searched his eyes, hunting for something solid, something she could trust. Handsome faces and pretty words had fooled her before.

Declan watched her carefully. "Have you noticed anything or anyone out of the ordinary?"

She tensed. Sharing her problems wasn't something she was used to.

"What is it?" he asked immediately, reading her expression before she could speak.

"A man chased me while I was out on my run yesterday."

His voice dropped, all seriousness. "What do you mean, a man chased you?"

Alex shifted, uncomfortable under his intense scrutiny. "Yesterday I went for a run. When I turned back, I noticed a man running behind me. I glanced over my shoulder and saw he'd turned around too. He was still following me. I got an uneasy feeling and picked up the pace, but he kept gaining on me. The last quarter mile, I was in a full sprint, and I could hear him right behind me."

"Luckily, Alyssa was outside when I rounded the corner to our house. I yelled to her. When I looked back, he jogged past and waved like nothing was wrong."

Declan didn't speak. His jaw tightened, and Alex could practically see the gears turning in his mind.

"That's not all," she added quietly.

His eyes snapped to hers. "What else?"

Alex swallowed. "I've been getting strange hang-up calls. Every day for the past week. Sometimes twice a day. No one ever says anything. They just… breathe. And then hang up."

Declan's expression darkened.

"And a few days ago at work," she continued, voice trembling slightly, "someone delivered flowers to the nurses' station. No card. Just a note that said, 'I hope the detective's visit last night was professional. You looked beautiful; you always do.'"

Declan went still. Completely still. The kind of stillness that meant danger.

"Why didn't you tell me this earlier?" he asked, voice low.

"Because I thought I was overreacting," she whispered. "Because I didn't want to seem paranoid. And because dragging you into my mess felt unfair. I don't know. I've just spent a long time handling things on my own."

The words left her mouth, and something inside her shifted. She'd known the entire time that someone was after her. She wasn't naïve, and she wasn't blind. The flowers. The note. The hang-up calls. The jogger. Declan's car exploding. The warning: Stay away from her. None of it had ever fooled her into thinking she was safe.

But saying it out loud… that was different.

A cold, creeping awareness slid down her spine, sharper than it had been in years. She'd lived with danger for so long that it had become background noise, something she managed, something she outran. Fear had dulled into routine.

Now, speaking the truth stripped away the numbness.

The threat wasn't distant.

It wasn't manageable.

It wasn't something she could keep outrunning.

It was here.

And it was closing in.

The realization settled in her chest like a stone, making it difficult to breathe. She had spent years convincing herself she was safe, that the past was buried, that she had outrun the shadows that once clung to her. But shadows had long memories. And they always knew how to find their way back.

Declan watched her closely, reading every flicker of emotion across her face. She felt his gaze like a weight settling against her skin, impossible to ignore.

"Alex," he said quietly, "there's more you're not telling me."

Her breath hitched. He wasn't wrong. There was more—so much more—but the words lodged in her throat. Telling him meant opening doors she had welded shut. It meant dragging him into a darkness he didn't deserve. It meant admitting that the life she'd built was more fragile than she let anyone see.

She forced a small, brittle smile. "I'm just... overwhelmed. That's all."

Declan shook his head, pacing in front of the window. His jaw was tight, his hands flexing restlessly at his sides. "The FBI thought the car bomb had to do with my new murder case, but it seems someone doesn't want me around you."

Alex's chest tightened. She'd seen him angry, focused, determined—but this was different. This was fear wearing the mask of frustration. For her.

Before she could second-guess herself, she stepped forward and reached for him. Her fingers brushed his hand, and he stopped as if she'd cut the power to his body. The moment their skin met, warmth rushed up her arm and into her cheeks.

"Hey," she whispered, giving his hand a gentle squeeze.

Declan exhaled, the tension in his shoulders loosening as though her touch had flipped a switch. He turned toward her fully, something raw and unguarded flickering in his eyes. For a heartbeat, she saw the war inside him—desire pulling him forward, duty holding him back. His jaw tightened, like he was trying to reel himself in, but the effort only made the moment feel more fragile, more charged.

He stepped closer anyway, giving in to whatever line he'd been trying not to cross, and wrapped his arms around her, pulling her against him like he'd been waiting for permission.

Alex melted into him, but her mind didn't quiet. She felt the steady thrum of his heartbeat beneath her cheek, strong and grounding, and yet she couldn't ignore the tension coiled beneath his skin. He was holding her, yes—but he was also holding something back. She could feel it in the way his breath hitched, in the way his hands hovered for a second before settling on her back, as if he wasn't sure he had the right.

Part of her wanted to sink into him completely, to let the warmth and safety swallow her whole. Another part whispered caution. She knew what it felt like to want someone who wasn't fully hers. She knew what it cost to misread a moment.

But right now, pressed against him, she could feel his restraint trembling at the edges. He wasn't unaffected. He wasn't indifferent. He was fighting himself—and losing.

And God help her, that scared her almost as much as it comforted her.

"I'm glad you came up tonight," he said in a low husky voice.

"Me too," she murmured against his chest.

Declan lowered his head, his lips brushing ever so lightly across hers. Alex rose onto her tiptoes, arms slipping around his neck as she leaned into him, deepening the kiss.

Her hands slid up the back of his neck, fingers threading into his hair. She felt him shiver beneath her touch, felt the restraint in the way his hands settled at her waist instead of pulling her closer, the way his body clearly wanted to.

Alex's pulse fluttered wildly. She hadn't let herself want someone like this in years. She hadn't let herself feel anything this intense in years. And the way he was looking at her, as if she were something he had been searching for, made her knees weaken.

She pressed her body against his just as his tongue began exploring her mouth. Her fingers began working their way up the row of buttons on his shirt. A small moan escaped her lips as her hands splayed over his chest. The moan shattered the last remnants of his self-control. In one fluid motion, he cupped her buttocks and lifted her effortlessly. Alex gasped in surprise, her breath catching in her throat.

He winced slightly, and she pulled back. "Your arm—" she gasped, wrapping her legs around his waist to help support her own weight.

"I'm fine," he said, though his voice was rougher now.

In three long strides, they reached the bed. Declan sat, pulling Alex onto his lap. Her hair fell around them like a curtain. She pressed her forehead to his and slipped her fingers beneath his collar to push his shirt off his shoulders. His fingers curled around her nape, possessive and hungry.

She sat back, admiring his rugged physique. Declan took the opportunity to pull her shirt off over her head, revealing the black lace bra she was wearing beneath it. He pulled the cup of her bra down, taking her nipple in his mouth. Heat spread throughout her body, settling between her legs.

"This wasn't covering very much to begin with," he said, holding her shirt up. "I almost dragged you off like some deranged barbarian in front of your friends tonight." He tossed the shirt to the ground and began rolling her nipples between his thumbs and index fingers. Alex couldn't tell if the spinning she was feeling was because of pleasure or margaritas. Declan had flipped their positions and was now on top of her, tracing kisses down her stomach. The wave of nausea came on fast and strong. She needed to get to the bathroom before she completely humiliated herself.

Alex pressed against Declan's shoulders, but he misread her urgency for desire and kept on with his ministrations, his fingers sliding beneath the waistband of her jeans. Her stomach lurched. She shoved harder, frantic now. "Declan, stop," she gasped, voice strangled.

He froze and looked up at her face. The moment their eyes met, he saw it—the pale sheen, the horror tightening her features. She was going to be sick.

"Bathroom's right there," he said, pointing.

That was all Alex needed. She bolted from the bed, sprinting into the bathroom and slamming the door behind her. The faucet clattered on as she brushed past it, water gushing in a futile attempt to drown out the sound of her retching. She dropped to her knees, barely reaching the toilet before her stomach revolted. Heat surged up her throat, splattering the bowl as her body convulsed.

Tears pricked her eyes. Mortification settled like a stone in her chest. Groaning, she flushed and staggered to the sink. The mirror offered no mercy. She stared at her reflection, willing herself to pull it together. Her gaze landed on the mouthwash. Grateful for something—anything—else to focus on, she poured a capful, swished, and spat. Then she splashed cold water on her face, hoping it would erase the worst of it. Or at least give her the courage to open the door.

She was patting her face dry when a soft knock sounded.

She froze.

"Can I come in?" Declan asked.

Alex cracked the door open and stared at his chest. She couldn't bring herself to meet his eyes. Declan held out a folded pair of pajama pants and a white T-shirt.

"You still want me to stay?" she asked, genuinely shocked.

"Of course I do. If you want to. I just figured you wouldn't be feeling well and would want to lie down. I can take you home if you prefer."

The thought of being in a moving vehicle made her stomach pitch again. She took the clothes with a quiet "thanks" and closed the door. They hung loosely on her frame, but she didn't care. The fabric was soft, worn, and carried the faint scent of him—clean, warm, grounding. It comforted her more than she had expected. Her head throbbed, each pulse a warning. She needed to lie down before her stomach staged another revolt.

Declan was leaning against the wall when she stepped out. He handed her a bottle of water and some ibuprofen. She accepted both gratefully before climbing into bed. Pulling the blanket up to her chin, she suddenly felt awkward. She hadn't shared a bed with a man since before her divorce, and the old instinct to guard herself flickered—hesitation tightening her chest even as exhaustion softened her defenses.

Declan stood in plaid pajama bottoms, his chest bare. Alex couldn't help but admire the solid lines of him, the quiet strength he carried so effortlessly.

"I'm sorry about tonight," she murmured.

"Don't worry about it," Declan said, sliding into bed beside her. He wrapped an arm around her and gently pulled her into his embrace. She let herself sink into him. His breath brushed her hair, slow and even, and the tension in her body melted. For the first time all week, Alex felt safe.

Before she could think too hard about any of it, the warmth of him lulled her into a much-needed sleep.

Chapter Thirteen
ALEX

Alex awoke just as the sun slipped through the curtains. For the first time in days, she felt refreshed. Declan lay beside her, peaceful in sleep, his features softened by the early light. She eased herself out of bed, careful not to disturb him, and pulled her shirt from the floor. Her stomach growled. Breakfast. She could at least do that much for him.

The hotel restaurant was just opening. She ordered two plates of French toast with bacon and hash browns, then added two coffees and two bottles of orange juice. Balancing everything felt like a juggling act, but she managed to make it back up the stairs without disaster.

At the door, however, she hit her limit. She shifted the drinks, the bags, the key card—nothing cooperated. She was seconds away from kicking the door to wake Declan when someone behind her cleared their throat.

"Do you need a hand?" an older blonde woman asked, already reaching to take a few items from Alex's overloaded arms.

Alex smiled gratefully and let her help. "Thank you. I really didn't want to wake him."

The woman was about Alex's height, slightly gaunt, her face half-hidden beneath a baseball cap and oversized sunglasses. Wearing them indoors struck Alex as odd. Something about her tugged at Alex's memory, but the connection stayed just out of reach.

She fished out the key card, slid it through the lock, and pushed the door open. The woman handed everything back.

"Thank you so much," Alex said warmly.

"Not a problem. Have a good day." The woman smiled, but something in it felt off.

Alex shut the door quickly. A prickle crawled up her spine. The way the woman had watched her—too intent, too familiar—made the hairs on her neck stand up. She knew that face. She just couldn't place it.

"There you are," Declan said behind her, making her jump. "I thought you'd slipped out without saying goodbye."

"I just went to get us some breakfast," she said, setting the food on the table.

Declan's smile softened. "This looks great."

They ate in comfortable silence until his phone rang.

"Wallace," he answered, irritation sharpening his tone.

His expression shifted almost immediately. His jaw tightened, his eyes narrowed, and he stood, walking into the other room with a clipped stride. The air thickened. Alex's appetite vanished.

It wouldn't take much digging into her past to connect her to Enzo.

She had never told anyone the full truth of what she endured—not even Henry. Eight years of silence. Eight years of proving she wasn't a threat. Not a single slip about Enzo's ties to organized crime or his overseas dealings. She had buried it all so deep that she sometimes convinced herself it belonged to someone else.

So why now? Why, after all this time, would he come for her?

Was it even him? The notes, the flowers, the calls—none of it fit. If Enzo wanted her dead, she wouldn't be standing here wondering about it.

She doubted he was behind any of this. Enzo didn't draw attention. That was how he survived.

But Declan was a cop. If he started pulling strings, Enzo would feel the tug. She didn't know how much of the truth she could trust him with, so for now, it was best to keep things to herself. She preferred to carry her own baggage. She'd grown accustomed to the weight of it.

Would Declan look at her differently once he knew the truth?

From across the room, she caught his glance. He spoke in a hushed tone, eyes flicking toward her. She didn't need to hear the words to know she was the subject. Her pulse quickened. She needed a way out—not a lie, she wouldn't lie to him, but a version of the truth. Something that would satisfy him without unraveling everything she had worked so hard to bury.

Declan reentered the room, and whatever fragile courage she had gathered evaporated at the sight of his face. Anger simmered beneath the surface, controlled but unmistakable. His gaze pinned her in place, heavy with questions he hadn't yet spoken.

The room seemed to shrink around her. Her throat tightened. She knew she had to speak, but the right words refused to come.

Declan

Declan hung up the phone with Martin and stood still for a moment, letting the silence settle around him. His thoughts churned. The FBI believed Alex had ties to the mob and wanted her brought in for questioning. The information hit him like a blow he hadn't braced for.

A quiet war stirred beneath his ribs. Part of him wanted to shield her from everything. The other whispered that he might be missing something, that she might not be who he thought she was. The conflict left him motionless, suspended between instinct and doubt.

He forced the emotions down, burying them beneath the practiced calm he wore like armor. He needed answers. And if there was one thing he was good at, it was finding the truth people tried to hide.

He squared his shoulders and stepped back into the room.

Alex sat at the small table, hands wrapped around her coffee cup even though she wasn't drinking it. She looked up when he entered, and whatever she saw in his expression made her straighten.

"You need to tell me everything you know," he said, his voice steady but stripped of warmth. "The FBI is taking over the car bomb investigation. They think it's mob-related. That was Martin on the phone. I have to bring you in for questioning."

The color drained from her face. Her fingers tightened around the cup until her knuckles whitened.

"Who is Enzo?" Declan asked.

He watched her carefully. The easy, relaxed man from earlier was gone. In his place stood the detective—measured, unyielding. Alex must have felt the shift. She sat up straighter, shoulders tense, as if bracing for impact.

A flicker of emotion crossed her face—fear, guilt, something else—before she smoothed it away.

"A man I used to work for back in New Hampshire," she said.

He waited. She didn't continue.

"What kind of work?"

"I was his barn manager."

"How long?"

"A year."

"How was your relationship with him?"

"Fine." Too quick. Her gaze dropped. Declan felt something cold settle in his stomach.

"Why did you leave?"

"I got married and moved to Arkansas."

He watched her closely. Her breathing had become shallow. Her shoulders were rigid. She was answering, but she wasn't talking.

"Did you ever see any illegal activity while you worked for him?"

She paled further. Her eyes darted away. Fear flickered there—real fear. Declan felt a surge of protectiveness rise, but he forced it down. The FBI wouldn't care about her feelings. And if he let his emotions cloud his judgment, he couldn't protect her either.

"Declan, I can't," she whispered, her voice trembling.

"Alex," he said quietly, "I can't help you unless you tell me the truth."

"I'm telling you everything I can."

That loaded statement set off all his warning bells.

"You're being evasive," he said, keeping his tone controlled. "Half answers. Deflections. Do you think the FBI is going to go easy on you? They won't. What are you involved in? Why do they want to question you about this man?"

Her composure cracked. Tears spilled over, silent and sudden. Her shoulders shook as she tried to hold herself together. Declan felt dread creep up his spine. She was in deeper trouble than he'd realized.

A small, broken sound escaped her. That was all it took. His resolve softened. He stepped forward and pulled her into his arms. She sagged against him, tension bleeding out of her as she pressed her forehead to his chest. After a moment, she steadied herself and drew back.

"Declan," she whispered, "he will kill me. He will kill Collin. He will kill anyone I care about. I can't talk to the FBI."

Her voice trembled with a desperation that made his anger rise—not at her, but at whoever had put that fear in her.

"Did you ever help commit a crime?"

"No."

"Did you ever know about a crime before it happened?"

"No."

"Did you ever help cover one up?"

"No."

Some of the dread eased. If she was telling the truth, she wasn't culpable. But she was terrified. And that terrified him.

"Okay, we need to go into the office. Just answer their questions as evasively as you answered mine, and you should be fine."

He walked to the closet and grabbed his coat. Behind him, Alex wrapped her arms around herself, drawing in a slow, steadying breath before following.

"And Alex," Declan said as he shrugged the coat on, his voice low, "this conversation isn't over."

Declan paced behind the two-way mirror, watching Agents Lopez and Mc-Murray question Alex. The weight of the morning pressed on him—Bubba's meltdown, the SAC insisting he needed a handler, and the tense phone call with Martin back at the hotel. He had told Martin everything then: the man who had chased Alex; the flowers delivered to her work, the repeated phone calls. Alex had thrown away the flowers and note, too shaken to remember the sender's company. The calls had come from an unknown number.

Now, standing in the dim viewing room, he wasn't sure what any of it meant.

His gaze drifted back to Alex. The woman sitting at the metal table was nothing like the one who had cried into his chest thirty minutes earlier. She was composed, steady, almost clinical. Every answer she gave was measured. She revealed just enough to satisfy the agents while neatly sidestepping anything that might pull her deeper into the mess.

They were asking questions they already knew the answers to. Testing her honesty. So far, she hadn't lied.

The door behind him clicked open.

Agent Stewart stepped inside, a short, sharp-eyed Black woman with a presence that filled the room despite her size. She carried a tablet under one arm and a steaming cup of coffee in the other.

"Wallace," she said quietly, joining him at the glass. "She's doing well."

"She's terrified," Declan murmured. "She's just hiding it."

Stewart tapped her tablet. "We pulled her phone records. The calls she mentioned? All from a burner. No subscriber info, no location data. Completely untraceable."

Declan's jaw tightened. "Burners don't automatically mean mob."

Stewart gave him a look. "Given her former employer, it's a reasonable assumption."

"Maybe," Declan said, crossing his arms. "But the flowers, the notes, the guy chasing her? That's not mob behavior. That's personal. That's someone fixated."

"You're suggesting a stalker."

"I'm saying it fits better than the mafia sending her anonymous bouquets," Declan replied. "If Enzo wanted her dead, she wouldn't be getting warning shots. She'd be gone."

Stewart considered that, her expression unreadable. "It's still a risk to assume this isn't connected."

"And it's a risk to assume it is," Declan countered. "If we chase the wrong angle, we leave her exposed."

Stewart exhaled slowly. "Either way, she needs protection."

Declan didn't hesitate. "I'll take the detail."

One of Stewart's eyebrows lifted. "You're volunteering."

"She trusts me," he said. "She won't trust a rotating team of agents she's never met."

"You're as much of a target as she is—if they're responsible for your car."

"I know," Declan replied, jaw tightening. "But I'm aware of the threat now. My guard's up. They won't get to me again."

Stewart studied him for a long, assessing moment. "All right. I'll tell the SAC you're taking point."

She turned to leave, then paused with her hand on the door. "Wallace... if this is a stalker, it's going to escalate."

Declan looked back at Alex through the glass. She sat perfectly still, hands folded, answering another question with quiet precision.

"If it's a stalker," he said, "I'll handle it."

"And if it's not?" Stewart asked softly.

He didn't answer, just shot her a sharp glare.

Stewart nodded once and slipped out, leaving him alone with the glass, the questions, and the unsettling possibility that the danger surrounding Alex might be coming from a direction no one expected.

Martin stood beside Declan, watching the interrogation unfold. Before the agents began their questioning, Martin had briefed him on everything the FBI had uncovered so far. The picture he painted of Enzo was far from flattering. Enzo sounded like a genuine piece of work—a manipulative, ruthless operator who treated the law like a suggestion. According to the Bureau, he was a prominent underboss in the Moretti crime family.

Enzo had been on their radar since the early nineties, but he was careful. Too careful. Despite decades of attempts, the FBI had never managed to infiltrate his circle. His meticulous nature and the fierce loyalty of his associates made it nearly impossible to gather enough evidence to bring him down.

The more Declan heard, the more uneasy he became. The FBI would do anything to topple a man like Enzo. They would leave no stone unturned, no witness unpressured. And that made Alex a liability—not just to Enzo, but to everyone tied to him. If she didn't navigate this interview perfectly, she was in trouble.

"Damn, man, take a breath. The tension radiating off you is suffocating me," Martin muttered, trying to lighten the air in the viewing room.

Declan exhaled slowly, realizing he'd been holding his breath. He trusted Martin. They'd been partners back when they both worked patrol, before either of them made detective.

"She's in deep, Martin," Declan said, eyes never leaving Alex.

"How deep?"

"Deep enough to run eight years ago, change her name, and live on a military base for protection. I don't know the details yet, but I know she was never involved in Enzo's dealings. She was aware of them, and that made her a liability. She's terrified of him."

He turned to Martin, voice low and steady. "We need to handle this delicately. She's been through enough. We can't let her fall through the cracks now. We protect her and her son. No matter what."

Martin nodded, the weight of the situation settling between them. Together, they watched Alex as the agents' questions grew sharper.

"Did Mr. Esposito ever take you to his car dealership?" Lopez asked.

"Yes. We stopped there sometimes when we went to buy feed for the horses."

"Did you ever meet any of his employees?" McMurray pressed.

"Only his son. I stayed in the car while he went inside."

"If you stayed in the car, how did you meet his son?" Lopez asked.

"His son would come to the barn sometimes."

The agents exchanged a look—frustration edging into their expressions. They were seasoned interrogators, used to slicing through ambiguity, but Alex's careful evasiveness was testing their patience.

"Let's cut the shit, Ms. Kelley," Lopez said, slapping a photo onto the table. "Have you ever seen this man?"

A yes-or-no question. No room to dance around it. Declan had told her before she walked in: Don't lie.

After a long, tense pause, she answered. "Yes. I saw him several times."

The agents shared another look. Declan recognized it instantly. He'd worn that same expression countless times in the field—a predatory gleam, the wolves circling before going for the throat.

"What was the nature of your interaction with this man?" McMurray asked.

"I had no interaction with him." She smiled politely. "Like I said, I always stayed in the car. The first time I saw him, Enzo was speaking with him outside the dealership. The second and final time, he showed up at the barn while I was riding. He and Enzo went into the office for a few minutes, then he left. That's all I know."

"Do you know who that man is?" McMurray asked.

"No idea," Alex said, irritation creeping into her tone.

"That," McMurray said, tapping the photo, "is Alonzo Moretti. The boss of the Moretti crime family."

Alex tempered her reaction so well it was almost imperceptible, but Declan caught it—the quick flash of fear before her mask snapped back into place. It lasted barely a heartbeat, but it was enough. He stayed alert, every muscle coiled, ready to intervene if the agents pushed her too far.

"What about this man?" McMurray asked, slapping another photo onto the table.

Alex paled. Not dramatically—just a slight drain of color, a tightening around her mouth—but Declan saw it.

"We know Enzo paid off customs agents to smuggle in his shipments from overseas," McMurray continued. "This is Agent Pike. He was deep undercover, posing as a customs agent. He disappeared shortly after making contact with Enzo."

A cold ripple slid down Declan's spine. He saw it—the flicker of recognition in Alex's eyes. Not guilt. Not surprise. Recognition. And fear.

That was enough.

Declan didn't think. He moved.

He shoved the door open so hard it ricocheted off the wall, the crack echoing through the room. Both agents jerked their heads up as he strode toward Alex.

"Let's go," he said, extending his hand.

Alex didn't hesitate. Her fingers slid into his, and she rose from the chair as if she'd been waiting for him to come get her.

"Excuse us, Sergeant Wallace," Agent Lopez snapped, pushing back from the table. "We aren't done with her yet."

Declan turned, his glare sharp enough to cut. "Is she under arrest?"

Lopez held his stare. If looks could kill, Declan would've dropped him on the spot.

"No," Lopez finally bit out.

"Then she's done here," Declan said, voice low and final.

He didn't wait for a response. He guided Alex out of the room, his grip firm but steady. She struggled to match his long strides, but he didn't slow until they were out of the building and inside his rental car, the door shutting with a decisive thud that felt like a line being drawn.

Chapter Fourteen
ALEX

They drove back to Alex's house in silence. Tension radiated between them, thick enough to press against her ribs. She knew she was going to have to tell him everything—maybe not all at once, but soon. The exhaustion from her morning with the FBI weighed heavily on her, and she was grateful for the quiet Declan allowed her on the short drive home.

Halfway down the road, Declan cleared his throat. "Before we get there, we need to talk."

Alex tensed. "About the interview?"

"About your safety." His hands tightened on the steering wheel. "Until we figure out what's going on, they've assigned me as your protective detail."

She blinked at him. "My what?"

"I'm staying with you," he said simply. "On the couch. In the house. Wherever you are, I'm there."

Her heart lurched. "Declan, that's unnecessary. I don't need a babysitter."

"This isn't babysitting," he said, glancing at her. "Someone chased you. Someone sent flowers with a note to let you know they're clearly watching you. Someone called and texted you from a burner phone. Oh, yeah, and someone tried to kill me. I'm not leaving you alone."

She shook her head. "You can't just—"

"I can," he said, his voice firm. "And I will. The SAC signed off on it. Stewart agreed. I'm your detail until this is resolved."

Alex opened her mouth to argue again, but the words tangled in her throat. She didn't want to need protection. She didn't want to feel weak. But the idea of Declan leaving her alone made her stomach twist.

She exhaled slowly. "Fine. But the couch. And only the couch." She wasn't ready for that conversation with Collin.

A faint smile tugged at his mouth. "The couch works."

She turned her face toward the window so he wouldn't see the relief softening her features. She hated how much safer she felt knowing he'd be there—but she couldn't deny it. Not even to herself.

As they approached the house, something felt off.

Alex leaned forward, squinting. "Declan... the door."

The front door stood wide open.

Her stomach dropped. Alyssa had been home alone last night.

Declan braked hard. Before the car fully stopped, Alex reached for the handle, panic surging through her.

Declan caught her arm, his grip firm but gentle. "Wait here. If I'm not back in five minutes, call Bishop." He handed her his phone, Bishop's number already pulled up.

Then he was out of the car, gun drawn as he moved up the steps and disappeared inside.

Alex stared at the clock on his phone. It was a quarter til nine.

Her pulse hammered. Maybe she should call Bishop now. Maybe she shouldn't wait. The idea of Declan being in there alone made her chest tighten.

She forced herself to set the phone down. He told her to wait. She would wait.

Two agonizing minutes later, Declan reappeared. Alex let out a breath she didn't realize she'd been holding. She rolled the window down, searching his face.

"It's not good," he said, voice tight. "The place has been ransacked. Whoever was here was looking for something."

Alex's heart plummeted. "Was Alyssa in there?"

He shook his head. Relief and dread tangled in her chest. She fumbled for her phone.

"What are you doing?" Declan asked.

"Alyssa was home alone last night. I need to find out if she's okay."

Declan's expression hardened. He reached through the window and grabbed his phone. "Call her. I'm calling this in."

Alyssa didn't answer. Neither did Emily or Memory.

"What is the point of having a phone if no one ever answers?" Alex snapped, her voice cracking.

Declan hung up and pulled her into a hug. "She's probably fine. Bishop and the guys are on their way."

"Can I go in and look at the damage?"

"No. They need to process the scene. And I'll have to let Martin take the lead since you're my—" He stumbled. "Since we have a personal relationship."

Alex managed a small smile despite the fear twisting her insides.

Two police cars pulled into the driveway. Bishop and another officer stepped out. Declan briefed them quickly, and the three headed toward the house.

Alex was about to climb back into the car when a black F-150 pulled in. Alyssa hopped out of the passenger side.

Relief crashed over Alex. She ran to her friend and wrapped her in a tight hug.

"Alex, what the hell is going on?" Alyssa asked.

"Someone broke in. The place is trashed. I tried calling you—I thought something happened to you."

Alyssa blinked. "I stayed at Dean's. My phone died. And he has an Android."

Declan approached. "Glad you're okay, Alyssa."

"Glad to be okay," she said with a shaky laugh.

"What do you say we grab coffee?" Declan suggested. "It'll be awhile before they finish inside."

They agreed. Alex jogged to her car to grab her sunglasses. She opened the door—

And froze.

A small package wrapped in white paper sat on the front seat. A folded note rested on top.

Now you'll have more time for me.

Alex's breath hitched. The words crawled under her skin like ice. Her fingers trembled as she reached for the lid, every instinct screaming at her to stop, to walk away, to pretend she hadn't seen it.

She lifted the cover.

Inside lay a severed pinky finger, the nail freshly manicured in glossy red.

For a heartbeat, her mind refused to process what she was seeing. The world narrowed to a pinpoint. A ringing filled her ears, drowning out everything else. Then reality slammed into her chest like a physical blow.

Alex screamed, stumbling backward. Her shoulder hit the doorframe, and she cracked her head against the roof of the car. The metallic tang of adrenaline coated her tongue. Her stomach lurched violently, and her vision blurred at the edges.

Declan was at her side in an instant, his presence a sudden anchor in the chaos.

"Fuck—please tell me you didn't touch it."

"I... I only touched the cover," she whispered. Her voice didn't sound like her own. It was thin, distant, as if it were coming from underwater.

"Okay. Go back to the car and wait for me."

She nodded, though she wasn't sure she understood. Her legs moved on instinct, carrying her away from the car even as her mind stayed frozen on the image of the finger in the box. Her breaths came in short, uneven pulls, each one thinner than the last. Sound dulled around her, as if someone had pressed hands over her ears, and her vision narrowed until the world tunneled into a single, wavering point.

Declan strode toward Bishop, already barking orders, but his voice sounded much too far away.

Today was a gift that just kept on giving.

The trip to the coffee shop passed in a blur. Alex barely registered the turns Declan made or the chatter from the radio. Her mind raced, looping through the break-in, the open door, the ransacked rooms. She kept her eyes fixed on her coffee, focusing on the warmth seeping into her palms and the steady rhythm of her breathing. She needed something—anything—to anchor her.

Until this morning, she'd convinced herself it was all a misunderstanding. A coincidence. A string of unnerving events that couldn't possibly be connected to Enzo. It made no sense for him to come after her after all this time.

But the break-in had shattered that fragile illusion.

They settled around a small table in the corner of the coffee shop. The low hum of conversation around them felt strangely distant, like the world was moving at a normal pace while theirs had tilted off its axis.

"Okay," he began, voice low but steady, "here's where we are."

Alex's stomach tightened. Alyssa reached for her hand under the table. Dean sat back, arms crossed, watching Declan closely.

"There are two working theories," Declan said. "Either Enzo or one of his associates is behind this, or you're dealing with a stalker."

He didn't dress it up.

"Based on what we have so far, it's hard to commit to one direction," he went on. "But right now, I'm leaning away from Enzo and toward a stalker. Nothing about this feels like someone from your past settling a score. It feels like someone who's fixated. Someone who's been watching."

Alex's breath hitched. She stared down at her coffee, hands trembling slightly.

Declan rubbed a hand over his jaw. "There's something else I need to tell you. Something I didn't want to bring up until I was sure it mattered."

Alyssa leaned in.

"What is it?" Alex asked.

"The murder case I'm working on," he said quietly. "My victim was missing a pinky finger."

Alyssa gasped. Dean sat forward. Alex felt the room tilt.

Declan nodded grimly. "Yeah. I know. The box this morning... it matches."

Alex pressed a hand to her mouth. "Oh, God."

Declan's voice softened. "The victim's name is Martha Cunningham."

Alex froze.

Alyssa whispered, "Wait—Martha? As in—"

"The Martha who comes into the ER all the time," Alex said, her voice barely audible. "Chest pain, migraines... she always asks for me."

Declan watched her carefully. "I figured you'd recognize the name."

Alex's eyes stung. "She was lonely. Sweet. She just... needed someone to listen."

"Exactly," Declan said. "And that's why this next part matters."

He leaned in, lowering his voice.

"Frequent flyers don't exist in isolation. They see who gets attention. Who gets comfort. Who gets kindness. And sometimes... someone fixates."

Alyssa's face drained of color. "You think someone at the hospital was jealous of her?"

"I think someone noticed how much attention she got from Alex," Declan said. "Someone who didn't enjoy sharing her. Someone who saw Martha as competition. Or perhaps the opposite. Martha noticed someone paying too close attention to Alex, maybe confronted them about it."

Alex's breath caught. "So Martha's murder... was because of me."

Declan shook his head firmly. "No. Martha's murder was because of a killer. A jealous, unstable person who made their own choices. But yes—whoever did this is targeting you now."

Silence settled over the table.

Declan reached out, his voice steady. "This is why you're not going anywhere alone. Not today. Not tonight. Not until we figure out who this is."

Alex nodded slowly, fear and relief tangling in her chest.

For the first time, the pieces formed a picture.

And it was far more terrifying than anything she'd imagined.

She felt Alyssa's discerning gaze on her as Declan laid everything out. His voice stayed calm, but the weight behind it was impossible to miss. He explained how someone connected to Alex's past, a former business associate, was coming after her and the people she cared about. Until they knew more, it wasn't safe for anyone to stay at the house. He remained vague and didnt give away anything to Alyssa and Dean.

Dean squeezed Alyssa's hand. "You can stay with me," he said, and Alyssa nodded right away.

Alex swallowed, feeling the pressure of their eyes on her. She could see the questions forming. Who was this man? Why was he after her? She owed them an explanation.

"Enzo was my boss back in New Hampshire," she said quietly. "He owned a horse farm and a car dealership. The farm was legitimate. The dealership wasn't." She rubbed her palms together, grounding herself. "He was connected to the Moretti crime family. I didn't know the extent of it at first, but once I did, I had no choice other than to run. I changed my name, built a new life, and kept a low profile."

Alyssa's eyes widened. Dean let out a low whistle.

Alex continued, "Enzo doesn't let people walk away. Not really. But it's been eight years. I thought I was safe."

Declan leaned forward, his tone steady and sure. "You're not going back to the house alone, and you're not staying there tonight. I have a place off the grid with no paper trail and no connection to me. No one knows about it. It's the safest option until we figure out what's going on."

Alex blinked, surprised by the certainty in his voice. "Declan…"

"It's not up for debate," he said firmly. "You and Collin will stay with me."

Alyssa looked relieved. Dean nodded in agreement.

Alex let out a slow breath. She didn't want to uproot Collin again, and she hated relying on anyone, but Declan was right. And the thought of being somewhere hidden eased some of the tension she was carrying.

"Okay," she said softly. "Thank you."

Declan's shoulders relaxed a little.

"It should be safe enough for you to go back into the house and grab some belongings," he said. "I need to head back to the office and get some work done."

Alex saw the hesitation in his eyes. He didn't want her alone.

"I was planning on spending the day at the barn," she offered. "I'll be with people. I'll carry my pepper spray just in case."

That seemed to settle him. She didn't want to intrude on Dean and Alyssa's weekend at the houseboat, and she didn't want to sit alone in a hotel room spiraling. The barn felt like the only place she could breathe.

They agreed to meet later that afternoon so she could follow Declan to the cabin. Dean and Alyssa offered her a ride back to the house to collect some belongings and her car. Although she was excited to spend another night alone with Declan she couldn't shake the feeling he was withdrawing from her.

Alex wrapped her hands around her coffee cup, letting the warmth steady her. Everything felt like it was shifting beneath her feet, but at least now she had a direction to move in.

And she wasn't moving alone.

Declan walked Alex to Dean's truck. Alyssa and Dean were already inside, their animated conversation a soft hum in the background. Alex took a small step toward Declan, instinctively seeking his steadiness. She needed an anchor, something solid in the chaos.

Declan stepped back.

The distance between them felt like a chasm. His storm gray eyes gave nothing away; his expression was unreadable. She searched for reassurance, for anything, but found only a wall. She didn't blame him. If their roles were reversed, she wouldn't trust her either.

"I'll see you tonight," Declan said with a curt nod. He turned and walked away without looking back, leaving a trail of unfinished words and tension behind him.

Alex climbed into the backseat and watched his car disappear down the road. The weight of everything pressed down on her. She owed him the truth. He had nearly been blown up because of her, and she was still holding back pieces of the story. Lying about her past had become so ingrained in her she wasn't sure she even remembered the truth herself.

Her phone rang, slicing clean through her thoughts. A local number flashed across the screen. Her stomach dipped. She almost let it go to voicemail, but her thumb betrayed her, and she answered.

Her real estate agent's voice exploded through the receiver. "Congratulations! Your offer was accepted!"

For a moment, she just sat there, stunned. With everything happening, she had completely forgotten she'd even put in an offer. After a brief conversation, she agreed to meet him at the office to sign the papers. She'd head to the barn afterward.

She hung up with a heavy sigh just as they pulled into the driveway. The house, once warm and familiar, now loomed dark and hollow.

Inside, the devastation hit like a punch. Every room had been turned upside down. Drawers dumped. Furniture overturned. Nothing left untouched. Martin had given them each one of his cards and told them to call if they noticed anything missing. Like they could notice anything missing in this mess.

Alex pulled out her phone and dialed Henry. She didn't want Collin to see the house like this. It would be safer if he stayed with his father for now. Henry answered on the third ring. The conversation went the way most things did with her ex: quick, frustrating, and leaving her wanting to punch him square in the face.

She tossed her phone onto the couch with an exaggerated huff, the kind that did nothing to ease the pressure building behind her ribs.

"Everything okay?" Alyssa asked.

"Just my ex being... my ex." Alex rubbed her forehead. "I asked him to keep Collin and explained what was going on. But apparently he's going TDY and can't get out of it. He agreed to keep him until Thursday; he leaves Saturday. Hopefully, we'll have answers by then."

Alyssa frowned. "What's TDY?"

"Temporary change of station. Shorter than a deployment, but long enough to be inconvenient."

Alyssa raised her brows in a figures kind of way. Alex righted a fallen lamp and surveyed the wreckage again.

"Let's just get out of here," Alyssa said, exasperated. "This mess will still be here later. We'll clean it up then."

They headed upstairs to pack. Alex grabbed a few outfits for herself and then went to Collin's room to pack his things. Alyssa and her ex had true joint custody of Luke, so he was with his dad until next Friday. Hopefully by then, the case would be resolved and they'd all be back home.

When Alex came downstairs, she found Alyssa kneeling in the living room, carefully gathering the shattered pieces of her grandmother's collectible plates. Alex's heart sank. Alyssa had been incredibly close to her grandmother, and those plates were one of the few things she had left of her.

"Oh my God, Alyssa, I'm so sorry." Alex's voice cracked with guilt. Tears stung her eyes, but she blinked them back.

Alyssa stood and pulled her into a hug, her own eyes shining. "It's not your fault, Alex. None of this is. We'll get through it together."

Her reassurance eased the tightness in Alex's chest. Alyssa pulled back with a small, wobbly smile. "Besides, spending the week with Dean isn't the worst fate."

Alex managed a weak laugh.

They said their goodbyes, and Alex headed to the realtor's office. Uncertainty hovered over her like a storm cloud. With everything happening, she might need her savings more than ever. Signing papers for a new property felt surreal, almost reckless.

But she walked inside anyway, still unsure of what her next steps would be.

Alex was now the proud owner of a fixer-upper.

After leaving the realtor's office, she headed straight for Tractor Supply. Freedom needed new tack, better feed, and a few supplements if she was going to put weight back on. Besides, stocking up for the mare felt productive, something she could actually control.

An hour later, her SUV was packed tight with feed, dewormer, and new halters for both horses. Maybe she had gone a little overboard, but retail therapy with a purpose beat letting her thoughts spiral. The smell of sweet grain and leather filled the car, oddly comforting, like she had bought herself a little control in a day that had offered none.

By the time she pulled into the barn two hours after leaving the realtor's office, the sun had dipped lower, casting long stripes of gold through the open bay doors. The familiar scent of hay, dust, and warm horse greeted her the moment she stepped out. A few geldings nickered from their stalls, the soft shuffle of hooves echoing down the aisle as if welcoming her back to solid ground.

She hauled the bags of feed into the grain room, the paper crinkling under her grip, then tucked the smaller supplies neatly into her tack closet. The rhythmic work steadied her breathing, each task a small anchor.

When everything was finally put away, she brushed the dust from her jeans and headed down the aisle in search of Pablo, the head groom. The barn lights hummed overhead, and the quiet rustle of horses settling in for the evening followed her as she walked.

She spotted him halfway down, starting the nighttime feeding.

"Hey, Pablo, how are you?" Alex asked, genuinely glad to see him. He was a down-to-earth, middle-aged gentleman who treated every horse like royalty and every boarder with kindness.

"Hola, señorita. I'm good. *¿Cómo estás?*"

"I'm good, too, thanks. Can I show you something really quick?" she said, turning toward the feed room.

"Of course," he replied, following her.

She showed him the feed she'd bought and explained she'd purchased the mare in stall twelve. Pablo nodded along, listening carefully as she told him what she wanted the mare to get and when.

When they finished, Alex headed back toward her tack closet to grab her bag before leaving. She swung the door open and froze.

A small piece of paper sat on top of her grooming kit. Not crumpled. Not tossed. Placed.

Her stomach dropped. She hadn't noticed it when she was unloading her car. Had it been there the entire time, or had someone placed it here while she had spoken to Pablo?

She picked it up with trembling fingers.

I can get to you anywhere.

Her pulse roared in her ears. The barn suddenly felt too quiet, too exposed. She glanced over her shoulder, scanning the aisle, the stalls, the shadows.

"Señorita?" Pablo's voice came from behind her, gentle but concerned. "Everything okay?"

Alex swallowed hard and held out the note. "Pablo... someone put this in my locker."

His expression darkened. "Who would do this?"

"I don't know," she whispered. "But I need you to keep an eye out. Anyone you don't recognize. Anyone hanging around my horses. Anything that feels off."

Pablo straightened, his jaw set. "I will watch. I promise. No one will touch your horses. Not while I am here."

The sincerity in his eyes eased some of her worry. He was someone who knew what it meant to work until your hands ached, someone who understood horses before he understood people. She trusted that far more than money or manners. She'd grown up beside people like him, not the polished riders who breezed in and out. She used to be him—the help, the invisible one in the background doing the real work while the wealthy boarders floated through without ever understanding what it meant to be a horseman. With Pablo, she didn't have to explain herself or her bond with her horses. He just got it.

"Thank you," she said softly.

"Always, señorita."

They exchanged a few more words about the mare's feeding schedule, but Alex barely heard them. Her mind was already racing ahead.

She walked out to her car, every instinct screaming at her to move faster without drawing attention. Her hands shook as she dug out her phone. Declan's name glowed on the screen, steady and calm in a way she absolutely wasn't.

For a moment, she couldn't breathe.

He had been here.

Close enough that she could feel it in her bones.

Close enough that someone should have seen him.

Close enough that she wasn't sure she hadn't imagined the brush of air at her back.

She swallowed hard, her thumb hovering over the call button. Declan was going to lose it when she told him. Not at her, never at her, but at the situation. He would go straight into that cold, controlled fury she hated almost as much as she relied on. He would demand details she didn't have, and insist she leave the barn immediately.

The barn was her safe place. The place she came to clear her head and steady her thoughts. She would not give it up. A sharp frown pulled at the corners of her mouth.

He had been close enough to breathe the same air.

Close enough that she could still feel the wrongness of it crawling along her skin.

The barn was her safe place, the one corner of her life he hadn't tainted. The idea that he had stood somewhere nearby, watching, waiting, made her stomach twist and her pulse spike with anger. She would not let him take this from her too.

Chapter Fifteen
DECLAN

Declan arrived at the office a few minutes after leaving the coffee shop. The drive over had been quiet, but not peaceful. His mind kept circling back to Alex—standing beside Dean's truck, looking at him like she needed something from him he wouldn't allow himself to give.

The threat against her was quickly escalating, and there needed to be clear lines. Clean boundaries until the mess was resolved. He wanted to pull her close, to take that fear out of her eyes for good, but wanting it and acting on it were two very different things. There was no room for impulse or emotions when so many lives hung in the balance.

Still, the look in her eyes when he stepped back from her...

He'd seen the hurt there.

He'd felt it like a punch.

He pushed the thought aside and pulled up Google on his desktop, searching for local cleaning companies. The cabin had sat untouched since Luther had moved to assisted living last year, and he was sure the place was in a desperate state of disarray. He dialed the first number that popped up.

After a quick conversation with Rebecca, the owner, she assured him that the cabin would be habitable in no time. He gave her his card information and told her where to find the spare key. Mixed emotions tugged at him. He wasn't thrilled about returning to the cabin, but he was tired of being cooped up in the city, and he needed a safe place for Alex and Collin. Somewhere no one would think to look.

The cabin was still in his father's late wife's maiden name, so tracking it to him would be difficult. Luther had signed everything over before moving to the Four Seasons, but Declan hadn't filed the paperwork yet. After Caroline passed, Luther's health had spiraled—loneliness, poor diet, grief. Declan had expected the worst when he visited him at the facility, but to his surprise, Luther had been thriving.

After the birth of Declan's older son, John, Luther had reached out to make amends. Declan had to give the old man credit. He really had changed. After a severe heart attack, Luther had decided he needed to make things right—with God, with his family, with himself. He quit drinking, quit smoking, started going to church with Caroline every Sunday, and reached out to his sons to heal old wounds.

It had taken Declan some time to trust the change, but eventually he began bringing the kids to visit. They'd formed a good relationship with their grandfather. Declan would never fully trust the man. He knew the demon still existed within him. The one that used to beat him, his brother and his mother, the old man had just gotten better at reining it in.

A knock on his office door pulled him from his thoughts. Martin stepped inside and dropped into the chair across from him.

"We wrapped everything up at the house," Martin said.

"Find anything?" Declan asked, though he already suspected they hadn't.

"Nope. Every print we pulled matched up. The place was such a wreck they haven't even figured out what's missing yet." Martin leaned forward, concern etched across his face. "Seriously, what the hell did you get yourself into?"

"I'm not sure," Declan's tone was clipped.

Martin cleared his throat and flipped open his notebook. "Does she have any enemies other than Enzo? Any legal troubles?"

"Err... I don't know," Declan admitted.

Martin raised a brow. "Surely you've run a check on her by now."

Declan exhaled. "I didn't want to find anything wrong with her, to be honest. So, no, I haven't."

Martin rose from his chair, shaking his head. "What is her date of birth?"

Declan averted his eyes and tapped his thumbs on the desk. He already knew where this was going.

"You don't even know her birthday?" Martin asked, incredulous.

"We've known each other for two seconds. No, I don't know her birthday." Declan pulled out his phone and opened their messages. "But I can find out."

> Hey, when is your birthday?

The reply came almost instantly.

> I'm going to kill Alyssa.

Not the response he expected.

> What happened?

> She told you my birthday is this Thursday. I told her I didn't want to make a big deal of it this year. It's not like thirty is special or anything.

Declan blinked. "Shit. Her birthday is on Thursday. She'll be thirty, so… January 15, 1995."

Martin jotted the date down and headed for the door. "I'll run her. You'd better figure out what you're doing for her birthday. And don't fall for the 'I don't want anything' line. It's a trap every time. Get her something if you know what's good for you."

Declan leaned back in his chair, exhaling slowly. A birthday gift. He shouldn't. Not when he was supposed to be keeping things professional. But the idea of doing nothing felt wrong. A gift didn't have to mean anything. It could be practical. Thoughtful without being intimate. Something that said I see you without saying I want you.

He scrubbed a hand over his face.

He was lying to himself, and he knew it.

He needed help. Luckily, he'd grabbed Alyssa's number that morning.

He scrolled to her name and hit call. After a brief conversation, Declan ended the call with Alyssa, feeling even more at a loss than when he'd dialed. She'd rattled off a handful of ideas, all practical things Alex would actually use—gift cards to Tractor Supply or the Farmers' Association, a subscription to some horse magazine she liked, even a United States Equestrian Federation membership she'd been eyeing. None of it narrowed anything down, and he hung up realizing Alex was both easy and impossible to shop for.

A gift card felt impersonal. He opened a new tab and searched USEF membership. Two thousand five hundred dollars for a lifetime membership. He blew out a breath.

He pushed the thought aside. He'd circle back to the birthday dilemma later. Right now, he needed to focus. He headed down the hall to Martin's office.

"Find anything juicy?" Declan asked, taking a seat.

Martin flipped a page in his notebook. "Not really. She worked at a couple of barns in New Hampshire and Maine between 2007 and 2011. Then she moved to Arkansas, got married, and joined the Arkansas Air National Guard. Divorced in 2015. Two speeding tickets, one accident. The bank repossessed her car after the divorce, but other than that, she's squeaky clean.

Declan felt something in his chest loosen.

Martin shrugged. "Honestly? She's boring on paper."

Declan huffed a quiet laugh. "I'll take boring." On paper she might look harmless, but in real life she was chaos wrapped in a pretty face. He'd take whatever boring he could get.

Declan shouldn't have felt relieved by Martin's report, and he told himself he didn't. She was his assignment, nothing more, and the clean background only confirmed what he already knew.

Until they found the danger that was circling her, that was how it had to be. The truth, however, was far more inconvenient. He wanted to protect her, claim her, and make her his in every sense of the word.

Returning to his office, he woke up his computer and pulled up the case files. He planned to spend the rest of the day digging into Martha's background, tracing every thread until something snapped into place.

Alex's social media tabs were already open from earlier—Facebook, LinkedIn, Instagram. One click and he could know more about her childhood, her friends, her habits, the pieces of her life she hadn't offered him yet.

His hand hovered over the mouse.

He wanted to know everything about her—every detail, every story, every scar. But he wanted it from her lips, in her time, not by sifting through the curated fragments of her past. Digging felt wrong. Too much like taking something she hadn't chosen to give. His job demanded that he look at every angle, especially with the threat closing in on her. Still, his conscience made him hesitate.

Her Facebook was mostly horse rescue posts and memes. Declan chuckled. At least she had a good sense of humor. Her photos were tame—nothing revealing, nothing concerning. Her last Instagram post was two years old, a sweet picture of her and Collin. She had only eighty-nine followers.

He clicked into the comments, scanning them with a detective's eye. Most were harmless—friends from the barn, a few coworkers, a couple of mom-friends. Still, he checked each profile, looking for anything off: burner accounts, obsessive patterns, strangers who interacted a little too often.

Nothing.

No unsettling messages.

No overeager men.

No one who even brushed the edges of a potential stalker.

If someone were watching her, they weren't doing it in the open.

He shifted his focus to Martha and opened the desk drawer where he kept her case file. He pulled it out and flipped through the pages. Her record was long: solicitation, drug possession, contempt of court. The only person Declan had ever seen with Martha was a woman named Cindy. Cindy would post her bail, and the next week, Martha was back in for some other petty crime.

Declan pulled up Martha's most recent arrest record and found Cindy's information. He jotted down her address and headed out of the station. Cindy lived two blocks away. He'd drive over and see what he could find out from her faithful friend.

Declan pulled up outside Cindy's rattrap apartment building. Carefully pushing the front door open, he immediately met resistance. Looking down, he saw a pair of legs blocking the door. Quickly but gently, he pushed it open further and found a man halfway inside his apartment, lying over the threshold, reeking of alcohol, and covered in his own piss.

Declan crouched beside him, two fingers pressed to the man's neck. A slow, steady thump pulsed against the pad of his fingers.

Just drunk.

He exhaled through his nose and shook his head. "All right, buddy. Sleep it off," he muttered, nudging the man fully inside the apartment so the door could close without crushing him.

He knocked three times and waited. Behind the door, Cindy's shadow shifted in the thin strip of light on the floor. She hesitated, staying just out of view.

"Ma'am, I can see your shadow under the door," Declan said, keeping his voice calm. "You are not in trouble. I just want to ask you a few questions about Martha."

A long pause followed, long enough for him to hear the faint catch in her breathing. At last the bolt slid back. The door cracked open, and Cindy appeared in the gap with tired eyes and slumped shoulders, looking worn down and unsteady.

"I don't want no trouble, officer," she said quickly.

"Neither do I, ma'am," Declan reassured her.

She unlocked the chain and opened the door wider. Declan stepped inside, and the stench of rotting food immediately assaulted his nostrils. Dishes overflowed the sink, and trash bags were piled beside the door. A cockroach scrambled up the kitchen wall, and Declan forced himself not to react as he turned back to Cindy.

"Ma'am, when was the last time you saw Martha?"

"Three days ago, I think." Cindy rubbed her arms as if suddenly cold. "She usually comes by once or twice a week. I heard she was murdered." Her voice cracked. "She always brought my groceries. I don't get out much." A sniffle, then a trembling breath. "I sure will miss having her around."

"Did she have any enemies that you knew of? Anyone who would want to hurt her?"

"No, Martha was a sweetheart. Everyone loved her." Cindy's voice dissolved into full-blown sobs.

Declan shifted, uncomfortable. Emotional women were not his strong suit. He crossed to the counter, grabbed a paper towel, and handed it to her. She accepted it gratefully and blew her nose loudly enough to make him wince. After a moment, she collected herself.

When he felt it was safe to continue, he asked, "Had Martha said or done anything out of the ordinary? Seemed agitated?"

Cindy let out a wet laugh. "Martha was always agitated, but it wasn't unusual for her," she sighed. "If anything, she was excited. She was planning a trip up to New Hampshire to visit her daughter."

Declan's head snapped up. "Did you say New Hampshire?"

Cindy nodded. "Yes. Her daughter went to New England College up there. After she graduated, she stayed. She loved her job training horses."

She reached into her purse and pulled out a worn photograph. A pretty young woman, late twenties, long red wavy hair, smiled up at him.

"This is Brittany, Martha's daughter."

Declan studied the picture. He couldn't blame the girl for staying far from Arkansas. Growing up with Martha as her mother couldn't have been easy.

"Do you have a number for Brittany?" he asked.

"I sure do." Cindy dug out her phone and rattled off the digits while Declan jotted them down.

"Great. Thank you, ma'am. We'll keep you updated."

On the way back to the office, he swung by the Flying Saucer and grabbed catfish to go. He had a working lunch ahead of him. Finally—finally—he had a lead worth chasing.

He set the takeout box on his desk and headed to Martin's office. The door was closed. Martin was gone. Declan pulled out his phone and sent a quick text:

> May have a lead. Call me.

He slipped the phone back into his pocket and returned to his office. He had just taken his first bite when Martin walked in and dropped into the chair across from him.

"What's the lead?"

"My murder victim has a daughter in New Hampshire. Went to college there, stayed on after graduation. Wanna guess what she does for work?" Declan lifted a brow.

Martin pretended to think. "Does she work with horses?"

"Bingo." Declan slapped the photo of Brittany onto the desk. "I'm going to ask Alex if she knows her tonight."

Martin was halfway out of his chair when Bishop burst through the door.

"Have you heard the news?"

Declan's stomach dropped. "What happened?"

"Enzo Esposito is dead. He died last week."

Declan felt the air rush out of his lungs. Their lead suspect—gone.

"Well, shit," Martin muttered, sinking back into his seat.

Bishop crossed his arms. "It's still most likely mob-related. The car bomb, the woman missing a finger, the attempted abduction. But maybe we were looking at it wrong. Maybe Enzo was protecting her all these years."

Declan and Martin exchanged a look.

It was a possibility Declan hadn't considered. That the timing of the attacks coincided with his death wasn't a coincidence. They had been looking at the case all wrong.

Bishop continued, "And look at the timing. The attacks started right after Enzo died. Practically to the day."

A cold weight settled in Declan's stomach.

If Enzo had been shielding Alex from something worse...

If his death had removed that shield...

If the person hunting her had been waiting for the moment she was unprotected...

Then, everything they thought they knew about this case was wrong.

And Alex was in far more danger than any of them realized.

Declan sighed, dragging a hand through his hair. "If that's the case, then we need to find out who the real threat is. We need to figure out who stands to gain something from her death. If Enzo was protecting her, his death might have set off a chain reaction."

The thought settled like lead in his stomach.

He was tired of playing catch-up. Tired of reacting instead of getting ahead of the danger. Tonight, he and Alex were going to have an honest conversation. No more half-truths, no more holding back. One way or another, he was going to get to the bottom of this.

Bishop and Martin excused themselves to chase down leads, leaving Declan alone with the quiet hum of his office. He finished his lunch, tossed the Styrofoam container in the trash, and pulled out his notepad. Brittany's number was scrawled across the top of the page. He picked up the office phone and dialed.

Straight to voicemail.

"Hello, Brittany. This is Detective Wallace with the Little Rock Police Department. I have a few questions for you. When you get this, please call me back at my office." He left his number and ended the call.

It was nearly four o'clock. He'd worked through his entire Saturday, but for the first time in days, he felt like he was finally getting somewhere. Tomorrow he wasn't coming into the office. He'd figured out the perfect birthday gift over lunch, and the thought of her reaction tugged a smile out of him before he could stop it.

He gathered the photos of Martha and her daughter, slid them into the case file, and tucked everything into his backpack. Slinging the bag over his shoulder, he locked up his office and headed downstairs. He gave a quick wave to the dispatcher behind the bulletproof glass before stepping out into the chilly afternoon air.

Five minutes later, he was climbing the stairs to his hotel room. The Chief would probably lose his mind when he found out Declan had checked out early, but Declan didn't care. He was done letting a psychopath dictate his movements.

Back in the room, he quickly gathered his belongings and shoved them into his bag. As he reached for the handle of his suitcase, his phone rang. A jolt of adrenaline shot through him when he saw Alex's name on the screen.

"Alex?"

Her voice came through in a shaky whisper. "Declan... he was here."

Declan froze. "What do you mean 'here'?"

"I—I found a note in my locker at the barn." Her breath hitched. "It says he can get to me anywhere."

The room tilted. His pulse roared in his ears.

"Alex, listen to me," he said, already grabbing his keys, already moving. "Where are you right now?"

But she didn't answer right away.

"I'm still at the barn."

"Stay there, I'm on my way!" Declan was already running out of the room when he disconnected the call.

The stalker wasn't just watching. He was escalating. And they were out of time.

Chapter Sixteen
ALEX

Alex ended the call with Declan, her hand trembling slightly as she lowered the phone. The barn aisle felt too quiet, too exposed, every shadow suddenly suspicious. The note in her pocket felt like it weighed a hundred pounds.

I can get to you anywhere.

Her stomach twisted. She didn't know whether to pace, hide, or run. Declan was on his way, but every minute felt like an hour. She needed to keep moving, keep her mind from spiraling, so she headed back inside to help Pablo finish feeding.

Connie, the barn manager, was leaving for the night. Pablo had his back turned towards Alex when she stepped into the aisle. He startled when he caught sight of her out of the corner of his eye.

"Sorry," Alex said.

He turned, and one look at his face told her something was wrong. His eyes were glassy; his expression strained. The man looked as if he were barely holding himself together.

"Pablo, what's wrong?" she asked gently.

He shook his head, retreating into himself. "It is nothing," he said with a forced smile.

Alex recognized that look. She'd worn it herself more times than she could count—shoulders tight, eyes distant, trying not to burden anyone.

"I can't help if you don't tell me what's going on," she said, lowering herself onto the trunk in the aisle. "Maybe I can help."

Pablo hesitated, glancing around as if afraid someone might overhear. Finally, he exhaled shakily.

"My wife and my son made it to the United States," he said. "They crossed the border three days ago from Mexico. They are on their way up here to me. When I talked to Ms. Connie about letting them stay here, she said no. I don't know what to do. I need money, but I need a place for my family to live."

His voice cracked with desperation.

Alex's heart clenched. Connie, the barn manager, was notorious for her rigid rules and colder-than-ice demeanor. The loft apartment flashed through Alex's mind. She had planned on staying there with Collin eventually, but nothing was pushing them out of Alyssa's place anytime soon. Pablo's family needed it far more urgently.

"Pablo," she said carefully, "would you be willing to come work for me if I opened a barn? I could offer you a place to live with your family."

"Yes!" he said instantly, without a hint of hesitation.

Alex blinked. "I wouldn't be able to pay you much at first. Not until I bring in some client horses."

"Yes, please," Pablo said earnestly. "I hate it here."

"Where are your wife and son now?" Alex asked.

"They are close to San Antonio, trying to hitchhike up to Arkansas."

"Hitchhike?" Alex's voice rose in alarm.

"They are illegal, señorita. No papers, no ID, no money. I don't have enough to get them a bus ticket. All our money went to the coyote who got them here."

Alex's chest tightened. "Call your wife and tell her to get to the train station in San Antonio. I'll have a friend meet them there and buy their tickets."

She pulled out her phone and opened Facebook, searching for Maria's profile. Maria, her friend from basic training, was stationed in San Antonio and had a heart of gold. After a quick exchange of messages, Maria agreed to meet Pablo's family at the station and get them safely on a train.

Sixteen hours on a train wasn't ideal—but it was a hell of a lot safer than hitchhiking.

Alex exhaled, feeling a small measure of relief settle over her.

Now she just had to survive long enough for Declan to get here.

"I'll bring you to the train station tomorrow morning to pick them up. We'll find a place for all of you to stay, so don't worry about that. But you need to talk to Connie. Don't quit yet—not until I can get the power turned on at my new place and make sure it's livable. Just tell her you need Monday off to spend time with your family. I'll pick you up at the groom's lodging around quarter past eight."

Pablo's face crumpled with relief. Before Alex could react, he swept her into a tight, grateful hug.

"Thank you, Miss Alex. I cannot tell you how much this means to me!"

Alex smiled at his exuberance. "It's truly not a problem."

Headlights washed across the barn aisle, and Alex glanced toward the parking lot. Declan's car rolled to a stop beside her car. She opened her mouth to say goodbye to Pablo, but Declan was already out of the car looking tense, scanning the shadows like he expected a threat to jump out at any second.

His eyes locked on Pablo immediately as he strode forward into the barn.

"Declan, this is Pablo, the head groom." Alex rushed to reassure Declan all was fine.

Declan didn't relax right away. His gaze flicked from Pablo to Alex, assessing, protective, coiled tight. Only when he saw no danger did his shoulders ease a fraction.

Pablo offered a polite nod. "Hello."

Alex stepped between them slightly. "Pablo, this is my... friend, Declan. Declan, this is Pablo, the head groom."

They shook hands, and Pablo excused himself to finish feeding, noticeably lighter than he'd been earlier.

Declan waited until he was out of earshot before turning to Alex, his voice low and serious. "Where's the note?"

Alex swallowed and reached into her vest pocket, handing it over. Declan unfolded it, jaw tightening as he read the message.

His eyes lifted to hers, "show me where you found it."

She led him to her tack stall. Declan inspected the locker, the latch, the aisle, the shadows—every inch of the space. He crouched, checking the floor, then stood again, expression grim.

"He was close," Declan said quietly. "Close enough to watch you. Close enough to know your routine."

A chill ran down Alex's spine.

"When I bought Freedom... the guy who sold her to me, Jeremy—he gave me a weird feeling." She rubbed her arms, remembering the way his eyes had lingered on her, too sharp, too assessing. "He works here sometimes. Helps out. He knows the barn. The layout. The routines. He could move around without anyone questioning him."

Declan's expression hardened, the shift subtle but unmistakable. "Did he say anything to you? Anything that felt off?"

"Not exactly. Just... the way he looked at me."

Declan folded the note and slipped it into his jacket. "We're leaving as soon as you're ready."

Alex nodded.

As they stepped out into the aisle, Declan's hand brushed her elbow, guiding her toward the exit. "We're taking my car," he said firmly. "I need to have yours swept for bugs before you drive it again."

Alex's breath hitched, but she nodded again, grateful for his steadiness even as fear coiled tighter in her chest. On the way out of the barn, Alex stopped at Zorro's stall. The gelding perked up the moment he saw her, ears forward, eyes bright. Alex kissed his muzzle.

"This is him," she said.

"He's pretty," Declan admitted, reaching out a hand.

Zorro pinned his ears and swung his head just out of reach, then turned around and planted his butt squarely in front of Declan.

Declan blinked. "Well. That's clear."

Alex laughed. "He just wants a butt scratch."

"Yeah, I'm going to pass on that," Declan said, smirking despite himself.

Alex gave Zorro a pat and moved toward the stall on the other side of the aisle.

"This is Freedom."

Declan followed Alex across the aisle of the barn and stuck his hand out towards the mare. To Alex's surprise, the mare perked up and walked over to his outstretched hand.

"Oh, so it's like that, huh?" Alex said with a chuckle. "She ignores me."

That earned a half-smile from Declan. "I have a way with females."

Declan glanced once more down the barn aisle, then back at Alex.

"Come on. It's time to get out of here." His voice was firm. They walked to the car together, and Declan opened her door before circling around to the driver's side.

After a quick stop at the grocery store for dinner essentials, they headed toward the cabin. The hum of the tires on the highway was steady, almost soothing, but Alex couldn't shake the lingering tension from the note.

They exited I-30 at the same place she had earlier that day when she went to look at her new property. She stared out the window, trying to settle her nerves, when something caught her eye.

A gas station.

The same gas station they'd passed ten minutes ago.

Alex frowned. "Didn't we already go by that?"

Declan didn't look over, but his grip tightened on the wheel. "Yeah. I looped us around."

"Why?"

"Making sure we don't have a tail."

A chill slid down her spine. She swallowed. "Did we?"

"Not that I can see," he said, voice low and controlled. "But I'm not taking chances."

Alex nodded, her pulse thudding in her ears. She turned back to the window, watching the darkening landscape roll by. A few minutes later, she realized she was smiling—just a small, private curve of her lips.

Declan caught it. "What are you smiling about?"

She hesitated, then let out a soft laugh. "I was thinking it would be funny if your cabin ended up being near the property I just bought."

Declan slowed as they approached the familiar road. "When did you buy property?"

"This morning. My agent called to tell me my offer had been accepted, so I stopped by to sign papers on the way to the barn. I couldn't help it. I saw it and it just felt right. There's already a barn, pasture, and an outdoor arena. And I found the perfect spot for a house—up on this little hill." She pointed ahead as they approached. "That's it right there."

Declan eased the car to a stop, eyeing the land with a thoughtful expression.

"That's Browning's old place," Declan said, leaning forward slightly as he slowed the truck. "I grew up with their kids. The old man passed away recently, and all his kids live out of state, so I guess they sold it. My land adjoins theirs. What is it—seven acres?"

"Yeah."

"When my father moved into the assisted living facility, he left me his hunting cabin and fifty-four acres right up here. I haven't been out here in years, so it's just been sitting." He shot her a sideways glance, a mischievous glint in his eye. "Looks like we're neighbors now."

They drove another five minutes before turning onto a long gravel drive-way set far back from the road. Magnolia trees lined both sides, their branches arching overhead like a quiet, welcoming tunnel. The drive opened into a circular loop with a large fountain in the center, its water catching the last streaks of sunlight.

Alex's breath caught.

The "cabin" was unlike any cabin she'd ever seen. It looked more like a secluded luxury lodge—an expansive wraparound porch, rustic beams paired with elegant stonework, and towering Venetian-style windows flanking the double front doors. As Declan parked, the automatic porch light flicked on, casting a warm glow across the entryway.

Declan grabbed the grocery bags from the trunk, and Alex circled around to help. Together, they carried everything up the steps and inside.

Declan pushed open the double doors, and Alex paused just inside the threshold.

The interior was stunning.

An open-concept layout stretched before her. To the left, a massive stone double-sided fireplace divided the dining area from the living room. Vaulted ceilings soared overhead, making the space feel even larger. Straight ahead, the kitchen gleamed with polished countertops and warm wood cabinetry. A staircase off the living room led up to a loft and what looked like a couple of bedrooms. Beneath the loft, a short hallway disappeared into a cluster of doors.

For a place Declan claimed he hadn't visited in years, it was immaculate.

"I hired a cleaning service to come out today," Declan said, catching her expression.

Alex smiled, taking in the space again. "It's beautiful here. I can't wait to see it in daylight."

"My father used it for hunting. There are several smaller cabins scattered throughout the property where his friends would stay when they came out here."

"Why would you not want to be out here all the time?" Alex asked, genuinely baffled.

Declan's expression shifted, the lightness fading. "My father and I had a very complicated relationship. The idea of accepting anything from him is foreign to me." He exhaled and glanced around the cabin as if seeing it through fresh eyes. "I have just been sitting on this, trying to decide what to do with it. When we found ourselves in this little pickle of a situation, it seemed like a good option. I am glad I kept it." A softer look crossed his face. "My boys would love it here."

Alex smiled. "Collin will love it here too."

Their eyes met, sharing a quiet, unexpected warmth.

"Alright," Declan said, clearing his throat lightly, "if you want to unpack some of these groceries, I will unload the rest."

Alex grabbed the first bag and opened it. Cheese, deli meats, a few snacks. She carried it to the double-wide stainless steel refrigerator and pulled open the door. Cold air rolled out in a clean, metallic wave. The fridge was completely empty; the shelves gleamed under the soft interior light. She slid the drawer open and began placing the food inside.

The kitchen was stunning. If she had to design her own, this is exactly what she would want. The butcher block countertops were warm and smooth under her fingertips, contrasting beautifully with the exposed brick walls. Black metal-trimmed windows framed the space with a modern edge and tied in perfectly with the massive glass wall that separated the office from the kitchen. Off-white cabinets softened the industrial touches and gave the entire room a French country meets modern farmhouse feel.

She reached for another bag filled with crackers, chips, and pantry staples. Looking around, she spotted a door next to the fridge. When she opened it, a cool draft brushed her face. Inside was a large, empty walk-in pantry with shelves stretching from floor to ceiling. The faint scent of fresh wood polish lingered in the air.

By the time she stepped back out, Declan was returning from the truck with a bag of frozen vegetables in hand. Together they moved around the kitchen in an easy rhythm, opening cabinets, sliding drawers, brushing past each other in the narrow spaces. The domesticity of it all felt strangely intimate, almost as if they had done this a hundred times before.

Declan set two filets, a couple of potatoes, and a can of green beans on the counter. "What do you think about this for dinner?"

"That looks amazing to me," Alex smiled. "I will cook the sides if you want to cook the steaks. I always overcook them."

"Deal."

His answering grin was warm and relaxed, something she had not seen from him all day.

For the first time since finding the note, Alex felt her shoulders loosen just a little. She got to work preparing the sides. After pouring two glasses of wine, she stepped outside to join Declan. The cement patio stretched out behind the cabin, part of it covered, part of it open to the night sky. The air smelled faintly of pine and wood smoke. Declan sat in a rocking chair, the grill hissing beside him. He was so lost in thought, he jumped when she handed him a wine glass.

"What were you thinking about?" Alex asked softly.

Declan stared out into the darkness. "I was remembering the last time I was here with my dad. I was thirteen, and we were down at the pond over the hill over there." He motioned to the right, though the night was too dark for her to see anything.

"We had the boat out, and he was drunk. I was hot, miserable, and tired of listening to him ramble about how different his life could have been. When he refused to bring me back to shore, I jumped out and swam back. He passed out soon after and spent the whole day out there. By the time he woke up and made his way back to the cabin that evening, he was so sunburnt and hungover that I couldn't help but laugh. While I was laughing, he took a swing and knocked me out cold." Declan wrung his hands. "My dad was a big guy and knew how to land a punch."

Alex's breath caught. She recognized that distant look in Declan's eyes, the one that told her his past was heavier than he let on. Hearing it out loud made something inside her twist. Suddenly, his cool detachment made sense. The way he kept people at arm's length. The way he could shut down emotion in an instant and slip into that calm, controlled detective mode. It was survival. It was learned. And she wondered, not for the first time, if that same detachment bled into his personal life too. If he ever let anyone close enough to see the parts of him he kept locked away.

"Did he hit you a lot?" she asked quietly.

"Whenever the mood struck him." Declan's voice was flat, almost clinical. "It wasn't long after that day my brother and I ran away. We were tired of being his punching bags."

He lifted his eyes to hers, and she could tell he saw the questions forming on her tongue. Questions about scars that went deeper than skin. Questions about how much of that boy still lived inside the man sitting in front of her. But he shut the door on the conversation with a slight shift of his shoulders.

"Tell me about your childhood," he said, redirecting the conversation.

Alex took a slow sip of wine, her heart still aching for the boy he had been. She wasn't sure where to begin, but she knew one thing for certain. Declan Wallace made a lot more sense now.

Alex took a deep breath. "Well, it is not as interesting as yours. My older brother Mitch decided he did not want to see my father anymore when he was nine, so he stopped coming over. I grew up spending every weekend at my grandmother's farm, riding horses and learning the business. I played soccer and did track and cross-country for a few years before I realized I really did not like running that much." She gave him a small grin.

"I am sorry about your brother. Do you talk to him now?" Declan asked. His voice was gentle, curious, not prying.

"Yes, Mitch and I text and get together whenever I go up for a visit. He and my dad are still not very close, but they are civil. I can tell it hurts my dad that Mitch keeps him at arm's length, but I do not feel it is my place to push a relationship between them."

Declan nodded slowly. "Speaking as someone who had a complicated relationship with their father, I would say you are probably right."

He rose and walked to the grill. When he lifted the lid, a wave of heat and the rich smell of searing steak rolled across the patio. Alex's stomach growled, loud enough that she hoped he had not heard it. Declan took a sip of wine, the glass catching the warm glow from the porch light.

"About five more minutes, these will be done," he said.

"Oh, I forgot to tell you earlier. I have to bring Pablo to the train station in the morning at nine to pick up his family."

"Alright. I will go with you."

Alex looked out toward the dark horizon. The faint shimmer of water caught her eye, a narrow ribbon of silver cutting through the land. "What is the name of that river? It runs along the back of your property, doesn't it?"

"Whiskey River," Declan said.

She studied the water again, surprised by how peaceful it looked in the fading light. "I have heard people mention it, but I have never actually seen it."

"It is good for fishing," he said. "My brother and I used to cast from the bank and sit out there for hours." A small, almost reluctant smile tugged at his mouth. "My parents got married on the bank, right where the oak tree splits. They always said the river was the heart of this land."

Something in his voice softened the air between them. Alex cleared her throat and stepped toward the cabin. "I'm going to pull the sides out."

Inside, the kitchen felt cooler, calmer. She dished out the potatoes and green beans, the scent of garlic and butter rising with the steam. She slipped into the pantry, grabbed the A1 sauce, and poured a small puddle onto her plate. The screen door slid open behind her, and a moment later Declan was at her side.

They walked back to the table together, the night air brushing against her skin.

Declan glanced at her plate and scoffed. "I know you are not disrespecting my steak with A1 sauce."

Alex laughed. "Do not make fun of me. I have always used A1 or Worcestershire sauce on my steaks."

Declan shook his head and took a bite of potato. His eyebrows lifted. "This is amazing."

"I know," Alex said, still focused on her plate. The quiet between them felt comfortable, almost soothing. They finished the rest of their dinner in companionable silence; the soft chirping of crickets filled the space around them.

Declan's hand closed gently around her wrist, warm and steady, but there was nothing soft about the way he looked at her. His posture shifted, shoulders squaring, the easy warmth from dinner draining from his expression. The man standing in front of her wasn't the one who'd just praised her cooking. This was the detective—focused, controlled, assessing every flicker of her face like it might hold the missing piece.

"We need to talk." His voice was low, firm, leaving no room for misunderstanding.

Alex's breath caught. The change in him sent a ripple of nerves through her, tightening low in her stomach. She knew that tone. She'd heard it in the interrogation room earlier this morning. Her pulse kicked up, not from fear of him, but from the knowledge that whatever came next mattered.

"I know," she managed, though her voice felt thinner than she wanted. There would be no going back after this. No more hiding in the shadows and pretending she could outrun the past forever. So much had shifted since this morning; the woman who'd walked out of that hotel room with Declan wasn't the same one standing here now.

She wasn't naïve enough to think he wouldn't take what she told him straight to the FBI, but at this point, what did it matter? She could continue carrying the weight of her past alone, as she always had, or she could choose to trust the man standing before her.

Chapter Seventeen
ALEX

Declan stood and guided them both toward the couch. Alex's pulse thudded in her ears as she sat beside him. She had already made peace with telling him everything. Despite how little time they had known each other, she trusted him. He had already done more for her than anyone ever had before, and the only thing he wanted in return was the truth.

The one thing she had always struggled to give.

"I started working for Enzo just after my twenty-second birthday," she began. "My uncle and I were not getting along, and he had run into some financial trouble. He stopped paying me. It was hard to leave, but I knew I needed to get out on my own and see if I could run a business myself. And honestly, a big part of me wanted to rub his face in it after I became a successful trainer. He had been stifling my career for years, underplaying everything I did and letting customers think he handled it all. I was sick of it."

She caught herself rambling and took a breath. "Sorry."

Declan shook his head slightly, encouraging her to continue.

"Enzo posted a job looking for someone to exercise his horses, so I applied. I needed money, and it seemed perfect while I figured out how to start my own company. We talked about my experience, and he pointed out I was overqualified. Then he pitched the idea of starting the business there. He had a huge indoor arena, empty stalls, everything I needed. He said he would cover the upfront costs, and when we sold a horse, we would split the profit."

Her stomach tightened at the memory. "I knew in my gut something was off. But I wanted it so badly that I ignored it. At first, nothing seemed suspicious. He owned a car dealership and a few other businesses, so the money he spent didn't raise red flags. But over time, I noticed things. He wrote inflated receipts. The totals didn't add up to how much he actually spent. I was there for most of the trips to the grain store and the vet's, so I knew how much it cost. Even then I stayed quiet, telling myself it wasn't my business."

She rubbed her palms against her jeans, grounding herself. "The first real red flag was the next year when he sent me a 1099 for way more than I actually made. When I asked him about it, he told me not to worry, that he would cover my taxes. After that, he stopped hiding things from me."

Alex swallowed hard. "One day, we went to his house for lunch with his wife. He showed me one of his offshore account with forty-four million dollars in it. He thought it would impress me. Then he tried to force himself on me right there in his office. Told me that account could be mine, His wife was in the next room."

Her voice wavered, but she pushed through it. "I shoved him away and ran to Helena, thinking she would help. He followed me out and told her what had happened. She looked me dead in the eye and said, 'Sometimes it is easier just to keep him happy.' I was so shocked I walked straight to my car and left."

Alex's throat tightened. "Things got worse after that. When I finally got the nerve to go back, I brought my cousin and my best friend, Molly, with me. I told him I would never sleep with him, and if that was a deal breaker, he could fire me."

She paused, finally looking at Declan.

His face was deep red.

"Are you okay?" she asked quietly.

"Yep, continue," he said through clenched teeth.

But Alex could see the storm behind his eyes.

"After that, he stopped trying to hide things from me. Whenever we went to buy supplies for the barn, he always needed to make a detour. Sometimes to his dealership. Sometimes to the docks. Sometimes to places he never explained." Alex's voice felt distant, like she was narrating someone else's life. "I saw them take cars apart and pull drugs out of hidden compartments. Weapons too. I never asked questions. I told myself the less I knew, the better."

She rubbed her palms against her thighs, grounding herself. "He started getting hostile about how our business relationship wasn't profitable enough for him. Then he brought Brittany on. He said she was there to be my assistant, but it was obvious she was there to replace me."

Alex let out a humorless breath. "She was sleeping with him. They weren't subtle. I could hear them in the office, behind the barn, wherever he felt like it. The only thing she was good at riding was him. She couldn't train a horse to save her life."

A cool, bitter smile touched her lips before fading.

"One day he set up a showing without asking me. He wanted me to show Zorro to a buyer, but Zorro wasn't ready. I told him that, but he made me do it, anyway. And of course, Zorro was awful. The buyers were furious. They had driven hours to see him." She swallowed. "As soon as they left, Enzo took his rage out on me."

Out of the corner of her eye, she caught the vein in Declan's forehead pulse. He stayed silent, every muscle drawn taut, listening with the kind of focus that made the air feel thinner.

Alex forced herself to continue. "He threatened to kill me that day. And I knew he wasn't bluffing. I had already been thinking about leaving, but that pushed me into action. I called Zorro's previous owner because I knew she had a barn Enzo wouldn't think to check. I couldn't leave him there. Enzo threatened to shoot him in the head over that showing."

Her throat tightened. "She agreed to help. The next day, my mom and I drove to the barn in a huge snowstorm. I knew Enzo wouldn't be out in that weather, so it was the perfect time to get everything out without being seen."

She paused, letting the memory settle. "I never saw Enzo again. A few weeks later, I hired a trucker to move Zorro. I married Henry the following week. There was a stable on base where I boarded him, and I barely left base for the first year we were married. I knew there was only a slim chance Enzo could get to me there. As the years passed, I thought the threat had passed too." She exhaled shakily. "I guess I was wrong."

Declan's voice cut through the quiet. "What about the undercover agent? You recognized him." It wasn't a question; it was a statement.

He cocked an eyebrow, daring her to deny it. Alex's stomach dropped. This was the part she had been dreading.

Tears welled in her eyes. "Two days before the disastrous showing, Enzo and I had gone to buy feed for the horses. On the way back, he started taking these side roads, and I thought he was taking me somewhere to kill me."

Her fingers picked at a loose thread on the throw pillow.

"We pulled into an abandoned lot. There were two other cars already there. As we approached, two men got out and yanked someone from the trunk. He was bruised and bloody. Enzo told me to stay in the car." Her voice cracked. "The man kept looking at me. He looked terrified. Like he was begging me to help him."

Alex swallowed hard, the memory clawing its way up her throat. "I pulled out my phone to call 911, but Enzo was already coming back, so I shoved it in my purse. As we drove away, the men were dragging him into the woods. When I asked Enzo about it, he said the guy had stolen from him and they were just going to rough him up and let him go. I knew it was a lie. But if I called for help, it would lead straight back to me. And I didn't have my escape plan ready yet, so... I did nothing."

A sob tore loose before she could stop it. Tears spilled down her cheeks.

Declan pulled her into his chest, his arms wrapping around her with a gentleness that contrasted sharply with the fury radiating off him. She felt the tension in his muscles, the way he held himself back. He whispered soft reassurances into her hair, but she could feel the storm raging beneath his calm exterior.

For a moment, she let herself lean into him, letting the warmth of his body anchor her.

"Do you remember where the abandoned lot is?" his voice was tight.

Alex wiped her cheeks and nodded. "There's an old Shell station on Main Street. It sits at the corner of Main and a dirt road. It was about half a mile down that road on the right."

Declan rubbed her arm once before standing. He stepped away, phone already in hand, and spoke in a low voice she couldn't make out. When he returned, he sat beside her again, closer than before.

His expression stayed controlled, but his eyes were sharp and unyielding, a protective focus that made her pulse stumble.

"Is there anyone other than Enzo who could be after you now?"

Alex eased back from his chest, confusion knitting her brow. "No. Not that I can think of. Why?"

Declan hesitated for a fraction of a second, just long enough for dread to bloom in her stomach. "Enzo is dead. He died last week."

The world seemed to tilt. "What?" Her voice scraped out of her. "How?"

"Heart attack." His gaze never left her face, watching every flicker of shock, every breath she struggled to pull in.

"So the attacks... your car... none of that was Enzo?"

"No." His jaw tightened. "It wasn't him."

"Then who—"

"We don't know." His voice dropped, low and grim. "Whoever this is, they've been close. Close enough to watch you. Close enough to follow you. And we have no name."

The bottom dropped out of her stomach, cold and absolute. The threat she thought she understood had just dissolved into something far more dangerous—someone who wanted her badly enough to hide in the dark and wait.

And now she wasn't running from a man she knew.

She was running from a ghost.

Declan exhaled slowly, "We are already moving on it. We subpoenaed the emergency department patient logs from every shift you worked in the last six months. We are cross-referencing the names to see if anyone shows up repeatedly on your days."

Alex blinked, absorbing that.

"We are also pulling security footage from the hospital for those same shifts," he continued. "Parking lot cameras, lobby cameras, hallway feeds. If someone was watching you or following you, we will find them."

Declan leaned back slightly, his expression tightening. "And we are digging into Enzo's contacts. Associates, employees, anyone he did business with. If he was protecting you from someone worse, we need to know who that was."

The idea of Enzo protecting her was almost laughable. He had never protected anyone but himself. But if, by some twisted chance, he'd been standing between her and someone else, then the person hunting her now was far more dangerous. Enzo had needed her, and that need had given her a thin, accidental layer of protection. Whoever was after her now wanted only one thing—her gone.

That thought chilled her more than anything else.

Declan reached out, brushing his thumb along her arm in a grounding gesture. "We will figure this out. Whoever is doing this, they slipped up somewhere. We just have to find it."

Alex nodded, though her mind was spinning. If it wasn't Enzo, then someone else had been watching her. Someone who knew her routine. Someone patient enough to wait for Enzo to die. The idea of a stranger lurking at the edges of her life for eight silent years sent a cold, crawling dread through her. It terrified her more than anything Enzo had ever done.

Chapter Eighteen
DECLAN

Declan had just finished the dishes when a soft snore drifted from the couch. Alex was curled into the corner, one hand tucked under her cheek, sleeping soundly. The exhaustion of the day had finally caught up with her.

He dried his hands on the dish towel and walked around the couch. When he bent to lift her, she didn't stir, only melted instinctively against his chest. He hesitated for a moment, glancing toward the staircase to the guest room, but turned toward the master bedroom down the hall instead.

He settled her gently onto the bed. When she sighed and turned toward the pillow, something hot and immediate punched through him. Last night in the hotel flickered through his mind, the feel of her mouth on his, the way she had melted against him, the way he had wanted her so badly it had scared him. That want was still there, sharp and insistent, rising the moment she relaxed into his hands.

He stood there, fingers buried in his hair, fighting the urge to reach for her again. Every part of him ached to pull her close, to feel her against him the way he had before everything went sideways. But she was vulnerable, raw from everything she had endured, and he refused to take advantage of a moment when she might choose comfort over clarity. Wanting her was one thing. Acting on it now would be something else entirely.

He forced himself to stay where he was, breathing through the need that clawed at him, reminding himself that she deserved more than a man who could not trust his own restraint.

Frustration simmered beneath his skin. They were no closer to finding who was after her. And the longer this dragged on, the more exposed she was. The more he wanted to wrap her in his arms and never let her out of his sight.

She shifted in her sleep, a quiet sound slipping from her lips, and heat shot through him so fast he had to grit his teeth. His body reacted instantly, traitorously, and he forced himself to step back before instinct overrode sense. She was exhausted, shaken, and far too vulnerable to be making choices she might not truly want.

He turned sharply and left the room before he did something reckless—like crawl into the bed and pick up where they'd left off last night.

In his office, he powered on his laptop. If he waited for the FBI to get a lead, he'd be waiting forever. He needed answers now.

Hacking into Enzo's email was easy. Too easy. The man had been meticulous in some ways and careless in others. Declan sifted through the inbox, but it was nothing but spam and mundane messages between Enzo, his wife, and his son. No business associates. No coded messages. No financial trails.

Declan leaned back, rubbing a hand over his face. He was about to shut the laptop in frustration when a memory surfaced—Alex mentioning the offshore account. Forty-four million dollars. Shown off like a trophy.

If Enzo was smart, and Declan knew he was, he wouldn't keep that kind of money anywhere U.S. law enforcement could access. The Cayman Islands were the obvious choice.

Declan leaned forward, determination settling over him like armor. If the FBI wanted to play by the rules, fine. He didn't have that luxury. Not when so many lives were on the line.

He opened his laptop and began digging, following the threads the Bureau had dismissed as dead ends. Minutes passed in a blur of searches, cross-checks, and half-remembered aliases. Then something clicked.

A shell corporation Enzo had used years ago.

An offshore account buried beneath it.

Declan tried a password. Wrong.

He tried another. No luck.

The third opened the account.

Except the account now held over four hundred million dollars. Declan let out a low whistle.

Declan scanned the recent transactions, but nothing jumped out. There were no large withdrawals, no sudden transfers, nothing that suggested an obvious trail. He kept scrolling until he finally spotted it, the wire number for Enzo's TD Bank account, the one he occasionally funneled money into.

Declan's pulse kicked up as he traced the routing information. He was seconds away from hacking into the TD account when something on the screen made him freeze. The account wasn't in Enzo's name alone. Listed beside it, in clean, undeniable text, was Alexandria Kelley. Joint account holders.

His stomach lurched, bile rising in his throat as he stared at the screen. He flexed his hands open and closed, trying to steady the rush of his pulse. A joint account. With Enzo. Her name, tied to his money.

His mind spun; a dozen possibilities slammed into him at once. Had she lied to him? Played him? Fed him a sob story while she sat on millions? Had she been working with Enzo the whole time?

He felt sick. He had believed every word, every tear, every tremble in her voice. A slow, deep breath did nothing to steady the suspicion clawing hot and relentless beneath his ribs. He leaned closer, ready to dig deeper and tear the account apart line by line, but froze as the outside floodlights snapped on.

Declan's instincts took over. He reached for his gun, drawing it from the holster in one smooth motion. The safety clicked off as he moved toward the front door, every muscle coiled tight.

Whoever was out there had picked the wrong night.

Alex

Alex awoke alone in an unfamiliar room, needing a moment for her surroundings to settle into place. She slid off the mattress and looked for her bag, spotting it on a bench at the foot of the bed, completely empty. Turning to the dresser, she opened the top drawer and found some of her things neatly folded inside. She moved down the right side and realized piece by piece that someone had unpacked and put away all her belongings with careful precision.

She found her pajamas in the bottom drawer, choosing a silk nightgown before heading to the bathroom. The shower's heat melted the tension from her muscles, and she stayed under the spray until the water ran cold. With a reluctant sigh, she shut it off, wrapped herself in a towel, and worked leave-in conditioner through her damp hair. Once dry, she slipped into the navy spaghetti-strap nightgown trimmed in white lace and lifted her gaze to the mirror.

She was pale as a ghost. She reached for her makeup bag, added a touch of blush, and smoothed her hair with her hands. Better. She stepped back, taking herself in. The silk nightgown hugged in all the right places. She grabbed the matching robe and tied it snugly around her waist.

Mustering her confidence, she went in search of Declan.

The house was eerily quiet.

A sudden thought struck her. What if Declan hadn't left of his own free will? A chill ran down her spine. She was completely vulnerable and unarmed. Her eyes darted around the room for something she could use to defend herself. In the basket of the coat tree by the door, she spotted a baseball bat and quickened her pace.

Alex was halfway across the living room when the doorknob rattled. A heartbeat later, she heard the unmistakable scrape of a key sliding into the lock. Her pulse lurched. She grabbed the bat just as the front door burst open.

She screeched and swung the bat up. The intruder screamed back.

A woman.

The lights flicked on, revealing an icy-blue-eyed, gray-haired stranger staring at her in equal terror.

Alex let out another decidedly unladylike scream just as Declan rounded the corner, pistol raised and aimed at the woman. She watched recognition flash across his face.

"Whoa! Whoa! Alex, hold on!" he shouted, lowering the gun and rushing forward.

Alex froze, breath shaking, the bat still lifted, cleavage on full display. Her eyes darted to him, searching for any explanation at all.

"Mom, what are you doing here?" Declan exclaimed, moving around the two women, taking a quick glance outside before shutting the door and relocking the latch.

Alex's eyes widened as she lowered the bat to her side. *Mom?* Heat crept up her neck as she tugged her robe tighter, suddenly aware of how little she had on.

"Your father is letting me stay in one of the smaller cabins," the woman said, brushing a strand of gray hair behind her ear. "Couldn't sleep tonight, and when I noticed a light on up here, it worried me. I thought someone might have broken in, so I used the spare key to check."

"What exactly was the plan, Mom? Lecture the intruder into surrendering? You should have called the police if you were worried. You could have gotten yourself killed." Declan glared at his mother.

His mother shrugged, completely unfazed. "Well, I was planning on grabbing the bat as I came through the door."

Declan shook his head and pulled her into a hug. "Good to see you, Mom. It's been a while."

Alex cinched her robe even tighter, grateful she'd had the sense to put it on before leaving the bedroom. Declan stepped back from his mother and turned toward her.

"Mom, this is Alex. Alex, this is my mother, Katherine."

The women offered each other a polite smile, though the awkwardness clung to the room like Arkansas humidity in July.

After a beat too long, Alex cleared her throat and turned toward the kitchen. "I was just about to make some tea. Would you like some?"

Katherine looked ready to make her excuses and leave when Declan cut in.

"Oh, come on, Mom. Have some tea with us."

She hesitated only a moment before nodding and following them into the kitchen. She settled onto the island stool beside Declan while Alex moved around the kitchen, preparing the tea.

"So... how did you two meet?" Katherine asked, trying to break the silence.

Declan didn't even look up. His voice clipped and impersonal.

"We met at the hospital. She is an ER nurse. A threat surfaced that was connected to one of my cases, and now I am assigned to protect her," Declan said, his tone clipped and impersonal.

The words hit harder than they should have. Alex froze mid-reach for the teacups, heat rising in her cheeks. After everything that had happened between them last night, she had let herself believe they were moving toward something real. Yet today she felt like nothing more than work to him, a responsibility he had been assigned rather than someone he wanted to spend time with. She tugged her robe tighter, suddenly aware of the low neckline of her nightgown and how foolish she must look to them both.

Katherine's eyes widened slightly as she absorbed the information. "Oh my, I'm glad everyone is okay!"

Alex forced a smile. "Thanks. Me too." She turned away quickly, pretending to focus on the teacups so neither of them would see the embarrassment burning across her face.

She ducked into the pantry. "Chamomile or raspberry zinger?"

"Chamomile," they answered in unison.

She grabbed three bags and returned to the kitchen. The kettle whistled, and she poured the hot water with hands that were steadier than she felt.

"Honey?" she asked.

"Yes, please," Katherine said warmly.

Alex nodded, keeping her eyes on the cups—anywhere but on Declan, who kept his gaze fixed on anything that wasn't her, as if looking at her might burn him.

"Yeah, I'll take some, too, please," Declan agreed.

Alex set a saucer in front of Katherine, then placed the next one in front of Declan. As she leaned forward, the edge of her robe shifted, the neckline dipping lower than she intended. She felt the cool air on her skin at the same moment she noticed Declan's eyes flick down. His gaze followed the line of her nightgown before he jerked it away, shoulders tightening as if the act of looking had burned him.

Heat rushed up her throat. She tugged the robe closed and stepped back, pretending to adjust the cups on the counter. Declan kept his attention fixed on the island, jaw tight, the muscle there working in a way she had seen only when he was fighting something he did not want to feel.

The reaction twisted something in her chest. If she had become nothing more than work to him, why did he look at her like that? Why did he seem angry with himself for noticing her at all? The confusion was sharp and humiliating, and she needed space before it showed on her face.

She stayed on the opposite side of the island, grateful for the barrier between them. Katherine accepted her tea with a warm smile, unaware of the tension threading through the room. Alex forced a polite nod, keeping her eyes on the cups, willing her breathing to steady.

"You don't sound like you're from around here, Alex. Where are you from?" Katherine asked, lifting her cup.

"I'm originally from New Hampshire. My ex was in the Air Force, which brought me down here, and I stayed after our split so my son could still see his dad." Alex took a sip of her tea before adding, "You also have an unusual accent. Where are you from?"

"Germany," Katherine replied. "Moved to the States when I was eighteen and married my ex-husband. He was in the 87th Airborne, stationed over there. It was a whirlwind romance followed by a tumultuous marriage that ended soon after it began. But he gave me my Megan, so I don't regret it for a second."

Alex blinked. Megan? Declan had never mentioned a sister.

"Why are you staying in one of the old hunting cabins? What happened to the apartment you were renting?" Declan asked, shifting the conversation.

"Oh, it was full of rodents, and the landlord refused to do anything about it, so I broke my lease and moved out. I was tired of living in the city, and your father needed help after Carol passed. So he stayed at his house, and I stayed here, and I would help him during the days."

Katherine pushed back from the island with a soft yawn. "Well, that tea did the trick. I best be going. Alex, it was so nice to meet you."

"Nice to meet you too," Alex said with a polite smile.

"I'll walk you, Mom," Declan said, already slipping on his shoes. "I'll be right back. Lock the door behind me."

After firmly sliding the bolt in place, she cleaned up the kitchen, grateful for something to keep her hands busy. The house felt too quiet now, and her thoughts raced. Declan had been warm just this morning, holding her while she cried and relived the darkest days of her life. His presence had been calm and grounding. And now... this. Cold, closed off, and professional.

Assigned.

Of course, he had soothed her. He had done what he needed to do to get the information for his case. Of course he did not want her, not with all the baggage she carried.

She rinsed the last saucer and set it in the drying rack, trying to make sense of the shift. Maybe she had imagined the warmth. Maybe exhaustion had made her read too much into the way he touched her hair, the way he stayed beside her until her breathing steadied.

Retreating to the bedroom felt like the only way to breathe.

The moment she shut the door, she collapsed onto the bed with a groan. Her earlier courage, her ridiculous plan to seduce him, felt laughable now. But even that embarrassment was not what twisted in her chest. It was the way he had looked at her earlier, as if she were a problem he needed to manage instead of someone who had fallen asleep in his arms the night before. The whiplash left her dizzy, unsure which version of him was real, unsure if she meant anything to him at all.

Declan

Declan walked his mother back to her cabin, waited until she was safely inside, and then headed toward the main house. The night air was cool, but it did nothing to settle the storm churning in his chest. He unlocked the front door and stepped inside, relocking it behind him. The kitchen was empty; the teacups washed and drying on the rack. The lights were low, and the entire house was quiet.

He looked down the hall toward the master bedroom. A soft glow spilled from beneath the door. For a moment he considered going to her, but he turned away and made for his office instead.

He sat down at the desk, jaw tight, and pulled up Enzo's offshore account again. The joint TD Bank account glared back at him. He clicked into the details, scrolling through the account history with a growing sense of dread.

Then he saw it: Alexandria Kelley—added as joint account holder one month ago. Declan froze. A month ago, not years. Not during her time with Enzo. Not when she'd been trapped under his thumb. A month ago, when she was already gone, when she supposedly had no contact with him. The discovery eased his suspicion, but not entirely. The timing made no sense. Why would Enzo add her name out of nowhere? What was he planning? What did he want from her?

Declan leaned back, rubbing a hand over his face. He wasn't ready to trust the situation—or her—fully. Not yet. But the knot in his chest loosened enough for him to breathe again.

He shut the laptop and stood.

He needed to check on her. The flinch she'd given at his gruff tone earlier had lodged under his skin, and the instinct to reach for her had been immediate and unwelcome. He'd shut it down fast. Distance was safer for both of them until he got a handle on the situation.

He moved quietly down the hall and eased the master bedroom door open just enough to slip inside. The room was dim, washed in the soft glow of the bedside lamp she had forgotten to turn off, shadows pooling in the corners and stretching across the bed where she lay curled on top of the covers, fast asleep. Her nightgown had ridden up to her hips, exposing smooth skin and the curve of her thigh.

Heat punched through him so hard he had to brace a hand on the doorframe, his body reacting before he could wrestle it under control. He forced his gaze away from her, locking it on the blanket instead of the soft lines of her sleeping form. Crossing the room, he lifted the covers and eased them over her shoulders, careful not to disturb her. She sighed and turned her face into the pillow, and something tight and protective twisted in his chest. He lingered for a moment, watching the steady rise and fall of her breathing, then stepped back and slipped out of the room, closing the door quietly behind him. The couch would have to do.

He grabbed a throw blanket, lowered himself onto the cushions, and let out a slow breath as he worked his shoulder with his fingertips. The pain had eased, but the tension always settled in deeper at night, coiling through the muscles no matter how much he tried to loosen them.

He stretched out and stared at the ceiling, sleep refusing to come. The image of her in his bed lingered; warm skin and tangled sheets burned into his mind. The case gnawed at him too, twisting into something darker with every new piece he uncovered. Worst of all was the knowledge that someone out there wanted her dead, and he could not shake the feeling they were closer than anyone realized.

Chapter Nineteen
DECLAN

Declan heard her alarm before her footsteps padded into the room. He'd been awake for an hour already, sitting on the edge of the couch with a cup of coffee that had gone cold. He'd forced himself to stay out here last night, exactly like she'd asked, even though every instinct had pulled him toward her door. Wanting something didn't make it the right call.

He showered, dressed, and started breakfast. The smell of bacon filled the cabin.. He glanced over his shoulder and found her standing there in jeans and a soft green sweater, her hair still mussed from sleep.

"Good morning," he said.

She offered him a small smile, "Good morning."

He turned back to the stove, flipping the bacon. He could feel her eyes on him before she spoke again.

"Where did you sleep last night?"

He nodded toward the couch. "The deal was that I slept out here. Remember."

Her gaze followed his gesture to the pillow and the folded blanket. Something flickered across her face before she masked it. Disappointment, maybe. He didn't let himself think too hard about it.

He slid a plate toward her. Bacon, eggs, toast, hash browns. "Breakfast is ready. What time do we need to be at the train station?"

"Nine," she said as she sat. "But we need to swing by the barn to pick up Pablo first, so we should leave by eight fifteen."

"Got it."

They ate in silence, the kind that settled heavily between them. Alex kept her eyes on her plate, and Declan kept his on his coffee, pretending the quiet didn't bother him. It did. A twinge of guilt worked its way under his ribs. He didn't look at her, not fully, but he caught enough in the edges of her expression to see the uncertainty she'd tried to hide when she asked where he'd slept. The distance he was putting between them was affecting her.

He pushed the thought aside and focused on the day ahead. By the time they reached the train station, the morning rush had already begun. The train pulled in just as they stepped onto the platform. Declan hung back a few steps, scanning the exits and the crowd while Pablo shifted beside Alex, practically vibrating with anticipation.

The doors opened. A small boy spotted Pablo and tore across the platform. Pablo dropped to his knees and caught him, laughing and crying at the same time. A woman rushed in behind the boy and wrapped her arms around both of them. Declan watched the reunion from a distance, letting Alex take it in. After everything Pablo had been through, he deserved this moment.

While they embraced, Declan's attention drifted to the far side of the station. The walls, the ceiling, the corners. He was looking for cameras, blind spots, anything that might explain how Martha ended up dead in an alley a few yards from here.

A metal door near a vending machine caught his eye. He moved toward it, jaw tightening. When he pushed it open, a piercing alarm filled the station.

An older man stormed over, face red and ready to yell, but Declan held up his badge before the man got a word out.

"Detective Wallace, Little Rock PD."

The man's anger deflated into a nervous swallow. "Sir, I didn't realize. That door isn't supposed to be opened without a key."

Declan stepped into the doorway and looked out into the alley. Razor wire. High fence. One way in without climbing. He turned back to the man.

"Who has access?"

"Only station staff. Me, the manager, and two maintenance guys. That's it."

"Do y'all have a gate key too?"

The man nodded. "We locked the alley down years ago. People used to slip behind the building and get into all kinds of trouble back there. After a few too many incidents with folks jumping onto the tracks, management decided it wasn't worth the liability and had the whole thing gated off."

Declan studied him. "Anyone ever prop this door open?"

The man hesitated, shifting his weight. "It's not supposed to be. Anyone with a key can turn the alarm off. I can't speak for what the other managers allow on their shifts."

Declan's jaw tightened. "Has anyone ever complained about it going off at night?"

"Not that I'm aware of."

Declan pulled out his notebook. "I'd like to take down your name and number in case I think of any further questions."

The man gave both, still flustered. Declan wrote them down, then asked, "Were you working last week when the body was found in the alley?"

The man swallowed. "Yes, sir. I was here that morning."

"See anyone hovering near this door?" Declan asked. "Anyone who didn't look like they belonged?"

The man thought for a moment, brow furrowing. "No, sir. Nothing out of the ordinary. Just the usual morning crowd."

Declan nodded once. "If you remember anything, even something small, call me."

"Yes, sir. Of course."

Pablo approached with his wife and son a few minutes later, his hand wrapped around the boy's like he was afraid to let go. Introductions were made, and relief softened Maria's face the moment she realized Alex and Declan weren't just dropping them off and disappearing. They were together again. Safe, at least for now.

Declan suggested breakfast before getting them settled, and Pablo agreed with a grateful nod. They walked to a small diner across the street, the kind with cracked vinyl booths and a bell that jingled every time the door opened. Jose pressed his face to the glass pastry case, eyes wide, pointing at everything like he'd never seen so many choices at once. Declan watched him, something easing in his chest. The kid had energy to burn. Collin would've liked him. They would've run circles around each other.

Pablo kept a hand on his son's shoulder, as if reassuring himself the boy was really there. He was quieter than Alex, but not withdrawn—just a man still finding his footing after a long night. Over breakfast he opened up in small, steady pieces. He talked about the horses at the barn, about Maria's cooking, about Jose's obsession with trains. There was a quiet pride in the way he spoke, the kind that came from holding his family together through things most people never had to imagine. Declan didn't know him well, not yet, but he recognized that kind of strength when he saw it.

Maria listened with a soft smile, her fingers brushing the back of Pablo's hand every so often. She thanked Alex for everything, her voice barely above a whisper. Declan didn't miss the way Alex's expression softened in return.

When the plates were cleared and Jose had finished his second chocolate milk, Declan drove them to the Red Roof Inn near the barn. It wasn't perfect, but it was close enough for Pablo to walk to work and gave the family a place to breathe while they figured out their next step. Pablo insisted on carrying every bag himself, refusing help with a quiet determination that made Declan respect him even more.

Once they were settled, Declan and Alex said their goodbyes and stepped back outside. The sun was higher now, warming the pavement, but the air still held a bite. As they walked toward the car, Declan kept his eyes on the parking lot, the rooftops, the shadows. The threat was still out there, circling. And Alex walked beside him, unaware of how many angles he was tracking at once.

She was the job. He reminded himself of that with every step.

But it didn't change the way he watched her. Or the way the danger felt sharper when she was near it.

On the drive back toward the cabin, Alex shifted in her seat. "Can we stop by my property?" she asked quietly.

He glanced at her, then nodded. "Yeah. Of course."

The gravel road leading in was familiar now, winding through bare winter trees until the land opened up. Her property stretched wide and quiet, the river cutting a slow curve through the back edge. The barn came into view first—red and white paint faded by sun and storms, but still standing solid against the landscape.

Declan parked beside the fence line. Alex stepped out, breathing in the cold air like it steadied her. He followed her up the gravel drive toward the barn. The building was bigger than it looked from the road, long and tall with sliding doors that groaned when she pushed them open.

Inside, four large stalls lined one wall, the wood worn smooth from years of use.

"This used to be a foaling barn," Alex said, her voice softening. "Mares would have their babies in here. They'd stay until the foals were strong enough to be moved."

Declan ran a hand along one of the stall doors. He could picture it—newborns wobbling on unsteady legs, Alex younger, smaller, probably standing right where he was now. There was something grounding about it. Something that made the place feel lived in even though it had been empty for years.

They walked out the opposite side of the barn. Alex pointed toward a gentle rise in the land, closer to the river.

"That's where I want to build my house," she said. "Someday."

Declan followed her gaze. The hill caught the late morning light; the river glinting behind it. It was a good spot. Secluded. Peaceful. Too far from him.

The thought hit before he could stop it.

He cleared his throat. "It's a good location."

She smiled faintly, then led him back inside and up the narrow staircase to the loft apartment. The space opened into a small living area, dust motes drifting through the light. Two bedrooms. One bath. A kitchenette that looked as if it hadn't been used in years. It needed a good cleaning, but it wouldn't take much work to make it habitable.

Alex stepped into the center of the room, turning slowly. "I'm going to offer this to Pablo and his family," she said. "They need it more than Collin and I do."

Declan looked around again, taking in the empty rooms, the quiet, the potential. It wasn't much, but it was the start Pablo's family needed. And it told him something about her—something he already knew but kept rediscovering anyway. She took care of people. Even when she was barely holding herself together.

He watched her for a moment, the weight of everything she didn't say settling between them. Then he nodded once.

"That sounds like a wonderful idea. They'll be grateful."

They left the loft and stepped back into the cold air, the barn settling behind them with a soft creak as the door swung shut. Alex led the way toward the river, her boots crunching over the gravel path that cut between the barn and the tree line. Declan followed a half-step behind, scanning out of habit even though the property felt quiet, almost peaceful.

The river came into view through the bare winter branches, the dark water moving slowly. Alex walked right up to the fence that separated the pasture from the bank. Declan stopped beside her, hands in his pockets, taking in the land she loved. She started talking about her plans—where she wanted the house, how she'd clear the brush, what she'd plant in the spring. Her voice warmed as she spoke, and he found himself answering, asking questions, pointing out the natural slope of the hill and how it would help with drainage. For a moment, the conversation felt easy. Almost normal.

He walked a few steps along the fence, eyes drifting over the ground out of habit more than suspicion. Then something caught his attention—a patch of grass pressed flat in a way that didn't match the rest of the winter-bent field. Not trampled. Not wind-blown. Flattened. Held down.

He crouched beside it, brushing his fingers over the matted blades. Cold. Undisturbed for at least a day, maybe longer. But the shape of it—the length, the width—wasn't an animal bed. Too straight. Too deliberate.

A sick feeling tightened low in his gut.

He lowered himself into a crouch, settling into the exact spot, letting his eyes follow the line of sight from that position. The barn sat directly ahead. The drive curved into view just beyond it. From here, someone would have had a clear vantage point of anyone coming or going.

He caught up to Alex, matching her pace as she turned back toward the barn. She looked relaxed, content even, her breath puffing in small clouds as she talked about the river in summer. He didn't want to take that from her. Not yet. Not until he knew more.

"I just remembered," he said, keeping his tone light, casual. "I need to swing by the office. Forgot something I should've grabbed yesterday."

Alex glanced over, surprised but not suspicious. "Oh. Sure. That's fine."

He guided them back to the car and headed toward the main road, keeping his speed even. If someone had been watching them, he wasn't risking leading them straight to the cabin. Not today. Not until he understood what he'd found. He'd swing by the station, switch into his unmarked cruiser, and use that from now on. It was the safer play.

Alex settled into her seat, unaware of the shift in him, unaware of the way his mind was already running through the timeline. She'd only owned this property for a handful of days. For someone to already know about it—and to already be watching it—meant they had access to something they shouldn't. Her email. Her phone records. Her bank account. Enzo's bank account.

That last thought hit harder than he expected. She told him she used her savings to buy the property, but had she? He needed to dig into her financials, make sure she hadn't touched the joint account with Enzo. Make sure no one else had either.

Declan's grip tightened on the wheel. The more he uncovered about the case, the more convinced he became that he wasn't dealing with one perpetrator. The attempted kidnapping and the home invasion had been impulsive and reckless. But the flowers, the notes, and the surveillance of her property were acts of someone more controlled, someone who liked to play with their prey before they pounced.

Two different patterns. Two different minds. Or one offender using someone else to do the reckless work while he stayed in the shadows. The contrast bothered him. It meant she was being hunted by someone meticulous enough to stay two steps ahead of the investigation, someone who planned every move, someone who either understood how an investigation worked or had close contact with someone who did.

Chapter Twenty
ALEX

It had been the longest week of her life. She and Declan had moved around each other like two ships passing in the night, sharing the same space without ever really meeting in it. He worked from home most days, hunched over his laptop or pacing the hallway with his phone pressed to his ear. When he wasn't making calls, he shut himself in his office and left her to her own devices.

He'd left several times to chase down leads, and whenever he did, Bishop or Martin showed up to sit with her. They tried to make it feel casual, but she knew what it was. Babysitting. Protection. Containment. The hours blurred together, long and heavy, and she couldn't remember the last time she'd had a real conversation with Declan that wasn't about logistics or safety.

So when she padded into the kitchen that morning and found him sitting at the island, waiting for her, she stopped short. He looked up, and something in his expression softened.

"Happy birthday," he said.

Before she could respond, he was already moving, pulling a pan from the stove, sliding a plate toward her. Breakfast. Hot. Thoughtful. Intentional. She blinked, unsure how to reconcile this version of him with the distant one she'd lived beside all week.

"Go get dressed," he told her once she'd eaten a few bites. "We're going out for the day."

She frowned. "Where?"

He shook his head, the corner of his mouth lifting just enough to count as a smile. "Not telling you. Just dress warmly."

Alex crossed her arms over her chest and didn't move. She hated surprises.

"Would you just trust me?" Declan cocked an eyebrow.

She muttered something under her breath but headed down the hall to her room. By the time she came back out, he already had the car warming in the driveway. They got in the car, the quiet of the morning stretching between them in a way that felt almost peaceful.

They were on the highway within minutes, heading north. Alex watched the scenery blur past her window, curiosity growing by the mile.

"Can you please tell me where we're going?" She asked, unable to help herself.

"Nope," Declan smirked.

Alex huffed and fought the tug at the corner of her lips. Her mother always told her she needed to work on her patience. Two hours and more dirt roads than she cared to count later, they finally pulled up beside a houseboat. They parked beside Alyssa's car.

"Phew," Alex said with a dramatic exhale. "I thought you were bringing me out here to murder me." She giggled, only half-joking. The last stretch of road had been nothing but trees, gravel, and questionable turns.

As they approached the boathouse, a head popped over the upper deck railing. Alyssa's bright grin appeared a second later.

"Come on up, you guys!" she called, practically vibrating with excitement.

Alex felt her own smile tug forward. Spending her birthday on the water with Alyssa had sounded perfect, a quiet day she could actually enjoy.

Declan led the way up the stairs to the upper deck. The moment Alex stepped onto the platform, a chorus of voices erupted.

"Surprise!"

She blinked, startled, her gaze sweeping across the deck. Emily, Dean, and Memory stood to her right, all grinning. She turned to her left and froze.

Beth and Molly.

Her best friends from high school. The girls who had held her together through heartbreaks, finals, and the chaos of senior year. She had not seen them since her nursing school graduation last spring.

Her vision blurred instantly. Before she could even process the shock, Beth and Molly rushed forward and wrapped her in a three-way hug. Alex clung to them, laughing and crying at the same time, overwhelmed by the sudden rush of familiarity and love.

"Oh my God, you're really here," she whispered, her voice cracking.

"Of course we are," Molly said, squeezing her tighter.

"You didn't think we'd miss your thirtieth," Beth added.

Behind them, a small table had been set up with a birthday cake and a jug of Carlo Rossi Sweet Red, her favorite wine. Emily and Memory came over next, pulling her into warm hugs. Memory pressed a glass of sweet red into her hand.

"Drink," Memory said with a wink. "You're officially old now."

Alex laughed, wiping her cheeks. The boat rocked gently beneath them as Dean, clearly overwhelmed by the number of people on his houseboat, retreated to the helm and started the engine. The hum of the motor vibrated through the deck as they drifted away from the dock.

The sun was bright overhead, unusually warm for January. Fifty-five degrees, according to her phone. The breeze was cool but pleasant, carrying the scent of lake water and pine.

Declan joined Dean at the helm, giving Alex space with her friends.

Alex turned to Alyssa. "Who planned all this?"

Alyssa grinned. "Declan and I came up with the idea together. He handled everything. Booked Beth and Molly's flights. Coordinated the timing. The whole thing. I'd say he's a keeper."

Beth and Molly nodded emphatically.

Alex's chest tightened. She looked toward the helm, where Declan stood beside Dean, hands in his pockets, watching the water. He wasn't smiling, but there was something soft in his posture. Something quiet. Something that made her heart ache.

No one had ever done anything like this for her. She had mentioned her friends only once, in passing, on the first day he came to her house. The fact that he remembered, that he cared enough to bring them here, was almost too much.

"How long are you guys here for?" Alex asked, turning back to her friends.

"We fly out in the morning," Beth said.

Alex groaned dramatically. "That's not long enough."

"We'll make the most of it," Molly promised.

They spent the next several minutes catching up. Beth talked about her new job. Molly showed pictures of her latest art project. Emily teased Alex about turning thirty. Memory kept refilling her wine glass.

Alex laughed more in those minutes than she had in months.

Eventually, the conversation drifted into its own pockets, her friends chatting among themselves. Alex leaned back in her chair, letting the sun warm her face. She closed her eyes, letting the gentle breeze brush across her skin. The voices around her softened into a pleasant hum.

For the first time in what felt like forever, she felt completely at peace.

When she opened her eyes again, she saw Declan had left the helm. He stood alone at the rail, looking out over the water, the wind tugging at his hair. His shoulders were relaxed, but there was a distance in his expression she couldn't quite read.

Something pulled her toward him.

She hesitated, unsure if she should leave her friends, unsure if he wanted company. But the gratitude swelling in her chest was too big to ignore.

She set her wineglass down and walked across the deck. He didn't hear her approach until she was right beside him.

"Hey," she said softly.

He turned, surprised. "Hey."

Before she could overthink it, she stepped forward and wrapped her arms around him. His body went still for a heartbeat, then his arms wrapped protectively around her waist.

"Thank you," she whispered into his chest. "This is the best gift anyone's ever given me."

His arms tightened around her, not protective this time, but something rougher, needier, like he'd been fighting the urge to touch her for far too long.

"You deserve it," he said, dipping his forehead to hers.

And for the first time in a long time, Alex believed it.

She lingered in his arms, letting the warmth of him settle something deep inside her. Before she could stop herself, she rose onto her toes and pressed a soft kiss to his lips. He didn't deepen it but he didn't pull away either. When she pulled back, she caught the look in his eyes before he blinked it away. He wanted her just as much as she wanted him.

By the time she made it back across the deck, Alyssa was waiting with a conspiratorial grin that practically sparkled.

Alyssa leaned in, lowering her voice as if sharing state secrets.

"I called Henry yesterday. He's keeping Collin until tomorrow afternoon after school. You can pick him up there."

Alex froze mid-step. Her mouth fell open.

"You... what?"

Alyssa's grin widened. "I explained that it was your birthday, and I wanted to take you out of town and we wouldn't be back until tomorrow." Alyssa shot a meaningful look in Declan's direction. "You can thank me later." She added a saucy wink for good measure.

Alex blinked, stunned. The realization hit her all at once.

She had the whole day.

The entire night.

No rushing home.

No juggling schedules.

No guilt for taking a moment for herself.

A laugh bubbled out of her, unexpected and bright. She threw her arms around Alyssa, squeezing her tightly. She'd just been thinking how much she hated to cut the day short, how they'd have to leave soon if they wanted to pick up Collin on time.

"You're unbelievable," Alex said, her voice thick with emotion. "In the best possible way."

Alyssa hugged her back. "I know."

Beth and Molly chimed in immediately.

"Girl, you deserve a break," Beth said.

"Yeah, and we're going to make sure you enjoy every second," Molly added.

Alex sank into her chair again, overwhelmed in the best way. The sun warmed her skin. The lake sparkled around them. Her friends were here. Declan was here. And at once, everything around her felt a little less sharp. The constant pressure she'd been living under eased, giving her room to breathe again.

She took a sip of her wine, savoring the sweetness.

Beth and Molly were still giving her matching mischievous grins, the kind that meant they were nowhere near done with her.

"Okay, listen," she said, lowering her voice. "Since the threats started, and they assigned him as my detail, he has been strictly business."

Beth raised a brow. "Strictly business. Right."

Molly snorted. "Yeah, because that man looks at you like he's been starving for weeks and you're the last donut in the box."

Alex felt her cheeks warm.

"I felt like we had something then it was like a wall slammed down between us and I don't know he barely looks at me now. I can feel his eyes on me when he thinks I'm not looking, but as soon as I look up, he looks away. He shuts himself in his office and works all day. Dinner is the only time we spend together. Afterwards, he walks around the house, checking all the doors and windows before he disappears back into his office."

"Well, that's frustrating," Memory said.

"Did anything happen when you went up to his room last week?" Emily asked.

Heat rushed up Alex's neck. "Things started to happen. But... three margaritas was apparently one too many." She dropped her gaze, mortified all over again.

The girls winced in perfect unison.

"Oh no," Alyssa said, bracing herself. "What happened?"

Alex walked them through the night—carefully, skimming the edges, focusing on the chaos and not the, almost. The girls hung on every word, gasping and groaning in all the right places.

"So after you got sick," Beth said, eyebrows climbing, "he just gave you his clothes and snuggled you?"

Alex nodded, and her eyes drifted across the deck. Declan stood beside Dean at the helm, laughing at something Dean said, sunlight catching the edge of his smile.

"That is so sweet," Molly said, pulling Alex back to the table.

"But," Alex went on, "now he won't make a move. Not even a little one. He told his mother I was his assignment."

"You've met his mother already?" Memory asked, eyes widening.

"Yeah," Alex said dryly. "I almost bashed her brains in with a baseball bat on my way to seduce her son. So I'd say it went exceedingly well."

Alex could tell she wasn't getting out of this without giving them the entire story. So she laid it out—her ridiculous attempt to seduce Declan, hearing someone at the door as she crossed the living room, standing there with a bat raised and her cleavage on full display, ready to take out an old lady. Then the three of them sitting around drinking tea while she tried to disappear inside a flimsy robe.

By the time she finished, her friends were in tears, clutching their sides.

"I was absolutely mortified. He's been nothing but professional since that night," Alex said, burying her face in her hands.

Alyssa let out a dramatic sigh. "Of course he is. He's a gentleman with a badge. They're all allergic to admitting they have feelings."

Beth tapped her wine glass thoughtfully. "Well," she said, drawing out the word, "if he won't make a move..."

Molly finished it with a wicked grin. "You make a move."

Alex nearly choked. "What? No. Absolutely not."

Beth shrugged. "Why not? You like him. He clearly likes you."

"Did you all miss what happened the last time I made a move?" Alex asked incredulously.

Molly shook her head. "Life is short, Al. Also, have you seen his arms? If I were you, I wouldn't waste another second not being tangled up in those arms."

Alyssa chimed in, eyes sparkling. "And the way he looks at you when he thinks no one's watching."

Alex groaned and covered her face again. "You guys are impossible."

Beth laughed. "We're right, though."

Alex peeked at Declan across the deck. He was leaning against the rail again; the wind tugging at his shirt, the sunlight catching in his hair. His eyes swept across the deck and locked onto her. He looked calm, but there was a tension in his shoulders she recognized now. A quiet protectiveness. A constant awareness of her.

Her heart fluttered. Maybe her friends were right. She hadn't known him long, but the way she felt when he looked at her or stood close was impossible to ignore. She'd noticed how his rough edges always seemed to ease when it was just the two of them. Fear had kept her still. She was afraid of misreading the moment, afraid of misreading him, afraid of wanting too much and being rejected. Waiting for him to make the first move had felt safer, but it wasn't getting her anywhere.

Maybe it was time to stop waiting.

Chapter Twenty-One
ALEX

They returned to the cabin a little after one in the morning. Alex had gotten fairly sloshed with her friends but had slept the entire ride back to the cabin and was feeling surprisingly refreshed.

She glimpsed her reflection in the mirror that hung in the entryway. Good grief. She looked like a raccoon who'd face-planted into a dumpster fire.

Nope. Absolutely not. She beelined for the bedroom, grabbed pajama shorts and a tank top, and headed straight for the shower.

Hot water spilled over her shoulders, washing away lake air, sweat, and the faint smell of spilled wine. The steady spray softened the world around her, giving her thoughts room to settle.

She wasn't the type to initiate intimacy. Waiting, reading the moment, letting someone else take the first step—that was her default. But Declan wasn't going to take any steps while he remained locked into that rigid, protective stance he'd adopted the moment the stalker entered the picture. He'd convinced himself that distance was safest for both of them.

And for all she knew, they might never catch whoever it was.

The thought tightened something low in her chest.

She braced her palms against the tile, letting the water run down her spine. Declan would retreat if she let him. He'd build walls out of duty and fear and that maddening sense of honor he wore like armor.

But she didn't want walls tonight. She wanted honesty. Warmth. Connection. She wanted him.

The water ran over her shoulders in a steady, soothing rhythm, but it could not quiet the thoughts that rose the moment she was alone. It was strange how quickly her mind could slip back into old patterns. One flicker of insecurity and suddenly she was remembering things she wished she could forget.

She hated that Henry's voice still lived somewhere deep inside her. It had been years, yet it could still fray the edges of her confidence. He had said it so often that the word sometimes rose unbidden in her mind, as if it belonged to her. *Broken.* As if something fundamental in her had been flawed from the start. Even now, the memory of that accusation could make her question the shape of her body, or the way she moved, or the simple act of wanting to be touched. She had left him and rebuilt her life. She had survived. But some wounds did not fade just because the person who caused them was gone.

She pressed her palms to the tile and let the spray run down her back. He had chipped away at her slowly, piece by piece, until she believed every cruel thing he said. She was undesirable. Difficult. Lacking in ways she could never fix. He'd twisted her so thoroughly that nothing she did ever felt right.

The worst part was how deeply she had absorbed it. How long she had carried the shame as if it belonged to her. Even now, with Declan, she felt the old instinct to shrink. To hide. To assume she was too much or not enough, depending on the moment.

She closed her eyes and breathed in the steam. Declan was nothing like Henry. There was no judgment in the way he looked at her, no silent tally of flaws she needed to fix. He never held her up against impossible standards or made her feel like a burden. With him, she felt seen in a way she had never experienced before. He listened. He cared. And he did it without making her earn it.

But knowing that and believing it were two different things.

She lifted her head and let the water wash over her face. Tonight felt important in a way she could not ignore. Reaching for him was not about seduction or proving anything. She wanted to reclaim the parts of herself she had learned to silence. The ability to speak her needs. The confidence to trust her own desires. The simple freedom to want closeness without feeling ashamed.

She was not broken. No amount of cruelty or criticism had the power to define her anymore. The version of herself her ex tried to mold had never been real, only a reflection of his insecurities. Feelings were not flaws. Desire was not something to apologize for. Taking up space in her own life was a right she no longer needed permission to claim. And for the first time in a long while, the idea of being held without fear felt possible.

Taking a deep breath, she squared her shoulders and turned the water off. She dried off quickly and slipped into her clothes, avoiding the mirror as much as she could. One glance was all it ever took for her eyes to find every flaw, every mark, every reminder of the years she had spent doubting herself.

She had no idea what she was doing. It had been ages since she had even thought about trying to seduce a man, and the attempt she made their first night there had crashed and burned so spectacularly that her cheeks still warmed at the memory. Confidence did not come naturally.

Before she could talk herself out of it, she stepped into the hallway and headed toward the living room, still unsure what her next move would be. Her pulse thudded in her ears as she rounded the corner, eyes sweeping the dim space until they landed on Declan's sleeping form stretched across the couch.

She stopped cold.

Now what? It was nearly two in the morning, and the day had been long for both of them. The sensible thing would be to turn around, slip quietly into the bedroom, and pretend she had never entertained this ridiculous plan.

She almost did.

Her foot even shifted back toward the hall before a thought flickered through her mind.

He had once dreamed of waking to her kissing him, but had woken to find his ex-wife instead. The disappointment in his voice was unmistakable. She could change that memory.

The idea sent a nervous flutter of excitement through her stomach. She bit her lip, torn between fear and a fragile spark of courage. This was reckless. Bold. Completely unlike her.

She crept forward until she stood directly in front of him. For a heartbeat she hovered there, nerves fluttering in her stomach, before sinking quietly to her knees beside the couch. In sleep, Declan looked softer, the usual tension gone from his features. Peaceful. Almost boyish.

Her breath caught.

Before she could talk herself out of it, she leaned in and brushed her lips against his. The reaction was immediate. His body went still, every muscle tightening beneath the blanket. He didn't open his eyes. He didn't move. He simply froze.

Panic flickered — but beneath it, something deeper rose, something she had been holding back for far too long.

She kissed him again, firmer this time, letting instinct guide her. A quiet ache pushed her forward, a need she barely understood herself. She searched for him in that second kiss, hoping he would meet her halfway, hoping she had not misread everything between them. Hoping she was not making a terrible mistake.

Declan

He sensed her the moment she stepped into the room. Even half asleep, his awareness shifted, sharpening around the soft sound of her movements.

He kept his body still, curious, waiting to see what she would choose. For a moment she hovered, the air tightening with her uncertainty, and he could almost feel her turning back toward the hallway.

Then her footsteps approached.

When her lips brushed against his, every fiber of his being became aware of her.

He did not move. He simply felt her: the gentle press of her mouth, the tremble of her courage, the quiet ache behind the kiss.

And in that suspended moment, he became acutely and painfully aware of her in a way he had been denying himself.

She was beautiful. Not in the polished, intentional way she seemed to think she needed to be, but in the effortless, unguarded moments. The way the sunlight danced through the highlights in her hair. The way her smile reached her eyes in a way he'd never seen before. Every time she threw her head back laughing, something in his chest tightened. The way she had been today was the version of her he always wanted to hold on to — free.

He had watched her all day, even when he pretended not to. It was impossible not to notice the way she lit up around her friends, the way laughter came easily, the way her shoulders loosened for the first time since he had met her. She had been relaxed in a way he had only glimpsed before, and the sight had eased something tight in his own chest. It also sharpened something else—an unshakable certainty. Whoever had been dimming that light was going to regret it. He would make damn sure of that.

He had tried to give her space today. It was her birthday, her friends, her day. She deserved to enjoy it without him hovering like some overprotective shadow. So he kept his distance, stayed on the edges of conversations, let her drift from group to group without interruption.

But he was painfully aware of her the entire time.

Every time she brushed past him, every time she glanced his way, every time her hand accidentally grazed his arm, he felt it. He felt her.

And now here she was, kissing him in the quiet dark of his living room, her lips trembling against his mouth while he struggled to hold on to the last of his restraint.

When she pressed her lips against his the second time, harder, more urgent, his restraint snapped. He pulled her onto the couch, pinning her beneath him.

He ran his hand up the back of her neck, fisting her hair, tugging slightly, exposing the curve of her neck to his lips. His head dipped as he brushed kisses along her collarbone, up the side of her neck to her ear.

A soft moan escaped her lips when he nipped her earlobe. Her hands slid under his shirt, exploring the lines of his chest and abdomen. fingertips tracing the warm lines of muscle along his torso. The contact sent a jolt through him. Declan shifted his weight onto his elbows, looked down at her, and stiffened.

The bank account. The murder. A stalker in the background of every moment. All the unanswered questions. She had not told him everything. He knew that. Part of him knew he needed to earn her trust. But the part of him trained to expect betrayal, to anticipate the worst, surged to the surface before he could stop it.

She must have felt the shift because her eyes fluttered open. Confusion flickered first, then something far more fragile. The heat he had seen there only moments ago dimmed, replaced by uncertainty. He watched her pull back into herself, watched the walls rise, watched the doubt settle over her like a veil.

The way she folded in on herself hit him with a force he wasn't ready for. "We shouldn't," he said in a ragged voice.

Alex shifted under him, hugging herself. She tore her eyes away from him, but before she did, he saw the sting of his rejection shining brightly, and he felt like a heel.

She moved to push him off, but he planted himself firmly over her until she met his eyes again.

Her eyes shimmered with unshed tears, and the sight of them nearly undid him.

"Alex," he said softly, but she flinched at the sound of her name, as if bracing for another blow.

A sharp curse burned through his mind. Hurting her had never been the intention. Slowing things down, getting his head straight, keeping both of them safe from the storm they were standing in... that was all he had meant to do. Part of it was self-preservation too. There were still unanswered questions circling her like shadows, and the part of him kept whispering that he needed to stay guarded.

But the look on her face cut straight through every defensive instinct he had.

The vulnerability in her eyes was not something a liar could fake. The way she seemed to shrink in on herself, the way doubt crept over her features, the way she braced as if she expected him to confirm every cruel thing she had ever been told... that was real.

He felt the weight of a choice settle in his chest.

He could retreat into suspicion, let fear dictate his next move, keep her at arm's length the way he always did when things got complicated. Or he could trust what he saw in front of him. Not blindly. Not foolishly. Just enough to meet her where she was instead of pushing her away.

She tried to turn her face aside, but he gently caught her chin, guiding her gaze back to his.

"Please," he murmured. "Look at me."

Her breath hitched. Something raw flickered across her features, unguarded and painfully honest. She looked like someone waiting to be told she had made a mistake. Waiting to be dismissed. Waiting for the worst.

It broke something in him.

"This isn't about not wanting you," he said, voice low and rough with emotion. "You have to know that."

She didn't say anything, still refusing to look at him. Her hand kept pushing weakly at his chest, more retreat than resistance. He caught it gently and guided it down between them, pressing her palm to the hard evidence of exactly how wrong her fear was. Her eyes snapped back to his.

"I want you," he said, breath unsteady. "Probably more than I've ever wanted anyone. But I'm trying to keep you safe and not blur the lines."

Something shifted in her expression. The hurt was still there, but it wavered. Her fingers curled around him, hesitant at first, as if she needed to feel the truth of his words for herself. Declan hissed a breath at the contact, his reaction sharp and involuntary.

That sound, raw and unguarded, pulled her up from the place she'd been sinking. Her eyes flicked to his, searching, and for the first time since he'd pulled back, she didn't look away.

Her fingers skimmed up his torso before she looped her arms around his neck. She shifted her hips beneath him and pressed her body into his, a tentative boldness replacing the fear that had been there moments before.

His forehead dropped to hers, his body trembling with the effort of restraint. Crossing this line meant there would be no going back; he would claim her in every way. "You're not making this easy," he managed, voice rough.

She bit her lip, gathering whatever courage she had left. When she finally spoke, her words were soft but steady.

"We could both be dead tomorrow. And before that happens, I want to know what it feels like to be with someone who actually wants me."

Declan furrowed his brow. That statement needed to be unpacked, but not now.

Did she really not see it? The thought hit him with unexpected force. How could she move through the world so unaware of her own beauty? Not just the kind that came from soft curves or delicate features, but the kind that lived in her laugh, in the way she cared, in the quiet strength she carried even when she thought she was falling apart.

She looked up at him with those wounded eyes, shadows lingering where light should have been, and something hot and dangerous twisted in his chest. Someone had put that doubt there. Someone had taught her to flinch at her own reflection. Someone had convinced her she was less than what she was.

He felt a surge of anger so sharp it startled him. Whoever had carved that insecurity into her did not deserve to breathe the same air she did. The urge to protect her, to shield her from every memory that still haunted her, rose like a tide he could not hold back.

"Fuck the lines," Declan said, crushing his mouth back to hers. A small gasp of surprise escaped her before his mouth consumed hers. He would deconstruct her walls brick by brick and heal the scars left by those who were unworthy of her.

Not because she needed saving.

Because she deserved someone who saw her clearly and chose her anyway.

After a few seconds, the tension in her body eased, and she melted into the kiss, answering him with a sudden, breathless urgency.

Her hands dropped to his waist, shoving impatiently at his waistband. When he sprang free of his pants, her hand closed around his velvety length. He moaned into her mouth, and her lips curved in response, brushing a quiet smile against his.

He reached between them and pulled the leg of her PJ shorts to the side and poised himself at her entrance. She arched into him, meeting him with a need that tore through whatever restraint he had left. He entered her with one hard, long stroke. Her touch scattered his thoughts; every brush of her fingers pulled him deeper into the moment. He kissed her again, harder this time, the last threads of control snapping as she answered him with the same fierce urgency.

It wasn't the slow, deliberate moment he'd pictured on all those nights he lay awake, imagining how it would feel when he finally let himself have her. It was feverish, hungry, and driven by every ounce of longing he'd tried to bury. The control he'd promised himself dissolved the second she reached for him. All he could do was meet her with the same fierce need that had been building in him since that night in the hotel.

Her hips met his thrusts with small thrusts of her own as if she couldn't get enough of him. Her nails bit into his back as she pulled him closer. His hand slid between their bodies, under the band of her pajama shorts, to her apex. He swallowed her gasp as his fingers began circling her clit. She pressed against him, whimpering with need.

Her breaths came fast and uneven as she approached her release. Declan forced himself still, holding her against him until her protest softened against his mouth. When he pulled back, the haze in her eyes cleared just enough for her to truly see him.

"You're mine," he said.

She froze beneath him, eyes lifting to his. He watched her, holding his breath without meaning to. He hadn't realized how badly he needed to hear her choose him.

Her eyes searched his; she nodded.

"Say it," he murmured.

"I'm yours."

A low, rough sound broke from his chest, something possessive he didn't bother to hide, as he claimed her mouth once again. His fingers resumed coaxing her back to the brink as he began moving inside her again.

"You feel so fucking good," he whispered against her ear, nipping at it.

"Please," she moaned against his shoulder as she ran her fingers through his hair. Declan hooked one arm under her knee, pulling her leg up and slid deeper into her.

Alex gasped, "Oh my God." She groaned, throwing her head back as his strokes came hard and fast.

He fisted his free hand into the hair at her nape and brought her face to his so he could watch her as she fell apart in his arms.

"That's it, just like that," Declan's voice was rough and strained.

Her eyes flickered open in what looked like surprise a second before they rolled back in her head and she cried out her release. Declan felt her spasming around him as he watched her unravel. She was beautiful like this, drunk with pleasure, body spasming around him. A few more strokes and he found his own release.

They lay there for a minute, bodies still intertwined, breaths coming in ragged gasps as they both came down from their high.

Her body shuddered softly beneath him. Declan went rigid, every instinct snapping to attention. Was she crying? A moment ago he'd been certain—absolutely certain—of her response to him. But this... this trembling... it felt different. His mind raced back over every second that had led them here, searching for any flicker of hesitation he might have missed, any sign she hadn't truly wanted this.

Declan pushed up onto his elbows, still catching his breath, and found her with a hand clamped over her mouth, shoulders shaking. A tear slid down her cheek, and for a beat he just stared, unsure if she was laughing or crying or both.

"I'm so sorry," she managed between little bursts of laughter. "I'm not laughing at you."

"Feels like you might be," he said, one brow lifting.

That earned another helpless snort before she finally got control, her laughter tapering into a shaky exhale. When she looked at him again, the humor had softened into something rawer. She reached up, palm warm against his cheek, as if grounding herself.

"I didn't know it could feel like that," she whispered. "I've never..." The words tangled, but the meaning was right there between them.

He opened his mouth—"You've never—"

She cut him off with a small shake of her head. "I've only ever been with my ex."

Declan stilled, the pieces shifting in his mind, but she wasn't done. Her gaze dropped to her hands, fingers twisting.

"He used to say there was something wrong with me," she said quietly. "If I wasn't enthusiastic enough, I was boring. If I tried, I was too much. Eventually, I just... faked it so he'd stop looking at me like I'd failed some test." She swallowed, voice thinning. "He told me I was broken. And after a while, I believed him."

Declan eased off her, guiding them upright, his expression softening in a way she didn't dare look at too long.

She let out a breath, almost a laugh, but not quite. "But tonight..." Her eyes lifted to his, steady now. "I guess it wasn't me who was broken."

Declan felt something cold and sharp slide beneath his ribs as she spoke. *Broken.*

The word echoed in his skull like a slur.

He'd heard men talk like that before, insecure boys masquerading as lovers, using shame as a shield for their own inadequacy. But hearing her say it, hearing the way she had folded that cruelty into herself like it was the truth... that hit differently. She had been taught to shrink herself inside someone else's ego.

Something hot and fierce rose in him at the thought. It wasn't just protectiveness, though that was part of it. It was a deeper pull, a possessive surge that made his pulse thrum with the urge to stand between her and anything that had ever hurt her.

She wasn't broken, but God, she'd been made to believe she was. And that was something he couldn't let stand.

"I'm not sure why I was laughing; there were just so many emotions and–"

Her nervous rambling cut off as Declan rose from the couch and pulled her up with him.

"Where are we going?" She asked breathlessly.

"To make you come so many times the only voice you hear in your head again is mine telling you how fucking beautiful you are."

Chapter Twenty-Two
ALEX

She awoke sometime in the early morning before the sun rose as the bed shifted under Declan's weight. She was sprawled out on her stomach in a deep sleep, limbs heavy, cheek pressed into the pillow. She had never been fucked so many times in a single night. The faintest groan slipped from her throat as consciousness tugged at her.

His chest hairs tickled her back as he pressed against her from behind trailing a row of kisses down her neck. There was no way he was human. Alex thought there was surely no way she could do this again but to her utter surprise, the muscles in her lower abdomen clenched in anticipation.

She moaned as he nipped her ear. And pressed back against him, feeling his erection. Declan slid a hand between her lower abdomen and the bed, lifting her hips just enough to slide into her, painfully slow. Her breath caught in her throat as his hand on her abdomen dropped lower and began working in slow, torturous circles.

Alex began moving, trying to increase the pace, but Declan's hand stilled her.

"Not this time. This time, we're taking it slow."

Alex groaned her displeasure.

"Be still. Feel what I'm doing to you."

Alex huffed, but stilled.

"You're beautiful," he whispered. A small smile tugged at the corner of Alex's lips. He had told her that more times than she could count tonight.

As well as sexy, gorgeous, and a million other variations. Had she really gone thirty years without this?

Declan rose to his knees, bringing her hips up with him. His other hand stayed coiled in her hair, keeping her head down. This new angle was hitting all the right spots, and Alex began to move against him again.

Declan stopped. Alex's eyes snapped open.

"Still," he said with a devilish grin.

Alex didn't think she could stay still; the knot in her stomach was begging for release.

She stilled, biting back the groan that threatened.

"That's my girl."

He began moving again, his fingers moving in unison with his thrusts. The coil began winding tighter until every nerve in her body was screaming for release. Just as she thought she couldn't take anymore pleasure exploded inside. Her vision went white and her body shook as wave after wave flowed through her.

She felt Declan jerk behind her before he collapsed on the bed beside her. She crumpled back onto the bed, her limbs completely useless, as if her bones had turned to jelly. A soft, frustrated sound escaped her; half-groan, half-sigh. The sound of a body pushed past its limits.

For a moment she just lay there, breathing hard, cheek pressed to the cool sheet. A faint tremor ran through her arms when she tried to push herself up. Every muscle felt hollowed out, drained, as if someone had wrung the strength from her and left only the echo of it behind.

Heat flushed across her skin, not embarrassment exactly, but the raw vulnerability of being so thoroughly undone. Before she could settle into that feeling, Declan pulled her close, tucking her head under his chin. He kissed the top of her head and held her close.

She watched him for a moment, the predawn light outlining the curve of his shoulder, the rise and fall of his breath. He looked softer like this, unguarded in a way she hadn't seen him before. The tension he normally carried in his jaw, the taut line of his shoulders, the no-nonsense way he carried himself around others all melted away as he drifted into sleep.

She let her gaze linger, tracing the softened lines of his expression. Without the weight of the world pressing on him, he looked younger. Kinder. As if sleep peeled back the armor he wore so effortlessly.

The steady sound of his breath coming and going and the feel of his heart beating under her palm was the only convincing she needed before slipping into sleep herself.

When she awoke again, she was alone in the bed, and the afternoon sun was spilling through the cracks in the blinds. She stretched lazily, muscles warm and loose, and lay there for a moment as the memories of the night washed over her. Heat crept up her cheeks before she could stop it.

After a quick search, she located her discarded pajamas, tugged them on, and padded out of the bedroom.

Declan was sitting at the island, a box of pizza open beside him, a cup of coffee in hand, his laptop glowing faintly in front of him. He looked up the moment he heard her footsteps and smiled.

"Good afternoon," he said, lifting his mug with a raised brow. "Sleep well."

"I did," she admitted, sliding onto the stool beside him.

She flipped open the pizza box and grabbed a slice. She hadn't realized how hungry she was until the smell hit her. As she took a bite, she could feel Declan's gaze on her — steady, assessing, almost amused.

"What?" she asked suddenly, self-conscious.

"Are you on birth control?"

Alex snorted. "It's a little late to worry about that now, isn't it?" She took another bite. "Yes, I am. But I forgot it at my house, so we'll have to swing by there when we pick Collin up tonight."

Declan nodded once, the tension in his shoulders easing. "Alright."

"What are you working on?" Alex asked, gesturing to the laptop.

Declan hesitated a moment before he answered. "Just doing a deep dive into Enzo."

He looked as if he were going to ask her something but didn't. The serious lines had settled back over his face as he slipped back into work like a second skin.

The shift reminded her she was scheduled to work tomorrow. A lump formed in her throat at the thought that the stalker could be someone from her job. Someone she saw every day. Someone who knew her routines.

"I have to work tomorrow," she said quietly. "Are they done with my car?"

Declan stiffened. "They are," he said, but the hesitation in his voice made her stomach dip.

"What?" Alex pressed.

He exhaled through his nose. "I don't like the idea of you driving around alone or going to work until we find this guy. He obviously knows where you work; it isn't safe."

"I can't just stay in bed with you all the time," she said, trying to lighten the mood with a smile.

"Why not?"

His deadpan delivery caught her off guard, and she laughed. He did too — a low, warm sound that eased the tension between them.

But beneath the humor, she could feel the truth humming under his words. He wasn't joking. Not entirely. That realization sent a strange, fluttering warmth through her chest.

"I will not let this person control my entire life," she said. Her gaze dropped to the counter as the words left her mouth.

Declan let out a slow breath. "Fine. We'll pick up your car tonight." He lifted his coffee, took a measured sip, and set the mug down with purpose. "While you're at the hospital, I'm working the case. They have security, and I'm putting an unmarked car outside your department for the entire shift."

Alex's head came up sharply. "Declan—"

"It is not negotiable," he said, cutting her protest off.

She opened her mouth to argue, but the look he gave her stopped the words before they formed.

Still, the knot in her chest tightened. "I do not want to feel like a prisoner. Or draw even more attention to myself."

"You won't," he said. "Go to work, do your job, live your life." He set his mug down and leaned in slightly, his eyes locked on hers. "I'm just making sure you get to keep doing all of that. You won't even know he's there."

He straightened again and went back to what he was doing, as if the matter were already settled.

She could tell by the set of his shoulders that he wasn't going to budge on the subject. She hated the idea of having a babysitter, but if it would make him feel better, she would accept it.

Alex slipped away to get dressed, leaving Declan absorbed in whatever he was reading on the laptop. She could feel his focus even from the hallway, a quiet intensity that seemed to settle over the entire cabin. He had a way of disappearing into work, while the rest of the world dimmed around him.

By the time night settled over the cabin, the mood had shifted back to quiet contentment. Alex and Declan sat curled together on the couch watching T.V. while Collin colored at the island. The pickup earlier had gone far better than she had expected. Alex had been nervous the entire drive, stomach in knots at the thought of Declan meeting her ex. She had braced for tension, awkwardness, and maybe even hostility. Instead, Declan and Henry ended up talking about football like old friends while Collin packed his backpack. The whole thing had been so... normal. Almost easy.

Afterward, they stopped by the barn to pick up her car, then drove to her house to grab clothes and school supplies for Collin, along with her birth control. She had been stunned when she walked inside and found the place spotless. Every dish washed, every toy put away, every surface gleaming.

Declan had only smiled and said he and Dean had called a maid service while they were out on the boat because they did not want her or Alyssa worrying about cleaning up the mess.

It was so much to take in. No one had ever done anything like that for her before. The kindness, the thoughtfulness, the sheer generosity of it all left her breathless. Everything in her life seemed to shift at once, and she struggled to find her footing in the whirlwind.

Collin seemed completely unfazed by the transition. His calm confidence was a stark contrast to the chaos inside her. He had run through the cabin, exploring every room, declaring everything was "awesome" before claiming the first bedroom upstairs as his own. He unpacked his things, jumped onto the bed, and announced it was the most comfortable bed he had ever slept on.

Alex had cooked pork chops for dinner while Collin and Declan talked animatedly at the island. The cabin had filled with the warm smell of seared meat and herbs, and for the first time in a long while, everything had felt strangely right. After dinner, they settled in for the night. Tomorrow would be busy, but at least she would get to see Alyssa and catch up on the past two days.

Nina, Collin's babysitter, had called earlier to say she was sick and couldn't watch him tomorrow. Alex had been ready to call out of work until Declan mentioned that his mother could pick Collin up and stay with him until he got home. She'd agreed, even if it made her a little uneasy. She'd only met Katherine once, but the woman had seemed warm and capable.

By ten, it was time for bed. Alex guided Collin upstairs and tucked him in. The familiar hum of his sound machine filled the room. Collin looked up at her with wide, uncertain eyes and asked if she could leave the lamp on. He was not used to sleeping in new places, and the unease in his voice tugged at her heart. She stroked his hair gently and whispered soothing words until his breathing slowed and he drifted off to sleep.

When she finally slipped out of the room, she paused in the doorway, watching him for a moment. She was about to slip out of the room when Collin's sleepy voice snapped her attention back to him.

"Where are you sleeping tonight, Mom?" he asked, patting the empty side of his full-size bed with hopeful eyes.

Alex froze. She hadn't thought this far ahead. Maybe sleeping with Declan wasn't the best idea yet. Collin had already been through so many changes in such a short time.

"Alright," she said softly. "I'll sleep in here with you tonight since it's your first night. I'm just going to go say goodnight to Declan, and I'll be right back." She kissed his forehead and slipped out.

Downstairs, the cabin was quiet. Declan's bedroom door was cracked, warm light spilling into the hall. She stepped inside and heard the shower running. Steam drifted from the bathroom, curling into the air like a beckoning hand.

The shower glass was steamy, but she could still see him, back to her, washing his hair. He hadn't heard her enter the bathroom. Alex slipped into the bathroom and quickly discarded her clothes and joined him in the shower.

Declan stiffened before relaxing as she wrapped her arms around him from behind.

"I hope you don't mind my joining you. I need a shower, too." Alex smiled up at him.

"Shower is all yours," he gestured with his hand.

Alex stepped into the water. The heat felt good on her body. She grabbed the sponge Declan had just been using and washed herself. The shower was big enough for the two of them, but barely.

She bent forward to wash her calves with the sponge, brushing her backside against Declan's groin. He hissed in a quick breath, letting her know she was having the desired effect. She threw a sly grin over her shoulder at him, but froze beneath his smoldering glare.

"Ma'am, if you rub your ass against my cock again, I won't be able to control myself." Declan said through gritted teeth.

"Maybe I don't want you to control yourself." Alex said breathlessly.

Declan let out a groan and, in one smooth motion, lifted Alex up and pinned her against the back shower wall. She wrapped her legs tightly around him as he lowered her down onto him. He had just begun moving inside her when Alex started sputtering. He looked up just in time to see Alex fighting for her life against the steady shower stream hitting her directly in the face.

Declan reached up with one hand and repositioned the shower head while stifling his laughter. Alex gasped for air. But soon joined him in his laughter.

"Take me to bed," she said, dragging a hand over her face, shedding some of the water.

Declan carried her to the bed, leaving a trail of water on the floor in their wake.

They fell onto the bed, soaking the sheets beneath them. Declan threw one of Alex's knees over his shoulder and thrust himself into her. Alex let out a loud moan that Declan quickly smothered with a deep kiss.

Alex felt goosebumps rise across her skin, a shiver running through her before she could stop it. For a heartbeat, she thought it was him; the way he touched her, the way he held her, the way he made her feel seen in a way she wasn't used to. But then the cool air from the ceiling fan brushed over her damp shoulders, and she realized the chill had nothing to do with nerves or anticipation.

Declan noticed immediately. He always noticed.

Without a word, he reached for the comforter and pulled it over both of them, shielding their damp bodies from the torturous fan. She tightened her legs around him, pulling him deeper. She arched her back as he began moving again. There was nothing slow and gentle about this, like there was last night. This was rougher, more demanding. She met him thrust for thrust, taking all of him as he filled every part of her.

She reached the pinnacle seconds before he did. They both lay in a heap, panting for breath, when a small, sleepy voice snapped their attention.

"Momma?"

Their eyes locked in panic.

"Fuck, I forgot to lock the door," Alex whispered. She yanked the blanket up to her neck and pushed up on her elbow.

"Yeah, baby?" she called, trying to sound normal.

"I thought you were going to sleep with me tonight. What are you doing?" Collin asked, rubbing his eyes with the back of his hand.

Alex froze. "Uh... I was just saying goodnight to Declan before I came up." She prayed that would be the end of it.

"Why were you crying?"

"I wasn't crying." Alex groaned aloud. "Hey, can you run to the kitchen and grab me a glass of water? I'll meet you upstairs in just a minute."

"Sure, Momma." Collin turned and padded toward the kitchen.

The second he disappeared around the corner, Alex threw the covers back and scrambled out of bed, frantically searching for her clothes. Declan lay back with his hands behind his head, a smug grin plastered on his face.

"That was not funny," Alex hissed.

"It was a little funny," Declan said, far too pleased with himself.

Alex shot him a look but couldn't help the smile tugging at her mouth. "Guess I should start saving for his future therapy sessions."

They both laughed. She tugged on the last of her clothes, then darted over to him and pressed a quick kiss to his forehead.

"I'll see you in the morning," she said, hurrying out of the room.

Chapter Twenty-Three
ALEX

It took all of Alex's willpower not to call in sick to work. When she pulled into the parking lot and saw four ambulances lined up in the bay, she wanted to put the car in reverse and keep driving. Instead, she gave herself a brief pep talk, squared her shoulders, and headed into the department.

All of her rooms were full except for her trauma bay. Several patients had full workups ordered that still weren't done, so she stuffed her pockets with IV supplies and got to work. Thirty minutes later, she returned to the desk to find her trauma room packed with people. Another patient had arrived while she was busy. Everything looked under control, so she finished labeling and sending off her blood samples before heading toward the commotion.

The patient was a man in his mid-thirties, barely conscious, high-flow oxygen hissing through the mask strapped to his face. He slumped sideways in the bed, and someone shouted that they had lost a pulse.

Denise, the charge nurse, cut the man's shirt open to place the AED pads and begin CPR. She jerked the shirt aside, revealing a device strapped to the man's chest—its timer blinking down with only two seconds left.

Before anyone could react, a cloud of white mist erupted from the canister.

The respiratory therapist and Denise tried to back away, but it was already too late. They had inhaled whatever was leaking from the canister. Both women collapsed to the floor almost in unison.

"Get out of the room!" Alex shouted from the doorway.

The doctor, recorder, ED tech, and pharmacist bolted past her. Alex slammed the door shut behind them, her heart hammering against her ribs.

"We can't just leave them in there!" Ashley the tech cried.

"We need respirators," Alex said, scanning the hall. "We don't know what was in that canister."

Her gaze landed on the firefighter who had brought the patient in. He was leaning against the counter, flirting with Amber, the new nurse.

"Hey!" Alex barked. "Do you have your respirator? The patient had something strapped to their chest, and whatever was in it took down two people before they could get out!"

Alyssa rounded the corner at a run. "What happened? How can I help?"

"Follow me," Alex said. She grabbed Alyssa and two other coworkers, leading them to the supply room. Within a minute, they were handing out gowns, gloves, and masks to the remaining staff.

"We need to get them into the decontamination shower as soon as they're out," Alex said, already tying her gown.

The firefighter sprinted toward the ambulance bay and returned with two more crew members, all three wearing full respirators. Alex, Alyssa, and the other nurses waited outside the decon room, fully suited in protective equipment.

Seconds later, the firefighters emerged carrying Denise and the respiratory therapist. They laid both women on the floor of the decon room. Alex dropped to her knees and checked for a pulse. Faint, but present.

She turned on the decon shower, icy water blasting down. Together, they cut away clothing and rinsed both women thoroughly before transferring them onto the gurneys Ashley had staged outside the door. The moment they were stable enough to move, the team wheeled them to separate rooms.

As Alex stepped out of the decon area, she saw a cluster of people in full HAZMAT suits gathering around Trauma One.

Movement at the far end of the ambulance bay caught her eye. The uniformed officer Declan had assigned to watch over her was pounding on the glass doors, trying to get inside. His radio was pressed to his shoulder, his expression tight with urgency as he spoke into the receiver. The bay was already in full lockdown—no one in, no one out.

He tried the door again, then met Alex's gaze through the glass. She shook her head once, signaling stay out. Whatever was in that room, she wasn't about to let anyone else get exposed.

The officer hesitated, jaw clenched, then stepped back, keeping his eyes on her as the HAZMAT team continued their sweep.

Alyssa took the respiratory therapist to an open room while Alex stayed with Denise. She hooked her up to the monitors, started supplemental oxygen, and covered her with warm blankets. The decon shower only had one temperature, and it was freezing. Neither woman had regained consciousness, but both were holding on.

They needed answers.

Alex stepped out to the nurses' station just as Alyssa joined her. Together, they watched the HAZMAT team work. One tech swabbed the canister, smeared the sample onto a small card, and sprayed it with a clear liquid.

The card turned blue.

The man closest to the door cracked it open and motioned for them to come closer.

"We think it is aerosolized fentanyl," the HAZMAT tech said before pulling the door closed again.

Alyssa and Alex locked eyes. "Narcan," they said at the same time, already sprinting toward the med room.

Alex grabbed a vial and rushed to Denise's room. She pushed the medication through the IV, her hands steady despite the adrenaline pounding in her veins. Narcan was used to reverse opioid overdoses, and if they were right about the substance, it was Denise's best shot.

Twenty seconds later, Denise's eyes flew open, darting wildly around the room.

"Denise, it's Alex. You're okay," she said quickly, leaning into her line of sight. "The patient in Trauma One had a canister of aerosolized fentanyl strapped to him. I just gave you Narcan. Try to lie back and breathe."

Denise blinked hard, trying to orient herself.

Alex stepped into the hallway just as one of the HAZMAT crew spoke to Dr. Carter. "With the size of the canister, it's hard to know how much got into the vents. It's probably confined to that room, but until a clean crew gets here, we need to divert traffic to surrounding hospitals and empty the ER as soon as possible."

"I'll call the medical director," Dr. Carter said. He turned to Alex. "Since Denise is out of commission, you're in charge for now. Call triage and evacuate the front. Overhead page a Code Orange for ED only. I'll start arranging transfers for anyone we can't discharge."

Code Orange meant an internal disaster. Alex didn't waste a second. She grabbed the phone, notified triage, then paged the alert overhead. The emergency department sat across the road from the main hospital, connected by a skybridge that could be sealed off to contain contamination. They were taking every precaution because an air-intake vent sat directly above the patient's bed, and no one knew how much of the drug had dispersed.

When Alex hung up the phone, she saw Denise waving weakly from her room.

Alex hurried over. "Everything okay?"

"Yeah," Denise said, pushing herself up on her elbows. "I can work. Where are my clothes?"

"Uh... I cut them off you," Alex admitted, wincing.

"Ugh, those were my favorite scrubs," Denise groaned. "Can you grab my phone so my husband can bring me something to wear?"

"Sure." Alex headed to the nurse's station. She chose not to mention that they were on full lockdown. Denise would need a ride home after they finished sorting the situation out. As she reached for Denise's phone, a vase of flowers caught her eye. It sat innocently on the corner of the desk she'd been using, as if it had always belonged there. Whoever delivered them must have slipped in and out during the commotion without anyone noticing.

She reached toward the vase... then froze, remembering the last time someone had sent her flowers at work.

A cold ripple slid down her spine.

Before the memory could fully take shape, the charge nurse's phone shrilled loudly beside her, snapping her back into motion. She snatched it up, forcing her voice steady.

"Alex."

The house supervisor's voice filled her ear. Alex shoved the unease down, burying it under the weight of everything still unfolding. There was no time to think about flowers.

"Alex, I have four beds upstairs for the most critical patients. The rest will need to be transferred to other local ERs."

"Understood." She hung up and stepped into the hall. "Dr. Carter, we've got four beds upstairs. The rest need to be transferred out."

"Got it," Dr. Carter called back, already moving.

The next ninety minutes blurred into motion. Stretchers rattled across the floor. Monitors beeped warnings as nurses disconnected lines and reconnected them to portable units. Someone shouted for more oxygen tanks. Someone else cursed when a gurney wheel snagged on a doorframe. Alex moved from room to room, checking vitals, signing transfer forms, steadying a trembling patient's hand while transport loaded him into the ambulance bay.

Outside, sirens rose and fell as ambulances arrived in waves, engines idling hot in the cold air. The bay doors opened and closed so many times that she lost count.

When the last patient was finally rolled out and the doors thudded shut, the sudden quiet hit her like a blow. Alex dropped into her chair, adrenaline burning off in a slow, shaky drain that left her hollow. Her gaze drifted to the vase of flowers on the desk. Bright. Cheerful. Completely out of place after the chaos of the last ninety minutes.

She'd told herself earlier they were from Declan. She'd wanted to believe that—needed to believe it—because the alternative was too terrifying to consider. But now, with the department stilling around her and her mind no longer racing from crisis to crisis, something inside her tightened. A cold, familiar certainty she'd been pushing away all afternoon crept back in.

The last time flowers had shown up unexpectedly, they hadn't been from someone who cared about her. They'd been from someone who meant her harm, someone who wanted her afraid. Her stomach twisted. She reached for the card nestled between the stems, dread already crawling up her spine.

RIP BITCH.

The words knocked the breath out of her. There it was, the confirmation she hadn't wanted, the truth she'd been trying to pretend wasn't staring her in the face. This wasn't random; it was deliberate. The weight of it settled hard. By pretending she could live like everything was normal, she had put everyone around her at risk. She'd grown so accustomed to living with her guard up, always looking over her shoulder, that she hadn't seen the danger right in front of her. It was time to stop running.

Declan

Declan arrived at the precinct a little after nine. The weekend break had been nice, but it was time to get back to work. As he sat down at his desk, he noticed a new voicemail blinking on his phone and hit play.

"Hello, Detective Wallace. This is Brittany Cunningham returning your call. You can reach me at this number. I rarely have any customers between nine and ten most mornings and will be available to talk." The message ended with a soft click.

Declan dialed her number immediately. The conversation that followed was polite, short, and left him with more questions than answers. Brittany had taken the news of her mother's death with unsettling calm — almost like she'd been expecting it. Or preparing for it.

He hung up and stared at his notes. If he could crack Martha's murder, he was certain it would lead him straight to whoever was targeting Alex. Martha's severed finger hadn't been left in her car by accident. It was a message. A taunt. And Declan felt the weight of it like a hand around his throat.

"Hey, Martha's bank and credit card statements finally came in," Edith said, appearing beside his desk with a thick stack of papers. Edith had been with the department so long she practically came with the building. Retirement wasn't a word she acknowledged.

"Thank you, Edith," Declan said, taking the stack.

He flipped through the pages quickly. Martha's last purchase was an Amtrak ticket from Durham, New Hampshire, to Little Rock, Arkansas. A layover in Chicago, a few Starbucks charges, and then nothing. No more credit card activity. No hotel. No food. No transportation.

She vanished financially the moment she hit Arkansas. As if someone had been waiting for her. Declan leaned back in his chair, a cold prickle running down his spine.

She must not have been home long before she was killed.

Declan picked up the phone again, calling contacts at both the Chicago and Durham Amtrak stations to request security footage. If the killer had ridden the train with Martha, the cameras might have caught a glimpse of their face. The requests were in motion now, but he knew it would take days before the footage landed on his desk.

He hated waiting. Hated being stuck in the space between suspicion and proof.

To keep himself from pacing a hole in the floor, he pulled up Martha's and Brittany's social media accounts. Martha's Facebook was sparse — old school photos of Brittany, a handful of poorly lit selfies, and endless reposts about rescuing animals. Nothing useful.

Brittany's page was the opposite. Over five hundred photos. Selfies. Friends. Parties. And dozens of pictures with horses.

He clicked through them mechanically until one image made him stop cold.

Brittany stood beside a bay horse in front of a big gray barn with a white sliding door.

Declan stared at it, something tugging at the back of his mind. It took a few seconds before it clicked.

Alex had a picture of herself and Zorro in front of that exact same barn.

His pulse kicked up. His gut told him he was finally brushing up against something real. A connection between Martha, Brittany, and Alex.

He printed the photo to add to the case file, snapped a picture with his phone, and sent it to Alex. He needed her to confirm whether Brittany was the same girl who'd replaced her after she fled Enzo's.

Declan's stomach growled loudly, pulling him out of his work. It was just before one in the afternoon, and the morning had evaporated without him noticing. He pushed back from his desk and headed down the hall to Bishop's office.

"Lunch?"

After a brief debate, they settled on McCallister's. Declan didn't care where they went; he was starving. They took a corner table and waited for their sandwiches.

"Any progress with your cases?" Bishop asked.

"Waiting on Amtrak footage for Martha," Declan said, rubbing a hand over his jaw. "Her last purchase was the train ticket from New Hampshire to Little Rock. I was going through Brittany's social media this morning and found a picture of her in front of the barn Enzo owns, the one Alex used to work at. I sent Alex a picture of Brittany, but she hasn't responded yet; she's probably slammed at work."

He paused, thinking back. "If I remember right, Brittany replaced Alex after she left Enzo's. I can't remember the girl's name exactly. We got, uh… sidetracked shortly after that part of the conversation."

Bishop snorted. "I'm sure you did."

Declan didn't rise to the bait. His mind was already spinning, connecting threads, waiting for Alex's reply, the reply that might confirm everything. If he could tie Martha's murder to her trip to New Hampshire, he was one step closer to closing in on whoever was after Alex. And the more he dug, the more convinced he became that this wasn't some coworker with a grudge or a stranger from the hospital who had fixated on her. Nothing about the flowers, the messages, or the timing fit that kind of profile. This felt older, heavier, rooted in the life she had tried to leave behind. Her past was reaching for her, and it was getting bolder.

"I could get sidetracked with that all day long," Bishop said with a mischievous grin, pulling Declan out of his thoughts.

Declan just stared at him. "No, you couldn't."

"Shit, man, I'm just playing." Bishop lifted his hands in surrender, the grin still lingering.

"McMurray said the New Hampshire FBI office checked that abandoned lot where Alex saw Agent Pike," Declan said, steering them back on track. "But they didn't find his body."

"Well, that'll be a load off Alex's mind," Bishop said, drumming his fingers on the table as he craned his neck to look for the server.

"Yes, and no. People don't just disappear. There's a body. It just wasn't where we thought it was."

"Unless he went native," Bishop said, raising an eyebrow.

Declan mulled that over. It wasn't impossible. Undercover agents sometimes blurred the line, started identifying with the people they were supposed to be investigating. Some even switched sides.

"It's possible," he admitted.

The server arrived with their food, interrupting the conversation. They fell into a comfortable silence as they ate, each lost in their own thoughts.

Halfway through his sandwich, Bishop's radio crackled to life.

"South East Regional Hospital has declared a Code ORANGE for the emergency department and requested a HAZMAT response team."

Declan froze.

"Isn't that where Alex works?" Bishop asked.

Declan was already on his feet. "Yeah."

"Go! I'll take care of lunch and meet you over there."

Declan didn't waste a second. He pulled out his phone as he sprinted to the car. The call went straight to voicemail. He tried again. Voicemail.

"Fuck!" he shouted as he slid into the Charger. The hospital was on the opposite side of the city. He flipped on the lights and sirens, gripping the wheel hard enough to make his knuckles ache.

He forced himself to think like a detective, to stay rational, to focus on the facts. But his mind kept drifting to images he couldn't control, flashes of Alex lying lifeless on the hospital floor. Sweat beaded along his brow and he swallowed hard against the bile rising in his throat. This was why he should have kept things professional. The slightest hint that Alex might not be okay and he was already unraveling.

He dialed Alex again. Straight to voicemail.

He swore under his breath and immediately called the uniformed officer he had stationed outside the ER.

The line picked up on the second ring. "Wallace?"

"Talk to me. What's happening over there?"

"Sir, the hospital's on full lockdown. They sealed the ambulance bay doors. I can't get inside."

Declan's grip tightened on the wheel. "Did you see Alex?"

"Yeah, I saw her about a minute ago through the glass. She looked okay. Shaken, but okay. They were moving staff around, getting people out of the trauma wing."

Declan exhaled, some of the tension in his chest easing. "Stay put. Don't leave that entrance. If she comes out, you call me immediately."

"Yes, sir."

Declan hung up and pressed harder on the accelerator, weaving through traffic as the city blurred past. The officer's update replayed in his mind, tightening something low in his chest. He should never have let her go in today. He knew better.

Someone had gone after Alex at the hospital. That alone told him everything he needed to know. This wasn't bold; it was reckless, the kind of move a man made when he was cornered and running out of options. Pressure was closing in on whoever was targeting her, and the bastard was slipping.

Declan felt the realization settle like a stone in his gut. He needed to figure out what had pushed the man to take a risk this stupid, and he needed to do it before the bastard struck again. Someone operating at this level of desperation would not stop on their own. They would keep coming until they succeeded or until someone put them down.

Chapter Twenty-Four
DECLAN

By the time Declan pulled into the parking lot, several patrol officers were already setting up a perimeter around the emergency department. He strode toward the nearest officer.

"What do we have?"

The officer straightened. "All we know so far is a patient came in with some kind of gas canister strapped to them. It went off. One dead, two in critical condition."

Declan's heart dropped. He didn't wait for more. He headed for the ambulance bay doors, but a HAZMAT team pushed out before he could reach them.

"No one goes in," one of the techs said, raising a hand. "Staff inside have protective gear. You don't."

He didn't waste time arguing. He was about to move around them when shouting erupted behind him. Several family members were trying to force their way past the officers. The officers were outnumbered, and the entire situation was seconds away from boiling over.

Declan stepped in without hesitation, placing himself between the crowd and the doors. His voice carried over the noise.

"Stop. All of you. Pushing your way in will help no one. You'll only make things worse."

The crowd faltered for a second.

"If you want answers, we do this the right way. Form a line. Give this officer your loved one's name. We'll relay it to the staff inside and get updates as soon as they come."

The fight drained out of them. One by one, they backed off and formed a line. The young officer pulled out a notepad and started taking names, relief written across his face.

Declan stayed where he was, eyes locked on the sealed doors. The air in the bay felt heavier than it should, thick with the chemical bite of disinfectant and the faint rubber smell from the HAZMAT suits. Sirens wailed somewhere outside, distant but constant, a reminder that this wasn't slowing down.

He reached into his pocket and pulled out his phone, fingers moving fast despite the adrenaline still burning through him. He found the hospital's main line, tapped through to the ER extension, and lifted the phone to his ear.

Around him, the crowd pressed in with a restless energy. Someone sobbed near the barricade. Others paced along the sidewalk. Officers worked to keep everyone back, but the tension hung thick in the crisp air.

The phone rang in his ear, each tone dragging longer than the last. Declan kept his eyes locked on the sliding glass doors, jaw tight, every muscle coiled and ready to move the second someone answered.

"ER, this is Leslie," a deep woman's voice answered.

"Leslie, this is Detective Wallace with LRPD. I'm trying to keep the crowd calm out here, but they're desperate for information."

"I can't give patient information over the phone," she said immediately.

Declan closed his eyes for half a second. His patience was already stretched thin. "I figured. Were any patients injured?"

A long pause followed. He could hear movement on her end, muffled voices, the distant hiss of something mechanical. "Hold on."

Declan lowered the phone and kicked at the rocks at his feet.

The line clicked.

"Sir? Are you still there?"

"Yes," Declan said. His voice came out sharper than he intended.

"All I can tell you is that there was one patient involved in the incident and two staff members. The rest of the patients are fine."

Declan swallowed. His mouth felt dry. "Are Alex and Alyssa okay? They're my... friends."

Another pause. He could hear typing, the faint shuffle of papers.

"Yes. They're both okay."

Declan closed his eyes and let out a breath he didn't realize he had been holding. The relief hit hard enough to make his knees feel unsteady for a moment. "Thank you, Leslie."

He hung up and returned to the crowd. "Everyone, I just spoke with the staff inside. Your family members are safe. They're asking for patience as they transfer patients to other facilities."

Just as Declan finished speaking to the crowd, he saw Dean's truck fly into the parking lot. Dean jumped out before the engine even stopped, scanning the chaos with wild eyes until he spotted Declan.

"They're both fine!" Declan called the moment Dean was within earshot. "I just got off the phone with the secretary—she said they're okay."

The relief that washed over Dean eased some of Declan's own tension.

"What happened?" Dean demanded.

Declan ran through everything he knew. Ambulances were lining up now, one after another, and patients were being loaded and hauled away. It wasn't until the fourth gurney rolled out that Declan finally caught a glimpse of Alex. She didn't see him, but she was on her feet and breathing. For now, that was enough.

He and Dean helped maintain the perimeter, directing frantic families and relaying information about where their loved ones were being transferred. By the time the last ambulance pulled away, Declan had counted fourteen patients.

Two hours later, Alex and Alyssa emerged from the hospital, arms linked, both looking wrung out. The moment the girls spotted them, Alex broke away and rushed straight into Declan's arms. He wrapped her up, burying his face in her neck, inhaling the cold scent of outside air and hospital antiseptic clinging to her skin.

When she finally pulled back, tears shimmered in her eyes.

"Tell me what happened," he said. His gaze raked over her, sharp with worry he didn't bother to hide. Her breath shook, and her hands were ice in his grip.

"The attack was meant for me," she said, her voice flat.

A cold shiver slid down Declan's spine. "What do you mean it was meant for you? How could you know that?"

Dean and Alyssa stepped up behind him, unnoticed until now.

"Because someone sent flowers to Alex during the attack," Alyssa said, turning her gaze from Alex to Declan. "The note said RIP Bitch."

Declan's stomach dropped. He held Alex at arm's length, searching her face. A tear slipped free, and she swiped it away angrily. She hated crying in front of people.

Another patrol car pulled in. Bishop climbed out and jogged over.

"Sorry I missed the commotion. Caught a call on the way out of the restaurant. What's the scoop?" he asked.

Declan didn't take his eyes off Alex as he answered. "Someone filled a canister with fentanyl and strapped it to a patient. When the charge nurse opened his shirt to start compressions, it released the drug into the air. The charge nurse and the respiratory therapist went down, but were able to be extracted and are stable. The patient with the canister is dead. And someone sent Alex flowers during all of this with a note that said, 'RIP BITCH.'"

Bishop's expression hardened.

Declan turned back to Alex. "Where are the flowers now?"

"I left them on my desk. The only thing I touched was the note."

Bishop looked between them. "Besides Enzo, who would want to hurt you?"

Declan felt the dread settle deeper. Whoever this was, they had failed today, and they would be back. That much he was certain of.

Alex's jaw tightened. Her eyes flicked away. She hesitated. It was small, barely a breath, but he caught it. He had asked her the same question several days ago.

"No one that I can think of," she said.

Declan watched her closely. Her words were steady, but something in her posture shifted. A flicker of uncertainty. A tell she probably didn't realize she had.

Her hand drifted toward her key ring, thumb brushing over something there. He followed the movement. A small flash drive hung from the ring, the metal catching the fading rays of sunlight.

His breath caught. Of course, she was hiding something. A flicker of irritation tightened his jaw. The woman was exasperating. Declan, the man, understood she needed space to unpack her traumatic past. Declan the detective knew they were out of time, and every hesitation, every inconsistency, every half-truth scraped against his nerves.

His brain wouldn't shut off. It never did. He filed it away. Now wasn't the time to push. Not with half the department watching and the situation still volatile. But he would circle back to this later. He needed the truth, and she'd give it to him.

He forced his focus back to the scene around him. The chemical bite of disinfectant hung in the air. Radios crackled. Officers murmured into comms. The HAZMAT team was already moving equipment toward the bay doors.

"We need to coordinate with HAZMAT," Declan said, shifting into command mode. "Make sure they don't touch the flowers. Once they're done, we track where they were sent from and get someone over there. Pull security footage from the hospital and the flower shop. The bastard could've been watching."

He grabbed Bishop's arm and pulled him aside. "I'm taking Alex home. I'll question her more there. I'll call if I get anything."

"Did you see her hesitate before she answered me?" Bishop asked quietly.

"I did," Declan said, jaw tight. "And I'll get to the bottom of it."

"Alright, Bossman. I'll be in touch." Bishop headed toward the HAZMAT team.

Declan turned back to Alex.

"Let's go home," he said, holding out his hand.

Alex nodded and laced her fingers through his. "I'll text you later, Alyssa."

Declan wrapped an arm around her as they walked toward her car. The air outside was cooler, carrying the faint chemical tang from the decontamination units. Gravel crunched under their feet. Alex reached for the handle.

Something in the scene shifted. A detail sat wrong, subtle but unmistakable. A prickle rose at the base of his neck.

"Alex, freeze!" Declan yelled.

She stopped instantly, hand hovering inches from the door.

Declan dropped to the ground, scanning beneath the car. A wire ran from the driver's door to a device strapped under the seat. A bomb. Rigged to detonate the moment the door opened.

"Back away. Slowly."

Alex stepped back, eyes wide. Declan rose and guided her toward the ambulance bay. Once they were under cover, he radioed for the bomb squad.

Bishop heard the call and sprinted over. "What's going on?"

"There's an explosive under her car," Declan said. "Door-triggered. We need a perimeter."

"On it." Bishop grabbed caution tape from his cruiser and began cordoning off the employee lot. Families still lingering in the parking area looked confused and frightened.

Declan raised his voice. "Everyone, we need to clear the area. There is a possible explosive device. If your car is parked in the front lot, go around the back of the building to reach it."

Reluctantly, the last of the families moved away.

Bishop finished taping off the area. Declan turned back to Alex. She was pale and trying her best to hide the tremble in her hands. He shrugged off his jacket and draped it over her shoulders.

"Thank you," she whispered.

She walked to the sidewalk and sat down, pulling the jacket tightly around herself. Declan stayed close, observing her. Her eyes kept darting toward the crowd, scanning faces one by one with a focus that bordered on frantic.

He followed her line of sight. The remaining onlookers lingered behind the tape. She was trying to find a threat she couldn't name. Nothing in the crowd stood out to him. No familiar faces. No one watching too closely.

The bomb squad truck pulled in, lights washing the scene in harsh red and blue. A stocky, middle-aged man stepped out, and Declan met him halfway. Declan pointed toward Alex's car and explained what he had seen before evacuating the area.

Two techs emerged carrying the EOD robot, its metal joints clicking softly as they lowered it to the pavement.

Declan returned to Alex's side and sat down beside her. She kept her eyes on the robot, shoulders tight beneath his jacket. He stayed close, scanning the perimeter, cataloging every movement, every face, every variable.

From the ambulance bay, Bishop called out, "Hey, Wallace! HAZMAT cleared me to enter. I'll process the flowers, determine where they originated, and look for fingerprints. I've got a call into the house supervisor for the last twenty-four hours of footage. Are you good out here?"

"Yeah, we're all set. Keep me updated."

"Will do," Bishop said, disappearing back into the hospital.

It was nearly five in the afternoon, and the winter light was fading fast. Declan pulled out his phone. "I better text Mom and let her know we're running late."

"Shit—Collin!" Alex blurted. She'd been so consumed by the day's chaos she'd forgotten Katherine was watching him.

"Don't worry," Declan said with a soft laugh. "If she survived raising me and my brother, she can handle Collin for a few extra hours."

After a quick conversation, he slipped his phone back into his pocket. Along the perimeter, the bomb squad had formed a line, and the EOD robot was trundling toward Alex's car.

"We should back up a little more," Declan said, rising and offering his hand.

Alex took it and stood just as the world tore open.

A violent crack ripped through the air, followed by a blast wave that punched into Declan's chest hard enough to steal his breath. Heat and pressure slammed into him at once. Training took over before thought could catch up. He lunged, grabbing Alex and driving her down as the shockwave rolled over them.

The ground hit his knees, then his shoulder, then his full weight crashed over her. The pavement vibrated beneath him. A high, piercing ring swallowed every other sound. Dust and debris rained down, peppering his back and arms. His vision flashed white at the edges.

For a beat, nothing moved. He forced air into his lungs, blinked until shapes steadied, until the world stopped tilting. Then he pushed himself off Alex and staggered upright.

Sound returned in jagged pieces. Radios crackled. Someone shouted. The bomb squad was already sprinting toward the blast site.

Flames engulfed Alex's car. Fire climbed through the shattered frame, black smoke twisting into the darkening sky. The heat hit his face even from a distance. The EOD robot sat untouched thirty feet from the wreckage, its metal shell reflecting the firelight.

Declan steered her toward his patrol car and eased her inside. He saw the bomb squad leader and Bishop converge on him, their mouths moving in rapid bursts as he strained to hear through the ringing in his ears.

The leader leaned in. "Detective, we found the trigger source. This wasn't timed. There had to be a remote detonator."

Declan's stomach tightened. "Range?"

"Close. Whoever did it was nearby when it went off."

Bishop swore under his breath. "We'll sweep the perimeter, check for anyone bolting right after the blast."

Declan nodded. "Coordinate with HAZMAT. I want the flowers untouched until they're cleared. Track the delivery. Pull every camera angle from the lot and the surrounding streets."

"We're on it," the leader said, already signaling to his team.

Bishop clapped Declan's shoulder once. "I'll update you as soon as we have anything."

Declan didn't waste another second. He turned, jogged back to the patrol car, and slid into the driver's seat. The ringing in his ears hadn't faded, but his focus had sharpened to a razor's edge.

Someone had been close enough to watch the explosion.

From the passenger seat, Alex absentmindedly rubbed her thumb over the flash drive. Declan saw it immediately. Even shaken and half in shock, her fingers went straight to the one thing she hadn't explained.

His stomach tightened. Whatever was on that drive, someone was willing to kill for it.

And he wasn't letting them get another chance.

Chapter Twenty-Five
ALEX

It was a quiet ride back to the station. Alex could feel Declan's anger simmering just beneath the surface. She didn't blame him. Over the past two weeks, she had turned his life inside out and dragged him into a nightmare he never asked to be a part of. If he wanted off the ride, she wouldn't blame him.

The shock of the day faded, and her own anger simmered just beneath the surface. She stared blankly out the window as her mind raced through recent events. She'd spent years rebuilding her life, clawing her way out of the shadows of her past. And now someone was trying to rip it all away.

Her thumb drifted to the flash drive on her key ring, rolling the smooth metal between her fingers. She had kept it hidden for eight years. Enzo had been the only other person who knew it existed. And now he was gone.

She should tell Declan. He deserved the truth. She hadn't meant to keep it from him. She had honestly forgotten it was even there. But if he was going to keep them safe, he needed the whole picture instead of the fragments she'd given him.

She exhaled slowly and rested her head against the window, the last of the adrenaline draining from her system. Exhaustion crept in to take its place. There was enough money tucked away to disappear with Collin if it came to that—she'd done it once, and she could do it again.

They were three blocks from the station when Declan's radio crackled to life.

"Residential burglary at 22 Pinnacle Mountain Road. Requesting EMS and police. Three injured, one unresponsive."

A chill shot through Alex.

"That's Nina's address," she whispered.

Her chest tightened as Declan's jaw began working overtime. He flicked on the lights and pulled the car into a sharp U-turn, the sudden shift pressing her back into the seat.

If anything happened to Nina because of her...

Alex's stomach twisted. Nina was barely eighteen, still finding her footing at UA Little Rock, still young enough to believe the world could be fair if she tried hard enough. She had slipped into their lives so easily that Alex sometimes forgot there had been a time before her. The thought of whoever was hunting Alex turning their attention toward Nina sent a tight, aching pressure through her throat.

Fifteen minutes later, they pulled into the driveway just as an ambulance was pulling out. Nina sat on the front steps wrapped in a blanket, her bottom lip split open, her left eye swollen and purple. The moment she saw Alex, she broke into sobs.

Alex's breath caught. For a second she could not move. Seeing Nina like that felt like being punched in the chest. Nina was supposed to be safe in her home. She was supposed to be laughing in her kitchen, scolding Collin for stealing snacks and helping him with his homework. Not sitting on the steps shaken and bloody.

The thought that someone had done this because of Alex hit with a force that made her vision blur. She pushed forward and dropped to her knees, pulling Nina into a tight embrace.

Declan arrived seconds later.

"What happened here, officer?" Declan asked a patrol officer standing nearby, taking notes.

"Home invasion," the officer said grimly. "Mother, father, and boyfriend were tied up in the living room. Daughter was taken upstairs. Father appears to have had a heart attack. EMS revived him and are transporting him to University Hospital now."

Declan turned to Nina, voice gentler. "Nina, tell us what happened."

Alex held her tighter, fury simmering beneath her skin.

Nina took a shaky breath. "We were all sitting in the living room watching a movie when they walked through the front door. There were two of them—a man and a woman. Both had guns. They made us get on the ground. The woman kept her gun on us while the man tied up Mom, Dad, and Jeremy. When he got to me, he sat me up on the couch."

Alex felt her pulse spike. She braced herself.

"He held the gun to my head," Nina continued, voice trembling, "and started asking me where Collin was."

Alex's stomach lurched violently. They were not just after her. They were after her son. Her teeth clenched so hard she thought she might crack one.

"I told him I didn't know," Nina said. "I told him I was sick and couldn't watch him today. He asked who else babysits him. I told him Alyssa was the only other person I knew."

Alex's hands curled into fists. A cold, controlled fury rose beneath her skin, hotter than fear and sharper than panic. Someone had come looking for her child. The urge to act, to find whoever was behind these attacks and end them, pressed hard against her ribs.

Nina swallowed hard. "After that, he grabbed my arm and yanked me off the couch. He started pulling me toward the stairs."

Something inside Alex snapped. The word rage did not even come close. It was a dark, consuming heat that flooded her chest and made her vision tighten at the edges. She pressed her eyes shut for a moment, bracing herself for whatever Nina would say next.

"But before we got to the top," Nina said, "the woman yelled at him. She told him they didn't have time for whatever he was trying to do and that they needed to stay focused. He got mad—really mad—but he let go of me and turned back toward the living room."

Nina's voice wavered. "Jeremy must have thought it was his chance. He tried to get free. The woman warned him to stop, but he didn't listen. He lunged, and she shot him."

Alex sucked in a sharp breath.

Nina continued, "Dad must've panicked when he heard the gun. He started breathing weird, and then he just... collapsed. Mom was screaming. The man and woman ran out the front door right after that."

She wiped her eyes with the back of her hand. "Jeremy was bleeding pretty badly, but it was his shoulder, so I knew he'd probably be okay. I untied Mom next. When I got to Dad, he wasn't moving. I started CPR and Jeremy called 911."

"Do you remember anything distinctive about either of them?" Declan asked.

Nina thought for a second before she spoke, "The man had a serpent tattoo on his left forearm."

Alex stiffened.

Another ambulance pulled in. An EMT jogged over. "We need to get her to the hospital. You can question her more there."

They helped Nina onto the gurney. Alex squeezed her hand one last time before they wheeled her away.

When Nina was out of earshot, she turned to Declan, "The man who delivered the flowers to my work a couple of weeks ago had a serpent tattoo on his forearm too."

Declan rounded on her, anger radiating off him. "What the hell are you mixed up in?"

His tone wasn't cruel. It was sharp and scared and too close to breaking. Before she could answer, he was already dialing. Alex heard the line ring and felt a flicker of confusion. Who was he trying to reach?

"Fuck." He hung up and hit redial. Straight to voicemail.

"Fuck!" he shouted again, louder this time. He turned toward her, face pale and furious. "My mother isn't answering."

The words hit her like a blow.

A cold weight settled in her stomach.

Declan sprinted for the car, and Alex followed with her heart slamming against her ribs. She barely registered the slam of the door before he threw the car into reverse and tore out of the driveway. He was already on the phone, voice low and urgent, but she couldn't make out the words. The sound blurred into the roar of the engine and the pounding in her ears.

Her hands shook as she fumbled for her own phone. She called Katherine. No answer. She tried again, pressing the phone so hard to her ear it hurt. Still nothing. A cold, suffocating dread wrapped around her chest, squeezing tighter with every ring. Her thoughts scattered in every direction at once.

If they touched Collin—if they laid a hand on Katherine—she didn't know what she would do, only that she would not stop until every last one of them paid for it.

Declan reached over and took her hand. She hadn't noticed her breathing had gone ragged until he squeezed her fingers and told her to slow down, to breathe with him. She tried. The air scraped in and out of her lungs, uneven at first, then steadier as she forced herself to match his rhythm.

The rest of the drive blurred into a smear of headlights and sirens and the sickening churn of dread. She had no sense of time, only the relentless forward motion and the fear that they were already too late.

After what felt like a lifetime, the cottage finally came into view. Declan tore up the driveway, gravel spitting beneath the tires, and the cabin loomed ahead in complete darkness. No lights. No movement. No sign of anyone inside.

He slammed on the brakes at the top of the circle drive.

"Stay here while I—"

Alex was already out of the car, the door barely open before her feet hit the ground. The cold air knifed into her lungs as she sprinted toward the porch, her mind refusing to accept the stillness of the house. Every instinct screamed at her to move, to get inside, to find her son.

The front door stood wide open. The interior was swallowed in darkness, a heavy, unnatural kind of quiet that made the hair on Alex's arms rise. Something was wrong. Deeply, unmistakably wrong.

She sprinted toward the porch, but Declan caught her and jolted her to a halt.

"Alex! For the love of God, you are making it exceedingly difficult to keep you alive," he snapped, his teeth clenched so tight the words barely made it out.

An Alexander police officer stepped out of the cabin with a flashlight, the beam cutting through the dark. Declan released her and flashed his badge.

"The place is torn apart. No one's here," the officer said.

The words hit like a physical blow. Alex let out a raw, guttural cry and dropped to her knees. Her baby. They had taken her baby.

Then a sudden burst of light flooded the yard as the motion sensor clicked on. Alex blinked against it, heart pounding, and saw a figure moving across the field.

Katherine.

She was walking up from her own cabin down the hill.

Alex surged to her feet and ran, legs shaking, Declan and the officer close behind her.

"Katherine, where is Collin?" Alex gasped.

"He's asleep in my cabin."

Alex didn't wait for anything more. She bolted toward Katherine's place, lungs burning, terror and relief crashing together so hard it made her vision swim. Katherine hurried after her, calling out, asking if everything was okay, but the words barely registered. Alex reached the cabin first and stumbled inside, her heart in her throat.

Katherine and Declan followed a moment later. Alex was already on the floor, cradling Collin's sleeping head in her lap, her fingers trembling as they threaded through his hair. Silent tears streamed down her cheeks.

"We went fishing at the pond after I picked him up," Katherine said, breathless from the run. "He said his stomach hurt, so I took him to my cabin. I had some Zofran. I was making him chamomile tea when he fell asleep on the couch. I must have dozed off watching NCIS. When I woke up, I saw lights up at your cabin and came to check."

Declan finished speaking with the officer outside before closing the door behind him. He took the high-backed chair across from her, his expression carved into something grim and unreadable. The weight of it settled heavily in the room.

"I think we need to talk," he said quietly.

Katherine hesitated in the doorway, her eyes soft with worry. "I'll let you two have a minute," she murmured before slipping down the hall, leaving Alex alone with the man who had just watched her world nearly fall apart.

The moment Katherine disappeared down the hall, Declan's entire demeanor shifted. Whatever patience he'd been holding onto evaporated, leaving something harder in its place. The fear, the adrenaline, the near-loss of Collin and his mother had burned through him, stripping him down to an exhausted, pissed-off man held together by sheer force of will.

"Look at your phone," he said. "I sent you a text earlier."

Alex wiped her cheeks with the back of her hand and opened the message. A photo filled the screen.

"Why did you send me a picture of Brittany?"

"So that is the woman who took over your position at Enzo's farm?"

"Yes," she said slowly, confusion tightening her brow. "Why?"

"Brittany is Martha's daughter. Martha had just returned from visiting her up in New Hampshire when she was killed."

Alex blinked, stunned. "I... I didn't know she had a daughter. She never mentioned Brittany."

Declan nodded, jaw tight. "It's a connection we can't ignore. Someone involved in all this is tied to your past."

"Could Brittany be the woman who attacked Nina and her family?" Alex asked.

"She said it was an older woman. Blonde. Could've been a disguise, but I doubt it."

Katherine reentered the room, but Declan didn't look away from Alex. His voice rose, firm and commanding, the tone of someone who had already made up his mind.

"It isn't safe here. We need to move. We're going to the station. Everyone. Mom, pack a bag."

He didn't wait for a response. He turned back to Alex, already shifting into motion.

"Call Alyssa and Dean. Tell them to meet us at the station. Nothing else over the phone. They could be listening. I'm going to run up to the cabin and pack us a couple of bags. I'll pull the car down in a minute."

Alex held Collin a little tighter, the weight of everything pressing down on her as Declan strode toward the door with a purpose that left no room for argument.

He reached for the door, then stopped. He turned back and locked eyes with her, and the air in the room seemed to tighten.

"What's on the flash drive, Alex?"

Her blood ran cold. "Declan, not now."

"Yes," he said, his voice hard and unyielding. "Right now."

Alex swallowed, her throat dry. Her thumb drifted to the flash drive on her key ring, the one she had carried like a secret for eight long years. Her last line of defense. Her last mistake.

"I downloaded files from Enzo's computer the night I left," she said quietly. "Inventory lists. Taxes. Bank information. Names. Anything I thought I could use as leverage to make him leave me alone."

Declan stared at her, stunned into stillness.

"I left him a note," she continued, her voice trembling despite her best effort to steady it. "I told him I had the files. And that as long as he left me alone, they would never see the light of day."

Declan closed his eyes, jaw clenched so tight it trembled. When he finally spoke, it was barely above a whisper.

"Jesus, Alex..."

"I was desperate," she whispered. "I didn't know what else to do."

Declan opened his eyes again, and something in his expression shifted. The fear was still there, but it had hardened into resolve. Whatever came next, he had already decided.

"I'm going to pack us a bag. We're leaving."

"Where are we going?" Alex asked.

"Somewhere they'll never find us," he said as he stepped out of the cabin.

They weren't supposed to find them here either. But they had.

Alex felt as though she had lived a hundred lives in the last two weeks. Exhaustion settled deep into her bones, a cold, dragging weight that made her limbs feel heavy. She was tired of running. Tired of reacting. Tired of pretending that the law alone could keep her and Collin safe.

One phone call could change everything. Eight years ago, she hadn't been ready to make it. But today, after they had come after her son, she knew she didn't have a choice anymore.

Katherine appeared in the living room with a duffel bag slung over her shoulder. She moved through the cabin with quiet purpose, checking windows, gathering essentials, making sure nothing important was left behind. The steadiness of it grounded Alex for a moment.

Alex pulled out her phone and dialed Alyssa. The conversation was short and tense, but Alyssa agreed to meet them at the station.

She nudged Collin gently.

"Hey, momma," he murmured sleepily, wrapping his arms around her neck.

She pressed her nose into his warm skin and breathed him in. "We're going on a surprise trip," she whispered with a smile she didn't feel.

Collin sat up and stretched. "Okay."

They stepped out of the cabin just as Declan pulled the car around. Alex climbed into the back with Collin while Katherine took the front seat. As they pulled away, FBI vehicles rolled up the drive. Declan slowed long enough to brief Agent McMurray on everything that had happened since the hospital.

The drive to the station passed in slow motion. Streetlights stretched into long gold smears across the wet windows, and raindrops splattered against the glass, slow at first, then gathering into a steady, heavy rush. Alex had always loved the rain. She loved curling up on the porch during summer storms with a book, listening to thunder roll across the hills. Rain usually made her feel free, as if the world was being washed clean.

Tonight, she felt anything but free. The storm outside only made the pressure inside her chest tighten. Every mile they drove felt like another reminder that nowhere was safe anymore. The darkness pressed in around the car, and the rhythmic thrum of the rain only amplified the fear she was trying to keep contained. She held Collin close, breathing in the warm, familiar scent of his hair, grounding herself in the one thing that still felt real.

When they pulled into the station parking lot, Alex was out of the car before it had fully stopped. She needed air. Space. Something to ground her before she shattered.

The wind whipped around her, pelting her with slushy rain. Each icy drop stung her skin, reminding her she was still alive. The cold cut through her clothes, but she barely felt it.

She drew in a long breath of winter air, letting it burn through her lungs. She tried to steady the storm inside her, tried to remember the version of herself who existed before tonight. The woman who believed she could outrun her past. The mother who thought she could keep her son safe by staying quiet.

But that woman felt far away now.

And the one she needed to become was already rising in her chest, forged from fear and fury and the knowledge that running was no longer enough.

Within an instant, Declan was beside her, shielding her with an umbrella. Her eyes locked with his, her chest heaving. His icy blue eyes battling their own war, mirroring the turbulent emotions that roiled within her. The stormy weather around them seemed almost symbolic of the tempest inside their hearts.

Declan steadied himself first. His large, warm hand closed around hers, as he guided them into the station. Katherine followed with Collin, who was happily chattering about how much fun he'd had fishing, blissfully unaware of the danger swirling around them.

Chapter Twenty-Six
ALEX

As they stepped into the lobby, Alex spotted Alyssa and Dean through the glass wall of a packed conference room. Several FBI agents lined the perimeter, arms crossed, expressions tight with irritation. Declan stopped at the front desk and asked the woman there to watch Collin for a moment. She nodded and lifted him into the chair beside her. Collin immediately launched into a stream of questions, his voice bright and innocent.

The two FBI agents who had questioned her over the weekend stood near the door beside another agent she didn't recognize. Bishop intercepted them the moment they stepped into the conference room, a folder tucked under his arm and a look on his face that made Alex's stomach dip.

"Got something you both need to see," he said, lowering his voice. "Surveillance from the hospital finally came through."

Declan stiffened beside her. "The flowers?"

"Yeah." Bishop flipped open the folder and slid a still frame across the table. A grainy image of a man in a baseball cap, head down, shoulders hunched. "Facial recognition hit on him this morning. Name's Alonzo DeLuca. Goes by Two-Face."

Alex's pulse kicked. "Two-Face?"

Bishop nodded. "Known associate of Enzo's. Low-level enforcer type. He's never been tied to anything big, but he's got a reputation for doing whatever he's told. No questions, no hesitation."

Guilt twisted in her gut. Nina had been hurt because of her.

Declan leaned in, jaw tightening. "Any priors?"

"Plenty," Bishop said. "But nothing sticks. And until today, we didn't have physical evidence placing him at any of the other crime scenes."

Alex swallowed. "Until today?"

Bishop pulled out another photo, this one clearer. "Nina's ring cam caught him and an older woman entering the house thirty minutes before the 911 call. Same build, same gait, same scar on the jawline. It's him."

Alex's breath hitched. "So he delivered the flowers... and he was at Nina's?"

"Yeah," Bishop closed the folder. "Whatever's going on, he's involved. How deep? We don't know yet. But he's not acting alone."

Declan's eyes narrowed. "Someone's pulling his strings."

Bishop shrugged, neither confirming or denying Declan's suspicions. "We'll get there."

Alex felt the room tilt, the truth settling like ice in her chest. Two-Face was no longer a shadow. He was real; he was close, and he had already crossed her path twice. If he was only the enforcer, then someone else was directing him. Someone smart enough to remain invisible.

She drew a steadying breath. "What about the older woman? The one with him."

Bishop slid another photo across the table. The woman's head was angled down, sunglasses hiding most of her face, a baseball cap shadowing the rest. But something about her—the posture, the sweep of her hair, the way she carried herself—

Alex's stomach tightened.

"I saw that woman that morning at the hotel," she said quietly. "She held my things while I opened the door. She was wearing the same cap and sunglasses then too. Something about her feels familiar, but I still can't place who she is."

Declan's attention snapped to her, his entire posture sharpening. Bishop's expression shifted as well, a flicker of concern breaking through his usual calm.

As frightening as Two-Face was, the idea of someone who could direct him and stay completely off the radar terrified her even more than having a name. And how did the woman fit into all this?

Declan gave her arm a squeeze, pulling her back to the moment, and then moved to the head of the table.

"Here's what we know," he began. "Conner Evans, thirty-eight, was brought into the emergency department earlier tonight. He was weak but responsive on arrival, then crashed fast. He was taken to Alex's room, but she was tied up with other patients, so Denise stepped in."

Alex's heartbeat kicked hard, a sharp, painful thud against her ribs.

"When the charge nurse cut his shirt open to begin CPR, a canister hidden under the fabric released a cloud of what we believe was aerosolized fentanyl. It incapacitated Denise and another nurse almost instantly. The room was sealed, the department evacuated, and in the middle of all that chaos, someone managed to get flowers to Alex. That tells us the attack was planned, coordinated, and timed to her exact location."

His jaw flexed, the only sign of how close he was to losing his composure.

"And they didn't stop there. As we were leaving the hospital, I spotted an explosive device under Alex's car. Whoever is behind this is escalating. Fast."

He turned to Bishop.

"The flowers were traced to Mary and Me Flower Shop on University Ave. You're there first thing in the morning.

Bishop nodded.

"Bomb squad confirmed the device was remotely activated," Declan said. "Whoever planted it was close enough to watch. They detonated it as the robot approached, likely to keep us from recovering evidence."

A ripple of unease moved through the room.

"While we were on our way back here, a call went out to Collin's babysitter's house. When we arrived, we found that two armed assailants had broken in and held the family at gunpoint. Nina was beaten. Her boyfriend was shot.

Her father had a heart attack from the stress. They were looking for Alex's son, who wasn't there."

Alex kept her eyes on the table, her throat tightening until she could barely swallow.

Declan lifted a sheet of paper. "The officer at the hospital sent over descriptions. Male, mid-thirties to early forties, five-nine to five-ten, around one-ninety, black hair, brown eyes. Female, mid-fifties to early sixties, bleach-blonde hair, five-five, around one-twenty."

Silence dropped over the room like a curtain.

Alex felt the weight of every stare, every breath, every unspoken question pressing in on her.

And she knew this was only the beginning.

Her heart stuttered as she remembered the woman from the hotel. Mid fifties. Bleach blonde hair. The same cold, assessing stare. Her pulse hammered. Declan's gaze flicked toward her, but he kept talking.

"Jeremy from the stables checked out. He was at work during the attempted abduction. Security footage confirms it."

Stewart spoke up from the corner. "And for what it's worth, a man and a woman working together does not fit the profile of a stalker. That kind of offender acts alone."

Declan nodded. "Exactly. Which brings us to what we found this afternoon."

Stewart continued, flipping through a thin folder. "We cross-referenced the last six months of Alex's ER shifts. Looked for repeat visitors, anyone who might have fixated on her. There were a few patients she saw more than once, but every single one of them checked out. No red flags. No patterns. Nothing that fits."

She closed the folder with a soft snap. "So we are operating under the assumption that this is connected to the Moretti crime family. Someone who worked under Enzo. Or someone who works under Moretti now."

Alex's stomach dropped.

Declan turned his attention to Alyssa. "Since these attacks have failed to kill Alex, they've started lashing out at her through her loved ones. It's possible you could be their next target. That's why we asked you here tonight. Until this is resolved, you and Luke need to lie low. It's safe to assume they already know about you."

He gestured to Dean. "Your place is no longer considered safe. Do you have anywhere else you can go?"

Alyssa exchanged a look with Dean. "We've been talking about going to California so he can meet my family. We could stay with my parents for a while."

Dean nodded. It wasn't the perfect solution, but it was far enough away from Alex to be safe for a few days.

"Perfect," Declan said. "You also need to lose the cell phones for a while."

He held out a basket.

Alyssa and Dean hesitated, then dropped their phones inside. Bishop handed them each a burner.

"All of us need to ditch the phones," Declan added, looking at Alex and Katherine.

Alex reluctantly placed hers in the basket. Katherine sighed heavily and followed suit. Bishop handed them both new burners.

"Use them only if necessary. Everyone's new numbers are already saved. I'll send updates as the case moves forward."

Declan waited until the room settled, then turned to Alex.

"Alex," Declan said quietly, "I need the flash drive."

Her breath caught. For a moment, she didn't move. Then she reached into her pocket and pulled out the small metal drive she had carried for eight years, the one that had felt like both a shield and a curse. Her fingers trembled as she placed it in his hand.

Declan closed his fingers around it and straightened. Without another word, he crossed the room to Agent Stewart, who had been watching from the corner with a stillness that made Alex uneasy. Declan spoke to her in a low voice, too soft for anyone else to hear. Stewart's expression shifted as she listened—curiosity first, then shock, then something far more serious.

She nodded once.

Declan handed her the flash drive.

Stewart slipped it into an evidence bag and tucked it inside her jacket. Her posture changed immediately, shoulders tightening, attention sharpening, as if the weight of that tiny device had just altered the entire direction of the investigation.

She had handed over the last bit of control she'd been clinging to, the final thread tying her to the choices she made the night she ran. Whatever happened next—whatever storm this unleashed—was no longer hers to manage or contain.

She was so lost in studying the hard lines of Declan's face that she didn't hear Bishop approach.

"He can be a bit prickly sometimes," Bishop murmured, stopping beside her, "but he's a softy underneath all that gruff exterior."

Alex wasn't sure she believed that anymore. She'd seen glimpses of something gentler in him—moments he probably hadn't meant her to notice—but he still kept her at arm's length. She couldn't tell if he was protecting her... or himself.

Bishop followed her gaze to Declan, his expression softening. "I was his partner during his divorce. That woman put him through hell. Used his kids as leverage, dragged the process out for years. It nearly broke him." He shook his head. "He doesn't trust easily, and he sure as hell doesn't let people close. But once he's loyal to someone? There's nothing he wouldn't do to protect them."

Alex swallowed hard. She didn't know what to do with that—what it meant for her, for the way Declan looked at her like she was both a responsibility and a threat to his sanity. She knew little about his ex—just the bare bones he'd shared in passing—but even that hadn't painted a flattering picture. She'd been so consumed with the threat circling her, with her own past clawing at her heels, that she hadn't stopped to consider the weight he carried too. The scars he didn't talk about. The ones that shaped every guarded look, every clipped word, every step he took between her and danger.

He wasn't cold.

He was wounded.

And he was still trying.

Bishop's voice dropped, gentler than she'd ever heard it. "I see the way he looks at you when he thinks no one's watching. He's fighting a battle he already lost. The only two people who don't know it yet are you and him."

Her breath caught. Heat curled low in her chest—fear, hope, something she wasn't ready to name. She drew a slow breath and met Bishop's eyes. "I'm not here to hurt him," she said quietly. "Whatever this is... I won't be careless with it."

Bishop studied her for a beat, then nodded—just once, as if he'd been waiting for that exact answer. Then he stepped away, giving her space.

Alex turned her attention back to Declan.

He stood rigid across the room, shoulders tight, jaw working as he spoke to Agent Stewart. Whatever he'd told her had shifted something—she could see it in the way Stewart's posture sharpened, in the way Declan's hand flexed at his side like he was bracing for impact.

Her future lay in the hands of the FBI now.

And there was no taking it back.

Chapter Twenty-Seven
DECLAN

Declan was just turning to leave when Agent Stewart's hand shot out and caught his sleeve. The touch was quick, almost surgical, and it stopped him mid-stride. He turned slowly, his expression sharpening as he faced her.

"Detective Wallace," she said, letting go as if the contact had never happened. "We found something else of interest while searching the cabin."

Her voice was calm, but her eyes told a different story. There was a flicker of intent behind them, a quiet calculation that made the air feel heavier.

"Something about Mr. Esposito's offshore bank account information. On your laptop."

Declan went still. A faint muscle jumped in his cheek, the only sign that her words had hit their mark. He didn't speak. He didn't look away. He simply held her gaze, and the silence stretched long enough for the room to feel colder.

Stewart watched him with the patience of someone who enjoyed watching reactions unfold. Her chin lifted a fraction, not quite a challenge, but close.

"Last I checked," she said, "hacking into a bank is a federal offense under the Computer Fraud and Abuse Act."

Declan's fingers curled at his sides.

"What do you want?" he asked. His voice was quiet, but something in it shifted the air. Stewart's confidence wavered for a heartbeat. Her chin dipped before she caught herself, and the steady focus in her eyes flickered.

Stewart regained her composure quickly and stepped closer. Not enough to invade his space, but enough that he could see the faint tightening at the corner of her eye, the subtle shift in her breathing.

"If I intended to arrest you," she said, "we wouldn't be having this conversation."

Declan's patience for this conversation was coming to an end.

Stewart cocked an eyebrow. "We are forming a task force for this case. It is bigger than anyone thought. We need someone with your tech skills on our team." Her voice stayed even, but there was a faint shift in her posture, as if she were bracing for his reaction.

A humorless laugh tore from his chest. "It'll be a cold day in hell before I work for the FBI."

She shrugged. "Suit yourself. I guess we'll just have to arrest you then."

Declan stepped in until he was inches from her face. To her credit, she didn't flinch. Or shrink back from him as he towered over her.

"My computer locks automatically after five minutes of inactivity," he said, voice like ice. "Which means you accessed it. Without a warrant. Violating my Fourth Amendment rights against unreasonable search and seizure. I was never a suspect. You had no probable cause to access my computer."

He lifted his wrists, daring her. "Go ahead. Cuff me."

For a long moment, they stared at one another. Then Stewart broke eye contact and stepped back.

"That's what I thought," Declan said. "Don't fucking threaten me again."

He turned to leave but stopped after two steps. The pause felt heavy, as if the air itself resisted what he was about to do. He hated the words forming in his throat.

He looked over his shoulder without turning around.

"Just. This. Case."

He could feel Stewart's triumphant smile burning into his back. His irritation flared as he turned back to face her.

"And since I'll be back in the field," he added, "you're going to arrange a protective detail for them. They don't go anywhere alone."

Stewart nodded once. "Already in motion."

Declan didn't thank her. He didn't trust her or the FBI, but he needed the jurisdiction and manpower. For now, he would do what needed to be done.

He turned to walk back toward Alex and his mother when Stewart spoke again.

"One more thing, Detective." She stepped closer, lowering her voice. "I've secured a safehouse for them tonight. Full protection. Secure location. Twenty-four seven guards."

Declan let out a humorless breath. "No."

Stewart blinked. "No?"

"An unusually high number of people get killed in FBI safe houses," he said flatly. "I'm not putting people I care about in one of your death traps."

Her jaw tightened, but she didn't argue.

"I have a place," Declan continued. He pulled a small notepad from his pocket, scribbled an address, tore off the page, and handed it to her. "Two agents. Rotating shifts. Starting tomorrow morning."

Stewart took the paper, her eyes flicking over the address.

"And Stewart," Declan added quietly, his tone shifting. "I'm choosing to trust you with this. Keep the location off the record. No reports, no logs, nothing digital. The two officers on rotation are the only other people who get this address."

She nodded once, understanding the weight of what he was giving her. He might sound paranoid, but very few people knew about the cabin. There were no paper trails connecting him or Alex to the location, which left another option. The thought settled in his chest like a stone, cold and unwelcome.

There was a mole.

"The place has been unused for years. See if you can get the power and water restored as soon as you can," Declan said. He didn't expect miracles; getting utilities back on tonight was a long shot.

"I'll see what I can do," she said as her eyes flickered to the paper.

As she folded the slip of paper, Detective Martin approached, curiosity written across his face. His gaze dipped to the note in Stewart's hand before he looked between the two of them, clearly sensing something he wasn't meant to be part of.

"Everything alright here?" Martin asked. His tone was casual, but his eyes were sharp.

"Just logistics," Declan said, his voice clipped. "We're done."

Stewart tucked the paper into her jacket. "We'll have your detail in place by 0800."

Declan gave a curt nod and walked away, feeling both of their eyes on his back as he headed toward Alex and his mother.

Alex was saying goodbye to Alyssa and Dean, exhaustion etched into every line of her face. The fluorescent lights overhead washed her out, making the dark circles beneath her eyes look even deeper. She looked like someone who had been holding herself together by sheer force of will.

"Bug-out house?" Katherine asked as Declan approached.

"Yup," he nodded.

"Bug-out house?" Alex echoed.

"I told you things weren't good in my house growing up," Declan said, voice dropping. "It wasn't just my brother and me who took the hits. My mom... she carried her share too."

He exhaled slowly. "When I was five—maybe six—she grabbed us and disappeared. We stayed gone almost a year. This place was where we hid. Only the three of us ever knew about it."

"I put the deed in my sister's name," Katherine added with a small chuckle. "She still lives in Germany. Never even been to the U.S., but she's a proud landowner."

"Where is it?" Alex asked.

"I'd rather not say out loud… just in case." Declan's eyes swept the room, instinctively assessing every corner.

He exhaled slowly, jaw tightening. "Only a handful of people even know where Alex and I have been staying. I kept that cabin off every report, every log. There is no paper trail, no digital footprint, nothing anyone could use to track us there."

Alex did not speak. She did not have to. Declan saw the way her shoulders tightened and the way her fingers curled against her thigh. It was almost as if she had been expecting this.

"I need to call my parents and warn them before we leave," Alex said.

"You should do it from your regular phone," Declan replied, rummaging through the basket of confiscated devices. "If they're monitoring your parents' phones, they can't trace the burner." He finally fished out her iPhone and handed it over.

"My mom never told my dad any of this," Alex murmured with a nervous laugh. "We worried he'd try to confront Enzo—or use him for target practice."

She stepped away to make the call.

Katherine turned to her son. "How are you holding up?"

Declan exhaled a long, heavy breath. "I wanna kill this bastard."

"You're not staying with us, are you?" Katherine asked, her voice warm but resigned. She'd seen that look in her son before. Once he committed to something, there was no pulling him away, especially now.

"No," he admitted. "I'll stay tonight and help you get settled tomorrow. But I already booked a flight from Nashville to Manchester, New Hampshire for tomorrow afternoon." He'd planned to go regardless of jurisdiction. The FBI's offer had simply cleared the murky waters he'd been wading through.

Alex slipped back into the conference room. "Did everything go okay?" Declan asked.

"Yeah. Mom's scared and wants me to come home. I told her about you and that we were going somewhere safe. She has a sister in New York—she and Dad are going to stay with her until this is over."

They headed to the lobby and collected Collin, who was happily chatting with the woman at the front desk. Martin had made his way back outside and was leaning against a black Chrysler minivan. He tossed Declan the keys.

"I had my brother-in-law rent this for you. Also, Amtrak sent over the footage you requested." Martin handed him the keys and a flash drive. "Safe travels."

"Thanks, Martin." Declan clicked the unlock button and moved quickly, transferring their bags from the unmarked car into the van.

Alex and Collin settled into the captain's chairs. Collin immediately spotted the built-in screen.

"Mom! Look! This van is awesome! You wanna watch a movie with me?"

"Of course," Alex said, softly. "Let's pick one out."

They were still scrolling through options when Declan pulled into the First Security Bank parking lot. He parked far from the ATM, stepped out into the cold night, and walked over to the machine.

He was back a minute later.

"No more cards until this is over," Declan said, dropping a thick wad of cash into the center console.

Alex nodded. Collin had already picked the movie Cars, the opening credits glowing across the screen.

"Mom, I'm hungry. We haven't had dinner yet," Collin said, leaning toward her.

Declan heard Collin pipe up from the backseat and glanced at the boy in the mirror. "McDonald's?" he offered, catching Alex's eyes in the reflection.

She didn't say anything at first, just gave a small, tired nod that told him enough. Today wasn't the day for rules or routines.

"Yeah!" Collin shouted.

"McDonald's it is," Alex said, managing a faint smile.

"Can I get a milkshake, Mom?" Collin asked.

"Yes, you can have a milkshake. I think I'll get one too."

"Me too," Declan and Katherine said at the same time.

Alex muttered something about hoping they found a McDonald's with a working ice cream machine. Declan huffed a quiet laugh, and even Katherine cracked a smile.

Ten minutes later, Katherine was handing out food bags while Declan merged onto I-40 East toward Memphis. The smell of fries filled the SUV, and the brief normalcy of it settled the tension in his shoulders a fraction.

"I know you didn't want to tell me where we were going," Alex said from the passenger seat, "but can you tell me how long the ride is?"

"I can tell you now," Declan replied. "We're going to Cottage Grove, Tennessee."

"Never heard of it."

"Few people have," Katherine said. "Tiny town near Paris. The population is probably under a hundred."

"It's about a four-and-a-half-hour drive," Declan added, taking a sip of his Coke. "Get comfy."

In the mirror, he saw Collin fully absorbed in his movie, milkshake in hand. Alex finished her fries and leaned her head back, her posture loosening as the adrenaline finally bled out of her system. Her eyes drifted shut, her breathing evening out within minutes.

Declan kept his hands steady on the wheel, watching the road stretch ahead while the car grew quiet around him. She didn't stand a chance against the exhaustion pulling her under, and he didn't blame her. Not after the day she'd had.

He adjusted the mirror just enough to keep her in view, then focused on the highway and the long drive ahead.

Alex

Alex startled awake. For a moment she had no idea where she was. The car was stopped, flooded with harsh white light from a parking lot lamp. Declan and Katherine were nowhere in sight.

Her heart lurched—until she spun around and saw Collin, still sound asleep in his seat, his little chest rising and falling in a steady rhythm.

She pushed her seat upright and blinked at her surroundings. Wal-Mart. Katherine and Declan were walking back toward the van, a buggy overflowing with bags between them.

The rear door opened, and Declan began unloading the haul. He noticed her stirring, phone pressed between his shoulder and ear as he shifted a bag to his other hand.

"Alright, buddy," he said softly, a warmth in his voice she rarely heard. "I love you. I'll see you soon. Listen to your mom and behave yourself."

A tiny pause, then a quiet chuckle. "Yeah, I know. I miss you too."

He ended the call and put the phone in his pocket, his expression tightening as he reached for another bag.

Alex's chest pulled tight. The threat she'd dragged into his life had kept him away from his kids. Every hour he spent protecting her was an hour stolen from them. The all too familiar guilt settled low in her stomach. She hadn't meant to upend his world, but that didn't change the fact that she had.

"Hey," he said in a hushed tone. "We're about forty minutes from the house, but this is the closest shopping center. We grabbed groceries, toiletries, and a few essentials."

He shut the back and headed off to return the buggy. Katherine climbed into the passenger seat, looking bone-tired.

As if sensing Alex's guilt, Katherine offered a soft smile. "I had to stay awake. Last time Declan was here, he was ten. He didn't remember how to get here."

Alex managed a small smile, though the awkward weight of everything she'd dragged them into pressed heavily on her chest. She scrolled through Netflix and put on the latest episode of Lost in Space. Declan heard the intro as he climbed back into the driver's seat.

"Turn it up," he said.

Alex watched him through the rearview mirror, silently begging him to meet her eyes. After a few minutes, he did—just briefly. His expression was unreadable, distant. It made something inside her twist.

She tore her gaze away and forced herself to focus on the screen.

Forty-five minutes later, they turned onto a long dirt drive. Alex leaned forward, peering out the windshield as the house came into view—a small cape-style home, white with hunter-green shutters and a wraparound porch. It looked surprisingly well-kept.

"When was the last time anyone's been here?" Alex asked.

"About twenty years," Katherine replied. "I pay the neighbor to mow the lawn and keep an eye on the place."

Alex glanced left and saw the faint silhouette of the neighboring house. Declan cut the engine. The interior lights flicked on as the front doors opened, waking Collin with a sleepy groan.

"You guys start taking the dust covers off everything," Declan said, opening the rear door. "I'll bring in the bags."

As Alex stepped out, she noticed the SUV that had followed them down the drive. She shot Declan a questioning look.

"FBI insisted on a security detail," he said with a shrug. "Under the circumstances, it's not the worst idea."

Oddly, it made her feel safer. Not because she doubted Declan—she didn't—but because even he needed sleep.

She and Collin followed Katherine inside. Katherine tried the light switch, and after a hesitant flicker, the bulbs warmed to life. She set her purse on the counter, relief softening her shoulders.

Declan stepped through the doorway a moment later, eyes lifting to the glowing fixtures. "Well, I'll be damned," he murmured. "Stewart actually came through."

The house was small and quaint: a round table to the left, a compact kitchen to the right, and a cozy living room straight ahead with a stone fireplace that looked like it hadn't seen a fire in decades.

"The master bedroom's this way," Katherine said, leading them through the kitchen. She flicked on another switch, and the overhead light buzzed before settling into a steady glow. "The master bath is through there." She pointed to a door on the left. "Why don't you take the dust covers off everything in here? Collin and I will get the other room ready. There are bunk beds. He and I will stay there, and you and Declan can stay here."

She turned to Collin with a grin. "What do you say, kiddo? Wanna have a sleepover with old Granny?"

Collin shrugged. "Sure." He trotted after her across the house toward the other bedroom.

Alex pulled the dust cover off the bed, folded it neatly, and set it in the corner. She did the same with the one draped over the chair. For a place untouched in twenty years, the house was surprisingly well kept—quiet, still, almost suspended in time.

She heard Declan drop the second load of bags on the kitchen counter and stepped out to help unload.

Declan was heading back toward the door when she rounded the corner.

"Do you want some help grabbing the rest?" Alex asked.

"Nope. I got it." His tone was clipped, and he disappeared into the night before she could respond.

The shift in him hurt more than she wanted to admit. She craved the safety of his arms, the calm he'd given her when everything else was falling apart. He'd withdrawn from her, and she didn't blame him. She'd blown into his life like a storm, upending everything he touched. She'd become one more mess for him to manage.

Exhaustion pressed into her bones. She swiped away a tear before it could fall and forced a steady breath.

She put the groceries away, trying to focus on the simple motions. Declan had picked up all of Collin's favorite snacks—a small kindness that made her chest ache.

The door opened again, and Declan came in with the luggage, shutting it behind him with a tired nudge of his boot. Katherine and Collin stepped out of the other bedroom a moment later, the house settling into a quiet rhythm around them.

"Momma! There are bunk beds in there and I'm gonna sleep on the top!" Collin announced, practically vibrating with excitement.

Alex smiled. "Just be careful climbing up and down, okay?" Coordination had never been his strong suit.

Katherine stepped forward and grabbed their bags. "Well, I don't know about y'all, but I'm exhausted. Let's go to bed, Collin."

Collin hugged Alex tightly. "Goodnight, Momma." Then he followed Katherine down the hall.

Declan locked the front door, the deadbolt clicking into place. Without a word, he bent for the remaining luggage and headed toward the master bedroom. Alex watched his back as he walked away, a heaviness settling in her chest. The distance he was putting between them felt like a widening chasm, and she couldn't shake the fear that she'd lost him before she ever truly had him.

She hesitated in the entryway, fingers brushing nervously against her thigh, unsure if following him would make things better or worse. But standing there alone felt worse, so she forced her feet to move.

The bedroom was dark when she stepped inside, and for a moment she couldn't see him at all. The shadows swallowed everything, including whatever welcome she hoped might still be there. She hovered for a split second in the doorway before stepping inside.

"I can sleep on the couch if you'd prefer to be alone—"

Alex's words died as he pushed her back against the door, slamming it shut behind her. His mouth crashed onto hers, hard and hungry. Relief flooded her so fast it made her knees go weak. She wrapped her arms around his neck as he lifted her, pinning her between his body and the door.

Declan broke the kiss just long enough to breathe. "I most certainly would not prefer to be alone."

His mouth found hers again as he backed her across the room, navigating the darkness as if he'd memorized every inch of it. The world narrowed to heat and hands and the desperate way he pulled her closer, as if he'd been starving for her.

They hit the bed in a tangle of limbs and need. Clothes vanished—she couldn't have said who moved first, only that the cool air on her skin made her gasp. His hands were everywhere, rough with urgency, reverent in the way they traced her. She felt the hard press of him beneath her, the unmistakable proof of how badly he wanted her, and relief surged through her so fiercely it almost hurt.

Alex broke the kiss, fingers sliding into his hair as she searched his face. For a heartbeat, raw emotion flickered there—want, fear, something deeper she couldn't name—before he shuttered it away behind that familiar mask.

Alex wasn't letting him retreat into it this time. Not when she finally had him close, not when his touch felt like the only solid thing in her world. She reached for him, guiding him back to her with a certainty born of need, pulling him into the space where their bodies fit perfectly together. Her hand slid between them and gripped his length as she guided him into her. Her other hand slid into his hair as she kissed him hard, refusing to give him even an inch of distance.

She rode him frantically, needing him like she needed air. He grasped her by the hips and slowed her pace. Her nipples brushed up against his chest hair, sending shockwaves through her body. A small moan escaped her lips. In one smooth motion, Declan thrust his right hip forward, throwing her off stride, and flipped her onto her back. He rose to his knees and threw her legs over his shoulders, lifting her bottom off the bed. His finger traced the small teardrop birthmark on her inner thigh. He bent forward and kissed it before he thrust back into her.

A loud moan escaped her lips. Declan quickly smothered it with his hand.

"Shh... Don't want Collin to think I'm making you cry again." He smirked.

Alex bit his hand before he could remove it from her mouth, earning her a hard smack on the ass. She didn't want to think about Collin, or Katherine, or anything other than the man inside her.

She clenched herself around him. His smirk vanished instantly as a low growl sounded in his throat. He slammed into her hard as she arched against him. The ache in her lower abdomen grew as he picked up the pace again. She buried her face in her pillow, muffling her cries as pleasure erupted throughout her body. She threw her head back as wave after wave washed over her.

Declan groaned and stiffened as he found his own release a moment later. Alex felt the last few pulses of his orgasm before he collapsed on the bed beside her. She curled into him, resting her head in the crook of his arm. His breathing slowed beneath her cheek, the tension easing from his body until she knew he'd slipped into sleep. She wasn't there yet—her pulse was still humming, her mind still spinning.

The truth crept in quietly, unsettling in its clarity: she was falling in love with him. The thought made her chest tighten, and she pushed it aside before it could take root. Instead, she tucked herself closer, letting the warmth of the bed and the steady rise and fall of his chest pull her under.

For now, they were safe. They were together. And that was enough.

Chapter Twenty-Eight
ALEX

Alex woke the next morning to the sound of Collin's laughter and the warm, buttery smell of pancakes. The blanket slid off her as she stretched, reminding her she was still naked. She dressed quickly in jeans and a T-shirt, brushed her teeth, splashed cold water on her face, and scraped her hair into a messy bun before heading toward the kitchen.

Declan, Katherine, and Collin were already at the table, plates full. The soft scrape of forks against ceramic and the low murmur of their conversation filled the kitchen. Collin spotted her first, his face brightening as he lifted his head.

"Good morning, Mom!" he shouted, launching himself from his chair and into her arms.

"Good morning, honey. Did you sleep well?"

"Yeah! I really like bunk beds. Do you think I can get one at home?"

Alex smiled. "I'll think about it."

She slid into the chair beside Declan and reached for a plate. "This looks delicious."

She added a couple of pancakes and took a grateful bite.

"Coffee?" Declan asked.

"Yes, please."

A moment later, he set a steaming mug beside her before sitting down again.

"Declan said we're doing target practice today, Mom," Collin announced proudly.

Alex turned to Declan, eyebrows raised. "Oh?"

"Yeah," he said. "I'll feel a lot more comfortable leaving knowing you know how to handle a gun."

Her heart lurched. She swallowed hard, pushing down the sudden rise of fear.

"You're leaving? Where are you going?" Her voice came out higher than she intended.

"I have a late-afternoon flight into Manchester," Declan said, standing from the table.

"You're still working on the case?" she asked, though she already knew the answer.

"Yes. If we wait for the Federal Bureau of Ineptitude to close this thing, we may as well enter witness protection. They march to the beat of their own drum. Urgency isn't in their vocabulary."

Alex took a sip of coffee, trying to smother the urge to argue. She wanted him here, with them, where she could see him and know he was safe. The thought of him going out alone tightened something low in her stomach. If anything happened to him—if he didn't come back—she wasn't sure how she'd survive it.

But she knew he was right. He had skin in the game, and he'd move faster than the Bureau ever would. Logic didn't quiet the fear, though. She pressed her thumb against the rim of the mug, grounding herself, forcing her breathing steady so he wouldn't see how much she was unraveling inside.

She heard him rummaging in the utility room. A moment later, he emerged holding a small kids' bow and arrow set.

"Look what I found!"

Katherine laughed. "Time just rolled back thirty years. He and Josh would shoot that thing for hours. We didn't have cable or internet the first time we came here, so they had to entertain themselves. They fought over that thing like cats and dogs. I could only afford one back then—working part-time at the diner while the boys were in school. But from what I re-member, you were a pretty excellent shot."

"Still am," Declan said. "You know where the old target went?"

Katherine's brows tugged in the middle. "I think I stuck it in the attic last time I was here."

Declan crossed the living room, opened a small door in the back corner, and disappeared up the stairs. A few minutes later, he reappeared holding a faded but intact target.

He grinned at Collin, "You wanna learn how to shoot this thing?"

"Yeah!" Collin jumped up from the table and ran to Declan.

Declan bent down and whispered something in his ear.

"Mom, is it okay if Declan teaches me how to shoot the bow?" Collin asked, practically vibrating with excitement.

"Yes—just be careful."

They all headed out the back door. Katherine and Alex settled onto the deck while Collin learned to shoot, Declan patiently adjusting his stance and grip. After a few rounds, Declan motioned for Alex to join them.

He walked to the old target, set it aside, and pulled a rolled-up paper plate from his back pocket. At a large mound of earth—clearly bulldozed into a pile years ago—he snapped a twig from a nearby branch, stabbed it through the plate, and anchored it into the hill. Then he returned to Alex.

Declan drew the nine-millimeter from his waistband.

"Okay. This is a nine-millimeter. Easy gun to learn on. This button ejects the clip." He demonstrated—clip out, clip in, rack. Smooth, practiced.

"Now there's one in the chamber. It's ready to fire once you take the safety off." He handed her the gun.

"The safety's right there," he said, pointing. Alex flipped it off.

"Red is dead," Declan reminded her, tapping the exposed red dot.

Alex nodded, playing along as he stepped behind her.

"See the sights on top?" he said, pointing. "Put whatever you're aiming at right between them. Then gently squeeze the trigger."

He adjusted her grip, her stance, then stepped back.

"Alright. Take aim. Breath in... breath out... and at the end of your exhale, pull the trigger."

Declan couldn't see the mischievous grin tugging at her lips.

Alex inhaled, exhaled, and squeezed.

The first shot hit dead center.

The second snapped the twig clean in half, sending the plate spinning into the air.

Alex fired twice more—each round punching the plate mid-flight. She flicked the safety on, tucked the gun into her waistband, and turned to face him.

Declan stood with his arms crossed, staring at her.

"Okay," he drawled. "Clearly you've shot a gun before."

Alex giggled. "Maybe you missed the part where I was in the Air Force?"

"I didn't think they taught you much about firearms in the chair force," Declan teased, eyebrow raised, waiting to see if she'd bite.

"I'll have you know I could disassemble and reassemble my M16 in forty-four seconds. I made marksman in basic. But you're right—that was the extent of our training. My dad taught me to shoot when I was eight."

Katherine cackled from the deck.

"That's enough out of you, old lady. Why don't you come down here and try it?" Declan called over his shoulder.

"Nah, I'm good," Katherine said, taking a drag of her Virginia Slim 120. "I'll stick with my trusty baseball bat. With her aim, I doubt anyone's getting past her."

Declan checked his watch and sighed. Ten thirty. His flight was at three, and Nashville was over two hours away.

Right on cue, a horn honked from the front of the house.

"That would be my ride," Declan said, turning toward Alex.

Her breath caught. She fought the urge to beg him to stay. She hadn't realized how shaken she still was until this moment.

"You two go on in," Katherine said, stepping off the deck. "Collin and I are going to practice some more with this bow." She hugged Declan tightly. "Be careful up there, son."

"I will. Bye, Mom."

Declan took Alex's hand and guided her inside. At the door, he drew her into a tight embrace, his arms firm around her, his breath warm against her hair. It was steadying... and tinged with a reluctance that said he wished he didn't have to pull away at all.

"I want you to have that gun on you at all times," he murmured against her hair. "And keep your head on a swivel."

"I will," she promised.

Her heart was already pounding at the thought of him walking out that door.

Declan eased back, cupping her face for a moment before pressing a soft kiss to her forehead. Then he bent to grab his duffel.

"I wish you weren't leaving," Alex whispered.

"I wish I wasn't either." He paused, searching her face like he was memorizing it. "I'm going to find whoever is responsible for these attacks."

"I know," she breathed, burying her face in his chest, clinging to the warmth she'd lose in seconds.

"I won't be gone long. I'll text when I land." He kissed her one last time—slow, lingering—before stepping through the open door.

Alex stood in the doorway as he loaded his bag into the trunk. He turned, gave her a small wave, and climbed into the back seat.

"See ya soon!"

"See you soon," she echoed, forcing a smile she didn't feel.

But dread coiled in her stomach, cold and certain. She didn't know why, but the fear that she'd never see him again settled deep, refusing to be shaken loose.

When the car disappeared down the long dirt drive, she stepped back inside and closed the door, the quiet of the house pressing in around her.

She forced herself to focus on something—anything—that didn't involve imagining Declan disappearing into danger. School was as good a place to start as any. She needed to check her coursework, send a few emails, pretend she still had a normal life waiting for her.

Collin and Katherine were on their way back inside. Alex drifted toward the attic door, searching for a quiet place to work. Pulling it open revealed a steep set of old wooden stairs leading into a cobweb-infested finished attic. She grabbed cleaning supplies from under the sink, a roll of paper towels, and a duster from the utility room before heading up.

At the top of the stairs, she almost turned around. The space was a disaster—dust, boxes, forgotten furniture. But she needed something to keep her mind off Declan. Busy was better than spiraling.

Two hours later, she descended the stairs feeling accomplished. She'd moved all the storage boxes to one side and cleaned the other half. She'd found an old table that would work as a desk and a small three-shelf bookcase that fit perfectly against the half wall. All she needed now was a chair and a lamp.

Collin sat at the kitchen table eating chicken nuggets. Katherine sat across from him—and beside her, with his back to Alex, was an older gentleman. The moment he spoke, the Italian lilt in his voice made her freeze. Panic surged through her, sharp and immediate. Her hand slipped toward the gun at her waistband on instinct.

Katherine spotted her before she could draw.

"Alex! This is Tony. He lives next door."

The man turned with a warm smile and rose to greet her. "Hello."

Alex forced her hand away from the weapon and took his instead. "Nice to meet you."

"What were you doing up there?" Katherine asked.

"I was cleaning the attic and setting up a little office so I can do my schoolwork. I need a chair and a lamp. Are there any furniture stores around here?"

"There's an antique mall a couple of towns over," Tony said. "They usually have interesting stuff."

"You wanna go into town?" Alex asked Katherine.

"Sure. It'll be nice to see my old stomping grounds."

"Well, I'll leave you ladies to it," Tony said, heading for the door.

Katherine walked him out, and Alex couldn't help noticing the faint flush on her cheeks and the nervous energy buzzing around her like static. A small smirk tugged at Alex's mouth as she watched them go.

Twenty minutes later, they pulled up to McKenzie's Antique Mall—a white building with bold red letters. It reminded Alex of the flea market she used to visit with her mom. Inside, the sheer amount of stuff crammed into every aisle was overwhelming.

Katherine grabbed a cart, and they started down the first row.

Alex spotted several lamps immediately. One in particular caught her eye, a handmade Victorian-style piece with a lace shade and dangling tassels. It reminded her of the lamps in her grandmother's barn-dominium, the ones that glowed softly in the evenings while she spent weekends and summers riding horses with her uncle whenever she wasn't in school.

She checked the price tag. Fifteen dollars. Not bad. She placed it in the cart.

"Mom! Can I please get this?" Collin called, pointing at an antique train set.

She almost said no. They really should save every dollar. But it would keep him occupied for hours, and that alone felt worth it. She gave in with a small nod. "Yes, you can get it."

Now she just needed a chair.

Katherine had wandered off to examine a tea kettle. Alex rounded the corner and spotted a section of office furniture. Several antique office chairs lined the wall. She checked the price of the executive-style one she liked and nearly choked. They had no idea how long they'd be here, and she wasn't about to spend a fortune.

Then she saw it: an Edwardian oak revolving office chair with an olive-green upholstered seat. Sturdy. Compact enough to fit up the attic stairs. Affordable. Exactly what she needed.

She lifted it and carried it over to Collin and Katherine, grabbing a power strip on the way so she could plug in everything she needed upstairs. They checked out and loaded the van. As she drove back toward Maple Street, her mind drifted to Declan. He'd only been gone a few hours, and she already missed him more than she wanted to admit.

Twenty minutes later, she pulled into the driveway. Collin immediately dumped his train set onto the living room floor and began assembling tracks while Katherine settled into the recliner to watch NCIS. Alex carefully stepped over the growing maze of train pieces as she carried her chair and lamp upstairs.

Thankfully, Declan—despite leaving in a rush—had remembered to grab her schoolbooks from the cabin. She made one last trip to haul them up to her new workspace.

She sat at the makeshift desk for a long moment, staring at her laptop. Where was she supposed to start? She couldn't exactly tell her professors she was hiding from violent criminals. Did she even want to? And what about Collin? It was the middle of the school year. She had no idea when their lives would return to anything resembling normal.

After a quick Google search, she submitted a Notice of Intent to homeschool him for the rest of the year. Then she emailed his principal, explaining there was a family emergency and asking her to approve the NOI as soon as possible.

Next, she sent a brief message to her academic advisor explaining that she had a family emergency, was out of state, and would keep up with her coursework. Then she logged into Blackboard. She opened each syllabus, scanning deadlines and assignments. With everything so uncertain, getting a jump start on the first few weeks felt like the only thing she could control.

Tomorrow, she would go to Walmart and pick up some kindergarten workbooks. Collin knew his ABCs, numbers, and a handful of sight words. Surely that was enough to get him ready for first grade. How hard could homeschooling be?

Chapter Twenty-Nine
HIM

A Marlboro Light dangled from his lips as he sat at his computer desk, the ember pulsing with each irritated breath. The glow from the monitor washed his face in a cold, bluish pallor, sharpening the furrow in his brow and the deep lines carved by months of sleepless nights. Mr. Beaumont's email was short—clinical, almost bored in its efficiency—but the meaning behind it struck like a hammer.

They were out of time.

His jaw clenched. Heat surged up his neck, flushing his face until it felt like his skin might split. Before he could think, his hand shot out, grabbing the antique Chinese blue-and-white porcelain vase beside the keyboard. It shattered against the far wall in a burst of ceramic shrapnel; the sound ricocheting through the house like a gunshot.

A string of inventive profanity followed the crash. A flash of movement in the corner of his vision drew his eyes to the mirror across the room. For a moment, he didn't recognize the man staring back. The dark circles beneath his brown eyes looked bruised, almost sunken, the kind of exhaustion that no amount of sleep could fix. His skin was sallow under the harsh monitor light, his hair flattened from the redeye flight out of Little Rock, and there was a wildness in his expression he hadn't seen before. He looked like a man unraveling, thread by thread.

The commotion summoned the older woman from down the hall. She circled the desk with the patience of a vulture and rested a hand on his shoulder before perching beside him.

"What is it, my dear?"

"Beaumont fucking located her," he muttered, lifting his head. His eyes were bloodshot, wild. "He's on his way to her first thing in the morning."

"Have we heard anything about her location?"

"Not a fucking thing. She and her cop boyfriend disappeared into the night. Ditched their phones at the station. Left their cars behind. They knew exactly how to make themselves ghosts."

He let his head fall into her lap, the way he had as a boy when the world felt too heavy. She had already seated herself on the edge of the desk beside him, but the comfort he sought was not what he received. She leaned back, studying him with a cold, measured appraisal, then slapped him sharply across the face.

The sting bloomed instantly. His hand flew to his cheek.

"You had one fucking job," she hissed.

Before he could respond, his phone chimed. He snatched it up and scanned the message, a slow, wicked grin spreading across his face.

"Wallace bought a one-way ticket from Nashville to Manchester this afternoon," he said. "Our contact at TSA came through. Detective Wallace has come out to play."

He rose, and the shift in his demeanor was immediate, like a mask snapping into place. In one fluid motion, he grabbed the woman by the throat and lifted her off the desk. Her feet scraped uselessly against the floor.

"If you ever lay a hand on me again," he growled, "it will be the last thing you do. Do you understand?"

She nodded frantically, gasping, her fingers clawing at his wrist. He released her, letting her collapse onto the desk. She coughed, then began to laugh, low and breathless, the sound tipping toward unhinged.

"What are you laughing about?" he snapped, pausing in the doorway.

"I'm just glad your balls finally dropped," she said, smoothing her blouse as if nothing had happened. "Maybe we'll make it out of this after all."

He didn't stay to hear more. Her voice followed him down the hall, muffled and indistinct, like a radio tuned between stations. He'd spent his entire life trying to earn her approval. He was done with that now. She could rot in her own bitterness.

For the first time, he saw her clearly—not as the mastermind she pretended to be, but as dead weight. A liability. A woman who thought she was still pulling the strings when she was nothing more than a pawn he'd allowed to live because she was useful. For now.

Outside, the night air hit him like a slap of its own, cool and damp, carrying the faint sweetness of the honeysuckle vines climbing the front gate. He lit another cigarette and inhaled deeply as he walked toward his car.

His prey was coming to him. And he had traps to set.

A memory flickered as he reached for the handle of his Audi.

Alex's car in flames.

The way she had frozen just in time.

The way her hand flew to her mouth and her eyes darted frantically around the parking lot.

He had waited for that moment.

He'd chosen to stay in the parking lot, tucked behind a row of vehicles, ready to finish the job himself if the plan inside the building fell apart. Watching her unravel had been almost better than doing it. Almost.

He'd crafted the scene with precision—just enough chaos, just enough personal detail—to make her believe one of the unstable men from her workplace had escalated. That Martha's death was the work of a stalker obsessed with her. Someone with no connection to her past.

He wanted her rattled.

He wanted her scared.

He wanted her to think of him. Wonder who he was and what he wanted.

And she had. She'd reacted exactly the way he expected.

Martha had been an unfortunate complication. Wrong place, wrong time, asking the wrong questions. He hadn't planned to kill her; he hadn't even known she was on the same train. But once she recognized him and saw the boy, her outcome was sealed. She could identify him, tie him to Brittany, tie him to everything he needed to keep buried.

He had taken her finger afterward, a small trophy to mark the kill. He hated giving it up. He enjoyed keeping reminders, little proofs of control. But discovering she frequented the hospital where Alex worked had changed everything. That coincidence had been a gift. A clean way to tie the murder to Alex's present life instead of her past. A way to make the threat feel close and personal.

Planting the finger in Alex's car had cost him something, but watching her reaction had been worth it. The fear in her eyes had been better than any souvenir.

Loose ends were dangerous, always tugging at the seams of a good plan. The babysitter had been one tug away from ruining his.

His mother and Two-Face had been responsible for that part of the plan. It should have been simple: quick, clean, decisive. Get the location of the boy. Kill everyone and get out. Instead, they had turned it into a disaster. The girl had survived; the family had survived, and Alex had slipped through their fingers yet again.

All because his mother never had the stomach to finish what needed to be done. She wanted the lifestyle, the power, the security he provided, but she refused to lift a finger to protect any of it. She expected others to do the work, to take the risks, while she reaped the rewards. And every time she hesitated, every time she flinched, someone escaped who shouldn't have.

The pattern was becoming impossible to ignore. Three plans. Three failures. And every one of them traced back to the same weakness.

He should have sent Two-Face to the house alone.

Irritation simmered beneath his skin, a slow, steady burn that threatened to flare. Time was running out, and excuses were no longer acceptable. He needed results, not apologies. That was why he had made the call. His contact inside the investigation had hesitated, but money had a way of turning reluctance into cooperation. Within the hour, he had the information he needed: a cabin, remote and quiet, the kind of place people believed would keep them safe.

The three of them had torn through it, searching every drawer, every vent, every loose floorboard for the flash drive. It was the one piece of leverage they needed, the one thing Alex had managed to keep hidden for eight long years. And still, they had come up empty.

He pulled out his phone and hit the third speed dial. It rang twice before a deep, raspy voice answered. "Two-Face, it's me. Meet me at the office in an hour. We have plans to make." He ended the call, slid into the driver's seat, and peeled out of the driveway, gravel spitting across the pavement as the car surged forward.

It wasn't Alex. But Wallace would do. Wallace would lead him straight to her.

And this time, she wouldn't escape.

As he drove, the cigarette between his fingers burned low, the ash trembling with each bump in the road. The night outside his windshield blurred into streaks of silver and shadow, but his mind was nowhere near the present. It drifted to a moment he'd tried to bury.

The day he asked Alex out.

He hadn't meant for it to matter. She was supposed to be a distraction, a pleasant curiosity, someone to pass the time with while he handled more important things. But she'd walked into the room with that quiet confidence, that easy laugh, that maddening way of looking at people like she actually saw them. And suddenly he'd wanted something he hadn't planned on wanting.

She tucked a loose strand of hair behind her ear while she sorted through the stack of paperwork, completely unaware of how easily the insignificant gesture drew his attention. A faint trace of her perfume drifted across the room, soft and clean and subtle enough to unsettle him. He had already practiced the invitation in his mind, shaping it to sound casual and effortless. Nerves were not something he usually dealt with. Hesitation was even rarer.

But with her, he had experienced both. He had leaned against the door-frame of her office, arms crossed, wearing the smile that usually got him whatever he wanted. "Dinner sometime?" He'd asked, voice smooth and confident, already expecting her agreement.

Instead, she had looked up at him with those steady eyes, warm and polite but unmistakably firm, and offered a small, apologetic smile that cut deeper than she could have known. "I'm flattered," she had said gently, "but no. I don't mix business and pleasure."

He had laughed it off at the time, made a joke, and pretended it didn't matter. But the rejection had burned. Not because he loved her; he hadn't even known her then. It burned because she had dismissed him. Overlooked him. Treated him as if he were forgettable. The word echoed in his mind, sour and persistent, and he tightened his grip on the steering wheel until the leather creaked. She had no idea who he was or what he was capable of. She didn't know how many people would have killed for his attention, his approval, his protection. And she had thrown it away without a second thought.

He exhaled slowly, letting the bitterness settle into something colder and far more useful. She would understand now. He would make her see exactly what she had walked away from—the life she could have stepped into if she had simply said yes. Influence, stability. The kind of protection most people only dreamed of. Instead, she had tied herself to a man with nothing to offer her, a man who could never shield her from what was coming.

If she had chosen him, none of this would be happening. The old man's betrayal wouldn't matter. Her possession of the flash drive wouldn't matter. She could have been his, and he could have kept her safe.

But if she refused to see that—if she insisted on choosing a life without him—then she had made herself a problem he could no longer ignore. Wanting her and needing her gone were not contradictions in his mind. They were the inevitable consequences of her choices. If she would not stand beside him, she stood in his way.

The Audi's engine hummed beneath him, steady and controlled, mirroring the resolve hardening in his chest. Wallace was on the move. Alex was out there. And the Lawyer's deadline loomed like a storm on the horizon. None of it mattered, not really. Because soon, she would see him clearly. She would understand what she had walked away from. And she would regret it—not because he wanted her love, not anymore, but because he wanted her to know she had never been the one in control.

Chapter Thirty
DECLAN

Declan landed in Manchester at nine o'clock that evening. The Enterprise counter connected to the airport was closing at ten, and the pickings were already slim. He begrudgingly settled for a red Kia Soul, choosing it only because he doubted he could fold himself into the Prius beside it. It wasn't dignified, but it would get him where he needed to go.

The Grand Bedford Village Inn sat across from Constitution Drive, directly opposite the NH FBI field office. Convenient. Impersonal. Exactly what he needed. He checked in, accepted the keycard, and made his way to the second floor.

The room was surprisingly spacious, with a four-poster king bed draped in crisp white linens and a small fireplace flickering quietly in the corner. A stocked minibar waited in the fridge, and he didn't hesitate to take advantage of it. The burn of whiskey did little to settle the ache in his chest, but it gave him something else to focus on.

Losing Alex was a thought he refused to examine too closely. The pain of it sat heavy and uninvited, like a bruise he kept pressing just to make sure it was still there.

He sat on the edge of the bed, elbows braced on his knees, head bowed into his hands. The last few days had stretched him thin, leaving every nerve wired and every muscle tight. He was used to pressure, but the attempts on their lives had pushed him somewhere he hadn't been in a long time. Shadows seemed to shift where they shouldn't. A soft noise in the hallway made his pulse kick. The entire room felt as if it were holding its breath with him.

He had pulled back from her over the last few days, telling himself it was necessary. Distance kept his head clear. Distance kept him focused on the case. That was the story he repeated whenever she looked at him with confusion in her eyes.

But deep down, he knew there was more to it than that.

She hadn't been completely honest with him. Not about the flash drive. Not about the things she'd carried alone for years. And he hated how easily that unsettled him. Half-truths had unraveled his life before, not once but twice, and he couldn't shake the fear that he had a blind spot where she was concerned. That he wanted to believe her too much. That he wasn't seeing something he should.

He'd tried to keep that fear contained, tried to keep his distance so it wouldn't bleed into the way he protected her. But last night, when she stood in the bedroom doorway looking so hurt and so unsure, every bit of control he'd been clinging to snapped. One look at her and the walls he'd spent years building didn't just crack—they gave way.

He wasn't sure when it had happened. Somewhere between her stubbornness and her softness, between the way she challenged him and the way she trusted him, she had slipped past every defense he had. She had worked her way into the quiet places he never let anyone touch.

And standing there now, he finally understood the truth he'd been trying not to see.

He was in love with her. Completely. Helplessly. Irrevocably.

He wanted nothing more than to put the chaos behind them and claim her in a way that left no room for doubt. To let himself want her without fear, without restraint, without the constant threat hanging over their heads. But wanting her didn't erase the old instincts that had kept him alive. It didn't silence the seeds of suspicion that had started to take root.

The unanswered questions.

The flash drive she'd hidden.

The things she hadn't said.

Her name on Enzo's bank account.

Pieces that didn't fit cleanly no matter how he turned them.

He hated those thoughts existed at all. Hated that they crept in right alongside the feelings he could no longer deny. But they were there, threading through the cracks left behind by a lifetime of betrayal and hard lessons.

He couldn't afford to ignore them. Not now. Not with someone hunting them. So he forced the emotions down, burying them beneath the discipline that had carried him through far worse. Focus was the only thing that would keep them alive. Focus was the only thing that would keep her alive.

Even if it meant holding himself together with nothing but grit and the hope that, when this was over, the truth wouldn't break them both.

But she made it harder than she realized. A quiet smile. A hand brushing his arm. The way she looked at him as if she trusted him without hesitation. Each small moment slipped past his defenses before he could stop it, loosening something he needed to keep locked tight.

A knock at the door pulled him from his spiraling thoughts. Room service. He took the tray from the bellhop and handed over a twenty for the trouble at such a late hour. After mixing himself another drink, he settled at the small table in the corner and put on the latest episode of *Game of Thrones*, hoping the noise would drown out the noise in his head. Two Benadryls went down with a swallow of rum and Coke. With his mind racing the way it was, sleep wouldn't come unless he forced it.

Once he finished eating, he turned off the television and climbed into bed. He set his alarm for the ungodly hour of six a.m., then scrolled through his contacts until he found Alex's burner number. He sent a brief text letting her know he was safe in his room and heading to sleep.

When the alarm blared the next morning, he wanted to hurl the phone out the window for daring to interrupt such a perfect dream. Groggy and irritated, he dragged himself into his suit and tie and headed downstairs for the complimentary breakfast. He inhaled eggs, toast, and coffee, then made his way to the federal building, arriving by seven as instructed. The lobby was quiet, sterile, and far too bright for the hour. He waited impatiently for someone to collect him.

Fifteen minutes later, the secretary answered a call, rose from her desk, and asked him to follow. She led him to a conference room near the back of the building where three agents sat waiting. Declan introduced himself and ran through the facts of the case as he understood them.

The agent closest to him extended a hand. "Special Agent in Charge Meeker."

Meeker looked to be pushing sixty, clean-shaven, with salt-and-pepper hair cut in a high and tight. Sharp eyes. Direct posture. Declan liked him immediately.

The other two agents, however, looked like they'd rather be anywhere else. Dalton, the one Meeker had addressed earlier, chewed his gum with loud, wet smacks that made Declan's jaw twitch.

"Dalton," Meeker said without looking away from Declan, "if you smack your gum one more time, I'll introduce your face to the table."

Dalton froze, then spat the gum into a napkin.

"Good choice," Meeker said, finally turning back to Declan. "Now tell me if there's anyone else we should be looking at."

"Not at the moment," Declan said. "But we need to talk to the people who worked directly under Enzo, and his boss." He paused, searching for the name.

"Antonio Moretti," Meeker supplied.

Declan nodded. "Alex knew things about how their operation worked. Enzo used to try to use his money and connections to pressure her. The man was a scumbag, but maybe we've been looking at this wrong. Maybe he was keeping something off her."

Meeker's expression tightened. "It's possible."

"I still want to speak with his family and with Moretti."

Meeker pushed back from the table and stood. Declan followed him into the hallway. As they walked, Meeker fired off instructions to the other agents to track down Moretti's location. They stepped outside into the parking lot and stopped beside Declan's rental car.

"That belong to you?" Meeker asked, eyeing the red Kia Soul.

"It was that or a Prius," Declan said, a touch defensive.

Meeker chuckled. "Come on. We'll take the SUV."

Declan followed him to a black Chevy Tahoe and climbed into the passenger seat.

"We'll start with Enzo's family," Meeker said as he pulled out of the lot. "They're just a few towns over."

He turned on the radio but didn't speak again. Declan didn't mind. Silence suited him just fine.

Twenty minutes later, they turned onto a short dirt road marked by a wooden sign: Great Valley Farm. Straight ahead stood the large gray barn with white doors—the same one Declan had seen in the photo on Alex's mantle.

"Enzo's house is a little further down," Meeker said. "But I figured we'd talk to the employees first. Maybe someone remembers Ms. Kelley."

They entered through the side door of the barn. Stalls lined both sides, and a wide riding arena stretched out ahead. Meeker veered right while Declan went left, but neither found anyone. Then Declan heard the rhythmic thud of hooves and followed the sound to the arena.

A slender redhead was dismounting a horse as he rounded the corner. She flipped the reins over the horse's head and turned toward the stables.

She spotted them and slowed her steps. "Can I help you?"

"Agent Meeker, FBI," Meeker said, holding up his badge. "This is Detective Wallace with the Little Rock PD."

Recognition flickered across her face at the mention of his name.

"Detective Wallace. We spoke on the phone about my mother."

"You're Brittany," Declan said.

She nodded, fingers tightening briefly on the reins. "Is this about her?"

"In part." Declan pulled a photo of Alex from his pocket and handed it over. "We're trying to confirm whether you knew this woman."

Brittany studied the picture, but her eyes didn't move the way they should if she were actually searching her memory. They stayed fixed on one spot, too still. "There was a girl who worked here before me. She left a couple of weeks after I started. It might be her. It was nine years ago." She smiled, but the muscles around her eyes didn't shift at all.

Declan felt the first prickle of doubt.

"We heard about your boss's passing," Meeker said. "Sorry for your loss."

A flash of anger crossed her face before she smoothed it into something softer. "Thank you."

"What happens to the farm now?" Declan asked.

"I'm not sure. His family doesn't care about horses. If they inherit it, they'll probably sell." She shifted her weight, boot scuffing the dirt. "Enzo told me he planned to leave it to me, but there's been a delay with the will. I don't know how long I'll have a job."

Her voice wavered on the last sentence—genuine fear there. That part rang true.

"Did they tell you what the delay was?" Declan asked.

"No." Her gaze flicked toward the barn, then back to him, a quick dart like she was checking for an exit. "Junior stopped by a few days ago and told me to keep working until they figure it out."

Declan let a beat of silence stretch. People filled silence with truth or lies; he waited to see which she'd choose. She swallowed and looked away.

"Brittany," he said, pulling her attention back to him. "After we spoke last week, someone left your mother's finger in a box inside this woman's car after breaking into her home."

Her hand flew to her mouth, but her eyes didn't widen until it was too late. "Oh, my gosh."

Delayed reaction. Performed shock. Declan's jaw tightened.

Meeker stepped in. "We believe Enzo may have had ties to the New England Mafia. Do you know anything about that?"

Brittany blinked, startled by the abrupt change of subject. "No. I had no idea."

Her shoulders rose slightly, a defensive posture. She was lying.

"Did your mother ever visit you here?" Declan asked.

"Yes. We went riding together."

Her voice softened, and her eyes dropped to the ground. That was genuine.

"Did she ever meet Enzo?"

"No. He had passed a few days before she came up."

Her breathing remained steady, and she held eye contact. Truth.

"What about his family? Junior?"

She hesitated, eyes flicking to the side—classic recall-avoidance. "She might have been here the day Junior stopped by about the will. I don't really remember."

She remembered. She just didn't want to say how clearly.

Declan stepped a little closer, lowering his voice. "Tell me about Alex Kelley. When did you last see her?"

"She worked here for a short time. We weren't close."

"That wasn't my question," Declan said.

Her throat bobbed as she swallowed. "I... I don't know. She left suddenly. People come and go around here."

The horse behind her stamped a hoof, the sound sharp in the quiet morning. Brittany flinched hard enough that the reins jerked in her hand.

Declan didn't miss the tremor in her fingers, or the sheen of sweat at her hairline despite the cool air, or the way she kept glancing toward the house like someone might be watching.

She was hiding something.

And she was terrified he'd figure out what.

A thought tugged at the back of Declan's mind—the older woman Nina had described during the attack. Confident. Controlled. Someone who moved as if she'd done this before. It was unlikely to be Helena, but he couldn't shake the possibility. Helena had already shown her colors years ago when Alex went to her for help after Enzo cornered her. Instead of protecting her, Helena had encouraged his behavior, proud of the influence it gave her.

If Helena were capable of that, then Brittany's reaction to her would be telling.

"What about Helena?" Declan asked. "Were you two close? Did she ever talk business with you?"

Brittany's shoulders stiffened before she even opened her mouth. "Helena and I rarely see each other. She knows nothing about business dealings. She's too busy getting Botox and manicures."

The bite in her tone was sharp enough to cut. Her grip on the mare's lead rope tightened, the leather creaking under her fingers. Declan watched the way her jaw clenched, the way her eyes flicked away as if she'd said more than she meant to.

Helena was a sore subject. That could be useful later.

"Why are you asking so many questions about the family?" Brittany asked. Her voice wavered, and she blinked hard, as if trying to steady herself. "You can't honestly think they had anything to do with my mother's death."

She swallowed, throat tightening. "My mom... she lived a messy life. She trusted the wrong people. She made choices that put her in dangerous situations." Her breath hitched, barely noticeable unless you were looking for it. "That's the kind of thing that gets someone hurt. Not... this."

Her fingers curled into the mare's reins, knuckles whitening. She wasn't just defending her mother. She was trying to convince herself of something. Declan saw it in the way her gaze kept darting away, in the way her shoulders trembled for a second before she forced them still.

Grief softened her features, but fear lingered just beneath the surface.

"Just standard procedure," Meeker said. "We look at everything from all sides."

Before Declan could press further, the mare Brittany held began pawing at the ground, restless and impatient.

"If you will excuse me, I need to put her away."

Meeker and Declan stepped aside as she led the horse toward the stables. Her shoulders were tight, her steps too quick, as if she couldn't get away from them fast enough.

"She knows something," Declan said quietly.

"Oh, yeah," Meeker replied.

They followed her into the stable; the air was warmer inside and thick with the scent of hay and leather. Brittany kept her back to them as she guided the mare into her stall, movements brisk and practiced.

"If you think of anything that might help the case, here is my card," Meeker said, handing it to her.

Brittany smiled over her shoulder as she guided Walla into her stall. "Alright," she said, slipping the card into her pocket. "If anything comes to mind, I'll let you know."

Declan doubted that very much.

As he and Meeker walked back to the SUV, Declan's thoughts churned. Brittany was not directly involved. His instincts told him that. But she was absolutely hiding something. The way she dodged certain questions. The way her expression tightened at Alex's name. The way her shock at the finger had been just a little too dramatic.

And Martha.

Every time he thought of her, a knot tightened in his chest. Her murder was not random. It was not a coincidence. It was connected to the attacks on Alex. Someone was tying up loose ends and sending messages, and Brittany's evasiveness only made the picture murkier.

The ride to the Espositos' house passed in heavy silence. Declan stared out the window, jaw clenched, watching the trees blur by. He hated feeling behind. He hated knowing Alex was still in danger. Most of all, he hated that Martha Cunningham had become collateral damage in a war she never chose.

They pulled into a long, gated driveway. Meeker pressed the buzzer.

"Can I help you?" a woman's voice asked over the speaker.

Meeker held his badge up to the camera. "Agent Meeker, FBI. I have some questions regarding your late husband."

A long silence stretched between them. Declan braced for the gate to stay shut, but then the lock snapped and the iron bars slid apart. Meeker eased the SUV forward and followed the winding drive toward the house.

A slender blonde stepped out onto the porch to greet them. She wore stilettos, red capri pants, and a white flowy blouse with black polka dots. The outfit screamed vanity and money in equal measure.

Petite. Bleach-blonde. Mid-fifties.

Declan stilled in the driveway, every instinct locking onto her. She fit the description perfectly.

"You gentlemen caught me just in time. I was on my way out. Helena Esposito," she said, offering her hand.

Declan shook it, forcing a polite smile. "Nice to meet you, ma'am."

"Oh, a southerner. I love your accent," she said with a flirtatious smile.

Declan felt an immediate wave of distaste. Everything about her seemed hollow and practiced, as if she were performing a version of herself she wanted the world to believe.

"We were sorry to hear about your husband's passing," Declan said. "We came to ask about a former employee of his." He pulled out the picture of Alex. "Do you recognize this woman?"

Helena studied the photo for a moment, her expression softening in a way that felt practiced.

"Oh heavens, yes. That is Alexandria. She worked for Enzo, training his horses ages ago. I always liked her. She had spunk."

Declan kept his face neutral, though unease prickled along his spine. Everyone remembered Alex just enough to sound helpful, yet not enough to offer anything real. And every single one of them was lying about something. He could feel it in the way their eyes shifted, in the pauses that lasted a fraction too long.

He did not know what the lie was yet.

But he intended to find out.

"Several attempts have been made on her life recently. It was brought to our attention that your late husband made threats against her when she worked for him," Meeker said in a steady, matter-of-fact tone.

Helena let out a light laugh. "Oh, honey, whose life did he not threaten? He threatened mine every day, and I am still standing."

The casual dismissal tightened something in Declan's chest. She treated violence like a personality quirk. Enzo's death, the delay with the will, the escalating attacks. None of it aligned cleanly, and Helena's polished charm only made the tension in his gut coil tighter.

"So you are saying he meant nothing by it?" Meeker asked.

"Oh, I am sure in the moment he did. He was Italian. His passions ran high. Once he calmed down, everything would be forgotten. Enzo loved Alexandria. He would not have hurt her."

Declan's gaze drifted past Helena toward the window beside the door. A curtain shifted, barely noticeable, but enough to catch his eye. Someone else was inside. Someone who did not want to be seen.

"Is Enzo Junior at home?" Declan asked.

"No, he is working at the dealership. He has an apartment near the city."

Declan didn't believe a word of it, but without a warrant, there was nothing to be done.

"Do you have a good number for him? We would like to ask him some questions," Declan said, pulling out his notebook.

"Of course," Helena replied with a bright smile. She grabbed the notebook and pen from Declan and scribbled down a number before handing them back.

Declan held her gaze. Something cold and calculating hid behind that sugary expression, and he felt it like a chill down his spine.

"Thank you for your time, ma'am," he said as they turned back toward the car.

"Are you getting the sense these people are trying to bullshit us," Declan muttered once they were out of earshot.

"Sure am," Meeker replied. "Did you see the curtain move?"

"I did. Probably Junior hiding behind his mommy's skirts. Apartment in the city, my ass."

Meeker's phone rang as they pulled out of the driveway. "Meeker," he answered. A few grunts later, he hung up.

"Moretti is out of town today, but agreed to come in tomorrow morning for an interview. I'm sure his entourage of lawyers will be in tow."

Declan felt a surge of impatience. He wanted to wrap things up and get back to Alex. Tomorrow morning would have to be soon enough.

Once they were back at the office, Declan placed a call to Junior. He refused to use his burner, not with the risk of it being traced. The line rang several times before going to voicemail. Declan kept his tone professional and brief, leaving a message requesting a callback and providing the office number for follow-up.

He spent the next several hours on the phone, pushing through requests for phone records and credit card statements for Brittany, Junior, and Helena. The work was tedious but necessary, and by the time he wrapped up, the cramped room they called his office felt suffocating. He was ready to call it quits for the day.

Meeker stepped inside, shoulder brushing the doorframe. "Moretti said he would be in the office by nine tomorrow."

"I will be here," Declan replied, gathering his things.

As he approached the glass double doors, he noticed the snow coming down in thick, steady sheets. A good foot had already accumulated, and the cold hit him like a slap the moment he stepped outside. He pulled his jacket tighter around his body, hurried across the lot, and climbed into his rental car. The heater roared to life, blasting his face with blessed warmth.

He had lived in Ohio for a short stretch while trying to make things work with Brianna, so he knew how to handle winter driving. That did not mean he missed it. Not even a little.

Back at the hotel, he spotted a restaurant tucked into the first floor. It was a little after three, and the thought of going straight to his room felt depressing, so he headed inside. The bar was packed, and the Patriots game blared from every screen. He ordered a club sandwich and a Blue Moon and watched a snow advisory crawl across the bottom of the TV. A nor'easter was on the way.

He briefly considered driving to the dealership to see if Junior was actually working today. Maybe ask around. Maybe catch him in a lie. But with the weather turning, it made more sense to stay put.

If he were going to be snowed in, he could use the time. He needed to comb through the Amtrak and hospital security footage. Bishop and Martin had already gone over both sets several times and found nothing. Declan wanted to see it for himself. The more eyes, the better.

He took a long drink of his beer and felt the weight of the day settle in. Tonight, he would comb through every frame.

The Patriots scored a touchdown, and the place erupted. A petite blonde slid onto the barstool beside him. Declan glanced her way. She looked barely old enough to be drinking, with long wavy hair, a narrow face, and buck teeth that made her pout look more comical than seductive.

"Buy me a beer?" she asked, leaning her shoulder into him.

"No," Declan said, shifting away.

"What? You don't think I'm pretty?" she demanded.

"I don't see how those two things correlate," he replied. "But since you asked, no. I don't think you're pretty."

Her mouth fell open in outrage.

"Did you hear that, Rusty? This man called me ugly."

A large man in Carhartt coveralls pushed back from the table behind them. He had the build of someone who lifted hay bales for fun and the slurred speech of someone who had been dipping since breakfast.

"Did you call my sister ugly?" he asked.

Declan turned in his chair to face him. "If you want to be technical, she asked if I thought she was pretty. I said no."

It had been a long time since Declan had been in a bar fight. His blood thrummed with the old, familiar rush. His younger self would have already had Rusty on the floor before the man finished his sentence. But he could not afford to spend the night in jail and miss the meeting with Moretti in the morning.

Annoyed by his own restraint, Declan pulled out his badge and held it up.

"Settle down, Hillbilly Joe. There will be no fist-to-cuffs today."

Rusty grumbled, but sank back into his chair. His sister scoffed and ordered her own beer.

Declan finished his drink, paid his tab, and headed upstairs. Once in his room, he turned the game back on for background noise and set his laptop on the desk. Instead of opening his design files, he pulled up the Amtrak footage and let the first clip load. With the storm rolling in, he had nothing but time.

Chapter Thirty-One
ALEX

Alex had finished all her assignments for the semester in two days and had been going stir-crazy ever since. Collin was too. For the past few afternoons, she had been taking him to a small park she had spotted on their drive back from the Antique Mall. It sat tucked behind a row of bare winter trees, only a ten-minute walk from the house, and the cold air always stung her nose as they made their way down the sidewalk.

It had been four days since Declan left. She had only heard from him once, a short check-in that did nothing to quiet the ache his absence left behind. The silence since then felt heavier than she wanted to admit, settling into her chest like a weight she carried everywhere.

The playground had been empty each day they visited, and today was no different. Collin sprinted straight for the monkey bars, his breath puffing in little clouds. A narrow track circled the play area, and Alex slipped into her now familiar routine, jogging laps while he played. She could see him from every point on the loop, which eased the knot of worry that had taken up permanent residence in her chest.

But even with the clear view and the quiet park, she could not shake the hollow space Declan had left behind. His absence was getting harder to ignore, and the silence between them felt louder with every passing hour. She knew it was for everyone's safety, but she didn't have to like it.

"Collin, I'm going to run around the track while you play. Stay on the playground and don't wander."

"Okay, Momma."

She checked her watch and set a timer. The cold air burned her lungs in a way that felt almost cleansing. During her second mile, she noticed a woman and a small boy walking toward the playground. The boy clung to his mother's sleeve, his shoulders hunched, his eyes downcast. Something about him looked... tired. Or resigned.

Collin immediately ran over to greet him, eager for a new friend. The boys began playing, but the other child stayed quiet, glancing back at his mother every few seconds as if checking for permission.

Alex finished her laps and slowed to a walk, her pulse still thudding in her ears. As she approached the bench, a familiar anxiety crept in. A cover story had not crossed her mind. Small talk had not crossed her mind. Anything that required her to act like a normal person had definitely not crossed her mind.

She sat down beside the woman.

"Hi, I'm Alex. That one belongs to me," she said, nodding toward Collin.

The woman startled slightly, as if she had not heard Alex approach. "I'm Myra. And that one is mine." She pointed to the dark-haired boy, who was now half-heartedly climbing the slide. "I haven't seen you here before. Are you from around here?"

"My mother-in-law owns a house on Maple Street. We're staying for a while."

Myra nodded, but her eyes flicked toward the parking lot, then back to Alex. Her fingers twisted the hem of her coat. She looked like someone waiting for something. Or someone.

"Do you homeschool?" Myra asked.

"Uh... yeah. I just started recently. Still trying to get the hang of it."

"We homeschool too. We should get the kids together a few times a week. Either to play at the park or go over lessons."

"I would love that," Alex said, and she meant it. Myra seemed kind, if a little distracted.

The boys came running over.

"Mom! Look what Brenden and I found!" Collin held up a turtle, grinning.

"Wow, look at that," Alex said, forcing enthusiasm.

"We should probably take him to the pond," she added, standing.

Myra rose quickly, almost too quickly. "We actually have to get going. Brenden has a doctor's appointment."

The boy's face fell. He looked up at his mother with a flicker of something like fear before he masked it. Alex's stomach tightened.

"Let me grab your number," Alex said, offering her phone.

Myra typed it in, her hands trembling slightly. "There you go."

They said their goodbyes. As Myra and Brenden walked toward the parking lot, Alex noticed an SUV idling there. A man sat in the back seat, his face shadowed, his expression hard. He did not look at Myra. He looked at Alex, and his scowl made her skin prickle.

Myra opened the door and ushered her son inside without a word. The boy glanced back once, eyes wide and sad, before the door shut.

Alex swallowed the uneasy feeling rising in her throat.

She and Collin walked to the pond and set the turtle down at the water's edge. It slipped beneath the surface and disappeared.

"Mom, what is the difference between a tortoise and a turtle?" Collin asked as they stepped onto the road to begin the walk home.

Alex took his hand, her gaze drifting back toward the park. The SUV was gone.

But the uneasy feeling stayed.

"Well, a tortoise spends most of its life on land and grows to be much bigger than a turtle. A turtle spends most of its time in the water and is usually smaller than a tortoise. I am not completely sure, but I think turtles are omnivores and tortoises are herbivores."

"What is an omnivore and a herbivore?"

Alex took a steadying breath. It was technically a school day, so this would count as science.

"An omnivore is an animal that eats both meat and plants. A herbivore only eats plants."

"Okay. When can I see Brendan again? I like him."

"I am not sure. I will text his mom today and set up a time for us to meet again."

Warmth from the roaring fire washed over them as they entered the house. Katherine and Tony were curled up on the couch with a bowl of popcorn, watching *The Sopranos*. The irony was not lost on Alex. She could tell they were intruding and scrambled for an excuse to leave again.

"Collin, do you want to go into town with me and get some lunch?"

"Yeah. Can we go to Chili's?" he asked, practically vibrating with excitement.

"Chili's sounds good. Katherine, what do you want me to bring back for you?"

Katherine thought for a moment. "Southwest egg rolls, please."

"You got it. Tony, would you like anything?"

"No, thank you, dear," Tony said without looking away from the screen.

Alex and Collin climbed into the minivan. She plugged the restaurant into the GPS and pulled out of the driveway. Collin immediately launched into rapid-fire questions about turtles, tortoises, Godzilla, and whether Chili's had chocolate milk. Her nerves frayed, but she reminded herself it had been a long time since she had spent uninterrupted time alone with him. She took a slow breath and answered each question as patiently as she could.

The restaurant was quiet, and they were seated immediately in a corner booth. Collin didn't wait for the hostess to hand him a menu before rattling off his order. The hostess laughed and promised their server would be right over.

Alex scanned the menu, torn between the southwest rolls and the Texas cheese fries. When the server arrived, Collin repeated his order with the same enthusiasm.

Alex smiled. "I will take the southwest rolls, and can I get an order of those to go?"

The server collected their menus and disappeared toward the kitchen. Collin worked on the maze on the back of his coloring sheet, humming a tune she did not recognize.

"Collin, I wanted to tell you something I forgot until now."

"Yeah, Momma."

"I bought some land and a barn a few days ago. I am going to move the horses out there and start building a house for us."

"Are Alyssa, Luke, and Declan going to live with us?"

"Probably not, but I am not sure. Things are a little crazy right now. Once things settle down, we will figure everything out."

Collin accepted that answer easily. Alex wished she could do the same. She had no idea what would happen between her and Declan once this nightmare was over. Their relationship was still new, still fragile, and had been forged under pressure neither of them had asked for. The thought of not waking up beside him sent a quiet ache through her chest. They hadn't talked about what they were, and the uncertainty of his feelings left her uneasy.

They finished their meal in comfortable silence. Collin asked if they could split the molten chocolate lava cake, and Alex agreed. After paying the bill, they grabbed their to-go order and headed across the street to Walmart. Alex wanted a bottle of wine. Collin immediately negotiated for a toy.

"You can pick something under twenty dollars," she said.

He chose a Godzilla figure and tore it open the moment they got back in the car, plastic crackling as he freed the toy from its packaging.

Alex started the engine, watching raindrops drift across the windshield. For a moment, she let herself breathe. It felt almost normal.

Almost.

The weather had taken a sharp turn. The sky had gone nearly black, and rain hammered the windshield as they climbed back into the van. A warning alarm blared over the radio, and Alex turned up the volume. Tornado warning. Perfect. They were thirty minutes from home, and she had no intention of being on the road when the twisters made an appearance. She merged onto the highway and pressed the accelerator.

Twenty-five tense minutes later, they pulled into the driveway. Katherine sat on the front deck, wrapped in a shawl, watching the storm while German news murmured from her phone. Alex handed her the egg rolls and carried the wine inside. Collin immediately dropped to the floor with his Godzilla toy and his train set.

"Is Godzilla taking the train somewhere?" Alex asked.

"Yeah, Mom. Godzilla can only move fast in water. He is slow on land, so if he wants to travel, he needs to take the train," Collin said with complete seriousness.

"Oh, excuse my ignorance. I am not a Godzilla expert."

"It's okay, Mom. You didn't know."

Alex pulled the corkscrew from the kitchen drawer and opened the bottle of wine. She poured herself a generous glass and headed upstairs to her office. The urge to journal hit her hard, a need to unload the chaos of the last few weeks. She used to write every day before school swallowed her life whole. She sat down, opened her laptop, and let her fingers move.

Rain pelted the large picture window beside her, and a strange surge of energy ran through her. She loved storms. They made her feel alive. When she finished her entry, it was time to start dinner. Collin was still on the floor with his toys when she came downstairs, and Katherine was still outside, unfazed by the weather.

Alex chopped potatoes and carrots, tossing them into the stew pot. She seared steak tips in a skillet until they browned, then added them to the mix. Beef stew on a stormy night felt perfect.

"What are we having for dinner, Mom?" Collin asked.

"Beef stew."

There was a short pause. "What am I having for dinner?"

Alex rolled her eyes. "Dirty socks if you do not sweeten up."

"Momma... you know I don't like soup. Or vegetables."

"I will make you a grilled cheese, but you are at least going to try the stew."

Collin huffed. "Fine."

Alex finished assembling the stew and set the crock pot to high. She curled up on the couch with a blanket and turned on the TV. After a few minutes of channel surfing, she settled on *Titanic*. It had been years since she had seen it, and the movie was still near the beginning. The storm raged outside, hail pinging off the roof like scattered gravel.

Katherine came back inside and sat beside her. "Oh, the *Titanic*. I love this movie." She pulled another blanket from the trunk behind the couch and settled in next to Alex.

For a moment, they found something that resembled normal life. The more Alex got to know Katherine, the more she liked her. She snuggled deeper into the couch; the warmth of the blanket and the steady hum of the storm lulled her toward sleep.

"Momma, don't forget to text Brenden's mom, please."

Alex blinked awake and reached for her phone. The brightness stung her eyes, and she scrolled to the bottom of her contacts in search of the number she had saved earlier that afternoon.

Her thumb stopped cold. Maria hadn't saved her number under her own name. Instead, two words stared back at her.

Help us.

A chill slid through her. The storm outside faded beneath the heavy thump of her heartbeat. She replayed the moment at the park, the one she had tried to shrug off.

The woman had scarcely spoken. Her voice was soft, almost apologetic. Her son clung to her side, silent and watchful. Both of them carried a tension that didn't belong on a playground. And the van parked across the street—dark windows, engine idling—had made Alex's skin crawl. A man sat in the back, half-hidden, pretending not to watch them.

She had ignored the unease then. She couldn't ignore it now.

Alex stood abruptly, grabbed her coat, and stepped into the cold. Rain misted across her face as she hurried toward the agent's car across the street. She waved him down, breath coming fast, and poured out everything she remembered. A mother who barely spoke. A boy who clung to her side. The van idling near the playground with a man watching from the back. And the unsettling discovery of the woman's silent cry for help.

The agent's expression grew serious.

He took her phone without a word, lifted his radio, and stepped toward the curb with sudden urgency.

"Go inside," he said quietly. "Lock the doors."

Alex hesitated, rain soaking through her hair, but he was already speaking into the radio, voice clipped and sharp.

The street felt suddenly, unnervingly still.

Chapter Thirty-Two
DECLAN

Moretti called and postponed the meeting to the following day. The storm had hammered the coast for three straight days, and Declan had spent every hour holed up in his room, living off room service and drowning himself in security footage. When his eyes needed a break from the hospital cameras, he switched to the Amtrak files. When those blurred together, he went back to the hospital. The cycle repeated until time lost its shape.

The first Amtrak clip showed Martha stepping off her train behind a man and a small boy. She watched them slip out a side door, the same one he had opened earlier, the one that should have triggered an alarm. She unfolded a piece of paper, scanned it, and hurried after them. The door never sounded. Neither time.

The alley footage was grainy, warped by distance and shadows, but Declan could still make out the man's general build. Broad shoulders. Average height. A posture that suggested confidence or familiarity with what he was doing. The struggle over the child was brief. Martha tried to intervene. She tried to run. The man raised a gun, and she dropped out of frame. The rest was lost to darkness, but the shape of it was clear enough.

Martha's final act had been trying to save a child.

Declan isolated a still of the boy's face and ran it through missing persons databases. A match came back almost immediately. Seven years old. Missing from Massachusetts. Reported two days before Martha's murder.

He sat back, staring at the screen.

Whoever had taken that child was part of something larger. Something organized. Something that had been moving in the shadows long before Alex ever stepped into the picture.

He just didn't know how the pieces connected yet.

He was just about to call it a night when his phone rang.

"Wallace."

"Wallace, it's Stewart. We finished examining the flash drive, and we came across something. It looks like a roster of horses… names, ages, prices… hundreds of them. It's code, Wallace. They aren't horses. I think your girl may have stumbled ass-backwards into the middle of a trafficking ring."

Declan froze, belt half undone. "The old man?"

"I don't think so," Stewart said. "The locations of the sales and the dates line up with his son's movements. Enzo Senior was old-school. No computers, no phones, everything face-to-face. That's how he never got caught. I think the son was doing this with or without his father's knowledge, and he used Senior's computer to keep track of everything. That would explain why the old man never went after Alex. He wasn't aware she had anything that could hurt them."

Declan's stomach dropped.

Declan froze. The boy from the footage stared back at him in his mind, small and terrified. And the man dragging him away had turned just enough for the camera to catch part of his face.

A cold realization crept up Declan's spine.

Could the man have been Junior? He only had a ten-year-old mug shot to go on, but the size and build fit.

His conversation with Alex flashed through his mind. The note… the one she'd left for the old man. If Junior had found it after his father's death—if he'd realized what she had on him—this was it. Everything clicked into place with sickening certainty. Declan could feel it in his gut. Junior was their guy.

Now he just needed proof.

"I'll swing by the dealership and talk to Junior on my way to the airport this afternoon," he said.

"Be careful, Wallace. And before I forget—the officers sitting on Alex's house phoned in a while ago. An older gentleman stopped by looking for her early this morning. He wouldn't tell the officer what it was regarding, but he gave his name. Mr. Beaumont. He's Enzo Esposito's lawyer."

"Do you have a number for him?" Declan asked, already reaching for a pen.

Stewart read it off, and Declan scribbled it onto the nearest scrap of paper before ending the call.

What the hell did Enzo's lawyer want with Alex?

He was about to call the lawyer when his phone rang again.

"Wallace."

"Agent Price at the safe house," the man said. His voice was tight, the kind that only came out when something was wrong. "I need to update you on an incident that happened earlier."

Declan straightened. "Go ahead."

Price regurgitated everything Alex had told him about the interaction from earlier, details about the woman and the boy, the hidden message in Alex's phone.

Declan listened without interrupting; the room shrank around him.

When Price finished, silence stretched for a beat.

"I'm sending you a picture," Declan said. "Show it to her. Ask if this is the boy she saw."

He pulled up the still image from the Amtrak footage and sent it.

Price's phone buzzed on the other end. "She's asleep," he said quietly.

"First thing in the morning," Declan replied. "I want an answer as soon as she's up. And put out a BOLO on the van she described. Every detail she gave you."

"Understood."

"And, Price, keep your head on a swivel tonight. This case is bigger than we thought. If that boy is who I think he is, they may be closing in already."

"Got it."

The line went dead.

Declan stared at the wall, the weight of it settling in his chest.

If Alex confirmed the boy, the entire case would tilt in one direction, and Junior would be at the center. Declan lay back, staring at the ceiling. Sleep wasn't happening. Not tonight. Something in his gut told him the next twenty-four hours were going to change everything.

Junior

The storm hammered the metal siding hard enough to make the walls vibrate, but Junior barely heard it. He sat at the scarred wooden table with his men, cards in his hand, pretending to focus while cigars burned low in the ashtrays and stale beer soured the air. The generator hummed as if it were running on fumes. None of it held his attention. His mind kept circling back to what had happened earlier.

He'd been at the dealership, halfway through a sales pitch, when the front door chimed. He looked up expecting a customer, maybe someone desperate enough to brave the weather. Instead, Moretti walked in. A blast of frigid air knifed through the showroom as the door swung wide, snow whipping in behind him. The wind rattled the glass, carrying the sharp scent of winter and exhaust, and Moretti stepped inside like the storm itself had delivered him—coat dusted with ice, shoulders squared, eyes cold enough to freeze the room solid.

Junior felt his stomach drop. The boss of the family. The man he answered to now. And the kind of man who never showed up anywhere without a reason.

Moretti didn't speak at first. He just stared at Junior, unreadable, then jerked his chin toward the back office. Junior followed, palms sweating.

The moment the door shut, Moretti spoke.

"Why is the FBI asking about Alexandria Kelley?"

His voice was calm, almost bored, but the weight behind it made Junior's pulse spike. He tried to brush it off, muttering something about not remembering her, about it being years ago, about the agents probably fishing. The excuses sounded weak even to him.

Moretti didn't buy a word of it. He watched Junior with a flat, patient stare, the kind that made the room feel smaller. When Junior finally admitted the truth—that Alex had taken a flash drive from his father's office eight years ago, and the FBI might have it now—Moretti's expression didn't change. He simply gave a small nod to the two men standing behind Junior.

They stepped in fast. A fist to the ribs. Another to the jaw. A third to the gut that knocked the air out of him. Not enough to do real damage. Just enough to make a point.

When they stepped back, Moretti finally spoke. "Kids and their computers," he said, almost amused. "Your father and I stayed out of prison because we didn't leave trails. No phones. No emails. No digital footprints. We kept everything face to face, and that's why no one ever touched us."

"Eight years," Junior said, wiping blood from his lip. "That's how long it's been. They don't have anything current. Most of those locations are no longer in operation. They can't tie us to anything," Junior croaked.

Moretti's gaze sharpened.

"Make sure all the locations have changed," he said. "Every one of them. And make sure there is nothing—nothing—that leads back to us."

Junior nodded quickly, throat tight. Moretti didn't raise his voice. He didn't need to. The message was clear, and it carried more weight than the beating ever could. Junior could feel it in the way Moretti looked at him—like this wasn't just about the flash drive anymore. Like Alex Kelley had just become another problem on a list Junior didn't even know existed.

And now that list was his responsibility to clean up.

Hours later, Junior brushed his fingers over his split lip, the skin tender and swollen. The ache pulsed in time with the storm outside, a steady reminder of how badly he'd screwed up and how little patience Moretti had left for him.

Across the room, Two-Face lounged on the couch with the stolen tablet balanced on his knee. Alex's tablet. He kept checking it as if he expected it to suddenly light up with her location. Junior didn't know why he bothered. The thing had been dead quiet since she vanished, nothing but a useless slab of glass and plastic.

Out of the corner of his eye, Junior caught the way Two-Face suddenly went rigid, and sucked in a harsh breath.

Junior's head snapped up. "What is it?"

Two-Face didn't answer. He just stared at the screen, eyes narrowing. Junior pushed back from the table and crossed the room, ignoring the muttered complaints from the men he'd been beating at cards.

A single notification glowed on the tablet.

Gremlin Cloud: New workout uploaded.

Junior's stomach twisted.

No, she shouldn't have been anywhere near a device. She shouldn't have been anywhere near anything that could leave a trail. Either she was dumber than he thought, or she had no idea her watch logged workouts automatically.

Two-Face tapped the alert. A three-mile run logged earlier today.

A slow heat crept up the back of Junior's neck, something sharp and electric. She was alive. She was moving. And her smart watch was recording her movements.

Two-Face dug through the menus, muttering as he navigated deeper. Junior leaned in, pulse thudding in his ears, anticipation bubbling up like pressure under his ribs.

Then something on the screen shifted.

A new option.

Locate Device.

Two-Face tapped it.

A loading circle spun, the pulsing icon reflected in his glasses. Junior held his breath without meaning to.

The map appeared. A blinking dot. Somewhere in Tennessee. Two-Face zoomed in, fingers moving fast, until the town name sharpened into view.

Junior's mouth went dry. Two-Face finally looked up, waiting for him to speak.

Junior forced himself to stand straighter. "Where is she?"

Two-Face turned the screen toward him. "Cottage Grove, Tennessee."

Junior stared at the blinking dot on the screen, a slow, mean smile pulling at his split lip. Look at that. Turns out he was the smart one after all. The girl who'd upended his life, taken what was his, and rejected him like he was nothing was sitting out there broadcasting her location like a gift.

And this time, she didn't have her protector hovering around her.

No cop boyfriend to swoop in.

No one to pull her out of the fire she'd lit.

She was alone, and they were coming. She'd slipped away once, but that had been a lifetime ago, before she'd taken what was his and left him to deal with the fallout. Her future had been taken out of his hands the second Moretti walked into the dealership. There would be no more escapes. Not if he wanted to keep breathing.

He dragged a hand over his face, jaw tight. He'd planned to deal with Declan tonight and tie off that loose end before it could unravel anything else, but the storm had shut down half the state. Roads were closed. Flights were grounded. Every route he tried to take had been blocked.

But this… this was better.

Declan could wait.

Finding her was the real prize.

Junior turned to Two-Face, who was still clutching the tablet as if it might vanish. "Book a flight," Junior said, voice low, steady. "First one out when the airports open."

Two Face blinked. "For you?"

"No." Junior's gaze slid back to the pulsing dot on the map. "For you. Go alone. And this time, you don't come back without finishing it."

Two-Face swallowed hard. Junior would've loved to be the one watching the life drain from her eyes, but Wallace had called him several times in the past few days. That alone told him he was on the man's radar. He needed distance—space between himself and Alex—so no one could tie him to her death.

Two-Face could be dealt with later. Junior would wrap this problem up with a neat little bow for Moretti and prove exactly how valuable he could be.

And then everyone would finally understand where he belonged.

Junior leaned in, letting the weight of the words settle. "Her death is the only thing that will keep us alive. You understand me."

Two-Face didn't flinch, didn't back down, didn't give him anything. Just that hard, flat stare that said he'd done worse for less. Junior hated that look. Hated the reminder that the men around him weren't afraid of him the way they'd been afraid of his father.

Moretti never had to repeat himself. Moretti never had to explain.

Junior swallowed the heat rising in his throat. He wasn't his father. He wasn't going to die because of someone else's mistakes. Because of her mistakes.

She should've stayed gone. Should've stayed quiet. Should never have taken what wasn't hers. But she had to come back, had to dig, had to ruin everything the way she always did. And now he was the one with a target on his back. His father's mess. Her fault. All of it.

One of them had to die, and it wouldn't be him.

Chapter Thirty-Three
DECLAN

After three days of being trapped in his room, Declan was more than ready to wrap up his trip to this snow-choked wasteland. His rental car sat buried under nearly two feet of powder, the roads were still coated in slush thick enough to swallow a tire, so he walked across the street to headquarters and put off digging out his car for later. Snowbanks towered over him, walls of white at least six feet high. Even during the two years he lived in Ohio, the storms had never dumped this much snow.

He shoved his hands deeper into his pockets and kept moving, the cold biting at his cheeks. Today he would get answers. Then he was going home.

He picked his way across the slushy street, his dress shoes soaking through almost immediately. With every step, melted snow pooled inside them, making a soft, miserable squishing sound he couldn't stop fixating on. By the time he reached the conference room, his feet were freezing, and the steady seep of cold through his socks had become all he could think about as Meeker began questioning Moretti.

Declan didn't believe Moretti was responsible for the attacks on Alex. The man was smart, calculating, and ruthless. If he wanted someone dead, they would be dead. Moretti didn't make mistakes, and he didn't leave loose ends. However, if the trafficking ring existed, he was the one orchestrating it, and that alone was worth sitting through the interview.

If Moretti truly didn't know about Alex or the information she possessed, they risked tipping him off to a threat he might not know about. And in doing so, they could add to the danger already circling Alex. They were locked in a high-stakes dance with a man who thrived in the shadows, and every question they asked had the potential to shift the balance in ways they couldn't predict.

He circled Mr. Beaumont's number with his pen. Stewart had given it to him yesterday, but by the time he ended the call, it was after nine, and he'd had all the news he could handle for one night. He planned on reaching out to the man when they concluded their business with Moretti.

Every time he tried to get information about the will, he hit the same wall. Brittany claimed she knew nothing, and Helena had danced around the subject with the polished vagueness that only came from years of practice. Neither woman would say a word about what Enzo left behind or why the estate was taking so long to settle. Declan didn't buy it. Enzo Esposito hadn't been the type to leave loose ends, and probate didn't stall this long without someone benefiting from the delay.

Junior was the obvious candidate. If there was a financial motive buried in that will, something that could explain the timing of the attacks, Beaumont was the man they needed to talk to. If his theory were right, and the delay in the will had anything to do with Alex, then Beaumont would know. And Beaumont wouldn't be able to hide behind attorney-client privilege once a federal investigation was involved.

Meeker's voice pulled him back to the present. Declan shifted in his chair and refocused, pen in hand, jotting down questions and observations as Meeker pressed Moretti. The man answered with the smooth confidence of someone who had spent years lying to law enforcement, but Declan listened anyway, letting the exchange unfold while his mind worked ahead, circling the thread he intended to pull the moment this interview ended.

"Do you know this woman?" Meeker asked, sliding a picture across the table.

Moretti studied it for a moment before pushing it back. "Never seen her before in my life."

"Have you heard the name Alexandria Kelley?"

"Can't say that I have," Moretti said, his tone clipped with annoyance. His gaze shifted to Declan and stayed there. He didn't look away when Declan met his stare. His gaze lingered, as if he were trying to decide what kind of man he was dealing with. A calculating look. The way predators sized up other predators, searching for weakness.

Meeker continued. "She used to work for Enzo Esposito. Recently, several attempts were made on her life. An abduction attempt. A canister of aerosolized fentanyl strapped to one of her patients. A car bomb. Several home invasions. They even attacked her babysitter."

Moretti's brows lifted a fraction. "Aerosolized fentanyl," he repeated, almost amused. "Creative. Messy, though. Whoever planned that one wasn't thinking ahead."

Declan looked up from his notes. "Why do you say that?"

Moretti shifted his attention to him, the faintest hint of condescension in his eyes. "Because it's unpredictable. Too many variables. Airflow, dosage, timing... you can't control any of it. Whoever set that up either didn't know what they were doing or didn't care who else got caught in the crossfire." His mouth curved, not quite a smile. "Professionals don't make a mess like that."

Declan watched him, the explanation settling into place with a clarity he didn't like. Moretti would never openly cooperate with law enforcement, not even to save himself, but his words carried more weight than he intended. A professional wouldn't have used aerosolized fentanyl. A professional wouldn't have risked collateral damage or left a trail that sloppy. And Moretti was nothing if not a professional. The attack hadn't been sanctioned. It had come from someone reckless and emotional. Someone with nothing to lose.

Someone like Junior.

Moretti looked as if he was about to speak. His mouth parted, a thought forming, then he pressed his lips into a thin line as though he'd reconsidered at the last second.

Declan caught it. "What were you about to say?"

Moretti's gaze slid to him, steady and unblinking. "We don't attack the family," he said. "It's our code." He lifted one shoulder in a small, dismissive shrug. "I think you're barking up the wrong tree looking at Enzo's associates."

Declan had entertained that same fleeting thought back at Nina's house. The mob wasn't usually this messy, and for a moment he'd wondered if they were getting tunnel vision. But then they'd identified Two-face and were without a doubt moving in the right direction. Moretti was good—better than Declan had expected—subtly trying to steer them away from Enzo's circle without making it obvious.

Meeker pressed on as if Moretti hadn't spoken at all. "Enzo threatened her life before they split ways. Probably not a coincidence that these attacks started immediately after his death. And we believe the motive ties back to a flash drive Miss Kelley copied from Esposito's computer before she left eight years ago."

That landed. Shit. He should've talked to Meeker before they walked in here. The whole point was to keep Alex off Moretti's radar for as long as possible.

Moretti didn't move, but something in him went still. His gaze sharpened for a single breath—an involuntary tell, the kind a man gives when a new variable hits the board. One he hadn't accounted for. He recovered fast, smoothing his expression back into bored indifference, but Declan had already seen the slip.

Moretti's mouth curved, not quite a smile. "Sounds like she's made some dangerous friends. Or enemies. Hard to tell the difference these days." His tone stayed mild, but the words had an edge. "Enzo was old-school, like me. No computers, no cell phones. The flash drive is of little concern."

The way he refused to meet their eyes on that last line told Declan the flash drive was anything but insignificant. And the longer he watched him, the more certain he became that Moretti had walked into this interview already knowing exactly what it was really about.

"I guess we'll find out," Declan said, forcing calm into his voice. "The FBI took possession of the flash drive." He threw that last part out there as a desperate attempt to steer attention away from Alex.

"Any idea who's behind these attacks?" Meeker barreled on. Subtlety wasn't in his toolkit. The questions mattered, but Declan preferred a slower squeeze—get a man comfortable, get him talking, then drop the hammer when he couldn't wriggle free.

Moretti scoffed. "What do I look like, a nark? I don't know anything about that."

A sharp knock broke the moment. An agent stepped in, murmured something low to Meeker, and slipped out again. The interruption lasted only a few seconds, but it was enough. When Declan looked back, Moretti had settled into a practiced calm. His shoulders eased, his expression smoothed, and the hint of tension he had shown earlier was gone.

Meeker moved on, asking about shipments, associates, and the last time Moretti had spoken to Enzo Esposito, his tone steady and unhurried. The questions came one after another, a quiet rhythm that filled the room. Declan listened, pen tapping lightly against his notepad, the faint squish of his still-wet shoes grounding him in the moment. The radiator in the corner clicked as it struggled to warm the space, and the air carried the stale scent of old coffee and disinfectant.

Meeker glanced over, checking whether Declan had anything to add. Declan gave a small shake of his head. Moretti's answers were consistent, his posture steady, and nothing in his reactions suggested he was involved or had any knowledge of the recent attacks.

Even with that realization, unease settled in his chest. Moretti might not be involved now, but he had taken an interest. Men like him rarely let something like this pass without inserting themselves. The interview felt less like closing a loop and more like setting something in motion that could easily spin out of control.

"Alright, Mr. Moretti, thank you for coming in today. We will be in touch if we have any further questions."

"Anything for my friends at the FBI," Moretti said, rising from his seat. "Good luck, gentlemen."

When the door closed behind him, Meeker exhaled. "I believe him."

"So do I," Declan said. He stood and walked to the window. "But he spoke in code. If he or Enzo wanted her dead, she would be. Someone else is behind this. Someone with less power. And Moretti knows it. My money is on Junior."

Meeker nodded slowly. "It makes sense. Junior was close to Enzo, and the timing lined up. The attacks started right after Enzo died." He crossed his arms, thinking it through. "Now we just need to figure out what triggered them."

"I've got a flight out of Boston this afternoon," Declan said. "I'm going to stop by the dealership on my way to the airport and see if I can catch Enzo Junior. He's been dodging my calls. I want to look him in the eye. Size him up. My gut says he's behind the attacks." He tapped the corner of his notepad where he'd scribbled Beaumont's number down last night. "I'll be calling Mr. Beaumont today, too. Enzo's lawyer should know what's holding up the will. I checked with the local court this morning, and it hasn't even been filed yet."

Meeker nodded, flipping to a fresh page in his own notebook. "The agent who stepped in earlier passed along something you should know. He's identified a handful of potential locations along the New England coast that might be tied to the trafficking ring. Old warehouses, private docks, a couple of shell companies leasing waterfront property. We'll be checking them out over the next few days." He met Declan's eyes. "We'll keep you apprised."

Declan gathered his things and said his goodbyes. He still needed to pack. He marched back across the street, cursing the snow with every stride. After brushing off the mountain of accumulation on his rental car, he headed up to his room. The moment the door shut behind him, he pulled out his phone and dialed Mr. Beaumont. The call rang until it rolled to voicemail. He set the phone aside with a tired exhale. A long, hot shower and a pair of warm wool socks to thaw out his feetsicles were definitely in order before he tried again.

He had just peeled off his wet socks and was unbuckling his belt when his phone rang. Agent Price's name lit up the screen. The update was brief but enough to punch the air from his lungs: Alex had confirmed the boy in the photo was the same boy she'd seen with Myra. The ring was real. And if they had any hope of finding that kid before he vanished for good, they needed to move now.

He forgot the shower and pulled on dry socks. He grabbed his bag and packed with quick, efficient movements. The plan hadn't changed. He still intended to stop by the dealership and speak with Junior on his way to the airport. Worcester was an hour from Boston and nearly two hours from his hotel, which meant he was already behind.

He checked out, tossed his bag into the Kia, and punched the address into the GPS. As he pulled out of the lot, he toyed with the idea of telling Junior he planned to speak with Mr. Beaumont, then dismissed it. Better to keep that card close. The stakes were rising by the minute, and the pull to get back to Alex tightened in his chest. Another attack felt inevitable. They'd overplayed their hand telling Moretti about the flash drive. If he figured out the information it contained, they wouldn't just be dealing with sloppy attempts and close calls. If Moretti got to Alex first, she was as good as dead.

Chapter Thirty-Four
DECLAN

The drive to the dealership passed without incident. As soon as he stepped into the service area, an eager sales associate beelined towards him. Declan flashed his badge, and the man's enthusiasm evaporated.

"I'm looking for Junior Esposito," Declan said.

"He's through there," the associate said, pointing toward a glass-walled office.

Declan approached the door. Junior was inside, pacing behind his desk, clearly in the middle of a heated phone call. Declan knocked on the glass, and Junior jolted, eyes snapping toward him. Irritation flashed across his face. He held up a finger, signaling Declan to wait.

Declan had no patience left for courtesy. Three days of being ignored had grated on him, and he refused to let Junior dictate the pace any longer. He pushed through the glass door and dropped into the chair across from him, arms loose, expression calm and indifferent. A slow smile tugged at his mouth; the conversation was happening now, whether or not Junior liked it.

Junior glared at him, clearly offended by the intrusion. Declan immediately noticed the black eye and split lip.

"I've gotta let you go. Some schmuck just walked into my office. I'll call you back." Junior slammed the corded phone into its cradle and turned his full attention on Declan. "What can I help you with?" he asked, irritation dripping from every word.

Declan leaned forward and offered his hand. "Sergeant Declan Wallace. I've left you several messages. Since you couldn't bother to call me back, I figured I'd swing by."

Junior shook his hand reluctantly. "It's been crazy around here with the storm."

"Right," Declan reached into his coat and pulled out a photo. "I wanted to ask you a few questions about the case I'm working on. Do you know her?"

He held up the picture of Martha.

Junior barely glanced at it before shaking his head. "No. Never seen her."

Declan watched him closely. The denial came too fast. A flicker of recognition tightened the muscles around his eyes, gone as quickly as it appeared. Junior looked away a beat too soon, as if afraid the truth might slip out if he held Declan's gaze.

He knew her. He just wasn't admitting it.

Declan didn't look away from Junior as he slipped the photo back into his pocket. "That's interesting," he said lightly. "Brittany told me you met her mother while she was up for a visit."

Junior hesitated and forced a casual shrug. "Oh. Yeah. I guess I did see her. Briefly. A few weeks ago."

Declan nodded as if the answer satisfied him, though the truth sat plain as day. Junior recognized Martha the moment he saw the photo. He just hadn't expected to be called on it.

Declan let Junior's weak correction hang in the air for a moment before sliding the photo back across the desk. "Someone murdered her when she returned from that trip. Know anything about that?"

Junior's jaw twitched, a tiny pulse beneath the skin, and he shifted in his chair as if the cushion had suddenly become uncomfortable. The office smelled faintly of motor oil and stale coffee, and the hum of the fluorescent lights overhead filled the silence between them. Junior cleared his throat, eyes dropping to the clutter on his desk. "No. I don't know anything about that."

Declan watched him closely. The denial was flat, but the tension in his shoulders told a different story.

"Of course not," Declan said in an almost placating tone. "How about her?" He held up the picture of Alex.

Junior studied it. "Oh, yeah, I know her." His eyes darkened. "Several of us know her."

Declan's spine stiffened at the way he drew out the word *know*. "How exactly do you know her?"

Junior's reaction shifted in a way that made the hair on the back of Declan's neck lift. The defensiveness he'd carried a moment ago slipped away, replaced by something slower and darker. His shoulders eased back, his posture loosening as if the question amused him. A lazy confidence crept into his expression, and the look he gave the photo held a smug, insinuating edge, meant to provoke. His eyes lingered on Alex's image with a familiarity he wanted Declan to notice, a silent suggestion that whatever he knew about her was intimate.

The air in the office felt warmer, heavier, thick with the scent of motor oil and the faint rubber tang drifting in from the service bay. The fluorescent light hummed overhead, sharpening the tension between them.

"She used to work for my father. Started out as a horse trainer, but eventually became more of a personal assistant. She handled everything. His meetings, his business dealings, all of it. He depended on her more than anyone else. She walked away about ten years ago."

Declan felt his shoulders tighten. *She handled everything.* That was not a small claim. He studied Junior's face carefully, watching for the twitch of an eye, the shift of a jaw, anything that hinted at exaggeration or a lie. He found nothing. Junior looked almost bored as he spoke, as if he were reciting a list he had memorized years ago.

"How was their relationship?" Declan asked.

"Good at first. She was damn good at what she did."

"What changed?"

Junior leaned back, a slow smirk pulling at his mouth. "He found out she was sleeping with me and decided he wanted a turn. When she shut him down, he did not take it well."

Declan kept his expression neutral, but something cold slid down his spine. Junior was a sensational liar or delusional enough to believe every word coming out of his mouth.

"So you had a personal relationship with Miss Kelley?"

"Yeah. Things were getting serious until I found out she was sleeping with a couple of my guys."

Declan watched him closely. There was something in Junior's eyes, a glint of satisfaction, almost like he enjoyed twisting the knife. It made Declan wary, but the confidence in the man's voice was unsettling.

"Those guys still work here," Declan said.

"Yeah. In fact—" Junior pushed open the office door. "Jared, come here a sec."

A mechanic in a grease-stained polo stepped inside, wiping his hands on a rag. The smell of motor oil drifted in with him, mixing with the stale coffee already hanging in the air. He looked between them, curious but wary, the way employees do when the boss calls them in without warning.

Declan watched Junior with a growing sense of certainty. Something in the man's reaction was off. Junior leaned back in his chair like he was relaxed, but the tight set of his jaw betrayed him. He was trying too hard. He held his shoulders a little too square, as if bracing for something. A thin sheen of sweat clung to his temple despite the cold air drifting in from the service bay.

Junior was performing. And Declan could feel the performance slipping.

Declan kept his voice even. "Miss Kelley denies ever having any kind of relationship with anyone in Mr. Esposito's organization. She says the only tension came from the old man trying to sleep with her. She claims that is why she left."

Junior scoffed, then turned to Jared, holding up Alex's photo. "You remember her?"

Jared studied it for a moment, then let out a low whistle. "Oh yeah. Hard to forget her."

Declan's stomach tightened. Jared looked genuinely amused, almost nostalgic.

Jared leaned in a little, lowering his voice as if he were sharing a memory he had no business sharing. "She had that little birthmark on her inner thigh. Right side. Shaped like a teardrop."

Declan went still.

He knew that birthmark.

He'd seen it.

He'd kissed it.

The room seemed to shift under him, his vision blurring at the edges. His pulse roared in his ears, drowning out the hum of the dealership lights. Junior watched him carefully, a slow smile spreading across his bruised face, as if savoring every second of Declan's unraveling.

Declan forced himself to breathe. He tried to tell himself they were lying, that this was some coordinated stunt meant to shake him. But how else would they know about the mark? That detail lived in a place no one else should ever have seen.

Junior's version of events was horribly logical. It explained why the old man had never gone after her. Enzo didn't leave loose ends. If she had betrayed his son, that alone would have been enough to make her disappear quietly, but not enough to bring down the wrath of Enzo Senior. He would have left his son's mess for his son to clean up.

Declan studied them both, waiting for the slightest slip that would let him dismiss this as a lie. Jared lounged back, bored and unbothered. Junior wore a smug certainty, the kind of confidence that came from believing he held the upper hand.

If they were lying, they were doing it with surgical precision.

If they were telling the truth...

Declan swallowed hard, fighting the rise of bile in his throat. His mind railed against every word coming out of their mouths. The picture they were painting of Alex did not just contradict the woman he knew. It shredded her. It twisted her into someone unrecognizable. Someone calculated. Someone deceitful. But he could not ignore the cold, brutal fact that they had described something only a lover would know.

Junior began clicking his pen rhythmically. The sound drilled into Declan's skull. Tap. Tap. Tap. Each click felt like a taunt.

"I didn't know she was the boss's girl. When I found out, I broke things off with her and told Junior what happened," Jared said with a shrug.

"Yeah," Junior added, leaning back like he was settling in to enjoy the show. "She denied everything when I confronted her. I broke it off, and a few weeks later she just... vanished. Luckily, my dad hired Brittany right before Alex left." He shrugged. "She was a social climber, really putting in work for that ring, if you know what I mean." He let out a low whistle. "God, I miss that mouth."

Declan's jaw clenched so hard he thought he might chip a tooth. He took a slow breath through his nose, fighting the violent urge to put Junior through the glass wall behind him. He tried to drag his thoughts back to the case, to something solid, but their words kept slipping through the cracks and pulling him under.

"That is all very interesting," Declan said, his voice tight. "But your father threatened her life. And in the last few weeks, there have been several attempts to make good on that threat. She was also in possession of files taken from his computer."

Junior barked out a laugh. "My father could barely turn a computer on. You really think he was keeping files on anything?"

Declan narrowed his eyes. "No," Declan leaned in just enough to make Junior feel it, his gaze sharpening to a hard point. "But you can."

Junior's smirk faltered for half a second. It was small, but Declan caught it.

"Where were you last week?" He asked, keeping his tone even.

Junior straightened a little, the confidence returning to his face. "I was here. Working. Ask anyone."

He looked toward Jared, who still hovered near the door as if he wanted to disappear.

"He was here," Jared said immediately. "Every day."

Declan studied them both. Jared's voice was steady, but his eyes flicked to Junior before he spoke. Junior sat too still, too composed, like a man who had practiced this moment in the mirror.

Declan let the silence stretch, then nodded once. "No bother. The FBI has the drive now. They are going through every piece of information on it."

He watched the way Junior's eyes tightened at the edges, the way his posture shifted a fraction. Junior had no idea the Bureau already knew about the trafficking ring. That ignorance was the only leverage Declan had left, and he was not about to waste it.

Let him think the FBI was still in the dark.

Let him believe he still had time.

Let him scramble to cover tracks that were already exposed.

A man who believed he still had a chance always revealed more than a man who knew he was finished.

Declan settled back in his chair, letting Junior stew in the uncertainty, waiting to see what fear would make him do next.

A slight flare in Junior's pupils gave him away, followed by a faint quickening of his breath.

Declan was done with the games. "Is there any reason your father's lawyer is in Arkansas asking to speak with Miss Kelley?"

Junior's expression flickered again, sharper this time. For a split second, something hot and ugly flashed across his face—rage, pure and unfiltered. It was gone almost as quickly as it appeared, buried under a practiced smirk, but Declan had already seen it. Any reasonable person would have asked for a lawyer by now. Anyone with sense would have slowed down, shut up, and stopped trying to charm their way through a federal investigation. But Junior wasn't thinking clearly anymore. He was reacting.

And that reaction told Declan everything he needed to know.

Junior had been trying to avoid this exact line of questioning. The moment the topic brushed against the will and the man who drafted it, his composure cracked. Declan felt the pieces click into place. Whatever answers they were missing, whatever motive tied this all together, lived with the lawyer. Beaumont wasn't just a name on a notepad. He was the key.

"I'm sure the old man left her a horse or something," Junior said, recovering quickly. "She was one of the best trainers he had, according to him."

Declan watched him, letting the silence settle again, letting Junior think he was still in control.

Declan pointed to the camera in the corner. "These security cameras work."

"Unfortunately, no. They stopped working last year, and Dad refused to replace them. Cheapskate. They work as a deterrent, though. Keep the guys honest."

Declan didn't buy a word of it, but without a warrant his hands were tied. Every instinct he had was pointing straight at Junior, and his instincts had never steered him wrong. He shifted tactics, letting his questions jump tracks without warning, keeping Junior off balance and denying him the chance to settle into the conversation.

"What happened to your face?" Declan asked.

Junior's smug grin faltered. "Got into a fight two nights ago. Poker game with a few of the guys. Things got heated."

"This guy have a name."

"None of your concern," Junior snapped.

"I don't think it was one of your guys. I think it was your boss. You see, we spoke to him earlier today. He knew nothing about the attacks on Miss Kelley. He didn't seem happy about all the attention he was getting from the FBI. If I were him, and one of my employees was doing side jobs and attracting unwanted attention from law enforcement, I'd be in a hurry to put a stop to that."

"I work for myself."

"We're holding to the 'I'm not in the mafia' story, I see."

Junior stared back with a blank, irritated expression.

"Aren't you a little out of your jurisdiction?"

"I'm working on a joint case with the FBI."

"Well, you're barking up the wrong tree. I have nothing to do with the attacks on that whore."

Declan squeezed the arms of his chair until his knuckles ached. He counted to three. Then three more. "Well, I'm off. I'm on my way to the airport. I'm flying in to speak with Mr. Beaumont about his business regarding miss Kelley." He rose and headed for the door.

"Safe travels. I heard a storm front is moving over Missouri, Arkansas… northwestern Tennessee." The last three words dropped into a lower register, almost a purr. Junior's voice dipped just enough to make Declan's pulse hitch. And as he spoke, a sly grin crept across his face.

Declan froze.

The hair on the back of his neck stood up.

Junior knew.

He knew exactly where Alex was.

He was baiting him, watching for a reaction, but Declan didn't care. Something inside him snapped. In three long strides, he was back at Junior's side, his hand clamped around the man's throat. The anger that had been simmering since he walked into the dealership erupted. Junior didn't even have time to flinch before Declan's fist connected with his face. Once. Twice. A third time. Junior slid down the wall, unconscious.

Declan stood over him, chest heaving, vision tunneling. He wiped his bloody knuckles on Junior's shirt and walked out. Jared was gone. The remaining employees stared but didn't move to help their boss.

Once inside his rental car, Declan shut the door against the biting wind and immediately called the FBI detail stationed outside Alex's house. He instructed them to stay on high alert. When he hung up, he scrolled to Mr. Beuamont's number from earlier and hit call.

Mr. Beaumont answered on the third ring. He had a thin, nasally voice, like someone perpetually recovering from a cold.

The conversation that followed was short, tense, and far more revealing than Beaumont intended. The lawyer tried to stonewall him at first, insisting he couldn't disclose anything without Alex present. Declan didn't bother arguing. He simply informed Beaumont that Agent Stewart had already obtained a federal warrant authorizing the seizure of any information he possessed regarding Enzo Esposito or Alex Kelley.

That was all it took.

Minutes later, Declan ended the call, the phone slipping from his fingers and landing in the passenger seat. His hands trembled as he stared through the windshield, the world outside blurring into streaks of snow and street-lights.

Beaumont's words echoed in his skull, each one slicing deeper than the last.

Alex wasn't just mentioned in Enzo Esposito's will. She inherited the bulk of the estate, with only a few minor items left to Junior and his mother. Enzo had given her the stable, several restaurants up and down the East Coast, and his entire bank account—four hundred million dollars. The number throbbed in Declan's mind, loud and insistent, a warning he couldn't ignore.

Junior's accusations surged back with brutal clarity. Alex hadn't simply been in the wrong place at the wrong time. She had been tied to the center of everything, woven into a world she claimed she feared. And if any of this were true, she hadn't just kept secrets—she had played him. Every moment they shared, every confession, every touch, all of it twisted now, poisoned by the possibility that she had been using him from the beginning.

A tightness spread through his chest as old wounds tore open—betrayals he had buried, humiliations he had sworn he would never relive, the sting of trusting another human being completely only to be gutted by it. He had promised himself he would never make that mistake again, never lower his guard, never let anyone close enough to hurt him the way others had.

And yet, he had let Alex in. He had believed her. He had wanted her. The realization twisted hard in his gut, leaving him unsteady, unsure where the truth ended and the lies began. His mind spun out, a storm of doubt and betrayal. He wanted to confront Alex, to demand answers and drag the truth into the open, but the thought of hearing her confirm any of it tightened his throat until he could barely breathe.

A blaring horn jolted him back to the present. The light had turned green. He hadn't even noticed. He pressed the accelerator, but his body felt numb, disconnected, like he was watching himself from somewhere outside his own skin.

He had been a fool.

A naïve, lovesick fool.

And he hated himself for it.

Chapter Thirty-Five
ALEX

It had been a long day. Tony had his grandkids up for the week, and Alex, Katherine, and Collin had spent the afternoon grilling out in Tony's backyard. The weather had been mild, almost sixty degrees, and the sun still hung warm and golden over the treetops. Alex sat in a rocking chair, wrapped in her white sweater, jeans, and lace-up brown knee-high boots, listening to the kids shriek and laugh as they chased each other across the grass. Katherine and Tony eventually slipped inside to watch a movie, leaving Alex alone with the children and the fading light.

She hadn't felt well all day. A heaviness clung to her limbs, a sluggishness she blamed on stress and too many sleepless nights. She finally headed back to the house for a nap. Collin didn't want to stop playing, so Katherine agreed to stay outside with the kids.

Alex crossed the wide yard, rubbing her arms against a sudden chill. As she neared the house, a yellow cab pulled up beside the parked FBI vehicle. Her heart skipped. Declan wasn't supposed to be home until tomorrow.

Then he stepped out.

The white button-down hugged his shoulders and chest in a way that made her breath catch. His stride was confident and purposeful, and the sight of him, solid and familiar and impossibly handsome, sent a warm rush through her. It had only been a week, but it felt like a lifetime. She quickened her pace, excitement bubbling up inside her.

He set his bags down on the porch just as she reached him.

"Hey!" she said brightly, racing up the steps and throwing her arms around him.

Declan didn't move.

He didn't hug her back.

His body went rigid beneath her hands, as if she'd startled a stranger instead of the man she'd been aching to see.

Alex pulled back, confusion tightening her chest. "What's wrong?"

Declan met her eyes with a look so closed off it felt like a door slamming in her face. The warmth she expected wasn't there. Not even a flicker. It was like staring into the eye of a storm—quiet on the surface, but danger circling just beneath it.

"Nothing. Where are Collin and my mom?" he asked coolly.

"They're over at Tony's house."

"We need to move. They know we're here."

"What? How?" Alex's brow furrowed, concern tightening her voice.

"I don't know." Declan stepped around her and headed down the stairs toward the parked agent. Alex followed, her pulse beginning to race.

"This position has been compromised. Keep an eye out while we pack. You'll need to take Miss Kelley and her son to a safe house," Declan instructed.

The agent nodded.

Alex's heart dropped.

He hadn't said we.

He hadn't said all of us.

He hadn't included himself. Or Katherine.

Declan turned toward Tony's house. Alex reached for his arm, desperate for grounding, for reassurance, for anything familiar. He jerked away as if her touch burned him. The rejection hit her like a slap.

"Declan, please tell me what is wrong," she whispered, her voice trembling.

His lips pressed into a hard, unforgiving line. Tension radiated off him like heat rising from asphalt in the thick summer sun.

"Are you coming to the safe house?" she asked, swallowing the rising panic clawing up her throat.

"No," he said, the finality in his voice colder than anything she'd heard from him before.

He didn't even look at her.

Her stomach plummeted. He was leaving. Leaving her. Leaving Collin. Leaving everything they'd built in the last few weeks. Tears stung her eyes, but she blinked them back, refusing to fall apart without understanding why.

"What happened?" she asked again, her voice cracking.

A low, humorless laugh escaped him, sharp enough to cut. It didn't sound like him. The sound froze her where she stood.

His eyes finally met hers, and the contempt in them stole the air from her lungs.

"I've been risking my life for you because I believed you. Because I lo—" He stopped himself, jaw tightening. "Now I don't know if I can believe a single word that's crossed your lips."

"What... what are you talking about?" she managed, stepping toward him instinctively, reaching for the man who had held her through nightmares, who had kissed her like she mattered, who had promised she was safe.

Declan stepped back, denying her even an inch of closeness.

"You know," he said, bitterness roughening every word, "I didn't want to believe them when they said you'd slept your way through their inner circle. I told myself they were just trying to get under my skin. But they knew things they shouldn't have known. They knew about your birthmark." He let out a sharp breath, something like disgust or hurt twisting through it. "And then I spoke to Beaumont, and he told me about the inheritance. After that... the pieces fell into place."

Alex staggered back as if he'd physically struck her. Her breath hitched, her chest tightened painfully. For a moment, she couldn't speak. Couldn't think. Couldn't breathe. She couldn't make sense of what he was saying. Birthmark? Inner circle? Inheritance? None of it connected. None of it made sense.

"Declan..." Her voice scraped out, barely there, her throat too tight to form anything stronger.

"How could you, Alex?" His voice was a low growl, thick with hurt. "How could you sell yourself to those lowlifes?"

The accusation didn't land all at once. It seeped in slowly, like cold water finding every crack. She shook her head, not in denial but in confusion, her mind scrambling for something solid to hold onto. She had no idea what he was talking about. No idea how they could know things they shouldn't. No idea why he suddenly looked at her as if she were a stranger.

Her stomach dropped. "Sell myself?" She whispered mostly to herself.

Her knees nearly buckled. "What are you talking about? I never—"

"Don't lie to me!" he shouted, the force of it making her flinch. "I spoke to Mr. Beaumont. I know everything."

Everything inside her went still.

She had never heard that name in her life.

She stared at him, wide-eyed and hollow, unable to reconcile the man in front of her with the one who had held her in his arms and told her she was beautiful. His expression was carved from something cold and unforgiving, and the look in his eyes made her feel small in a way she hadn't felt in years.

Her throat tightened painfully. "Declan... please... I don't even know a Mr. Beau—"

"Save it," Declan spat, his voice dripping with contempt. "I thought you were different, Alex. I thought you were someone I could trust. But you're just like everyone else, willing to sell yourself for a quick buck. Your feigned modesty." He scoffed. "Our first time together was a nice touch. Very believable." His tone sharpened into something cruel. "Your ex was right. You are broken.

Her heart shattered into a million tiny shards, the sharp edges scraping against scars that had only just begun to heal. The wounds tore open again, raw and bleeding. It wasn't a loud or dramatic collapse. It was a devastatingly quiet assault that left her standing on unsteady ground with nothing solid to hold on to. A slow and brutal unraveling she doubted she'd recover from.

Broken.

He had taken her deepest insecurity and thrown it back at her with precision. The worst part was how easily the word fit in this moment. She felt it settle inside her, as if it had been waiting for a chance to resurface. All she could do was stand there, holding herself together with shaking hands, while the man she loved tore her apart with a few careless words.

"Go. Pack." His jaw was clenched so tightly that the words barely made it out. Hostility radiated off him in waves.

Unable to stand one more second of his scornful stare, Alex retreated into the house. She barely made it to the sink before her stomach lurched. When the heaving finally stopped, she clung to the counter, shaking. Cold water splashed over her face, but it did nothing to steady the storm inside her.

How could she have been such a fool?

She had trusted him with the parts of herself she never let anyone see—her fears, her insecurities, the fragile truths she kept buried beneath her armor. She had handed him her most vulnerable pieces, and he had wielded them against her like a weapon.

Her insides felt flayed open, every nerve raw and exposed. She pressed her palms to the counter, trying to hold herself together, but the pieces kept slipping through her fingers.

Broken.

One thing became painfully clear: she couldn't stay here.

Not with him.

Not after what he'd said.

Not after the way he'd looked at her like she was something dirty he'd stepped in.

She couldn't breathe in the same space as him, couldn't stand the thought of being trapped in a car or a safe house with the man who had just gutted her.

She had put off this call, hoping Declan and the FBI would sort things out legally, hoping he would come back to her with answers instead of accusations.

Her hands trembled as she picked up the phone. The device felt impossibly heavy, as though it carried the weight of her entire future. She dialed the number, each ring echoing through the quiet kitchen, matching the frantic beat of her heart.

"Hello," an elderly gentleman answered on the fourth ring.

"Uncle Richard... it's Alex. I need help."

The elderly man listened intently as Alex told him everything. She hadn't spoken to her great-uncle in years, but he had always been a constant presence in her childhood. After a quick conversation, he assured her that everything would be taken care of. Despite his reassuring words, as she hung up the phone, a sense of dread washed over her. The wheel had been set in motion, and there was no going back now.

Alex walked to the bedroom to pack. She pulled open the drawers of the dresser and began placing her clothes in her suitcase. As she folded a shirt, a movement in the mirror caught her eye. She froze. Behind her in the doorway stood a man, holding a knife, a knife covered in blood. Her heart pounded in her chest, but she forced herself to keep packing, pretending not to see him. She was a good ten feet away from the nightstand where her gun lay in the drawer. Every muscle in her body tensed as she calculated her chances. She knew she had to get to the gun before the man got to her.

Alex closed her eyes and said a quick prayer before she made her move. She had just grabbed the gun when she felt the full weight of the man tackling her from behind. She held onto the gun for dear life.

Alex hit the floor hard, the impact knocking the breath from her lungs. Before she could recover, the man was already on top of her, driving her down against the bedroom floor with his full weight. He straddled her hips, one hand clamped around her wrist, forcing her arm to the floor and keeping her from getting a clean shot. His other hand lifted, the knife angled above them, catching the dim light of the room.

She twisted beneath him, trying to shift her weight, trying to roll, trying anything to break his hold. But the hardwood floor offered no traction. Her feet slid uselessly, giving her nothing to push against. Every attempt to move only let him tighten his grip and settle his weight more firmly over her. Her muscles strained, her breath coming fast, but he had her pinned, and he knew it.

She couldn't die like this. She couldn't leave Collin. She couldn't let him find her dead when they returned from next door. The man wrenched the gun from her grip and sent it skidding across the room. Before she could reach for it, he trapped her arm beneath his knee, pinning her in place. His other hand fisted in her hair and yanked her head back, exposing her throat.

She cried out, the sound torn from her before she could stop it. The man's fury exploded, and the world became a blur of impact and disorientation. Her vision fractured. The floor rushed up. Pain flared along her side, sharp enough to steal her breath. She couldn't tell what he'd done; everything was happening too fast.

Her head was yanked back again, the movement violent enough to make her stomach roll. Darkness crowded the edges of her vision. She felt herself slipping, her body too heavy to fight, too battered to understand.

Just before everything went black, she saw Collin's face in her mind. Then Declan's. A single tear slid free. She couldn't give up. Not yet. Not while they were out there.

Instinct took over. She threw her free hand up to shield herself, bracing for the strike. Pain flared as the blade sliced across her palm, a sharp, burning line that forced a scream from her throat. The shock of it snapped her back into herself, clearing the fog for one brief, desperate moment. She held her ground, refusing him access to her neck, refusing to let this be the end.

Death didn't scare her. She had seen enough of it to think of it as an acquaintance she'd get to know better some day. But she had always imagined that day would come when she was old and had lived her life fully. After she watched Collin grow into a man and build a family of his own. After she finally knew what it felt like to be truly loved by someone who saw her, all of her, and stayed.

There was so much she wasn't ready to leave behind. So much unfinished. So much she still needed to fight for.

She strained with everything she had to free her trapped arm, but it was useless. His weight held her in place. She turned her head, searching for anything—any angle, any chance—and caught sight of his arm braced beside her. His hand clenched around the knife, supporting his weight as he shifted. The sleeve of his jacket slid up just enough for her to see the ink beneath it.

A serpent coiled along his forearm.

Recognition hit her like a blow. This was the man who had delivered the flowers to her work.

His arm was close. Close enough to bite.

If he killed her, they could match his DNA to the bite mark. They could tie him to her. And she knew—down to her bones—that Declan wouldn't stop until he found the man responsible. No matter what he thought of her now, no matter how deeply he'd cut her, he was relentless when it came to justice. He would hunt this man to the ends of the earth.

And she just needed to give him something to find.

She lunged for his arm and sank her teeth into his flesh as hard as she could. She tasted blood in her mouth and got a moment of satisfaction before a blow came down hard on the back of her head. Her vision went black. She felt the cold steel blade press against her throat. The warmth of her blood dripping down her throat was strangely comforting. She took a slow, deep breath that was sure to be her last and felt the blade slice.

There was no pain, only pressure as adrenaline surged through her body. The blade was halfway across her throat when the gunshot cracked through the room. The man's grip on her hair vanished, and the knife slipped from his hand, clattering to the floor a heartbeat before he collapsed on top of her.

Relief flooded her. Declan had come home in time. He had saved her.

But the man's weight was crushing. She struggled to push him off, her muscles shaking with the effort. When she finally rolled free, she staggered to her feet, bracing herself against the edge of the bed. Black spots flickered at the edges of her vision, and she knew something was wrong — a concussion, maybe, or the shock catching up to her.

She blinked hard, trying to focus on the figure standing in the doorway. It wasn't Declan.

She had never seen this man before. And it took a full second for her to register that the gun was still raised — and pointed at her. She froze; the relief she'd felt a moment earlier evaporated in an instant.

"Miss Kelley, my boss would really like to have a word with you," she thought she heard him say. His voice sounded distant, muffled, as if she were underwater.

Her head throbbed. Every muscle in her body ached. She pressed her uninjured hand to her throat, trying to slow the bleeding, and stumbled to the bench at the foot of the bed. Six feet away, near the bathroom door, she saw her gun.

The man saw it too.

"Don't do it, ma'am. I don't want to hurt you," he said, stepping farther into the room.

He didn't want to kill her—that much was clear—but she wasn't going anywhere with him. Not willingly.

Alex lunged for the gun.

She didn't make it. He was faster, already closing the distance. His arm hooked around her, lifting her clean off her feet. The room tilted as he swung her over his shoulder, her vision blurring at the edges. She heard him muttering under his breath about getting blood on his new shirt as she fought to stay conscious, her body growing heavier with every step he took toward the door.

Warm blood from her own neck wound slid down her cheek as she hung over the man's shoulder. She turned her head toward Tony's house just in time to see Declan rushing out the front door. He looked impossibly small from this distance, swallowed by the space between them.

The hatch of the SUV opened, and a moment later she was tossed inside. The impact knocked what little breath she had left from her lungs. Darkness swallowed her as the door slammed shut, pressing in from every direction. Her heartbeat thundered in her ears while gravel pinged against the underside of the vehicle as they peeled out of the driveway.

A second later, she felt hands on her, moving with practiced precision. The man had climbed into the back with her. His palms pressed firmly against her neck, trying to slow the bleeding. His voice was low and urgent as he spoke to the driver, but she couldn't make out the words. Everything sounded muffled, as if she were slipping underwater.

Her vision tunneled, the darkness closing in like a tide she couldn't outrun. She held on for one last breath, a fragile, fading thing. The warmth of her blood-soaked shirt was her only comfort as the darkness finally claimed her.

To be continued…

Acknowledgements

I owe deep gratitude to the people who helped bring this book to life.

To Christina Lykaios at Crafthouse Editing, thank you for your sharp eye, steady guidance, and the care you poured into every page. Your proofreading made this story stronger in all the ways that matter.

To Zainab at The Blue Couch Edits, your line and copy edits were a gift. You refined the voice, polished the rhythm, and helped the heart of this book shine through. I'm endlessly grateful for your talent and dedication.

To my mom and my mother-in-law—thank you for every hour of babysitting, every "go write, I've got this," and every quiet moment you carved out so I could chase this dream.

And to my husband: thank you for believing in me on the days I didn't believe in myself. Your support made this possible, and I'm so lucky to walk this path with you.

Coming Soon

Whiskey River Redemption, Book 2 of the Whiskey River Series

The scars of Whiskey River haven't healed, and the danger waiting in the shadows hasn't forgotten her. Alex's abduction exposes the truth she's spent years burying, pulling her family's criminal past into the light and sparking a war no one is safe from. Declan will stop at nothing to bring her home, but the path back to each other is tangled with betrayal, obsession, and enemies who refuse to let go.

Book Two of the Whiskey River Series dives deeper into obsession, betrayal, and the cost of survival.

Can Alex and Declan find their way back to each other, or will the growing danger pull them under before they ever get the chance?

About the author

A.J. grew up in a small New Hampshire town, splitting her days between her family's farm and whatever book she could sneak away with. She moved to Arkansas in 2012, joined the Arkansas Air National Guard as a medic, and later earned her Doctor of Nursing Practice from the University of Arkansas for Medical Sciences in 2023.

These days she's a homesteading, homeschooling mom who spends her time wrangling kids, chasing loose chickens, negotiating with stubborn horses, and pretending the ducks aren't plotting against her. When she isn't tending her garden or rescuing a cat from somewhere it shouldn't be, she's writing stories built on emotion, sharpened by suspense, and rooted in the grit of everyday life.

Her debut novel, *Secrets of Whiskey River*, began in 2020 as a journal to survive the emotional weight of working in healthcare during COVID.

It didn't stay a journal for long. The story grew teeth, heart, and a life of its own, becoming the first book in the *Whiskey River* Series.

You can find A.J. at authorajturner.com